A Measure of Rhyme

Praise Page

The **most jaw dropping conclusion to any book written this century**…fans of the **incredible** first book **must read** this one.

— *NN Light's Book Heaven 5+ star*

Never want to stop to eat or sleep-reading experience… writing style as a mixture of Stephen **King**, Dan **Brown** and (without the slightest stretch) **Dante**'s Divine Comedy.

— Lex Allen, *Readers' Favorite*

One of the **strongest female lead characters this reader has ever seen**…a fabulous continuation to **an incredible story**.

— *Feathered Quill*, Gold Award

Couldn't put the book down and finished in record time...**the perfect formula** for a nearly **perfect series.**

— *READER VIEWS*, BRONZE AWARD

Hand over heart, I struggled to find a spot to press pause and take a break...**exceptional**.

— ASHER SYED, *READERS' FAVORITE*

A **rich and satisfying** cocktail of literary goodness...a **gripping read from start to finish...a must-read**.

— *LITERARY TITAN*

Excitement was off-the-charts...the first novel in the series was **fantastic, but the sequel tops it by miles.**

— RABIA TANVEER, *READERS' FAVORITE*

Like Katniss of Hunger Games fame...Rhyme is an especially **fascinating character**...a **sensational** continuation of the series.

— LEX ALLEN, *READERS' FAVORITE*

Heart-pounding...readers **will not want to put it down**...is **beautifully written**.

— SEMI-FINALIST, BOOKLIFE PRIZE BY *PUBLISHER'S WEEKLY*

Gold Award, Feathered Quill
Silver Award, Feathered Quill
Bronze Award, Reader Views

Semi-finalist, BookLife Prize
by Publisher's Weekly

BookLife Elite

Embers of Shadow, Book III available Spring 2024.

"Unpredictable and gape-worthy"
"Cinematic…like one is watching a movie"
"Masterfully written"

Follow Lloyd at www.lloydjeffries.com

A Measure of Rhyme

Ages of Malice, Book II

Lloyd Jeffries

For Sage

PROLOGUE

This place bristles; vibrant, opalescent. Red and yellow, subtle orange, pearl, onyx; shimmering, sliding.

I'm not numb, not unaware. Consciousness hovers, floats, teeters on the slick edge between reality and something else, something all-consuming, something awesome. I'm unafraid.

The place I left: twinkling, beeping, harsh, has become this corridor. The light, a super nova. Yet I don't squint. I'm calm, my body whole. I glide along.

I should be frightened, I think, more inquisitive. Yet, those emotions have abandoned me. Am I senseless? Mentally deficient? Dead? My heart should be racing, hands trembling.

There's a figure in front of me, a shadow, if such a thing can exist in a place this brilliant. It steps close, and I realize I know the man.

"Emery, welcome," he says.

I should be surprised but my emotions are muted. I can't remember how I got here.

"John?"

His smile is genuine, his embrace comforting.

"I was sent to collect you and answer your questions," he says. "You have a very specific task."

I laugh, feel somewhat joyous. "Where am I?"

John's beard crinkles around a smile, warm and soft. I see the gleam in his eye. The peace, the unshakeable confidence.

"You're not going to believe this," he says, "but this is Heaven."

My mouth falls open as I squint into the brightness. "I made it to Heaven?" I look down the corridor, realize it has no walls, no floor or ceiling, just an endless rainbow of space. "Shouldn't I feel more elated? More, I don't know, overjoyed?"

John laughs. "Ah, curiosity. Waiting for the other shoe to drop, eh?" He slaps me on the back. "I've missed you Emery."

Is it possible to miss someone if you're in Heaven? Do emotions exist here? They seem so distant, like every other care: hunger, anger, jealousy, revenge.

Before I can ask, John speaks again. "You're a very special guest. A wonder, if I might venture such a statement. I think if these were normal times, you'd be surrounded by angels who'd examine you from head to foot. You'd be a hit for sure." He raises a finger. "If times were different. For now, though, you're a guest of the Father. One of only a handful of humans who've ever seen this place while still alive."

"I'm not dead?" I say. "Not here because I'm dead?"

John grasps my hand, and we start to move. Upward it seems. I see an endless expanse, an ocean of light and space. No clouds above, no structures below, floating in the void, holding the hand of the Apostle who speaks as we rise.

"You are to witness and record as I did on Patmos so long ago. You are chosen. You cannot be harmed, neither can you interact. The Father decided to show you these things for whatever His purpose. Please observe carefully."

The light parts as if breaking through a cloud. I'm presented with endlessness, a tourist at a scenic overlook on some mountain highway. I've never witnessed such vastness in my life, certainly not on Earth, as if I'm standing atop the Empire State Building and can see all the way to California.

As we rise structures become visible. Curved, shining, beautiful, shimmering with the same opalescence as the corridor through which I entered. There are levels, or sections, above, below, under, beside me. Figures move between them, serene, unhurried, content.

You'd think I'd be an oddity as we rise through these levels, bend around these structures, but these *people*, if they are people, either don't see me or don't care. Perhaps they're shielded from seeing me. Perhaps not people at all, bipeds maybe, in the tradition of a good sci-fi novel.

We gain speed as we rise. The structures become a blur; the bipeds, shooting stars. Then, high above, we approach a castle, an estate maybe, but something grander, something larger than anything a human could possibly hope to build, as if some Beverly Hills neighborhood took all its mansions and joined them together, then every other mansion from every other elite zip code in the world was joined with that, creating a sort of super mansion, a super colossal mega mansion, the mother of all mansions, stretching for as far as I can see.

I squint as if it will improve my vision. I see angels of every race and color. They're stunning. Their wings glorious, glistening. Not feathered, yet something feather-like, splaying colored arrays in breathtaking hues. They seem crazed with haste, dashing around the huge structures, wings flapping easily, moving them with great speed.

One streaks toward me and I flinch. Its face is stern, eyebrows creased above alert eyes, hair curled and flowing behind as wings, every bit of ten feet, pump the air and push the being along.

I reach out as it flashes by, but it flows through as if I'm made only of air. I crane my head as it zips past, white robes flowing, full of speed and wind like boat sails in that famous Rembrandt.

I look to John, who looks skyward. Or I guess up, as I can't tell if there is a sky per se.

"War has come." His features are stern yet serene. He betrays no fear.

"War? Didn't you say we're in Heaven?"

He averts his gaze to me. "Yes," he says, "we are. That's why you're here."

"Great. I get to Heaven just as it gets wrecked."

John laughs. "Same old Emery," he says. "We don't get much sarcasm here."

I look up and see the multitude. So hard to describe, so many beings at once. My mind scrambles, unable to process the enormity of what's before me.

War rages. Millions of angels collide and spin and whirl. They clash and flip, crash into one another, through my entire field of vision. Some fall, dropping with speed from the heights. Others rise on enormous wings and seek advantage over their foes.

We move into them, through them. Then we stop full in their midst. Explosions of light and color surround, rise, burst. In front of me an angel falls, an explosion of cloud and brilliance, different from some other angels who burst to an empty darkness, a soulless black spot. A cosmic period at sentence end, brief but definite.

Then, across the expanse, I see the first different thing, the first obvious contrast against the backdrop of light and wing. Black specks. At first thousands, then millions, streaking toward the fray. The most glorious thing leads in flowing gold. Larger than the others, more brilliant than anything thus far. Gorgeous with a delicate face, perfect muscles rippling beneath golden robes. Its wings, easily twenty feet across, are a kaleidoscope of shimmering color, spread rays in thick hues across the expanse. A snarl appears, movie-star teeth through a wrinkled mouth.

It streaks forward as the angels closest to us shift and race toward him.

A million against a million, light and wing and elegance, bolt at speeds too fast to follow. My mouth hangs open, my eyes won't blink. My mind becomes a supercomputer at max speed.

They collide in a sizzling nebula of wing and weapon and vapor. Thousands fall, streak downward, implode like upside down fireworks. There's no sound. No sense of anger or fear or bewilderment. Although the beings fight with unnatural fury, no screams accost, no calls from the wounded, no clamor of steel on steel. Just a sense of smoke, a mist of war's fog, of a brief confusion amongst the ranks, barely perceptible, like a single hair being dragged across one's skin.

They battle, test one another, hand to hand combat in three dimensions. I watch as the largest angel smashes an opposing line two-hundred strong. Its speed is brilliant, the speed of sound times the speed of sound. Velocity times velocity, V-squared. Seconds pass; explosions follow. Each of the two-hundred burst, flail. Some fall, bodies contorted, wings limp and fluttering with the speed of descent.

The large angel speeds on, sizzles like lightning. Can he possibly move faster? He circles, then dives into the next throng.

"Just what in the…" I start.

John raises a finger, has the same expression he wore at the Vatican when he told me not to profane God's name. I snap my lips shut.

"Lucifer," he says, "one of the best. Nearly unmatched. He wages war on Heaven."

I feel a sense of horror, that single hair tickling my skin. "For what —" Purpose? I start to say but the words freeze in my mouth. Another angel rises above the tumult, hovers majestic, a Giordano painting come to life, golden sword raised high as flames dance on its edge.

"Michael," I whisper, the Archangel who bested Cain in the Temple.

Lucifer pauses mid-flight, then turns a course so abrupt, I'm surprised his body stays together. Nothing human could endure that speed, those forces.

He sees Michael, smiles like he's posing for a sunny-beach snapshot. A smile of joy, of objective long sought and finally known.

The battle rages as if all the beings fuse their fear and anger and wrath into some sublime form that quickens them.

I look for Lucifer, realize I can only see what's going on by flashing my gaze from place to place. Like watching a ceiling fan spin and trying to pick out a single blade. These are statues to me, and I see them in brief, paused glimpses that last a nanosecond.

Lucifer, sword raised, teeth bared, hand on Michael's throat.

Then Michael above Lucifer, flaming sword poised to strike his heart.

Then, Lucifer behind Michael, arm locked around his neck.

Then, Michael in a half spin, landing a kick, eyes raging, teeth bared.

Lucifer rockets past us, a streak of white and gold.

In a blink, he changes direction, comes whistling back.

I see Michael, unmoving, framed in brilliance, golden hair, raging eyes, resplendent wings.

I'm engulfed in popping light; other angels move too fast to follow, each burst, one who's fallen.

Lucifer sizzles through the endlessness, a ballistic missile screeching towards its target, fire flowing in his wake.

Then a voice like thunder, a mix of clanging bells and deepest bass.

"The Father rebukes thee!"

It's the Archangel, wings spread high and dazzling, eyes reflecting the fire dancing on his sword.

Flames leap from the weapon to strike Lucifer full in the chest.

There's a singular, pregnant pause, an event horizon traversed.

Heaven ripples like a raindrop on still waters.

Lucifer freezes, his mouth a frozen O, his eyes black orbs, smoke trailing from wing tips.

Then he falls.

Around us, the angels stop. None show signs of battle; no contusion or blood, no rent flesh or torn skin, no sign of damage to wing or body. They float on gilded wings, watch as Lucifer streaks toward the unknown.

There's another series of flashes, not fireworks, but streaks of pure sable. Before my eyes, some turn gray as radiant wings become something leather, something pterodactyl. Gorgeous faces become snarling, fanged beasts and then, one after another, fall and follow Lucifer into the depths.

Michael hovers radiant, his face calm. He is elegance and wrath, fury fused with contentment.

I pry my eyes away, look at John.

He smiles, mouths something, and is gone.

All becomes white, still, perfect. The mansions and structures and angels gone.

I float in the original opalescence of this space.
Then I wake.

———

Jerusalem, Israel

"No need for speed, Uri," Daniel yells. "This guy's already dead." He glances at Yosef, his partner. "And keep the damn siren off!"

A husk of charred flesh lies on the gurney before him. The poor bastard, burnt to a crisp, as they say. Yosef attends the corpse, searches a charred arm for a place to start an IV.

"Man, this guy stinks."

"I know, I hate the burnt ones. Any idea what happened back there?"

Yosef looks up from his work. "None," he says. "The police wouldn't tell me anything." He repositions the massive limb, retightens the thin rubber tourniquet. "Hand me that saline."

Daniel flips open the transparent storage area. "You're wasting your time."

"I don't think so."

"Even if he *isn't* dead, and even if you *can* get an IV, it won't matter. He won't live another hour, two tops. I've seen it before. Burning is one of the worst ways to go. Never quick."

Yosef ignores the remark, returns to the task of searching for a vein. After a few seconds, he plunges the needle, feels a familiar pop. "I think I got it!" He rolls the stopper on the IV tube and saline begins to drip. "Ha!"

He looks at Daniel, then realizes the EMT doesn't care. He's holding a sword, examining it from blade to pommel. "Wonder what this writing means," he says. Light flashes from steel, flares in his eyes. "Some other language." He gives the sword a shake. "Sounds like there's something in the pommel."

Yosef takes a seat on a long blue bench that runs the length of the patient compartment. "You shouldn't have taken that," he says, nods at the sword. "The thing looks old as hell."

Daniel lifts the sword to shoulder level. "It's heavy too. Seems well balanced."

Yosef sighs, pushes ten milligrams of morphine. "The police will come looking, it's not right to take souvenirs."

Daniel lowers the blade and gives Yosef a look. "We were the first ones on the scene. Thank God the other squad was attending to the one that got stabbed. They would've gotten the prize instead of us. I mean, how do you think this guy gets burnt to a crisp? By that other guy? He probably won't make it either. And who even called us? And why a sword? I mean, of all things. A sword? Really?" He stares at Yosef for a few seconds. "The way I figure, it's a trophy for having to put up with his stench. And is he big enough? We barely managed to squeeze him in here, even with the power gurney." He spins the sword. "No, this thing is mine. It's gonna look great on my wall. I mean, maybe it's an antique." He runs his finger along the blade. "Maybe it's worth a few million."

Yosef laughs, watches desolate streets roll by. "Another great idea. Try selling that and we'll both be in trouble."

Daniel snorts. "You're such a rookie. I've been doing this for five years. Everyone takes a souvenir from time to time. Consider it a fringe benefit." He turns the sword once more, then offers it to Yosef, pommel first. "Take a feel."

Yosef reaches but stops short when he notices something peculiar.

"Were his eyes open before?"

Daniel looks. "Hmm," he says. "I don't think so. Surprised he still has eyes after whatever burnt him."

Yosef places a stethoscope on his chest. "His heart's still beating. Too bad we can't get those damn leads to stick. A heart monitor would really help us."

The ambulance lurches and they both hear a quick siren blast, something ambulance drivers do to warn inattentive cars.

"Easy up there!" Daniel yells to the front. "We're playing with sharp objects back here."

"Sorry!" Uri yells.

Yosef tightens his seat belt, glances into the overhead for another bag of saline. The patient spills over the gurney, charred arms like scorched tree trunks. "This guy's a beast," he says, "and I'm certain his eyes weren't open."

The burnt giant groans, sits straight up, then rips the IV from his arm and swings his massive legs over the gurney's side. Eyes burn with an evil flame, a stare that blisters. "Ye lads have me sword."

Yosef's words catch in his throat. He stares, wonders how words can form through the black char of face, scalp and body.

Daniel places a hand on the man's shoulder. "Easy partner," he says, gives Yosef a reassuring nod. "You'll be fine, just lay back and we'll give you more happy juice."

In a flash, the burnt man has Daniel by the shirtfront.

A blurred motion of a single massive arm sends him crashing through the ambulance's rear doors.

Yosef watches him bounce down the street and slide to a stop near a curb.

The sword clatters to the floor between them.

They both look down, then fly forward as the ambulance driver slams the brakes.

Uri appears in the narrow passage from cab to patient compartment. "What was—?" He stops, stares at the charred zombie. "How in…" he starts, then the sword appears in his chest. Eyes go wide, then fade as life leaves.

Yosef leaps, but the seat belt holds him tight. He's amazed Uri hasn't slumped to the floor, realizes the sword holds him affixed to the vehicle's wall.

He raises his hands. "I'm trying to help you man. You can leave anytime you want." He nods toward the open doors, tries to control the fear in his voice. "See? Just go. I won't tell anyone."

The zombie yanks the sword. Uri slides to the floor.

Yosef cringes, steels for the killing blow.

When he opens his eyes, the man is gone, sword and all.

CHAPTER 1

JERUSALEM, ISRAEL

Laslo Slabav stares with astonished eyes through the limo's dark glass. The fact it's Easter Sunday and the last day of Passover is not lost on him.

Providence, he thinks. God at work. All as it's meant to be.

People move like a swarm, filling the sidewalks and crowding the streets. They smile hand in hand, some arm in arm. Children perch on parents' shoulders as older kids chase each other through the crowd and play made-up games.

At last, peace has come.

Had some reporter asked even two months ago if this were possible in his lifetime, the Israeli Prime Minister would've responded with a solid "No!". But times were different, even two months ago, and today he stares with wondering eyes.

The crowd gives way to the disabled and elderly, quick to offer aid to those in need. All seem joyful, even serene as they enjoy the cool temperatures and the company of those around them. A group of women pass wearing broad smiles, chatting in excited tones. The streets are full, as if all of Israel has emptied into Jerusalem.

A shame we even need security, he thinks. But alas, the past informs the future. He dips his head and mouths a prayer. "Through

Your grace, oh Lord, our enemies have seen reason and our flocks embraced peace. Use me as a worthy tool. Bless this place and its people."

The radio squawks. "Getting close. Everyone in position."

The Temple glows as sun rains upon it. It's perfect, inviting, waiting to embrace all who enter. It grows large as they approach, as if God himself has increased its grandeur for this occasion alone. Slabav thinks of the time this was a myth. Of the time Longinus, the hulking Roman, had invaded his home and asked for Israel's help in rebuilding the place.

He leans into the seat's soft leather and sighs. Peace has come, at last, at last, and with it an end to the cares of strategy, and enemies, and terrorists.

And all it cost was the life of a single man.

He thinks to all that's happened since the man's assassination. Thaddeus Drake: *The Dove*. A saint. A worker of wonders. A martyr for peace.

Now Muslim and Christian, Jew and gentile, all dance in the streets, within the Temple's courtyard, along the Temple's perimeter. Their joy creates its own energy, cascades over the people and through Jerusalem. Tonight, they'll feast together, will be tolerant and display love, will embrace each other's gods and accept each other's cultures.

Yes, for now, much has changed.

Even the prophets of old couldn't have predicted how all of this would come about. To Slabav, Thaddeus Drake had been an enigma. A man above the fray, but not above using violence to meet his ends.

"I will have my Temple," Drake said the last time Slabav had seen him. Then he'd taken out a pistol and killed the man to whom he was speaking.

Maybe not a saint, Slabav thinks, but God works in mysterious ways.

The limo stops and Laslo exits to a deafening cheer. The crowd presses, beams, reaches out, yells his name. "Blessings to you!" a man shouts. An older, chubby woman squeezes through security, offers a pen and paper.

"Have you a camera?" Laslo asks. She produces an iPhone from her bra. Laslo slides next to her and snaps the photo. "A selfie for you," he says, "along with my blessings." She beams.

He waves, moves through the crowd. He hasn't felt safe in a crowd since, well, never. His smile grows as he moves toward the stage. He's having trouble forgetting the decades of terror, the oceans of hatred hanging over this place. Yet there have been no incidents; no riots, no bombs, no uprisings. No anything since Drake was assassinated. Simply wondrous, he thinks; God has it well in hand.

A reporter steps forward, holds out a microphone. "Prime Minister Slabav, how do you feel?"

Laslo's cheeks stretch. He's trained himself to hide emotion but today can't hold it in. The crowd sings and celebrates. The new Temple rises to the heavens and fully solidifies God's place on this Earth and among His people forever more.

"I..." Warm tears fill his eyes. A sign of supreme elation, of witnessing God's hand among His people. Friend and enemy are united; hate, washed away, cleansed like the sins of the world.

He clears his throat, wipes an eye. "I feel enchanted. Enthralled. Elated. I am joyous, more than joyous, more than thrilled. I celebrate Israel. I celebrate Jew, Muslim and Christian. I celebrate tolerance and acceptance, but mostly what I feel is humility. From this day, the world will change as never before. Gone is war, violence, hate. Peace reigns and I am overjoyed."

Those around him cheer, which sparks further cheers as his words spread through the crowd. Laslo continues. "Today I sign the Religious Tolerance Treaty on the steps of the new Temple and while surrounded by my new Muslim friends." He stops here and looks to the sky. "Even as I say that, I'm struck dumb. I never thought those words would pass my lips.

"But today is not only a day of joy, but a day of miracles. A day to look to the heavens and to thank God for making such things possible. We will assure peace reigns. That all viewpoints are tolerated and accepted. We will sign this pact between our religions and our nations. This treaty, bartered by the great Thaddeus Drake, may God rest his soul, for the benefit of all mankind. I feel today Drake is somehow with us, feel him smiling down from the heavens. I feel he knows what he's accomplished and knows the outcome of his sacrifice."

The crowd erupts at the mention of the Dove. Energy flows over, seems to ignite as it reaches the Temple's courtyard.

He waves, moves up the steps of the grand stage. The Temple smiles down on him. Its stone rises into the blue sky, a symbol of peace and hope. A foundation for enterprise and godliness. An appropriate backdrop, he thinks. All religions, at long last, peaceful, devoted, tolerant.

He approaches a table in the stage's center. It's draped with a single white cloth. A large book sits on it and holds the treaty. Oshi Khalifa, Laslo's oldest enemy, rises and offers his hand.

Slabav clasps it with both hands. "Drake would've loved this," he says.

Khalifa's expression is warm and, dare he believe, jubilant. Such a drastic change from the decades where, at every encounter, the man's face was strained with worry and stress. Today, the Muslim appears without a care.

"How does the transport go?" Khalifa says.

"Very well," Slabav says, "my people are relocating from all over the world. This land will thrive through the toil of both Muslim and Jew. We've done it, Oshi." He searches the man's eyes. "My new friend," he adds with a smile.

Khalifa inflates, seems to energize. "Yes, my friend, we will thrive."

Slabav looks offstage at the assembled gallery of world leaders. The president of the United States of America, a gruff man and staunch ally, gives him a wink and a smile. The Russian president also nods. China, the European Union, Iran, Saudi Arabia, representatives from almost all the world's major nations are in attendance. Their smiles stoke the marvelous wonder in Slabav's heart.

Slabav nods to the podium. "Why don't you say a few words, Oshi?"

"Eloquence isn't my strong suit, Laslo. Why don't you speak for both of us?"

Laslo grins and steps to the mic. He stares over the crowd, realizes every space is filled. People sit on rooftops of surrounding buildings and the square is packed with humanity stretching for as far as he can see. People have climbed to the tops of stone fences, nested atop lamp posts, even statues. Any spot that can afford a better view.

This is truly what the people want. What they've always wanted.

He raises his arms then waits for the crowd to quiet.

"*Chag Pesach sameach*," he starts. "Happy Passover and happy Easter!"

The crowd roars, embrace each other, pump their arms, jump in the air. They're radiant, jubilant. Laslo's smile broadens as the people celebrate all that's passed, all they've endured. Khalifa beams as well.

When the crowd settles, he starts to speak.

"On the day he was assassinated, Thaddeus Drake gave a speech not too far from here.

"The words he spoke were simple to follow, yet hard to understand.

"You see, he spoke of decency and fellowship.

"He called on us to be more godly. More godlike. That is to say, more *like* God. He called on us to forgive and unite. He called on us to share common blood, not spilled blood. He called on us to embrace what we have in common and to relish our differences. He called for an end to hate. An end to violence and discord.

"He called on us, *as humans,* to embrace the bonds we *share.*"

He looks over the crowd.

"He gave his life for those words.

"But he also gave his life so that we could be here today. Rejoicing. In peace and harmony."

The crowd starts to applaud and Slabav raises a hand to stop them.

"He helped us free our minds and free ourselves.

"He helped us to be better, and we have proven worthy of his trust.

"When he spoke that day, he started each sentence with the word *today*. He was telling us that we could choose to change *this instant*. That we were bound only by attitude and prejudice. He told us if we cast these aside, we could endure and thrive. He called for that today. Now. Without delay."

He glances at Khalifa. "So, *today*, Mr. Khalifa and I represent the last two nations to sign this accord."

The masses cheer.

"Today, we end the terrorism and mistrust that plague our lives.

"Today, we complete the tapestry that ties us together. And today, *this day*, we assure lasting peace for all people, all religions, and all cultures.

"Today, we complete a Temple built on trust. As the Temple behind me offers closeness to God, this treaty offers a more intimate humanity. One where we fill chasms of hate with waters of love.

"Today –"

He pauses, notes something at the throng's farthest periphery. A stream of light shines from the heavens, a giant spotlight moving toward the stage as the crowd turns to look.

It pierces, blinds, tenfold brighter than normal sunlight.

Security assembles in front of the stage. Six men, guns exposed but holstered. They're a show of force, a gesture of mistrust, an expectation of terrorism from Israel's enemies. Slabav wishes they would've stayed behind the stage.

Then, another security detachment joins them.

He glances to Khalifa.

The Muslim read the situation and dispatched his own security team.

Thank God, Oshi, Slabav thinks, breathes a quick sigh. It's vital to preserve this show of unity if they wish for lasting change.

The beam continues its approach and although Laslo expects the crowd to scatter in fear, they don't, simply stepping aside, eyes wide, hands raised to surprised mouths.

Then Laslo sees him. A man perched atop a white Arabian stallion.

All eyes follow, yet no one seems alarmed. The beam intensifies as the man draws close.

Slabav gasps.

Thaddeus Drake has come.

CHAPTER 2

JERUSALEM, ISRAEL

Drake's dead. Confirmed dead. The funeral extraordinarily well attended and televised to all nations.

Thoughts rush through his mind. It's some sort of trick. Some Muslim antic to turn his shining moment to foolish self-indulgence. He glances at Khalifa, then to the gallery of world leaders. Security forms a line before them as well.

No one's run, Slabav thinks. There's no panic or even a sense of concern as all stand and watch Drake approach.

Drake makes a slight gesture. The light snuffs. He glances toward the security detail blocking the stage.

They draw their pistols. The detail's leader says, "Acquire," and each takes aim as the stallion approaches.

It *is* Drake. Same chiseled features, same perfect silhouette, same fit form, but somehow, he's changed. Gone are the trademark gloves, but that strikes Slabav as not quite right, not the real difference. Then Drake comes more in focus, and Slabav realizes his hair is completely white. Not gray, or salt and pepper, nor the tinted silver of advanced age. No, this is brilliant, luminescent, like a halo. A glowing radiance enshrouds, casts calm rays over the crowd.

Drake doesn't smile, yet neither does he seem perturbed. He looks stoic, confident. Classic Drake style on full display.

Slabav steps from the podium just as Khalifa steps forward. They stand next to each other wearing quizzical expressions.

The Arabian continues a few strides, then stops before the twelve-man security team.

Drake regards them, says nothing.

"Hands up!" a security man shouts.

Drake doesn't move.

"Get your hands up now!"

Drake looks to Slabav and their eyes meet.

Slabav gasps, realizes Drake's eyes are crystal blue, piercing, breathtaking.

Drake nudges the horse, and it starts forward.

"Another step and we'll shoot!"

Drake continues.

Slabav yells.

Security fires.

Drake moves his hand. A subtle twitch of the index finger, the casual movement of a single digit.

Twelve bullets rattle to the ground; twelve men rocket backwards as if struck by a battering ram. They slice the air, collide with stage and chair and rigging. Their pistols clatter, glowing as if heated to extreme temperatures. They blaze like molten iron from a Steel City smelter, then become smoking lumps of lead.

There's a commotion from the gallery where the world leaders stand. Those security personnel have also dropped their weapons; those weapons have become smoldering lumps.

Drake dismounts the stallion and ascends the stage. His clothes are of the same excellent quality as before. His features seem young, yet more mature, more refined. His hair is as white as new fallen snow, but glowing, radiant, mesmerizing. When he speaks, perfect teeth flash from a perfect mouth. Crystal blue eyes regard Slabav, deep, like a Caribbean pool. Slabav thinks of Zeus, the mythical god of thunder.

Drake nods as he passes. "Laslo. Oshi," he says. His expression is reverent, determined, calm yet resolute.

Drake stands before the microphone as all the world watches.

Silence falls thick over the crowd. No one dares to move. Even the security men lie where they've landed, unable to speak or rise.

Drake takes them in, glances to the gallery of world leaders, looks into the cameras.

Then he speaks.

"I am he that was dead. But now I live."

Silence reigns, grows more glaring with each second like the very Earth holds its breath. All stare, solemn, awed, dumbstruck.

"Drake is gone," he says. "I am Cain. Sent by the Father."

CHAPTER 3

JERUSALEM, ISRAEL

Every day I startle awake and look for her.

Every day she isn't here, and I kick myself for believing she could be.

Get used to it, she's dead. Not coming back.

My stupid hospital gown is soaked again, and I rise from the bed with only a slight groan. My wound is healing nicely. Almost completely. Record time, the docs say.

I move to the cheap cabinet, ass flapping, and retrieve a new gown. These hospital folks must have a butt fetish. Must take great joy in watching an idiot try to snap all the buttons together, and in a very certain way. A real brain teaser. A Rubik's gown. What price for a decent change of clothes?

The nurses here have been nice though. There's one in particular who is very kind. When I first got here, I kept calling her Rhyme. You see, they resemble, and in my drug-induced couple of weeks here I'm sure she's heard a snootful of my stories.

I suppress thoughts of Rhyme. Just my psyche coming up to try and comfort me as I heal. "Missed your aorta by a sliver," the doc said, "a single inch saved you."

Yeah, lucky me, sometimes a sliver makes all the difference.

I assemble the stupid gown, slide it over my shoulders, then try to tie the little ropes in the back. This isn't easy either. These hospital folks are real wise crackers. You're sick and then have to monkey around trying to figure out the Rubik's robe. The reward for success: a cool breeze up your ass.

During my time here, I've been presented with various clothing items to try. Some from lost and found, some from a charity box. None fit. Or are comfortable. Or don't stink. Or all three.

I return to my chair. An ugly blue thing with cheap wooden legs that'll slide out from under you in a heartbeat. I ease into it and pull today's meal closer. The bedside table squeaks across speckled linoleum.

"Drum roll please," I say as I lift the lid.

I'm presented with some kind of meat. It's brown and square and its odor doesn't help discern what it actually is. Next to that, a smattering of peas. It seems peas look the same no matter where they're served. There's a carton of milk, a cup of gelatin, lime today, and some cheap metal silverware. The silverware is bent, and I examine it closely for stains.

I scoop some peas with a bent spoon and slide a heap in my mouth. They're tasteless; more jokes from the hospital folks. Ass-baring, unsolvable gowns; unidentifiable food; bent silverware, and tasteless peas.

Chewing, I lean back and sigh, then look out the window at Jerusalem's timeless structures and myriad streets. I heft a remote control clipped to the sheet of the bed. Another great gag, a remote that's attached to the wall with a thick electrical cord. Not many people know this, but the cord is magic. It has the ability to wrap around everything and anything. All the time. I eye it with disdain. The cord and I are not friends. I bet the jokers love it.

I thumb the button, a great round thing that says TV in faded red. Across the wide chasm of this room, about five feet, the TV blinks on. And here's the really fun part: I understand almost none of what's being said. You see, I speak only English. Like any dumb American, I've relied on the people of other countries to learn *my* language while

I've been relieved of the burden of learning theirs. Sometimes I can make out the gist of whatever's on, but most times I'm searching for something visual: music, dancing, magic shows. Anything where I don't really have to know what's being said to understand what's happening.

The channels roll by. I've become adept at flipping them using this remote. With each button press, it takes a second for the screen to change. If you press the button without waiting between each press, the lazy TV will pause for about five seconds, then advance three or four channels at once. This greatly reduces the chances of finding something amusing. I've learned the jokers have many traps and can't help but feel like I'm on some reality show. One where things are designed to make you crazy while the home audience laughs their asses off.

I can hear the announcer now. "Here's Emery. He going to change the channel. Let's watch. Ooh! The cord's wrapped around the bedside table. There goes the gelatin, splat! Emery bends to get it. The chair slides out from under him. Down he goes. Oof! That linoleum must be cold on his bare ass!" The home audience howls as they watch me struggle with each new obstacle, all while recovering from a wound that should've killed me.

That, folks, is entertainment.

In any event, I'm just writing to write these days. I don't really know what to do next. I have no money. The expensive Italian clothes the Apostle provided are long gone. Hanging, I'm sure, in some orderly's closet. Seems my wallet ended up there too. I haven't been asked how I'm going to pay for these weeks either and as the days pass, I expect everyone who walks in to be the "finance person."

"Mr. Merrick, it seems you owe us a couple million dollars. Have you a plan for paying or do we need to take back the Rubik's gown and toss your naked ass in the street?" I'm sure it will go something like that, the final joke on this reality show.

When they ask, though, I have the perfect plan. I'm going pull a Ramirez, going to act like I don't speak the language. If I can't understand, I can't pay, right? They'll never see it coming.

But here's some light in the darkness: I'm on drugs. I just drew a big smiley face at the end of that sentence. A handwritten emoji like we did in the old days. Score a point for Emery, if you're watching at home. He's found a way to get his fix. Pulled one over on the jokers themselves. Seems when you've been run through with a sword, you can just ask, and they show up with that sweet syringe and provide your high. It's beautiful. Although a word of warning, don't try and name your poison.

"I want Fentanyl."

"Only Dilaudid works for me."

"Pardon me, but have you any Demerol?"

That sort of thing puts them on high alert and then they ask a bunch of questions designed to keep your fix away. More hospital jokes. They ask the questions but won't give the fix.

I shouldn't be writing this, but here's the trick: refuse the medication. Simple as that. Grimace when they touch you or change the bandage or whatever they're doing, but when they ask if you need your meds, say, "No, I'll live with the pain. I mean, I don't want to get hooked."

Imagine my surprise. When you refuse your meds, they get all sorts of compassionate and offer the fix every few hours. It was pure glee when I figured that out. Those fixes are important. And probably the reason I keep seeing Rhyme. And I'm sure my ingenuity earned me some points with the home audience.

But now I find myself in a quandary. One of the doctors said they're discharging me today. First thing I asked about was the pain and he said he'd write me some scripts. So, bonus for me.

The quandary: I have no clothes, no money, no *one*. No idea where I'll go or what I'll do. Maybe I can find a bridge and live under that. Or maybe the *Jerusalem Post* will hire me to write my musings on healthcare and I can earn a few bucks. That's if they don't mind all of my articles in English. Might be a way to earn some dough though, possibly enough to get back to Carter's Glen to see if Sig has waited up. I've mentioned before how impatient he is.

And here's the real joke in my luscious comedy. I think I'm loaded.

Like literally rolling in money. I remember Igneus telling me my money was secure. Which, to me, meant it was available. Like, mine to use. You know, my money. The problem: I was pissed off and had convinced myself I didn't care about money. Thinking about it, I'm not sure what I cared about then. I was on a real high horse. I stormed out and everything. Got piss drunk. Arrested. Bailed out by Longinus. Flash forward to the Temple. I get the centurion's blade through my gut. Then everyone disappears and I wake up in this place.

Oh! And I never mentioned the problem. I never asked Igneus how to get my money. Never thought to ask the obvious: Is there a bank account? A credit card? Um, in what country does this money reside? An address would also be helpful? And one other thing, is the account in my name, or is there some way to, you know, actually access this money?

I'm such a dumb ass.

I look up from my notebook to see the nurse. Peggy? Pearl? I can't remember and am too embarrassed to ask.

She holds some clothes draped over her left arm. What looks like corduroy pants in diarrhea brown and a T-shirt. Then, she hands me a Cadbury egg.

"What's this?" I say.

"It's Easter."

"It is?"

I look at the clothes, look at her, then the egg. I feel some relief she isn't the finance person. I realize I might be able to make my escape before the finance people actually come knocking.

"Are you ready to go?" she says.

"Um, I guess so. Although I wouldn't mind staying a little longer." I feel stupid saying this, showing my fear. Practically begging.

Her smile is nice, she really does resemble Rhyme. The auburn hair, round lips, great body. "Nonsense," she says. "You'll be fine at home."

I nod, think to tell her I'm homeless.

"We're going to miss you Emery," she says. "And look, I've brought you some clothes."

"I see that," I say, as she places them on the bed.

"You get changed and we'll bring a wheelchair to get you downstairs."

"I don't mind walking."

She tuts me. Purses her lips and says, "Tut tut, hospital policy."

Like the Rubik's gown and the lazy TV, I think.

I have a vision of how this is going to play for the home audience. "Here's Emery thinking he's being discharged. He's in the wheelchair. Oh no! It seems the orderly in the Italian suit is dumping him down the stairs. Wow! That Emery is a good sport."

"Okay," I say.

She shuts the door as she leaves but it stays open a couple of inches. I've never figured out if it just isn't capable of shutting or if this is the jokers at work. Seems hospital people don't like doors being shut. Maybe it blocks the home audience's view.

I pull off Rubik's robe and slide on the corduroys. As soon as I let go of them, they fall to the floor. Great, hope they have a belt. I slip on the T-shirt, noticing as it goes over my head I can see through it.

I also realize how accustomed I've become to not wearing underwear. They haven't even crossed my mind until this second. Does Peggy know I need underwear? Should I ask? She seems like a person who would've thought of that. I decide to go commando rather than ask the question.

Then the orderly is there with the wheelchair. I look him over, examine his clothes to see if any of them are mine. I grab my dopp kit, full of hospital-issued toothpaste, a toothbrush, a small bar of soap and shower hat. I took the shower hat on purpose. Not that I wear one, but it feels like my only way to protest.

To my relief they don't dump me down the stairs, just roll me onto an elevator and then back off the elevator on the first floor. We pass a white van. Children are everywhere, their chaperones hushing and wrangling them toward the vehicle. We weave around them and it feels like we're moving at a breakneck pace.

The orderly shoos the kids from a metal bench bolted to the concrete, then assists me onto it.

"You can wait for your ride here," he says.

I decide to tell him I don't have a ride. I hope he'll take pity and tell me of a shelter or something. I'm scared, broke, hungry and my pain meds are wearing off.

I unwrap the chocolate but before I can speak, the egg slips from my hand and rolls into the parking lot. I move to get it, but a stretch limo pulls up, squishing it flat.

A well-dressed and well-built man exits, walks around the front of the vehicle and says, "Mr. Merrick?"

He wears a chauffeur's hat and a smile. "Yes," I say.

He moves to the rear of the vehicle and opens the door, then motions me inside.

I stare for a second or two, then stand.

My corduroys hit the floor exposing my bare ass to chauffeur, child and chaperone.

Cue audience.

Cue laugh track.

In the back of the big limo, I revel in the luxury and take in the sights.

Jerusalem in the daytime appears like any other place in the world. People busy themselves with common tasks as do any world of ants, lemmings, really, when you think about it. A man rushes by, bends to tie his shoe. Another exits a store, nearly trips over the first. Then, a woman emerges and there's a three-human pile up. The home audience roars. I laugh with them.

Only when we stop at a red light, do I realize I've no idea where we're going. I haven't asked, and the driver hasn't said. I'm just going with the flow, riding the wave, if you will.

The limo must have something to do with Cain. Or Igneus. One of them sent it, which means one of them has been keeping tabs on me this entire time. If forced to guess, I'd say Igneus. I'm sure Cain, if he's even still alive, has forgotten about me, and the fact I've received no visitors during my time in the hospital makes me think my benefactor is my friend the Jew.

I wonder where he's been and find myself looking forward to seeing his face again as his was the last face I'd seen before I'd gone unconscious after being stabbed by Longinus.

I have to admit, I miss the skinny bastard.

It all makes sense. Igneus wouldn't visit because he'd be exposing himself to Cain. I'm certain Cain isn't happy with him, and by extension, Igneus would lay low, fearing Longinus is now unleashed. Although, thinking about it, maybe it doesn't make much sense. A limo is rather conspicuous and can be easily followed.

A shudder runs through me. If the limo has been sent by Cain, I'm screwed. I remember our deal. "You will not interfere, take sides, etc."

Well, I've done all of those things, had even worked up the courage to try and tackle the big Roman when he was about to skewer the Apostle. I should've just sprinted headfirst into a concrete wall for all the good I did. It felt the same either way. Man, that guy is just a monster.

I press the intercom button on my right.

"Yes sir," the driver says.

"Hello. Would you mind swinging by a pharmacy so I can get my prescription filled?"

"Of course, sir."

I lean back. I'll get my fix, then face my pending doom properly dissociated.

I inhale the fragrance of the luxury vehicle, leather mixed with… honey, apricots? Well, something fruity and pleasant. I glance out the window, then notice a line of bottles on the left side of the limo's interior.

Oh, this is too good. I forage and find a brand-new bottle of Macallan 12. I grab a glass and fill it to the brim.

This is luxury, riding through Jerusalem in a stretch limo, scotch running happily down my throat. Once I get this prescription filled, I'll have a real party on my hands.

The limo takes up four spaces in the pharmacy parking lot.

I leap out, holding my corduroys at the waist.

Inside there's no line and I'm greeted by a portly pharmacist with dark hair tied up in red ribbon. She greets me in a foreign language.

I say, "English?"

She shakes her head.

I hand her the prescription.

She goes in the back, then returns and says something else while holding up all ten fingers. I imagine this means ten minutes. So, I smile and nod.

I go back to the limo for a couple of swallows of the luscious nectar I'd left behind. I stand beside it, wearing my see-through shirt, scotch in one hand, corduroys in the other.

I giggle at the looks I'm getting. People are trying to figure me out, questions written on their expressions. "Does he own that limo?" "Is it some rich guy helping a homeless guy?" "Should we call the police?"

I down the liquid and head back inside. My prescription is ready, at least that's what the pharmacist's smile tells me and my mouth starts to water. I can't wait for my fix. The scotch is starting to kick in and when I add a couple of Percocet, well, my mind will be thoroughly uninvolved in whatever other insults await.

She says something I don't understand, then glances at the cash register. The green LED shows a *480* with a squiggly little square next to them. I realize I need to pay.

I realize I have no money.

My heart sinks. Despite the effects of the scotch, I understand I have no money of any kind, let alone four-hundred and eighty of the squiggly box currencies the register demands.

Maybe I can borrow it from the limo driver? He looks like a pal and will probably be happy to help an old junkie. Maybe I can trade some of the pills? Ooh now we're talking; except I don't really like that idea because it means less for me. Junkies are notoriously stingy with their stash.

The pharmacist looks at me, her dark eyes reveal patience and kindness. Maybe I can just explain to her the issue and she can help.

Then I remember I don't speak the language. My friend Macallan is kicking in just when I need my brain to work one last time.

Then a different idea lands.

I make a writing motion in the air and the pharmacist catches my meaning. She hands me a sticky note and a pen.

I draw an X with a P through it. The Labarum, the great symbol of X'chasei and all its power.

It's a long shot but I'd seen Drake use the symbol in the Burj Khalifa and it'd worked for him. I slide the paper to the pharmacist. Then try to look regal and important, corduroys bunched in my left hand, chin tilted slightly toward the ceiling.

She looks at it and slides it back. Her face tells me she doesn't know what the hell the symbol means. My heart deflates, all my cells moan in disappointment. I'm going to have to wait for my fix.

She must notice this deflation, my entire body slouching. She takes the paper and disappears into the shelves of the pharmacy. I hear her talking to a man I can't see.

I'm not sure if I should stand or go. Maybe they're calling the police. Maybe they think this is a bribe or something. That sort of thing doesn't fly in the U.S. and I have a feeling won't fly here.

The need for my fix makes me stand firm. If I'm arrested, I think, the limo driver will probably get a nice day off. When they come for me, I'll plead an ignorance of the language. I'll act like this sort of thing is totally normal in my country.

But then she's back, smiling, white paper bag in hand. She opens it, shows me the drugs, shows me the printout for the drug's instructions, then points to an electronic pad.

She wants me to sign, I realize. I scribble my name, she hands me the bag, and off I go, almost losing my corduroys again in my haste.

Back in the limo I pop the lid and swallow two Percs like they're a last meal. I refill my scotch, signal the driver and lean back. Whatever happens next, whether Cain or Igneus, I won't mind. Not now. The chemicals find their mark and I'm pleasantly adrift.

The lyrics for "Comfortably Numb" by Pink Floyd float through my mind. I hum along. Jerusalem has become a blur of green and brown outside my window. We're cruising, the limo and me. It's my magic carpet, my pet dragon, my flying chariot. I'm a king now and all outside, peasants. The Percs mix with the Macallan and I ride the wave. I sip my scotch, think how much the home audience at the hospital must miss my hijinks. I give my corduroys a gentle tug.

Then just like that it's over. My door opens and the huge driver stands there. It takes me a moment to notice him and when I do, he seems even more massive than before.

I stare up at him, then blurt, "Do you work out?"

He reaches in and helps me out. He may as well lift me for as much effort as I put into standing, but he's gentle enough and even catches my corduroys when they begin to slide off.

I gaze up at him. "You're my best friend."

CHAPTER 4

JERUSALEM, ISRAEL

Completely naked, I wake in a gorgeous room and wonder if the driver has taken advantage of me. I'm not that kind of girl, I think.

I sit up with my head on a swivel. I'm in a king bed adorned with pillows of various size and texture. Each of them feels expensive, comfortable. The sheets are crisp and white, and on the wall in front of the bed hangs a giant TV. Seventy-five inch plus, I think. The whole room is large, maybe twenty by twenty. I look for the remote and notice a bottle of water on the nightstand. I'm consumed by thirst. I twist the cap and chug half of it.

I swing my legs over the bed and my feet hit the carpet. After that stay in the hospital, my feet have forgotten the feel of carpet. It's amazing, soft, cool, padded, smooth. I wriggle my toes as my smile grows. Someone should write a song about this.

I rise, walk into the bathroom and marvel. It's like an elite spa. Everything marble and glass. Finely etched reliefs adorn the walls. Beside the sink, a stack of three towels. I think to the towels in my apartment on Mulberry Street. I could've stacked ten of them and they wouldn't have been as high as these three.

I move to the commode and relieve myself, then turn to the shower, a walk-in made entirely of marble. The spotless glass door slides easily, and I step in to discover there's no faucet. Only four square buttons, each about four inches. There's writing on these, but I can't read the language. I press one and nothing happens. I press the other three in turn and get the same result.

I'm frustrated. "How do you get the goddamn water to turn on?" Then, as if on command, the jets spring to life.

I jump at first, then realize the water's the perfect temperature.

Guess I'll take a shower.

I haven't the vocabulary to explain how marvelous this feels. There's a rain jet above me, two more on the walls beside, then, on three sides at just above waist level, six more. I experiment with the square buttons and realize they change the order and intensity of the jets.

This becomes great fun and I press the buttons with enthusiasm. I'm learning this shower and really don't intend to ever leave. I lather myself paying careful attention to every nook and cranny. Then I wash the wound on my abdomen and am quite astonished at how much it looks like a scar instead of an open puncture.

I find I can speak for temperature changes. "Turn up the temperature." And the water becomes warmer. This is amazing, and I take my time basking in the jets, the soapy lather, the succulent warmth. I haven't had this much fun in a shower since I was a child.

I step out, wrap myself in one of the thick towels, use another to wipe the fog off the mirror. A homeless man looks back at me. My beard is full. And scraggly. My hair is long. And scraggly. My face is aged. And scraggly. My eyes peep from a perch above large dark bags that were once my lower eyelids.

"Sweet Jesus," I say. I do my best to recover my appearance. There's a hairbrush, which doesn't seem to enjoy going through my hair. It feels like I pull half of it out as I struggle to get rid of the snags. Various cosmetic products line the counter, and I apply a healthy dollop of deodorant, spritz myself with a cologne called French Lover, then exit the bathroom.

Past the bed there's a sitting area. A couch and two chairs arranged around an antique coffee table. Past that, daylight squeezes around thick drapes that cover the windows.

I move that way, look for my corduroys and threadbare T-shirt. At a long low dresser, I rifle through drawers and find a selection of socks, underwear, and undershirts. I glance around the room before pulling out a set and sliding them on. They're cool and clean, a perfect fit. I then move to double doors which appear to be a closet. When I open it, I gasp.

Four pairs of shoes sit in a shoe rack. Above them, hanging neatly spaced, are seven different suits, each with jacket and pants. On the left, a selection of neck ties in various colors and patterns. On the right, a selection of dress shirts. My mouth hangs open. I touch the fabric, realize these are every bit the quality of what the Apostle had given me when I'd left the Vatican. I select a shirt and slide it on. It's a perfect fit. Same for the pants and jacket. I turn, excited to look at myself in the bathroom's mirror, and notice there's a selection of belts hanging from the inner side of the closet's doors. I select one that's braided and brown and slide it through the loops of my pants. Again, perfect. I slip on a pair of brown Oxfords and tie the laces.

On my way to the bathroom, I notice a gray, square valet atop the long dresser beneath the giant TV. My pill bottle is there. Next to them is a bifold leather wallet, two breath mints and a small tube of lip balm.

I pop the lid of the balm and coat my lips. Then I open the wallet. It's crammed with shekels, euros, and dollars. There are even two credit cards.

Impostor. That's the thought that hits me. That perhaps all the things I'm taking liberties with aren't mine at all. That the real owner of the place will walk in to find me dressed in his clothes, using his products, rifling through his money. I glance around the room, see the door that leads to whatever's beyond. I slide a credit card from the wallet. At least I'll know who my benefactor is, I think. Then a great smile crosses my face. Both cards are embossed with the name EMERY MERRICK.

I slide the wallet into the suit jacket and move to the bathroom. I look good, not James Bond good, but pretty good for a junkie.

I search the products on the bathroom counter and find a nice hair gel, one infused with VITAMINS FOR LUSTER. I slick my hair back and regard myself in the mirror. Not perfect but certainly passable, too bad I can't do anything about these wrinkles and the dark luggage my eyes carry.

I put on a tie, struggle to tie the perfect knot, then go back into the living area and take two Percs. I stand between the bed and the TV. I've exhausted my very productive search of this room and now the time's come to leave this sanctuary and greet my host.

God help me.

My heart starts to thrum. I feel shaky. I finish the water beside the bed, think to take another couple of Percs.

Quit being such a sissy, I scold myself. If they wanted you dead, you'd be dead. Just walk out there like you own the place.

I move to the door, grip the doorknob.

I take a deep breath and pull.

I'm greeted by a scowling Roman.

The tip of his sword at my throat.

Will the insults never cease?

CHAPTER 5

JERUSALEM, ISRAEL

Laslo Slabav enters the room and starts to speak. They meet today in a conference room at the Israeli Prime Minister's office building, a last-minute thing that's upended the PM's schedule. Laslo has many meetings today and doesn't really have time for this.

"Mr. Drake," he says, "that was quite an entrance yesterday. Care to explain yourself?"

Oshi Khalifa rises. He's positioned on the far side of a long conference table in the room's center. Laslo is momentarily surprised by the man's presence, but then remembers how things have changed. This is normal, he thinks, one's oldest enemy now a close friend. A new world with new rules. He smiles at the Arab, then looks to the far end of the room.

Cain stands with his back toward them. He looks at the Standard of Israel, a menorah flanked on each side by olive branches.

"Nations will come to your light," he says softly, "and kings to the brightness of your dawn."

Khalifa resumes his seat, looks to Laslo.

"Isaiah sixty," Laslo says. "I'm impressed." He glances toward Khalifa. "And surprised you know that scripture, Mr. Drake."

Cain turns to face them. "There are many things about me that would surprise you, Laslo. And please, call me Cain. Drake is dead."

Laslo moves to the table's far side and takes a seat. Cain moves from the standard, smooths his jacket. Meticulous as always, he wears a dark suit in faint pinstripes and sterling blue tie. He assumes a seat across from the Prime Minister and Khalifa.

"As for my methods, dear Laslo, they are my own. Much has changed since we last met, and as I said to the world, I am sent by God." In front of him is a yellow legal pad provided by Slabav's staff. Cain slides it a few inches toward the table's center. "God has a plan for this Earth, and you both are vital to it." He glances at Slabav, then Khalifa.

Slabav eyes him, marvels at the changes in his appearance. He has the same olive skin tones as before, the same method of dress, even the same manner of speech. But there's a distinct change. His formerly walnut eyes are now a deep, crystal blue. They look like lasers, focus intently on whatever they regard, no detail missed. They're clear and focused, intense in the way of a raptor. And the hair, brilliant, bright white, opalescent if one stares too long. Laslo can't shake the feeling that with Cain's arrival, bad things are coming for Israel. Peace must be preserved, Laslo thinks, and so I must deal with this man.

"What plan?" Slabav asks. "What more is left?"

Cain picks a piece of lint from the sleeve of his jacket, then regards Slabav. "You don't think this is finished do you, Laslo? Think that Israel's achieved its true station?"

Laslo considers all that's happened in the past few months. "I thought it a rather good start," he says. "Too much change, and too quickly, will make people nervous."

"Nonsense," Cain says with a dismissive wave. "The people are the same. They'll enjoy what we build. All nations will supplicate to us, be drawn to our light. We will be the shining city on the hill."

"I could argue that we are now," Laslo says.

"And you'd be wrong. Come Laslo, are you so short-sighted? Is this your grand plan for your nation?"

Laslo thinks of this. His place in history is assured. He'll be considered one of the best PM's in Israel's existence. But Cain's right, there's still work to be done. Perhaps my sight has been short.

"You're experiencing great prosperity now, yes?" Cain says.

Laslo eyes him before answering. "We are."

"And peace?"

"That as well," Laslo says. "It's truly amazing what your death heralded. But I can see that you're not dead. That you sit here before us. I also sense that you're different in other ways and that makes me uneasy. Makes me guarded and distrustful."

Cain flashes his perfect smile. "And you, Oshi? What are your thoughts?"

Khalifa sits to Slabav's right. He leans forward a bit. "I'm glad you're alive, Mr. Cain. It matters not how you appear, neither do your theatrics impress me." He adjusts his tie, a gesture that seems foreign, as if the tie's too tight. "All you promised has come to pass. There remain only a few loose ends which I'm sure will be tied up very soon." He winks at Cain with his right eye. He's positioned such that there's no way Slabav can see this. "I remain at your service."

Cain flashes that smile, looks back to Laslo. "You're right to be suspicious, Laslo. I'm suspicious as well. Much of this I don't understand myself. If I did, I would seek to allay your concerns and to offer a more complete accounting. As it is, I know only God has sent me to you as an advisor. I don't know why He crowned me with such an apparition as my hair or changed my eyes to this wretched blue. But I can assure you, it is, indeed, me."

He shifts his attention to Khalifa. "As far as loose ends, there remain a few monetary transactions that will be complete within a day or two. As for other concerns, they'll need to stay on the back burner for a time. You see, God's plan," he frowns a bit here, "will supersede any of my own."

Khalifa looks at the man and his expression becomes stern, on the verge of anger. He leans back, seems to collect himself, then glances at his watch. He rises. "Gentleman, I must go. I've just realized I'm late for another meeting." He nods at them both. "Peace be unto you." He departs the room.

"Rather abrupt, that," Laslo says. "It's not like him to depart with such haste. Unless he's angry. But what could he possibly be angry about?"

"I'm sure he's just distracted, sometimes keeping peace is more difficult than waging war. Do forgive him, Laslo."

Laslo looks at the door. "And what of you, Cain? What plans has God entrusted to you?"

"He's commanded me to guide you." He looks to the ceiling, chooses his words. "All we've planned has been delivered through God's hand. Your Temple is built. Your nation, sovereign and joyous. Do you not find it strange how the rest of the world has become so acquiescent? How Israel now thrives? How other nations supplicate to your wishes? Your economy is booming, your people enjoy peace. Do you think that's because of Thaddeus Drake or Laslo Slabav or Oshi Khalifa?" He holds Laslo's eyes for a moment. "Only God can perform such miracles. But He tells me we're not finished. That there are those who work against our goals. That's why I'm here, to offer guidance. To ensure that these miracles endure. I'm here today, Laslo, to offer you my services."

Laslo hesitates. "To what end?"

"To assure Israel takes its rightful place as the world's true leader. I wish to see this nation as the leader of all things. To see this country serve as a fount of wisdom and peace and to unite the Earth as one global state. A state that's peaceful, joyous and god-fearing." He leans forward, blue eyes piercing. "Don't you see? We'll christen a new empire, one born from centuries of death and bloodshed. This is what God wants. This is why He sent me."

Slabav reclines a bit. *Beware the bearer of gifts for a dagger they may conceal.* "And if Israel doesn't want your help?"

Cain's expression doesn't change. He leans back, slides his right hand onto the table. It appears burned, scalded, as if someone branded him with a hot iron. Laslo doesn't want to be rude but can't stop from looking closer. The brand is round like the sun with rays moving off in all directions. As he stares, a myriad of small triangles comes in focus. A Zentangle of squiggled lines and sharp angles whose pattern grows deeper and more elaborate the longer he stares. He sees movement within these lines, as if each is imbued with a fluid, blood maybe, moving at speed, joining, intersecting, crossing, fusing.

"If you don't want my help, dear Laslo, then say so. I'm sure God wouldn't want me to force such a thing on His chosen people."

His manner is calming, the white locks on his head beam with some invisible light, some radiation. Laslo feels his words are true. But then he also remembers Drake emptying his revolver into another man's chest, saying "Now you know the price of betrayal." Is this the same man? Is he sent by God? Perhaps he should be arrested and kept safe in a cell until such time as Laslo can say with accuracy that he poses no threat.

Laslo remembers Cain's arrival. The symbolism of a returning hero on a white horse hadn't escaped his notice. He remembers how easily Cain defeated the security detail, with just a flick of his index finger. Not natural, but in alignment with his claims he's sent by God. The media hasn't started asking these questions yet, and Laslo is sure when they do, Cain will have a very good answer. The world can't get enough of him, even now throngs of reporters wait outside for even a glimpse of the man.

"Why the name change?" Laslo asks.

Cain laughs, smooths his tie. "Because that's my real name, Laslo. I am Cain. Drake was a persona. A tool in God's hands. After my unfortunate death, God freed me from such nonsense. I am who I was, am, and shall be."

Laslo watches the man, searches for signs of deception. He must tread carefully. He's seen what Drake can do. Is this Cain so much different? Has God intervened? The evidence tells him, more now than ever before, God *is* working wonders. Israel is sovereign and at peace. Muslim, Jew, and Christian live in harmony. The Temple has been rebuilt and the people are happy. All of his dreams have come true. Perhaps Cain is who he says he is. Besides, could it be so bad to use this man's fame for Israel's benefit? Announcing Cain has joined the administration will certainly cause a stir, and one most probably supported by the masses.

"Very well," Slabav says. "You'll be Minister of Communication. Your job will be to do what you do best. To be a diplomat, an orator. You will convey Israel's messages to the world."

Cain rises and smiles. "Excellent." He buttons his jacket and moves toward the door.

Then he stops and turns. "I'm excited to start, but first I must meet with the U.S. president. After that, some other pressing business. Rest assured, though; I will carry the message of Israel to the world."

Laslo stands, raises a hand, chuckles. Cain has his hand on the doorknob; the puckered brand twists on his skin. "Mr. Cain," he says, "you may have confused the duties of your new position. As Minister of Communication, you will direct *my* communications to the world."

Laslo doesn't know why, but he expects anger, an outburst of disagreement.

Instead, Cain flashes that perfect smile. "Of course," he says, and departs the room.

CHAPTER 6

JERUSALEM, ISRAEL

Oshi Khalifa considers his options, his assets. The pistol feels hard in the holster against his chest. He has friends, allies, plans of his own. Now these plans are in jeopardy. The personal loans he's taken, based on his word and reputation, on that goodwill he'd gained through the years, are coming due soon.

It wasn't easy convincing them. Even now he knows plans for his assassination are in motion. No, these allies won't wait. He's promised an end to all of the wars and feuds over land and religious territories. To achieve those ends he's worked to assure peace and aid in the rebuilding of the Temple. Aims he should've worked against, aims that serve a grander purpose.

Double-crossed, he thinks. The only words that truly describe what just happened. "On the back burner," is what Drake said, "God's plans had changed."

Nonsense, he thinks, the pistol's bulk pressing against him. Has Drake lost his nerve? Does he plan to renege on the promise of the complete extermination of the Jews?

And just when things were going so smoothly. Slabav, the ignorant ass, has been assisting Jews from all over the world in their relocation to the Holy Land, never thinking his "new friend" may have other plans.

Where Sundamir failed, Khalifa would prevail. But then this Cain shows up. He thinks he's fooling everyone with the name change and the different looks. More theatrics, more inanity from a talented liar.

Still, the gloved man was a powerful ally. This Cain will be as well. Or a powerful enemy.

Cooler heads must prevail, he reminds himself. He hasn't achieved his station through anything but sheer gall and a level head.

But now he's simmering, a pot about to boil. He doesn't know how long he can suffer these insults without acting. The blood of his lineage screams from the grave, for vengeance, justice, revenge.

It's been ten minutes since he sent the text to the only number he had, what used to be Drake's number. He has no idea if the man will show but waits, seething. The limo sits purring in the empty lot of an old construction company on Jerusalem's outskirts. He glances at his watch. Five more minutes, that's all I'll give.

He no sooner thinks this, and another limousine enters, makes a wide circle, then pulls alongside. Cain exits the vehicle, then enters Khalifa's.

His smile catches Khalifa off guard. Soothes much of his rage in an instant. Khalifa fights to retain the emotion, reminds himself what's at stake. He must be strong; he must be passionate. Anger is his edge, his fuel.

Cain slides in the back. His smile is sincere, his eyes kind. "Dear Oshi, are you okay?"

Oshi's pistol calls to him and he wonders if Cain can sustain another shot to the head. He thinks back to the security detail on Easter Sunday. The smoldering lumps that were their weapons. The *Easter Miracle,* the press calls it. A defining moment of peace, the guns serving as symbols of swords beat into plowshares. Khalifa suppresses his sneer, or at least hopes he does.

"I fear I'm not okay," Khalifa says, "but can be made whole by a simple answer to a simple question." He takes Cain in, meticulous, even beautiful. A king of the desert, a blessed pasha in a thriving oasis.

"Our deal, as I understood it, was that I would lend my support to your goals. In turn, I'd see my own goals come to fruition. I've bided my time, done everything I said I would. My promises remain unbroken." He pauses here, waits to see if Cain will speak.

The man remains silent, his expression as sincere as when he'd entered the limo.

Khalifa continues. "The relocation of the Jews is almost complete," he says. "Plans have been made for their extermination and disposal. Plans have been made to conquer Israel and to erase their history from the world once and for all."

He again pauses to let his words sink in. He slides forward a bit, looks Cain right in the eye. "Here is my question: Do you intend to keep that promise?" He holds Cain's eyes as he waits for his answer. The man shows no visible sign of expression or emotion, returns Khalifa's gaze without blinking.

Then his smile widens, glistening white teeth blaze.

"Dear Oshi," he says, "we cannot continue as planned. You must be patient for a little longer. Does all the new peace not warm your soul? Are your countrymen so consumed with hatred that they fail to see this new dawn? Will you not lead them through this as you've so deftly led them before?"

The words hang in the car's interior, echo through Oshi's brain, bounce around, jar things loose, crack his facade with each bounce.

Oshi looks down. His hands tremble with rage. Like boiling liquid coursing through his veins. Drake *is* backing out of the deal.

The pistol calls to him through his jacket. Khalifa looks up, wills himself calm, tries again.

"My dear Cain," he says, "it seems you've been dishonest with me. I've expended much effort, both personal and professional, to see your aims achieved. Now, you leave me to die in the desert. To rot under a blazing sun when you alone can provide an oasis. This cannot be. Might you elaborate so we can part today as friends?"

Cain is quick to answer. "Of course, dear Oshi, you see, it wasn't I that amended the plan, but God. Yes, the one God who is known by many names. He beckons us to be patient, to cherish peace and each other. I'm afraid the time may never come to eradicate the Jews and I'm sorry if that displeases you. But I serve a higher power and I must be true to that. If you wish, I can offer you my protection, which I assure you will be ample."

Khalifa leans back, forces a smile. "Forgive me," he says, "for my methods. I just needed to know so I can direct some changes and undo what has been done."

Cain smiles again. "Of course, don't give it another thought. And thank you for understanding."

As soon as Cain exits, Khalifa dials his phone.

It rings three times before there's an answer.

"You better have something important to say," a man says.

"I do," Khalifa says, "we've been double crossed. Drake just told me he has no intention of fulfilling his end of the bargain."

There's silence. A full five seconds or more pass before the man replies. "This changes nothing." The man's voice is cold, void of emotion. "Plans are in motion and cannot be stopped. What Drake *thinks* is unimportant. Proceed as planned. When it's over, we'll execute him as a traitor."

Khalifa smiles. Allies and friends. All is well. "Excellent," he says, "dosvedanya."

"Dosvedanya."

The line goes dead.

CHAPTER 7

JERUSALEM, ISRAEL

I stand frozen, sword pressed just above my Adam's apple.

The Roman's eyes are dark specks that defy description, not brown or cedar or mahogany. Just black ice, cold as a crow, dead. As if every person he's ever killed stole a kernel of his life on their way out.

I glance over his shoulder, around the vast room right and left. I'm looking for a savior, for someone to stop the killing blow.

I see no one.

"I missed me mark last time, lad," the Roman says. "I'll non be makin' that mistake agin."

I try to think of something to say, manage only: "But we're friends."

Longinus's eyebrows rise. He's surprised by this. Surprised, perhaps, at anyone ever considering him a friend. His eyes glance down and back up. There's a flicker there, a flash of remembrance, perhaps of some past friendship.

He holds my eyes for a few long moments, then the steel presses deeper. "Me friends do non mettle in me affairs." He leans close, his next words are a spit whisper. "I burnt because of ye."

I gulp and it makes a weird sound. This should be funny, but no one laughs. "I… We…" I lick my lips, flick my eyes at the steel. "You were going to kill us."

"Aye," he says, "ye were warned. And I trusted ye. I told ye leave it be."

"I'm sorry," I blurt. "Just so sorry."

He has me pressed against the wall now, sword to my throat. I know the power of X'chasei. I'll be mopped up and no one will ever be the wiser.

Then there's a commotion to my left, a shriek. The room is immense, two-stories, modern in glass and steel like a rich man's greenhouse. Someone streaks down the stairs to my left and races to Longinus.

It's Rhyme.

Tears stain her face, and there's panic in her voice. "No, Longinus! You can't, you can't." She speaks fast, each word a plea, tugging the Roman's arm. "Cain won't like it. Please don't. Please don't!"

I stare as she begs for my life. I'm not sure if the hallucinations have returned or if I'm watching a ghost.

The Roman's arm barely moves as she pulls. "Please.Please.Please."

Then I hear another voice.

"Dear Emery! You've returned."

Cain stands atop the stairs. He beams, glows from the top of his head. I think it must be the sun through large windows behind him, but as he descends, I realize his hair is completely white.

"Rhyme," he says, "do calm yourself."

She whirls toward him. "Stop this!" Auburn hair rolls like a thunderhead. Her scent invades my nostrils, vanilla and lavender. I know that look. That fire.

Cain reaches the bottom of the stairs and holds out his hand.

She accepts and he pulls her close.

"Stop him," she says. "Please."

He smiles at her. "How can I deny my wife anything?" He glances at me. "Our Emery has been a naughty boy. Thinking about it, I see why you're so fond of him. You're both very naughty. Very naughty, indeed." He cups her ass with his left hand and squeezes her tight. Their kiss is deep, long, and passionate.

When they part, Cain's lips are smeared with lipstick. "Dear Longinus," he says, "might you reconsider? Emery remains a valuable asset just now, and you are causing my perfect angel great distress." He looks into Rhyme's eyes as he speaks the last words.

The next few seconds appear as a family portrait painted in Dysfunction Junction. We all stand frozen in time.

Cain watches Longinus, a pleasant expression on his face. One arm around Rhyme, the other tucked in his pant pocket.

Rhyme nuzzles her head in his chest, eyes closed, left hand pressed against his abdomen.

Longinus stares, smoldering, sword held to my throat.

And I, the centerpiece of this macabre Gainsborough, horrified as I watch Rhyme and wish the centurion's blade to finish its job.

Seconds tick, all is silence.

The Roman flicks his wrist and I feel a sharp sting on my neck.

My hand shoots to my throat, to a trickle of blood.

He turns and crosses the long room to the bar, where he fills a glass with brown liquor and lights a cigar. He sits with his back to us and I'm struck by his posture. He appears a lonely teamster in a neighborhood pub contemplating his life's choices.

I sink to the floor and pull my knees to my chest.

My mind fights the Percs, tries to make sense of it all.

I raise my hands to my ears. They're trembling.

Then the tears flow.

I try to fight, but they're a tsunami. A thousand-foot wave consuming my soul and ravaging my flimsy breakwater. It drenches me, destroys the few defenses I have, logic, reason, and hope. My soul bleeds, sliced wide open. Despair fills my heart, drips through my veins to invade every cell and violate every breath.

I think of our love, our unborn child, of my misery at the news of her death. Of the anguish I'd suffered since then. I mourn my descent into the bottle, my lack of courage in all things. She is here, Cain's wife, and a new round of sobs flow as I realize she must've been here through the entire journey, must've known she'd forsaken and left me with only my memories and these madmen.

Our love is gone, I know that as if looking at a burnt-out home. A space filled with love and joy, reduced to charred rafters and ashen floors. A skeleton of what was.

I'm too bereft to be embarrassed. I've strayed too far in these wilds and am being consumed by monsters. I am Jonathan Harker in Dracula's castle. Alone. A lost traveler without defenses. I am blind, in the dark, hearing the beast approach.

I don't know how long I sit there bawling, but when I finally raise my eyes, I see Cain and Rhyme sitting at a large oval table. They're having breakfast and talking in quiet tones. I watch her. The sharp, high cheekbones. The flashing emerald of her eyes. Her full lips as she talks. She wears a turquoise dress, is a model of elegance and beauty. All that a woman should be.

She glances toward me and our eyes meet. I feel a scowl cross my features but am disarmed in an instant by her gaze. She pities me and wears it like a diamond brooch, large and glaring. One side of her mouth turns down and I see her deflate a bit.

"Dear Emery, do join us," Cain says, "you've endured much and are in need of something other than opiates." He sounds pleasant, like he's my best friend.

I rise, shaky, use the wall to brace myself.

Then I open the door to my sanctuary, the place where my drugs wait.

His next words are harsh and loud. "That was *not* a request."

CHAPTER 8

JERUSALEM, ISRAEL

Longinus sits drinking. To his left, the entire wall is a vast window that overlooks the entirety of Jerusalem. I sit at the oval table with Rhyme at the table's head to my right and Cain at the table's head to my left. My back is to the door of my sanctum, about fifty feet behind me.

To call this room spacious would be an understatement. It's spacious in the way of a cathedral. To my right is the room's entrance and to my left another huge floor-to-ceiling window. Stairs of glass and steel run in front of the vast transparent panel and rise to the second floor.

On the table everything is silver. Silver goblets, silver plates, silver napkin rings, silver pitchers, silver utensils. These sit atop a perfect white tablecloth, etched with white thread into a myriad of leaves and flowers without color.

Silver dishes reveal foods of all kinds. Bananas, apples, cherries, and oranges sit in a large bowl to my right. In the table's center are three serving dishes each with an assortment of meat: ham, bacon, and sausage. Next to that, various side dishes of eggs, hash browns, oatmeal.

Three silver pitchers are arranged on the table's opposite side. One has condensation, so it must be something cold, juice or milk. The others steam from narrow spouts, coffee or tea, maybe syrup.

An elegant hand grasps one of the steaming vessels. Rhyme collects a small silver cup from my place setting. The coffee smells black and strong. She doesn't ask if I want cream or sugar. She knows how I take my coffee. She slides the cup over and gives me a brief glance before turning to Cain.

"Do eat, dear Emery," Cain says. "I can't have you dying of starvation."

I stare at my empty plate. "How *would* you like me to die, then?" I raise my head, look straight at him. It crosses my mind to take my shot. Perhaps I can grab a knife and be fast enough to make for his eyes. Even though I know he can't die, I consider the risk possibly worth it. What's he gonna do, kill me? Take my woman? Leave me for dead in a Jerusalem ghetto? Turn me over to the psychotic centurion?

"Dear Emery," Cain says, "I never want you to die."

I look at my plate, see my pitiful reflection blurred in silver. I feel like a child between two parents. Silence hangs over us.

Then suddenly I realize I've made a decision. And without any help from such a nuisance as conscious thought.

I must die. I know now the insults will *never* cease, and I can't imagine what my life will become from this point. I've been betrayed. Forsaken. Abandoned. Everything of which I've dreamed has been ripped from me, and it would be a monstrous waste to continue this life. It's a decision made on instinct, but I know it's the right one. I'll rid the Earth of my presence.

Immense relief fills me, such an obvious and tangible answer. I kick myself for the idiocy of my recorded suicide note. Had I not taken the time for that little self-indulgence, I wouldn't be here today. My problems would be over, and I happily planted.

Yet here I sit.

Cain continues to eat. Fine and good then, I think; first chance I get, I'll end my role in this little theater of misery.

Then Rhyme speaks. "Please, Emery," she says, "I'm worried about you. You've lost so much weight. Please eat." Her voice breaks my concentration, makes me think of the times when she truly worried about me. The times when I could've held her, stayed with her. The time I'd squandered for a story, a Pulitzer or two, a line up my nose or shot down my throat. I'm tempted to look at her but just can't. I haven't the courage. I lack the control to look upon this woman and keep my emotions in check.

I long for my pills. Perhaps that's the way. Slam them all the first second I can, then drift off. A perfect coward's way out.

I don't reply.

Cain folds his napkin, tosses it on his plate. "Well then," he says, "shall we get started?" He doesn't wait for a response. "Emery, you shall accompany me to Washington where we have a meeting scheduled with the president. I'll need you there to record everything and have listed you as my personal envoy. All is in order, and I expect it to be a productive conversation."

Fine, I think, as long as you don't mind transporting a corpse.

"Rhyme," he says, "will you be joining us?"

I feel her look at me and struggle not to face her. The Percs call from my sanctum.

"Would you like me to?" she asks.

Cain's laugh is full and hearty. "A second without you is an eternity, my dear. I'd be honored to have so fine a woman in my entourage."

I stare at my plate, wait to be dismissed.

"I'm sure you and Emery have some catching up to do, perhaps some shopping as well."

There's a pause, then I hear: "As you wish, my love."

A spear straight through my bleeding heart.

I can hear the home audience groan as the announcer gives the play by play. He sounds like Vince Logan, a favorite commentator from a favorite show, *Challenge of Champions*, a spoof on Japanese game shows. "Here's Emery, the poor junkie. Looks like he's taken a shot to the bean bag."

"There *must* be a woman involved." This is Lenny Frankincense,

Vince's loyal, but off-color color man. "I have to hand it to him, Vince. He can really take a beating."

"Right you are, Lenny! He's not the best in the biz for nothing. Oh look, seems the love of his life has run off with another man."

"Ooh, that hurts!" Lenny says. "The little pansy cried real tears. What a puss."

I sit like an impotent turd. My stomach rumbles, but all I can think of is a quick end to this nightmare. Catching up? Shopping? What the fuck?

"Emery, would you care to escort my wife for an outing while we're in D.C.? It may lift your spirits." This is Cain. What a prick.

"Fuck you." I don't look up but can imagine the smug grin on his face.

I hear a chuckle, then a single hand clap. "Perfect," he says, "I'll take that as a yes."

I hear him rise from the table and walk to the bar where Longinus sits. I look up to see the Roman hasn't moved.

"Longinus, the time has come to retrieve your relic," Cain says. "Is it safe to assume you haven't misplaced it?"

"Aye," he says, "but t'isn't worth a frog's fart. Anon and agin, ne'er was."

"Marvelous then," Cain says, "retrieve your relic and meet us here in three days. We'll see if we can breathe some life into that amphibian's bowels."

Longinus draws long on his cigar then snuffs it into an ashtray. He exhales a pillar of smoke, then downs what remains in his glass. "I can non wait."

I watch Cain, the radiant hair, the icy blue eyes. He looks right at me.

"O ye of little faith," he says.

To my right Rhyme rises and I turn to see her smile at me. The pity is gone, and she looks genuine, even loving.

I snap my attention to the empty silver of my plate.

Her scent surrounds me as she walks past. I close my eyes and inhale with as much subtlety as I can manage. A single indulgence before I meet my maker.

I feel her hand brush my back, subtle, but definite.

She breezes to the steps and disappears above. I force myself not to watch.

I look at Cain, who is watching me. He shows his supermodel smile, then walks toward the steps as well. At the bottom of the flight he turns and holds my gaze for a few seconds more.

"Dear Emery," he says, "I'm glad you're back." He pauses to let the words hit home, then glides up the stairs to join my ex.

Longinus rises, turns, looks at me. His expression tells me he's reconsidering his earlier choice. He walks from the room, sword forgotten on the bar.

This strikes me as odd. Longinus is to his sword as a trucker is to naked lady mudflaps. Perhaps he's testing me. Giving me the opportunity to take the weapon and go marauding through the house. I consider this, then realize the only ones in the place who *can die* are me and the woman I love. Or loved. Pardon the slip, Freudian as it is.

I sit alone at the table and consider my options. Seems the only expendable one here is me. Remove me and the problems cease. My subconscious thinks it a good idea, and if Sig were here, he'd agree.

I take some small pleasure in the thought of Rhyme finding my dead body. Perhaps she'll save a tear for me.

I grab a handful of bacon and head for my sanctum.

Chapter 9

Jerusalem, Israel

If, indeed, you find me dead,
a hoard of pills stuffed in my head.
Please push them further down my throat,
and burn this little verse I wrote.
Then walk away, forget the thought,
of saving me, my life was naught.
No need for docs, no need for cops,
just leave me where I finally flop.
–Then dunk me in a ruddy plot.

I stare at the opiates. Round, light blue, beautiful; demons that alter the mind, then ensnare and enslave. Pure evil, deep and endless.

They're my salvation.

I munch on bacon and stare at the bottle. More than forty in there. Should be plenty.

I grab another water from the nightstand and think I should probably mark the occasion, say a few words. A lonely eulogy for a dead junkie.

"Oh no, he's gonna give a speech. I bet it'll be about love and all that."

"Easy, Lenny. Let's watch."

Real Romeo and Juliet shit. I'm going to end my life because my heart's broken. My lost love has returned. Has played the cruelest of pranks, faked her own death, then feigned concern about the Roman's blade at my throat.

I think of the sword in the next room. Think maybe I can call the police, then storm the house, inflict as much damage as possible to everyone. Except Rhyme. I don't know why, but to harm her seems ungentlemanly. But attacking everyone else, slicing and cutting my way through them, seeing the surprised looks on their faces, now that would be something. A fitting tribute to their inhumanity and my insanity.

When the cops arrive, I'll threaten them, and they'll shoot me. Now we're talking. A suicide, but not my fault. I imagine explaining this to John when I'm at the pearly gates. I feel a bit embarrassed as my imagination is too spot on as to what he'd say about it all.

"God knows your heart. Suicide was your goal."

Then I wouldn't be let into Heaven. I snort. Like I have a chance at getting in anyway.

I imagine Rhyme finding me, those black pearls falling from her eyes, faux pearls this time, made in China. But she'd know what she'd done, know she'd deserted me, know the cost of her claws.

Even as I think these thoughts, Vince and Lenny heckle me. Call me a sissy. Tell me I'm buying off on my own bullshit. In a rare moment of candor, Lenny actually warns that I've walked this road before, that my problems have been caused by my own actions and self-loathing.

Then Vince says I need to be accountable.

Then I have a moment of clarity. A parting of the fog, if you will.

I realize there's hope.

The woman I love lives and despite everything else, her abandonment, our divorce, her marriage, I realize I've caused her more misery than she has a right. I've shredded her heart to slim ribbons, abandoned her completely and fully. I drew first blood as John Rambo would say.

I see the plain facts.

She's here.

She's alive.

She's in the clutches of a monster.

I may be her only friend. I can't abandon her to this evil, can't leave her to these wolves.

I empty the bottle into my hand and stare at the little demons.

"Coward," Lenny teases.

"Pussy," Vince says.

I take two and dump the rest back into the bottle.

Then I think about it.

I open the bottle and take two more.

Sleep is what I need now, and these little beauts will do the trick just fine.

"Junkies always have an excuse, eh, Vince?"

"Right you are, Lenny!"

I think of Rhyme. The way she looked at me, the way she touched my back.

I sigh, make my decision. Today I'll choose strength and discard that which is easy. I make a choice to think of another before myself. For once.

Besides, the pills aren't going anywhere, and I always have tomorrow to reconsider.

I put the cap on the bottle and replace it in my valet. Then I exit the sanctum, cross the vast room and retrieve a bottle of Macallan from the bar.

Rhyme needs me.

"All jilted lovers say that," Vince says.

"I think he's a stalker."

I see Longinus's sword on the bar. I've never really seen it up close.

Intrigued, I lift it with both hands and examine it. It feels rugged and thick. Smells of blood and fear. A relic from a museum. The scabbard is gold, etched with a swirly design and strange writing. In the middle of this, an etching catches my eye, a profile of a man.

Probably an emperor, I think. I remind myself to ask Longinus about it, whenever he deigns to talk to me again.

I slide the sword from its sheath. The blade gleams silver and I see it's weathered its long life quite well. It hasn't a blemish, stain, or dent. I remind myself to research how Romans made their swords.

I hold the pommel and swing it through the air. Then I thrust it in front of me as if skewering Cain. As heavy as it is, it's surprisingly easy to wield. Must have something to do with balance, I think. I remember someone at some point saying something about blades being balanced. This must be what they're talking about.

I swing it through a wide arc, then spin it and hold it in front of me. Then a thought hits me: I'd been stabbed by this very sword. For some reason this locks me in place, and I can see my scowl as a bent reflection in the sword's blade. I lower it, look closely at its tip. I remember the feeling, akin to being branded, a loud pain, harsh.

I poke the point gently with my finger. It's razor sharp, ready to do precisely what it was made to do. The Roman takes good care of his tools. I'd better put it back before he comes looking for it.

I spin it once more and hear a subtle click. I start to sweat. I've broken the thing. It's survived all these centuries and then my dumb ass has to play with it, and it breaks.

Will insults never cease?

I swing it a few gentle strokes and hear the click again. From the pommel. I feel some relief with this. Perhaps a pommel is easy to fix. I raise it close to my face, examine the handle. It's gold like the scabbard but contains no etchings. It has ridges about the width of a large finger. These run from the hilt near the blade to a solid golf ball-sized orb made of some hard metal. Just enough room here for a human hand. I shake the sword, spin it again, zero in on the click.

It comes from the orb, and with each movement of the blade I hear it.

The orb appears attached by a single pin the caliber of a fountain pen. It juts from the orb a quarter of an inch. I grasp it, try to push it in, to tighten it. I don't know if the sword is supposed to click, but if it isn't, Longinus will have something to say about it.

I fiddle with the thing, try desperately to fix it. Then, suddenly, the pin falls into my hand. I panic a bit, glance around the vast room, pause to listen. The Roman will come looking any second. I grasp the orb, find it turns. Call it a reporter's nature, but I can't help but unscrew it. When I do, a key falls into my hand.

It's black, old, appears oiled. About two inches long, it looks like a skeleton key, something a pirate would wear on a necklace close to his heart.

From somewhere in the building, I hear a door shut.

With shaky fingers, I replace the key in the orb and screw the thing back on the pommel. I turn it as tightly as possible. Then I replace the pin and slide it to its original position, pushing with my thumb. The pin slides easily and seems secure as it becomes flush with the orb.

I glance up, swing the sword again, and am relieved the click has disappeared.

I reach for the scabbard, anxious to replace the sword and depart with my scotch.

Then I hear the voice, unmistakable.

"Ye up for some killin'?"

I turn to see the Roman. A shiver runs through me, I've no idea how long he's been there.

At least he's talking to me, I think. Vince and Lenny are silent.

Longinus stands with massive arms folded over his chest. His muscles bulge against the fabric of his button-down shirt, pink no less, which amazes me. He doesn't look pleased. I should've downed the bottle of pills when I had the chance.

I slide the sword in the scabbard, being very, very gentle. I manage a smile and try to look like an old friend who's just blown in for the weekend.

He moves toward me, holds out his hand.

I give him the sword and step back.

He eyes me, lowers the sword to his side, then says, "Ne'er agin."

I gulp and nod.

Then he hikes his thumb in the direction of my sanctum, the universal sign for "beat it."

I grab the Macallan and move past.

I'm stopped by the sword against my chest. Longinus reaches down and twists the bottle from my hand. The scabbard lowers and he lets me pass.

I hurry to my sanctum, shut the door and flop on the bed. I'm breathing hard, heart hammering. Most people never survive one encounter with the Roman, let alone two. And in the same day.

I exhale, feel the Percs working their magic.

I hear Vince and Lenny. They're congratulating themselves on saving me from suicide.

"You're great at giving advice."

"Why thank you, Lenny. So are you."

CHAPTER 10

JERUSALEM, ISRAEL

Igneus makes his way down the sidewalk as shadows grow long. The sun dips to the horizon and he knows tonight will be cool, better for sleep.

"God be with you," he says to a woman who carries a chubby child in her arms. She glances with a flash of disgust, then averts her eyes and hurries past holding the child close.

Igneus pushes through the throng. His thoughts turn to Cain. To his re-emergence. To the change in the man's appearance. The white hair, the new power. How had he disabled all that security? Igneus recalls the spectacle viewed on an old RCA TV in a laundromat frequented by the homeless. A chill tickles his spine as his mind runs. Cain disarmed them with no more than a flick.

None of it makes sense. Igneus knows the man, knows Cain, as Drake, wouldn't have missed a chance to speak to a worldwide audience. Wouldn't have squandered a chance to seduce them with words or to use his gifts again to his advantage.

But indeed, he *had* missed the chance. Or not taken it, in any event. He said only a few words, then announced himself as Cain. He departed quickly and left the world buzzing about Thaddeus Drake's inexplicable return.

What's he planning? What next steps down this sordid road?

He squeezes past a group of men outside a restaurant, then moves down an alley. He remembers a time when places like this filled him with dread, the darkness, the hidden spots. Good places to be waylaid. Good places to die, which come to think of it, had been the cause of his death on the day Cain found him.

Doesn't bother me now, he thinks. Since assuming this new identity, he's become one with the street, has grown bold and fearless.

Will wonders never cease.

He passes a dumpster that reeks of raw chicken too long in the sun, then past a collection of garbage, discarded pallets, empty soda cans, an old tricycle. The alley has green doors about every forty feet. Each needs a fresh coat of paint. He knows them to be closed and tightly locked, opening only when one of these businesses needs to eject some fresh waste into the alley's dark confines.

He approaches one, about halfway down. Painted words greet him, faded with thick scratches through the lettering. Lee's Chinese.

He knocks twice, waits.

An Asian man peaks through a crack. He looks suspicious, ready for trouble. His expression changes when he sees the Jew.

"Ah, Mr. Igneus," the man says, "are you here for your dinner?"

"I am, sir," he says, looking at his ragged shoes. He's embarrassed by his appearance. What little hair he has is disheveled, and he wears blue jeans covered with dark stains and stringy holes. A faded, plaid long-sleeve covers a threadbare cotton shirt, a BMW logo shows slightly above a buttonhole.

Mr. Lee disappears for a few seconds, then returns with a bag. The smells reach Igneus and his stomach makes a gurgling sound that even Mr. Lee hears.

Mr. Lee smiles but the expression isn't for joy, but for pity. "Come back three days. Honey chicken special. Plenty leftover." He winks and closes the door.

Igneus can hardly wait to tear into the bag. If it weren't for Mr. Lee and a couple of other restaurant owners, he'd be digging through that dumpster to explore just how nasty old chicken can get and still be edible.

He hurries down the street, the smell of lo mien and orange chicken tempting him to stop in some hidden corner and devour it all. He fights the urge, turns down a side street and into another alley. He hurries past two unconscious junkies who sleep it off on a collection of newspapers and cardboard. Another right, then left down a long alley which ends abruptly.

He freezes. A man he doesn't recognize pokes around near his box.

"Move away," Igneus says.

The man startles, then turns. A scar splits his right cheek. He's bigger than Igneus, looks like an alley cat morphed human.

"Is that food?" The man stares at the bag.

Igneus places the bag on the ground and steps forward. "Yes, it is."

A thick tongue pokes over the man's lips. "I'll be taking that."

Igneus glances at his box, his home. "Or you could just leave me in peace."

"Mr. Igneus?" Igneus cringes as Sebastian pokes his head from the box.

The man turns, sees the boy, licks his lips again. "Now who might this be?"

"No concern of yours," Igneus says. "Why don't you take the food and leave us in peace?"

The man shows a smile without a front tooth. "Why don't I take both?" He looks at the boy again and his smile grows.

The man sidles toward the child, then leaps at Igneus.

This isn't unexpected. Igneus closes the distance, ducks under outstretched arms.

The man spins, eyes him, circles. "A slippery one." He steps cautiously, throws a couple of weak jabs.

Igneus knows the setup. An attempt to draw him close. Knows the man's real objective is to catch him in a bear hug and get him on the ground. The man's size is his advantage. If he gets Igneus on the ground it will be over quickly. Then what of Sebastian?

Igneus keeps his distance, glances at the boy.

The man moves close, feigns a punch with his left then throws a full punch with his right. Igneus moves left, avoids the blow by half an inch, then punches the man's forearm an inch below the elbow.

The man jumps back, shaking his hand.

Igneus knows his arm is tingling, painful, probably numb.

The man leaps, punches in a flurry.

Although Igneus is frail, he's fast and intelligent. He knows his strengths and his weaknesses. The man attacking has no plan at all. As soon as he'd seen Igneus, he thought *easy target.* He hasn't had another thought since, just entered attack mode.

Igneus ducks the punches, slides to the man's left and gets in two jabs of his own. One to the same spot as before and the other to a soft spot on the underside of the man's upper arm.

The man yelps. "You little shit!" He rubs his arm, shakes it, holds it loose. "I just wanted the food and the boy. Now I'm taking your little box and everything in it."

Igneus glances at the box, tries to move closer.

The man rushes him.

If he tackles me, I'm done.

Then Igneus has another thought.

Just before the man has him, Igneus jumps in the air. Not very high, but high enough to ensure the man's hug falls around his waist and not in a spot where his arms will be trapped.

Igneus impacts the wall behind him, steels himself so as not to lose air or strike his head.

Then he goes to work.

Spreading both arms wide, he claps them together on the man's ears.

The attacker's eyes go wide. His hands shoot to his head.

Igneus sees the advantage, drives his index fingers into the man's eyes.

The man screams, hands dart to his face.

Igneus turns slightly, then stomps hard on the inner part of his attacker's foot.

The man gasps, hands dropping, mouth open, eyes squeezed tight. He throws his arms forward in a blind attempt to catch his target.

But he's too slow. Igneus is out of reach.

The man flails, blinded, arms searching. "You little shit!"

Igneus circles, sees his opening, rears his foot like a scorpion poised to sting.

He unloads, a full kick to his attacker's balls.

The man doubles over, his face turns purple; spit flies from his mouth as air rushes from his lungs.

He crumbles, eyes closed, holding his groin.

Igneus steps past, retrieves a three-foot length of wood from atop his box.

He winks at Sebastian, then spins and cracks the man upside the head.

The man falls limp, brain scrambled, spread-eagled.

Igneus retrieves the food and hands it to the boy. Then he stands facing the man, watches him stir, sit up, look around with a dazed expression. A trickle of blood flows from his ear.

He attempts to stand as Igneus taps the two-by-four in his hand.

"You've been a marvelous guest," Igneus says, "but I think it's time to call it an evening."

The man rises on shaky limbs, stumbles a few paces. He presents his middle finger, lets out a string of expletives, threats of what he'll do to Igneus and the boy.

He limps off down the alley, rubbing his eyes, his arm, his ears.

"You okay?" Igneus says.

Big blue eyes flash over a wide smile. The boy's hair is a mess, long, blonde and unkempt.

"Wow!" the boy says. "You're like Bruce Lee."

Igneus grins, leans the plank against the wall. "Hardly," he says. "If he'd got his arms around me, that would've been it." Igneus shudders at the thought. What if he lost? What would a man like that do to Sebastian? He shakes away the thought.

"Come," he says, "I brought Chinese from Mr. Lee."

"Oh boy!" Sebastian darts from the box and grabs two old milk crates. He flips them over and arranges them beside an old tire that lies flat on the ground. Upon this, he sets a small piece of plywood.

He grins, blue eyes peering beneath blonde locks. "Dinner for two?"

Igneus laughs and takes his place at the makeshift table. Retrieving the food, he hands each carton to Sebastian, who arranges them.

"Have we any water left?" Igneus asks.

Sebastian disappears into the old box and emerges with a one-liter bottle of Aquafina. Igneus frowns. He's worried sharing the same bottle too many times may make one of them sick. "We need a new bottle or two, eh?"

"Eh!" Sebastian says, opening the first carton and unwrapping the plastic utensils Mr. Lee enclosed.

"Save those," Igneus says. "We can use them for a few days."

Sebastian nods as a pile of Lo Mein slides into his mouth.

Igneus looks down the alley, a habit one develops on the streets, then starts to eat.

They devour the food like hungry dogs. No sense wasting time, especially when experience shows if you try and *dine*, someone may show up and take your food leaving you with only a horrible, hollow feeling gnawing your insides.

Igneus is glad he's been thin his entire life. It doesn't take much to fill him and he worries about Sebastian's growth. The lad is about twelve and Igneus is glad to have him as a companion, but growing boys need food.

After ten or twelve mouthfuls, Igneus slides his carton to the boy. Sebastian's expression says he's still hungry.

"I could burst," Igneus says, patting his stomach. "Would you like the rest?"

Sebastian doesn't hesitate, diving into the carton, plastic fork moving with speed.

Igneus laughs. The boy swallows without even chewing.

"Slow down," he says. "We've got time. I'll keep watch while you enjoy your meal."

Sebastian sets his fork down and takes a deep breath. "Okay," he says. "I'll try."

The benefits of immortality aren't lost on Igneus. Neither is the fact that he has plenty of money. Too much money to count, in fact, and in too many banks around the world. As he watches the boy, he feels a compulsion to take Sebastian to Jerusalem's finest hotel and set them both up in the presidential suite. Room service will flow, they can get clean. Sebastian can get his hair trimmed, get new clothes. From there they can figure out where on the planet they'd like to live. He'd enroll Sebastian in a fine school. A top-rated school: one of those schools where the kids all wear uniforms and play sports like polo. Sebastian can be a normal kid, not just some kid from a burned-out commune left for dead by the great Thaddeus Drake.

The boy finishes, cleans every noodle, carrot, onion, even licks inside the cartons. He's growing, and for adolescent boys, that means calories. He needs calories if he's to grow and thrive.

Igneus sighs, thinks of his apartment in the high rise in New York. His flat in the well-to-do section of London. He thinks of Prague, Hong Kong, Los Angeles, Vienna, Zurich. His mind goes to the various safe houses he can remember. He can free them from all of this. Easily. Can probably even rekindle his deal with Cain.

Sebastian rises, then starts to kick a rock around the alley. "I'm gonna be one of the greats," he says. "Sebastian…" He stops, looks at Igneus. "What's my last name?"

Igneus shakes his head. "I don't know. You're just Sebastian, I guess."

The boy holds his gaze for a second and Igneus wonders what he's thinking. Then he says, "I'll just be Sebastian, then. That way it's easier for everyone to remember my name when I'm famous. Easier to sign autographs, easier for the people who put the names on the shirts, easier to write…" He returns to his rock, kicks it against the alley wall, aims for a discolored brick that seems newer than the surrounding brick. A goal of sorts. He talks to himself as he plays, as if he hasn't a care in the world.

Igneus smiles as the boy scores an imaginary goal then prances around the alley. He thinks of the homes, the money.

No, he thinks, I made my choice at the Temple. If I reach for any of that, Cain will be on me before the money gets to my pocket. And what of Longinus? I burned him to a cinder. He's going to want pay back. Or perhaps they'll just plant me to never again see the light of day, and after a good round of torture just for kicks.

No, the decision's been made.

He feels strong, bold, confident. God uses him still, he knows. If this is where God wants me, then this is where I'll be. God will provide. He provided for John through all those centuries. We'll be fine.

His heart remains skeptical though and although he doesn't verbalize it, his real concern is Sebastian. The words *like a son* float through his mind.

Since finding the boy in the burned-out compound of the Children of the Rocks, he's grown to love the lad. Seems Drake shut the whole place down as soon as the ritual was complete. The people who lived there were scattered to the winds, utterly forsaken and deserted. By the time Igneus arrived, the place was in ruins, desecrated, empty. Except for Sebastian. He'd remained, telling Igneus he was "Waiting for Mr. Drake to come." Then he'd said something about Cain not wanting anyone else to be able to repeat the ritual. So, they'd been scattered.

Igneus can only imagine what happened to the rest of them. Knowing Cain, something horrific and inhuman.

The boy scores another goal against the brick wall.

Igneus rises. "Come, Sebastian. We must go."

Sebastian fires another shot, then moves to their cardboard home where he closes the flaps and disassembles the makeshift table.

He scampers to Igneus's side as they walk into the evening.

CHAPTER 11

JERUSALEM, ISRAEL

Three days later, Igneus searches for cardboard. A steady drizzle soaks his clothes, makes the breeze vicious in its theft of body heat. A shiver runs through him as he glances at Sebastian. He tries to hide the worry from his face.

The boy's been coughing for days, has become gaunter and paler as each day passes. Igneus has tried to bolster the boy, has even skipped his own scrounged meals in an attempt to support Sebastian's nutritional needs.

What the boy needs is antibiotics, Igneus thinks. The free clinic is only three blocks away.

He considers the option as he watches Sebastian slough along. X'chasei will be watching. They're always watching. Taking the risk may have consequences he isn't ready to deal with.

He dismisses the dangerous idea. The move will cause unnecessary exposure.

So far, they'd been successful in evading X'chasei, and Igneus would like to keep it that way. They'd become adept at evading police, ambulances, banks, clinics, any place that might expose them, which, as he thinks about it, is everywhere.

Who knows what Cain will do if he finds them? At a minimum, Sebastian will be taken, exposed to Cain and his evils, perhaps killed. Certainly abandoned and left to fend for himself. Igneus shudders at the possibilities; he's running out of options.

He climbs over a low, concrete wall into a parking garage with very few cars. The boy trudges along, then exerts tremendous effort scaling the low barricade.

Worrisome. A healthy Sebastian would've leaped the wall, sprinted toward it to see if he could clear it with a single jump. Now he's struggling just to walk.

Igneus thinks of the hotel, five-stars, another option. Thick carpets, soft beds, fine dining. It may be worth the risk, worth it to get Sebastian comfortable, even if just for a single night. There'll be an on-call doctor who could be summoned to examine the boy and get him better.

He pulls a piece of jerky from the pocket of his faded jeans and offers it to Sebastian. The boy waves it away, wipes the rain from his face and flops down on a parking block of yellow concrete. He shivers like a wet chihuahua.

If only they could find a decent box, a new home.

Yes, boxes have become valuable in the never-ending rain. Have become a vital form of protection from the endless downpour. What they need is a big box, something large enough to enclose them on all sides and provide some warmth for the night.

Despite the fair temperatures, the cold has been all-consuming. It's amazing how moisture can seep through one's psyche and into one's soul. How it can completely demoralize and drain all energy, a little demon that seizes the frail, the malnourished. The young.

They'd spent last night between a stinking dumpster and an alley wall. Igneus managed to build a slim roof from empty fruit boxes propped from a dumpster's lip to a random pipe. Not a bad shelter, certainly not the best, had lasted only part of the night before eventually falling in on their heads.

This can't last, he thinks. He's very much afraid the boy will become sicker as the days progress. He considers his options. No X'chasei physician can be trusted, no emergency room doctor or health clinic. No homeless shelter or community charity. No, he'll have to solve this himself, and can think of only a single option.

The boy props himself against the wall of the garage, sits on the parking block looking worse by the second. Glazed blue eyes peer at Igneus, but he can't tell if the boy is seeing him or just staring into the abyss.

"Come on, Sebastian," he says, "just a little farther."

The boy tries to smile, opens his eyes more fully, struggles to his feet. He leans on the wall as hacking spasms escape his body. He's lost more weight.

Some father I am, Igneus thinks. Enough is enough. He moves to the boy, slides under his arm. "Come on," he says. "We'll get through this."

Sebastian doesn't respond, just leans on Igneus's shoulder and trudges slowly beside as they move to the stairs.

These prove difficult for the youth and it takes nearly five minutes to ascend two short flights. Sebastian leans on Igneus, seems about to collapse.

Are his lips blue? Perhaps I can just drop him at an ER and retrieve him later. Igneus dismisses this quickly. He knows what will happen. He'll drop the minor off, and the lad will get treated, but he'll also be turned over to the authorities and placed in some facility.

No, there's still a way, one more thing to try. If that doesn't work, I'll have to take the boy to a doctor, exposure or not.

They struggle across the parking garage. Igneus looks ahead, to a door he hopes is unlocked. His time on the streets has taught him to be aware of his surroundings. To watch people and examine their actions.

A couple of days ago, Igneus used the garage as a shortcut to another alley where he'd hoped to find some cardboard, perhaps a tarp. During the journey he'd seen a custodian exit a maintenance closet at the rear of the garage. The man hadn't locked the door, giving Igneus the chance to explore the room.

He'd found nothing but large pipes and gray walls.

Now the room may be their only hope.

They reach the door and Igneus feels elation as the knob turns and the door opens. They duck inside, and Igneus locks it behind them.

It's warm in here, dry. Igneus removes his thin windbreaker and the sweater beneath. He folds the sweater and lays it on the cold concrete, some insulation for the lad. He then wraps the windbreaker around the boy's torso and helps him to a sitting position.

"Wait here," he says.

"Where—" Another round of hacking spasms pour from the boy. Sebastian spits, and Igneus notices the sputum tinged with blood. He has to hurry.

"I'm going to get some medicine for you," he says. "Wait here, sleep if you can. I'll lock the door behind me, but you must open it when I return. I'll knock three times, then twice so you'll know it's me. Think you can do that?"

Sebastian takes a moment to answer. He's consumed by sickness and this worries Igneus, makes him think the boy will be unconscious or even perish while he's out.

He weighs the choice; lock the door to protect from the people who prowl these streets, or leave it unlocked so Sebastian won't have to try and open it.

"I can do it," the boy says, eyes barely open. His head leans against the wall and Igneus notices the skin above his collar bones retract with each breath.

He'll have to take the risk. "Don't worry, dear boy. I'll leave it unlocked. Sleep, I'll be back in a flash."

Sebastian offers a weak smile. "In a flash of lightning?"

Igneus kneels before him, places a hand on his forehead. He's hot, smoldering in fact. He wants to embrace the boy, hold him close until he feels better, caress his head as he sleeps, provide him all the comforts he needs until his illness subsides.

"In a flash of lightning," Igneus says, ruffling the boy's hair.

He exits the room and scans the area for anyone who might see him. There's no one. A spot of luck in a miserable day. He closes the door and moves to the first floor and out of the parking garage.

Broad daylight has been made dark by looming storm clouds, made cold by wind and falling rain. The windbreaker provided some protection but now Igneus is fully exposed.

He crosses a street and moves down an alley, keeps a sharp eye for anything useful. He crosses another street, turns left, down an alley, across another street, takes another left up another long alley.

At the alley's far end, just inside the entrance, he surveys the street. He's become a sort of expert on Jerusalem and knows this area to be residential, inhabited by a more upscale type of person. He watches, fighting impatience as worry scratches his soul and clouds his judgment.

He shakes his head, clears his mind. Emotion can only hurt him now. He has to focus, getting caught may literally cost Sebastian his life.

Igneus stamps his feet against the cold, tries to stay concealed as much as possible and still maintain a view of the street.

People pass in ones and twos, none seem to notice the thin, shivering man. He sizes them up. This one a lawyer, probably. This one an executive, maybe a business owner.

The wait is unbearable. He needs someone who looks like a doctor.

Across the street, two women exit a three-story brick building. They move down a short flight of steps and toward his hiding spot. Both wear scrubs. Nurses or doctors, medical folk for sure. If Igneus knows anything, he knows the place to find meds is in a medic's house.

He moves out of the alley and leans against a wall. The women approach, eye him carefully. They don't seem too concerned, probably because its daytime and probably because he's become so thin he doesn't look like a threat to anyone.

One of the women speaks on her cell phone. The other walks to her left, closest to the street. As they near, Igneus holds out his hand, lowers his head. Says a single word in Hebrew. "Help."

He doesn't look at them, can't risk being identified later. He feels something press into his palm, then watches their feet as they pass and move up the walk.

They've given him money. He grins, breathes a prayer that God will bless their generosity.

He watches them go, then returns his attention to the street to wait for a time when there's very few people. No people at all would be perfect but he doubts he'll get that lucky.

A man passes, walks up the street toward the apartments. Igneus looks around, sees no one else.

He exits the alley and crosses the street as quick as he dares. Near the building, he slides between a hedge and a smooth, brick wall. He tries to be silent, tries to see everything and anything, to take advantage of even the smallest opening while minimizing his own risk.

He moves down the wall, tries to avoid bustling the hedge. If he sees anyone he can simply duck down, and the thick hedgerow will hide him. He moves fast, stays low until he reaches the building's rear corner.

The building's rear area is split into six gardens, small patios each separated by a decorative wire fence perhaps eight inches tall. This is vital information; the building has six tenants. Now he just has to surmise which flat belongs to the medics.

Perhaps both of them live here, he thinks. Perhaps he has two different apartments from which to choose. Unlikely though. Far more likely the two share a flat. The ladies looked young, in the prime of their lives.

This is going to be tricky.

Igneus crosses the building's back yard then slides behind a stout poplar. Behind him, a wood-slatted fence runs the property's rearmost edge. He hadn't wanted to cross the area, to gamble with the chance a resident might see him. But he needed a better vantage point to view the building's exterior and garner clues.

He waits a few minutes. Rain drips from his nose. His shirt sticks to his body, hangs below his waist soaking his jeans drop by drop. He eyes the building, ready to bolt at any moment.

The building is a three-story rectangle. Each story has four windows that look out over the patio area. Igneus realizes the windows aren't evenly spaced. On the lowest floor a glass door splits the rectangle in half. Using the door as a center point, the windows closest to it have more distance between them than the ones farther away.

The extra space must indicate a passageway, probably holds stairs or an elevator. That means each apartment has two windows facing the rear of the building. So, six apartments in three stories with stairs or an elevator in the center.

He pictures it in his mind, visualizes what he might encounter upon entrance.

Now, where do the medics live?

He examines each window. On the first floor all the windows are without decoration. On the second floor a Star of David hangs in a window of the apartment on the left. In a window of the apartment on the right, a relief of butterflies in stained glass.

Of the windows on the third floor, no décor can be seen. One of the windows appears caked with dirt as if it's left open on sunny days and has never been cleaned. Or perhaps the apartment lacks a tenant. The other windows are featureless.

Igneus makes some assumptions. First, rule out the dirty window. Although a possibility, he can't imagine those ladies keeping anything but a tidy apartment. He scans the other windows on the third floor. No clues there, still a possibility.

The second floor contains the most clues. The butterflies are certainly a possibility. Young women enjoy stained-glass bursting in sunlight. He moves it higher on his list.

Now, what to make of the Star of David? Could be just a Jew but could also be a medic. In this country the Star of David is used as a medical symbol, like a red cross on an ambulance in America. The symbol is usually red, though, and this one is blue. The ladies were young and seemed the type to enjoy their youth. Probably wouldn't hang a Star of David in their window, and, if they did, it would probably be red. Perhaps or perhaps not, either way he can't rule out the option. He develops a plan to try and explore both second-floor apartments.

The wind picks up, steals heat as it glides over his soaked T-shirt. He shivers, holds his arms close to his thin frame, ponders his route. The butterfly apartment is the most obvious choice, so that's the primary target. Secondary target, the Star of David apartment. He dismisses the apartments without window décor. They've provided no clues and he won't have time to explore them all.

The odds work against him. His chance of success, low. Of the six apartments, he's narrowed it down to one, at most two. Inversely, all his assumptions might be wrong. Which means of the six apartments, six could be possibilities, giving him about a seventeen percent chance of simply guessing the correct one.

He rubs his temples, shakes his head. Cold gnaws his bones. It's hard to think through the shivering, through his shredded morale. Sebastian is waiting, he has to move.

Go with your gut. Trust the few pieces of info you have.

After a final scan, he crosses the yard to the building's rear door.

He glances around, knows he's exposed. Needs to make a choice, flee or enter. He pulls the door, but it doesn't move, locked. He steps left, over a decorative fence, then moves to the first window. It's locked, as is the one adjacent.

He peers through the glass, into a tidy flat done with modern elegance. A sleek low couch sits before a modern coffee table flanked by two minimalist armchairs. Beyond these a small, gleaming bar surrounds a white kitchen with steel appliances. The place seems deserted.

Igneus pushes up on the window, tests it again, hopes it's just stuck. It holds fast.

The rain picks up, runs down his back, soaks him more with each second. He shivers, ignores the discomfort. He's going to have to try the windows on the other side which means more exposure, more chance of getting noticed. He crouches, needs a second to think, then realizes he's more conspicuous crouched than standing. He stands up. What would a real criminal do?

Two metal chairs sit on the patio before him. Each holds a faded blue cushion.

An idea forms.

He grabs a cushion, places it against the window, then punches it hard in the center.

The glass makes an enormous sound as it breaks. Igneus freezes, cringes. A real criminal probably wouldn't have done that.

He feels the pressure, glances around the yard. With no time to lose, he sets the pad on the windowsill and climbs through.

The room is elegant, well decorated. Perhaps the ladies live here. He crosses the apartment, past the furniture and up a hall. To his right a bathroom gleams in steel and white. He enters, pulls open the mirrored door of the cabinet above the sink, sees three prescription bottles. He reads them, Cardiloc, Odnatron, Serenada. He has no idea what the meds are or what they do. No idea if they'll help Sebastian at all. He also has no time to be choosy.

He grabs the bottles then stoops to the cabinet beneath the sink. Three rolls of toilet paper sit stacked atop each other. Beside them a plunger and four hand towels, but no pill bottles. He starts to close the cabinet, then sees a small, blue dopp kit. He pulls it out and empties its contents into the sink, replacing them with the pills. He zips the kit closed. A real criminal would've thought to bring a decent bag, he thinks.

He moves out of the bathroom, turns right toward a bedroom at the end of the hall. It contains a massive, unmade bed. Beside it a cluttered nightstand that holds nothing that looks like medication. Beyond the bed is a closet. The door creaks as it opens. Igneus stands frozen. The sound was loud, like someone stomping a toad. Did anyone hear?

Tense seconds tick as Igneus drips rain on the room's white carpet. He hears nothing, assumes it's safe to go on.

The closet holds an assortment of men's clothes. He rifles through the wardrobe, snags a stocking cap, a hooded sweatshirt, and a nice, tweed sport coat. All are too big, but he slides them on anyway. They engulf him, make him feel like a child playing dress up, make him realize how much weight he's lost on the streets.

He scans the room once more, then moves quickly to the apartment's entrance and looks through the peephole. The hall beyond is empty. He unlatches the door and exits.

The door across the hall has a paper flower taped to it. He hasn't seen anything like this before and can't guess as to its meaning. He moves close, tries the knob. Locked, which is just as well because he's wasted too much time on the first floor anyway. The second floor is the goal, and he needs to get there. He turns, then notices a flash of shadow break the light of the peephole in the door before him.

Someone's in there. They've seen me. Have to move.

His heart thrums as he slips a bit on the tile floor. He's leaving quite a trail from his mud-caked shoes.

He moves down the hall, then up a short flight of stairs nearest the building's front door. This hall is identical to the first, clean with a beige, tile floor and a single potted ivy resting in a waist-level bronze stand.

Time to make a choice. Igneus knows the Star of David is the medical symbol in Israel but it's usually red. Butterflies seem a more apt choice for ladies to choose as décor.

He looks at the door to his right, the apartment with the Star of David, then left, at the butterfly apartment.

Someone's seen him, is probably calling the authorities. It's all or nothing.

Butterflies it is. He moves to the door, rears back and kicks it in. The resounding crash is alarming, unmistakable, certainly nothing a real criminal would do. He's just announced himself to the entire complex, has broadcast that an intruder has entered.

He springs into the apartment, ready to flee at the first glimpse of anyone.

All the apartments have the same floor plan, so he moves left into a short hall, then into the bathroom. His reflection taunts him from the mirrored cabinet above the sink; sunken eyes with dark sockets, pale skin stretched taught over sharp cheekbones. Skeleton fingers reach for the cabinet and pull it open. It holds a few perfume bottles, two tubes of toothpaste, another tube of something with blue letters in French. No medication.

He opens the cabinet beneath the sink. Sees three towels, thick and neatly folded. He pulls them out, throws them behind him. A bag of cotton balls follows, then a curling iron and pack of Q-tips.

In the cabinet's rear corner, he sees a cheap plastic basket and a dozen pill bottles.

Trembling fingers fumble with the kit's zipper. His nerves are catching up, all the pressure, too important to fail.

He dumps the basket in the kit, then finds he can't close it due to the bulk of so many bottles. He doesn't dare leave one behind. The odds are better for Sebastian the more meds he can scrounge. He forces the bottles, squeezes the kit until trembling hands and stubborn zipper cooperate.

This is about as good as it gets, and he can't waste more time with other apartments. He moves to the front door stepping over shards of wood and his own muddy footprints. He offers the ladies a silent apology, then moves into the hall.

He pauses in front of the Star of David apartment, considers kicking it in, weighs the risk. It may yield more meds but will cost precious seconds. He shakes his head, decides against it. The kit is full, and he's been gone too long, is too exposed. Who knows how Sebastian's feeling or who he's encountered?

He speeds toward the stairs, races down.

Near the bottom, he hears a gasp and looks up to see an elderly man. The man is stocky with squinted eyes and sunken cheeks. His index finger trembles as he points at Igneus. His other hand holds the main entrance open.

A police officer enters, sees Igneus, reaches for his gun and yells something. Then another officer enters behind the first. They look big and capable and Igneus knows he's outmatched.

The first officer blocks his path, draws his gun, positions himself low and square.

Igneus flies toward him.

The officer fires and the bullet sizzles past his ear, a high-pitched ring that muffles all other sound.

Igneus steps sideways, ducks another shot, then plants his right palm beneath the officer's left arm just above the elbow. He pivots and pushes. The officer spins sideways, gun discharging into the ceiling. He falls into his partner who has also drawn his weapon. They become entwined in the door's narrow space.

Igneus breaks for the back, fueled by panic.

Running wild, he nears the back door, hears the chasing gunfire, feels his left shoulder ignite. The force throws him off balance, causes him to fly forward in a tight spin.

He crashes through the rear door. Hears the glass shatter, feels the falling shards bite his skin.

He rises, holds his wounded arm close, sprints for the back fence.

Gunfire follows, rushes past with a shriek. Small holes appear in the fence ahead.

He sprints through the backyard, reaches the big poplar and moves behind it. He looks up, tosses the dopp kit over the fence, hears it land on the other side.

The officers are gaining, will be on him in a second.

Igneus leaps to grab the top of the fence. He plants his feet on the tree, then forces his wounded arm to move. A scream escapes as his left arm stretches through the injury. The pain is overwhelming, sobering. One never gets used to the pain.

He forces the limb to work, to grasp the fence's top. A hand grabs his ankle, one of the officers is on him. He pulls, pries his ankle from the policeman's grasp, then pushes off the tree, up and over the wall.

He falls, off-balance, lands hard, feels a sharp pop in his right ankle. He hasn't time to be concerned with such nuisances as injured limbs or gunshot wounds.

He has to get to Sebastian.

Sirens scream in the distance, closing by the second, volume increasing.

Rain falls with added fervor, mixes with the blood dripping from his hand.

The dopp kit sits in a puddle to his left. He limps toward it, grasps it tight. His ankle rages protest as he sprints down the asphalt passage. His shoulder is numb, doesn't move properly, has become useless.

Twenty yards ahead, a police car screeches around the corner and enters the passageway. The driver's eyes light up. The engine roars as the officer accelerates.

Then, Igneus feels a sense of relief. Fear disappears, panic drifts off on the wind. He's clear. Everything else is just details. The officers have no chance. They're in *his* house now.

He races forward, foot numb and swollen in a too-tight shoe.

He leaps atop a small green utility box, uses it as a step to jump to the top of another fence.

Another scream escapes as he lands on the other side. He stands, feels blood flow from his shoulder, checks to be sure he hasn't dropped the dopp kit.

He races down another alley, crosses a street, then turns up another alley.

The passage opens to a bustling street of shops and restaurants. People enjoy a meal safe from the day's rain and oblivious to the world around them. Others cover their heads with umbrellas as they move in and out of the shops or scurry down the street.

Igneus slows. He can't appear frantic. Must try and look as normal as possible. He holds the dopp kit under his left arm beneath the tweed sport coat and above the stolen hoodie. He tries not to limp; knows he isn't pulling it off. His shoulder throbs, his breath is harsh and rapid.

He passes a garbage can and retrieves a discarded newspaper, rolling it to a ball as he walks, then sliding it under the sport coat to press against his wound. The bullet must've gone all the way through. The blood hasn't yet soaked through his clothes. Another bit of luck.

Head low, he walks fast but not too fast. No one gives him a thought as he passes, too concerned with their shopping or dining to notice their surroundings.

Sirens wail and draw near. Igneus grins. They're too late, they'll never find him in the city's underbelly.

He enters a convenience store, grabs a bottle that looks the closest to cough medicine, Tarodex. He heads to the counter.

The clerk is young with a round face and short clipped bangs. She takes the bottle and rings it up, then places it in a bag. She doesn't look at him as she processes the transaction, too busy snapping her gum and chewing like a cow.

Igneus slides her the money, hopefully it's enough.

She hits a button on the register, hands him a few coins, then places the receipt in the bag.

He keeps his gaze low, nods a single time and takes the bag.

On his way to the exit, he slides the dopp kit in the bag then stops at a rack of magazines and peers out at the street. A police car drives past. Blue lights flash, but there's no siren. They search for him; haven't realized he's already disappeared.

He smirks, watches the car move down the street and out of sight.

He leaves, then turns into an alley a few paces down. Here he removes the sport coat and the hoodie, grimacing against the pain in his shoulder.

It takes great effort to disrobe but he manages to switch the garments, slipping on the sport coat then pulling the sweatshirt over it. He stuffs the newspaper under the coat and presses it against his wound. It's not much of an appearance change, but probably enough.

He moves off toward his goal, doubling back occasionally and taking a roundabout route. The pace is maddening, slowed by his injured ankle and throbbing shoulder. Panic grows with each step as blood streams down his arm. The sum of his injuries will eventually subdue him. Will eventually lay him low and leave him unconscious in a puddle somewhere. He has to get to Sebastian before then. After that, it doesn't matter.

He presses the newspaper hard against the wound.

The rain is a deluge now, hammering the ground around him as lightning shreds the sky. Pressing through the rain, through the pain, fueled by his own panic, he finally steps into the parking garage and races to the second floor as best he can.

The closet door is closed, appears the same as when he left.

The pain in his shoulder relents a bit.
His heart rate slows as he limps closer.
Then the custodian walks out.
Sebastian lies in his arms.
The boy's unconscious.
Or dead.

CHAPTER 12

JERUSALEM, ISRAEL

Sebastian is pale, soaked, limp in the arms of the custodian. Igneus thinks to run but can't desert the lad. Never will he leave him to an unknown fate. No, the boy's his responsibility, his family, his ward.

"Stop!" Igneus speaks a little louder than he likes, and the custodian freezes.

"Look, this kid is sick. He needs some help," the man says.

Igneus steps close, a few paces from Sebastian. He thinks to attack, to subdue the threat and remove the boy. Fists clench, lips tighten to a snarl.

The custodian steps back as if seeing the thoughts in his head.

Then Igneus has a calming thought, soothing, coming from some far-off place, some distant wrinkle in his memory.

My God will provide all my needs.

"He's my son," Igneus says. "I'll look after him."

The custodian stares at the little man, seems to size him up. Igneus doesn't shrink but ventures another step closer. "Give him to me."

Blood drips from his hand to form a small pool. He stands with his weight on his left in an attempt to try and relieve the agony in his right ankle. He knows how he looks, knows the man won't believe a thing he says. He sees the confusion, crinkled eyebrows over dark eyes.

"I don't want trouble," the man says, "but neither will I leave the boy to die."

The man is stout with broad shoulders spread to a V over a slim waist. Dark eyes never flinch. A cool customer.

"I can't let you take him," Igneus says.

"You can't stop me." His eyes are steely, calm. "Although you can come with us, if you wish."

Igneus does the calculations. If he deserts the boy, Sebastian will get the medical care he so obviously needs but Igneus will never see him again, will have no way to track his whereabouts when he recovers. If Igneus fights and manages to free Sebastian, he won't be any further along than when he started, homeless with a very sick child.

Must be another way, he thinks.

"Listen," Igneus strains to keep emotion from his voice. "I know I don't look it but I'm very rich. I can pay any sum you want. How about a hundred-thousand American dollars?"

The custodian looks stunned. Takes another step back. "Yes," he says, eyeing Igneus, "I'm sure you've stashed the boy in this closet because all the hotels were full. Makes perfect sense."

Igneus realizes the inanity of the offer. Realizes he has no way to back it up or to make the man believe. Realizes that currently the largest sum of money he has are some coins in his pocket. Coins provided by a stranger who he'd subsequently burgled.

"Listen," the custodian says, "you look a bit under the weather yourself. How about you walk with me. We'll call an ambulance and then part on friendly terms."

"We can't go to the hospital," Igneus says. "Our home is the streets. Hospitals are too risky. Just give me the boy and I'll mend him." It sounds like something a criminal would say. He ventures a step, feels his ankle refuse the weight, feels the warmth of his own blood as it drips down his hand.

"Looks like you've done a fine job to this point," the custodian says.

Igneus realizes the impasse. The futility of further discussion. The boy needs care, and quickly.

He raises the dopp kit. Struggles to unzip it. "I have medicine for him. I've just come from the doctor."

Sebastian lifts his head. "Dad?"

He's never called Igneus dad before. He must've heard the conversation, must be playing along. Such a clever boy.

Igneus goes to him, runs a hand through his hair. "I'm here, Sebastian. How are you feeling?"

The lad's features brighten although his pallor remains unchanged. "Better now you're here." He glances to the custodian. "Who's he?"

Igneus glances at the man, examines his features. His eyes are focused but hold no malice. "A friend," he replies.

Sebastian smiles. "We can use a friend."

The boy closes his eyes, seems to fall asleep. Igneus is amazed he can drift off in the arms of a stranger. He looks at the custodian. "I'll level with you. I can't tell you why we hide but I assure you, we aren't criminals." He feels like a liar. Certainly, Sebastian isn't a criminal but Igneus feels he can't make the same claim. Feels he's committed more crimes than anyone in living history. Feels every bit as criminal as Hitler, and Pol Pot, and Lenin. "The reasons we live the way we live are our own," he continues, "but we're in need of aid just now. Perhaps you can look the other way while we use the closet for a few days? We won't be a bother and don't indulge in vices of any kind. We just need a place where he can recover."

The custodian stares such that Igneus feels he's under a spotlight, preparing to endure an interrogation. The man glances at the boy and his features soften.

"I had a son once," he says.

Igneus nods, looks to his feet, to the bloody puddle on the concrete. "Then you understand a father's instincts."

The custodian nods, glances at them both.

He moves to the closet door.

Igneus limps behind, holds the door as the man enters and lowers Sebastian back atop the sweater Igneus laid out earlier.

He turns to Igneus, glances at his arm then at his ankle which has swollen over the sides of his sneaker. "I think I can help," he says. "My brother is a doctor. If I call, I'm sure he'll come."

Igneus shakes his head. "No, no," he says. "I have medications. Sebastian will be fine."

A few seconds pass, seem unnatural in their length. Igneus realizes the risk he's taking. The man may have connections that can spell disaster. He also has no idea where the man will go when he leaves the room. He thinks again about an attempt to subdue the man. To keep him prisoner here until Sebastian recovers and they can be on their way.

The man's well built, obviously strong. He'd held Sebastian for an awfully long time without tiring. He's in good shape and healthy, even well fed. A physical confrontation will undo all the man has done for them so far, besides being completely pointless. He can't win a fight in his condition. He's weakening from loss of blood, becoming more exhausted, drained by the cold, by the pain of his ankle and shoulder, by lack of food, by fatigue.

The man's face shows the wrinkles of time, but barely. He's perhaps forty, maybe younger. Perhaps has time in the service. Or prison. Either way, Igneus realizes, he hasn't any other options, has no choice but to trust despite the fact the streets have taught him to *never* trust *anyone. Ever.*

The same thought whispers, calming in tone and message. It puts him at ease, makes him nod and accept assistance.

My God will provide all my needs.

CHAPTER 13

JERUSALEM, ISRAEL

An hour later the custodian returns with the doctor.

Igneus is not impressed.

He looks like a child, slight of frame with short, dark hair and wide eyes. He wears a black backpack with yellow stripes. It looks like something a poor kid would bring to school.

"This is the doctor?" Igneus asks.

"Yes. My brother, Ishmael. He's a doctor," the custodian replies.

Ishmael steps forward and offers his hand. "I'm not actually a doctor," the young man says. "I mean, I am, but still in my residency. I'll complete that in another year."

Igneus sits on the closet floor, legs extended, Sebastian's head cradled in his lap.

"Phenomenal," Igneus says, not trying to hide the sarcasm.

There's an awkward silence as the child-doctor shuffles his feet, glances at Sebastian. "Should I have a look?"

Any port in a storm, Igneus thinks. "May as well." He jostles Sebastian and the lad starts to rouse. Ishmael kneels beside the boy and places his hand on Sebastian's arm.

"How are you feeling?" he says.

"Not good. Feels hard to breathe."

The doctor looks to Igneus. "Has he been running a fever?"

Igneus nods. "Most definitely. He's felt hot to the touch and has had chills off and on."

Ishmael removes his backpack, rummages, then produces a stethoscope and an otoscope. He places the stethoscope on Sebastian's chest.

"Hmmm," he says, "sounds crunchy." He takes Sebastian's pulse, then uses the otoscope to look in his ears and mouth. He finishes by probing Sebastian's belly asking if anything hurts.

Exam complete, he leans back on his haunches and looks at Igneus. He seems to consider his words. Or, Igneus worries, he's over his head and has no idea how to proceed.

"Does he take any medications?" the young doctor asks.

Igneus hesitates. "Well, some of these." He hands the doctor the dopp kit. The doctor seems surprised, accepting the kit and examining each bottle.

"Some of these are for women," he says. "I'm not even going to ask how you got them." He sets each bottle on the concrete floor. "Only one antibiotic here," he says. "Fortunately, I think it will help." He hands the bottle to Igneus. "Give him one every eight hours."

Igneus nods, silently rejoicing that his crime hasn't been for naught.

"Also," the doctor says, "do you mind if I start an IV?"

"Why?" Igneus asks.

"Your boy is severely dehydrated. He needs fluids. I'd like to start an intravenous line and give him some saline. It will make him feel better and help him recover more quickly."

Sebastian cuts in. "Do you have to give me a shot?"

The doctor leans forward, appears not much older than Sebastian. "I'm afraid so," he says. "But I'm pretty good at starting these, and I think you're man enough to take it."

Sebastian inflates a bit. His eyes become firm. Comparing him to a man has bolstered his will. "I can be a man," he says.

The doctor looks at Igneus. "Is that okay?"

Igneus nods, looks at Sebastian, ruffles his hair. "This kid is tough."

The doctor produces the necessary supplies. A long needle, a few alcohol pads, tape, some tubing, and a large bag of clear liquid.

Sebastian handles the procedure like a champ, and soon the fluid flows into his arm. It seems to improve his color but Igneus can't tell if that's fact or just wishful thinking.

Ishmael produces a syringe and hypodermic. He screws the needle on, pulls a clear vial from his pack, then draws some of the fluid into the syringe. Withdrawing the needle from the vial, he pokes it into a rubber hub on the IV line. "Is he allergic to anything?"

A tricky question. Igneus has been posing as the child's father, but these men think he actually *is* the child's father. If the truth comes out, they may report him, cause other trouble, think he's kidnapped Sebastian. "I'm not sure," he says. "He's been healthy most of his life and hasn't needed medications."

Igneus has no idea if the lie will work, if the child-doctor will see through such a thing. To Igneus it sounds ridiculous.

The doctor nods. "Well, he needs this," Ishmael says. "We'll watch for a reaction and see how it goes. I think the benefits outweigh the risks." He pushes the plunger, slowly sends the medicine into the IV.

"What is that?" Igneus asks.

"Ceftriaxone, a wide-spectrum antibiotic. First-line treatment for sepsis." The plunger empties and Ishmael pulls the syringe from the tube. "He's very close to sepsis, I think. That's an infection that gets so bad it overwhelms the body's defenses and makes the patient very unstable. It kills a lot of people every year. This will help."

Igneus nods, his eyes fill with tears. Has he been so self-centered he's pushed Sebastian to the very verge of death? Has he been so blinded avoiding Cain, he's risked his son's life?

Ishmael takes Igneus's arm. "Don't worry," he says. "It's nothing you did. We have time and I think these meds will do the trick. Sebastian is very ill." He looks at Sebastian, smiles. "But also, very rugged. I think he'll do alright." He goes through the pill bottles again, picks out the cough syrup Igneus purchased. "Be sure to use this for the next couple of days."

Igneus nods, collects himself, manages a smile. "Thank you. Doctor."

Ishmael nods. "You're welcome," he says. "Now let's have a look at you."

This surprises Igneus, although it shouldn't. The custodian had seen his obvious injuries and knew they both needed a physician. "I'll be fine," he says. I'm immortal, he adds silently, nothing can kill me.

"Oh, posh," the doctor says. "I'm here now. May as well have a look. What hurts?"

Igneus decides to play along, knows he can't tell this stranger the truth about his immortality. "I injured my ankle jumping from a wall. Probably just a sprain."

"I see," Ishmael says. He removes Igneus's shoe and sock, which, again, surprises Igneus. It's a very compassionate act, to remove the shoe and sock of a homeless man. Most doctors would consider themselves above it. Ishmael slides them off, and Igneus is surprised at how filthy his feet are. He's also astonished to notice the ankle isn't as swollen as it was even an hour ago.

The doctor examines the limb, presses at various points, asks, "Does this hurt?" "How about this?"

When he completes the exam, Ishmael leans back on his heels. "It'd be nice to get an Xray." He looks at Sebastian. "Actually, an Xray would do you both good." He holds Igneus's eyes, waits for an answer to a question he hasn't actually asked.

Igneus tries to be polite. "Thank you, but no."

"If it's a matter of money—"

Igneus interrupts. "No."

Another awkward pause. The doctor glances at the custodian, then back to Igneus. "Very well," he says. "Let's have a look at that shoulder."

Did the custodian notice everything? "It's fine," he says.

The doctor holds his eyes for a second. "I'm sorry, Mister…" He pauses here, waits for Igneus to finish his sentence.

"Igneus."

"Mr. Igneus. I've come here to treat you per Jonas's request." He nods to his brother, the custodian. "You're not cooperating, and I don't know why. I have no interest in harming you. Jonas told me about your predicament, the reason you and your boy live as you do. You must know that I don't care what's going on with your personal life. I don't care what kind of trouble you're in or what illegal activities you perform. I care only about treating you and your child and seeing you both healthy. Now," he smiles, "may I look at your shoulder?"

Igneus is struck silent as his estimation of the child-doctor grows. The man is obviously professional and seems to know what he's doing. His words have also stripped Igneus of any protest he can think to make. Igneus realizes he's being rude and doesn't need to be. The nature of his predicament hasn't changed, but the doctor seems genuine.

He slides to the left, gently places Sebastian's head on the balled-up sweater. He stands, removes his bloody shirt, grimaces.

"Ah," Ishmael says, "judging by the amount of blood, I'd say you've been shot."

Igneus nods. "Yes, I was—"

The doctor raises his hand. "Tut, tut, tut. I don't want to know." He holds Igneus's eyes, seems to reassure himself he's made his point. "Very serious. The bullet could still be in there, infection setting up. Let me take a closer look, it's important to find the entrance *and* the exit wounds."

He rummages through the backpack again. Produces a large bottle of saline and some thick, white gauze pads. "First we clean," he says. He pours the saline onto the gauze and wipes away the dried blood on Igneus's shoulder and torso.

Finished, he steps back, looks at Igneus and then to Jonas. "I thought you were shot?" he says.

Igneus nods. "I was."

"Nonsense," the doctor says. "There are no wounds."

"I'm a fast healer."

The doctor's expression is deadpan. The kid would be an excellent poker player if he put his mind to it.

He knows I'm deceiving him, Igneus thinks.

"People don't just heal from gunshot wounds. Not in an hour or two. Are you sure you were shot?"

Igneus thinks, deception is not a skill at which he's adept. "Perhaps I wasn't. I mean, I heard gunshots and then my shoulder started to hurt. I didn't really have time to look."

"Uh huh," Ishmael says. "Let's see how it moves. Can you lift your arms above your head?"

Igneus tries, moves the arm only a few inches before a spasm of pain courses through it and makes his fingers tingle.

Ishmael places a hand over the shoulder joint, pushes in certain places. "You've dislocated your shoulder. Perhaps you weren't shot." His eyes lower as he contemplates. "But what about all the blood?" He speaks to himself, tries to connect dots that aren't connecting.

Jonas stands by the door. Igneus gives him a slight smile.

Ishmael returns from his thoughts. "No matter," he says. "Let's reduce it."

"Reduce what?" Igneus asks.

"Your shoulder. We'll pop it back in place."

"Oh," Igneus says. "Of course."

The doctor grasps Igneus's left wrist and bends his arm at the elbow. He starts to rotate the arm to the left. Igneus feels the pain as a building pressure. The joint doesn't want to turn.

"Breathe deep," Ishmael says. Igneus inhales, tries to concentrate on staying still.

He feels a pop and a burst of pain. A few seconds later the pain subsides, and the shoulder feels somewhat normal.

"There we go," he says. "You'll be good as new in no time."

You have no idea, Igneus thinks.

"Just try not to overdo it for a few days. It could pop back out."

Igneus nods, smiles. "Thank you…Doctor."

"You're quite welcome."

Jonas opens the door and steps out of the room. A few seconds later he returns holding a large, black garbage bag. "I've found some things for you two. Some food, clothes, nothing fancy."

The bag bulges with contents.

"Right," Ishmael says. "I must go. My shift starts in an hour. I'll be back tomorrow to check on you. Have Jonas call me if the boy gets worse."

Igneus shakes his hand, repeats his gratitude.

Ishmael exits and closes the door behind him.

My God will provide all my needs. Igneus can't believe his luck. These two are living proof, sent by God, angels in the flesh. He hasn't witnessed compassion for some time, had convinced himself it no longer exists. But these two men are compassionate, helping without consideration for themselves or any reward. It's been so long since Igneus has known anyone like that, he finds himself completely stunned. Completely speechless.

Jonas moves to the room's far corner, produces a tall walking stick stained dark. The branch bends near the top, shines in Jonas's hand. Someone's taken great pains to smooth and lacquer it. He hands it to Igneus. "For your ankle," he says. "Should help you walk."

Igneus nods again. Still can't speak. Still in awe.

"I'll be back this evening to check on you two," Jonas says. "Keep the door locked." He trades glances from Igneus to Sebastian. The hint of a smile crosses his lips. "Vagrants have a way of getting in here." He's teasing them, poking fun.

"Yes," Igneus says, "I hear those vagrants are a nasty sort."

CHAPTER 14

NEW YORK, NEW YORK

Months earlier

Rhyme watches the hulking man depart. Longinus of Misthli, he'd called himself when they'd been introduced. Seems like years ago.

Lucky break, she thinks, easier to deal with Drake.

The alley is long and dark, holds only a dumpster and shadow. Behind the dumpster, forty stories rise to the night. Fear makes her shiver. She inhales, holds it, then exhales in a rush that fogs the windshield.

Octavio headquarters, the organization Emery toppled on his way to the top. The offices should be deserted, *have been* deserted during her daily surveillance over the last week. Most of the workers were arrested or fled after Emery's story.

Seems tonight, that isn't the case.

Drake and Longinus had entered the building around twilight. Minutes later the windows on the top floor lit up. She stares up at them now, checks the side view mirrors to assure no one's around. With Longinus gone, Drake should be up there alone.

The night air is cold as she exits the car and tries to clear her head.

She'll only get one chance. One shot to save Emery's life.

What a stupid man, my husband, never content.

She remembers the conversation. Emery returning after God knows how long, booze and body odor wafting, tired, bloodshot eyes, promises tumbling from his mouth.

He'd done it, he said, broke the story that would serve as the crowning achievement of his career. Things would be different now, he said. Rehab, more time at home, back to how it was in the beginning.

Then he'd made her blood run cold with a single word. A word she'd thought she'd left behind.

Octavio.

She remembers the spikes of panic, the rush of thoughts in her head, the adrenaline surge and urge to urinate.

Never got the top guy, he said. A shadow in the night Emery called him. A clouded phantom in the back of one's closet. He'd used the word kingpin. Said he tried every trick, turned every stone, chased every lead, asked every question. In the end the kingpin remained a mystery. The only loose end.

She knew then, with her bladder begging to purge and her skin covered in gooseflesh. The kingpin Emery seeks is Thaddeus Drake, the Dove, the devil, the peacemaker.

The realization crushed her, infused her bones with rage of such magnitude that her vision changed to a harsh redness. Her mind scrambled, thoughts coalescing but unfocused, surrounded in crimson, jumbled, tripping over one another.

Then one thought chased away all the others. He's coming. He'll not be stopped. What she thought she'd escaped is now streaking toward her, toward them both with the fury of hell itself.

In a single second she knew the only way to preserve her family, her life, her love, was to go on the offensive.

She knew, for the first time in her life, she'd have to commit murder.

Her anger bubbled over, got the better of her. He'd ruined it. Fucked it up. Had to dig and dig and dig. Too dumb to see what's right before him, the riches surrounding him. He'd needed more, wanted more, couldn't resist. The story, an opiate over which he held no power.

She made the decision then, to deal with Drake forever, to end this nightmare. Swift and devastating, her mentor would say. Swift and devastating like a force of nature.

Emery tried to stop her, and she'd knocked him on his ass. Hell hath no fury.

Up to that point, she'd been successful hiding her past. Whether Emery didn't care or just didn't want to know, he'd never asked her about it, and, in that silence, they'd found contentment. Life was good and getting better. That stupid man!

They call it the human condition. The state where nothing good can last, like Frost said. Innocence, happiness, contentment, nothing more than chaff on the winds of time.

When humans get involved, good things get fucked up.

She then set out to find Drake, which is no easy task. Turns out, patience yields all things though. A few questions in the right ears started her up the vast network of Octavio underlings, slowly climbing the ranks until, after a week of watching almost 24/7, she found Longinus.

A lucky break where luck was short.

She adjusts her position in the Subaru, realizes she has to pee. Again. Like the eighth time in the few hours she's been here. She hurries across the alley, feels a shiver. Her body is a mess, pregnancy taking control. One second hot, the next cold. One second content, the next filled with an overwhelming urge to void.

I've been through worse, overcome worse. If Drake thinks he's going to mess with my family, he's got another thought coming.

She moves behind the dumpster and empties her bladder as quietly as possible.

She looks left and right, then moves to the door and slides the pick in the keyhole.

This is her maximum exposure, and she knows it. If a guard shows, or Longinus returns, she'll have to fight, and a fight isn't something she can win while seven months pregnant.

Her fingers feel fat and slow as she pushes the pick. Were they always this chubby? Like little sausages on game day?

To pick a lock requires subtlety, a certain fine dexterity. One need be able to feel the slightest vibration, hear the slightest click. She holds the tensioner, a metal tool bent to a right angle, then slides the rake in. The trick is to apply even pressure while gliding the rake over each tumbler. The complication: most locks have multiple tumblers, so when one clicks in place, the tensioner will move the tiniest fraction. It's miniscule but easily done in the right hands. Slim hands, not sausages.

Women's hands are perfect for this, if she's not pregnant.

And cold.

And full of urine.

Extra weight has caused everything to "fluff up," as her mom used to say.

The alley remains empty and dark, just the way she needs it. She feels another miniscule click, means she's tripped another tumbler. She retracts the rake a hair, carefully applies even pressure.

Another subtle click.

Almost there.

Another click and the tensioner turns. The door opens.

She eases in, crouches, closes it as quietly as possible.

She leans against the wall just inside the threshold. To her right, there's a door marked STAIRS. Before her, a long hallway. She glances at the stairs, thinks of the climb to the top. Her ankles are twice their normal size and she dreads the climb, unsure if she can even make forty stories.

She moves forward, congratulates her foresight in wearing her thief's shoes. A friend, a thief from Chinatown, had recommended these years ago, and he'd been right. Ninja shoes, he'd called them, although they look nothing like the traditional shoes of a ninja. They are, however, quiet, silent even, and silence is what she needs.

At the hall's end, she takes a small mirror and holds it low to the floor, angled out a centimeter or two. Another trick, a good way to see what's around corners before barging in.

It's a vast lobby. She keeps low, scans the area, knees aching from position and pregnancy.

About one-hundred paces to her left is a long, curved reception desk. A single guard reads a book, faces the entryway, feet propped up. His computer flashes the logo for the Octavio corporation, a thick O containing three dots arranged in a triangle.

She feels nauseated. Octavio, the worst of the worst.

She knows Octavio, knows their methods. If they find her, they'll kill her. Easy as breathing for them.

The front of the lobby are huge glass panes facing the street. Although less crowded than usual, people pass by in irregular intervals.

This is going to be tricky. Pregnancy makes it almost impossible. In her condition she's not sure if she can sneak up on the guard, and even if she can, she's not sure she can subdue him without raising an alarm. It'll have to be perfect and she knows things are rarely, if ever, perfect.

She considers her options, then has an idea. There's a bank of elevators between them. If she's quick, she might be able to pull it off.

She slides around the corner and moves to the elevators. The lobby is dimly lit this time of night and she stays to the shadows as best she can.

There are six elevator doors. She selects the second one because it has the best sight lines. A single pillar blocks the view from the street and some of the lobby's light. Shadowed, partially concealed, not perfect but not bad.

She slides up the wall to fully stand.

The guard remains consumed by his book.

She presses the UP button.

The door opens with a high-pitched ding, and Rhyme falls to the ground, careful to protect her stomach. "Help," she says feebly, then groans. The guard startles, then moves toward her with a quick and graceful assurance.

A pro, she thinks, moonlighting.

She holds her stomach, rocks as if she's in great pain.

He kneels beside her. His pistol is holstered, and she breathes silent thanks to Saint Cajetan.

"Are you okay, ma'am?"

"Yes…I think…the baby…" Her speech is stuttered, breathless. She wishes she could sweat.

He stands. "I'll call an ambulance."

"No!" she says, "I…already called."

He starts to crouch, but she stops him. "Doctor said…lift my legs…"

"Lift your legs?"

Stupid man! The elevator's gonna close!

"Yes…" She breathes hard and fast, manages another groan higher pitched than the last. "Please…the pain."

He must be a real sweet guy, she thinks. He moves to her feet and gently starts to raise.

Rhyme acts relieved. Says, "Thank you, thank you." She breathes and pulls her knees toward her pregnant belly. "Push them toward me." The guard smiles nervously, then gently pushes her knees toward her tummy.

When the guard's ankle is close enough, she flips a taser from her palm and plants it on the exposed skin of his lower leg. She clicks the button, then kicks with all her might.

The guard goes limp, then flies into the open elevator.

Rhyme slides on her butt, clears the doors just before they close.

I might've peed a little, she thinks, but first hurdle overcome. She smiles. She's a long way from the Carter's Glen library.

Removing the guard's pistol, she checks the load, sees one in the chamber. She kneels, takes the laces from his shoes then tosses them in the corner. She removes his socks too.

Soon he's tied, hands and feet, socks stuffed in his mouth. A final check shows he's breathing through his nose without issue.

She stands, pokes the button for the fortieth floor.

The guard stirs a bit but seems out of it as they reach the top floor.

She'll lose the element of surprise when the elevator stops and the distinctive ding calls.

Rhyme holds the gun low and steady.

Ding!

She raises the pistol.

The doors open.

The place is dimly lit. Directly in front of her is a reception desk, long and dark, decorated with the word Octavio in large glass letters. Past the desk, she sees doors of various offices, all closed. She steps in, crouches, looks left and right.

To her left a stream of light falls from a partially open door.

She moves toward it, knows Drake must be there.

The urge to pee cries out again but she can't tell if it's nerves or pregnancy. She creeps forward, closing the distance.

At the door, she pauses to listen.

No sounds come from the room and no movement breaks the light from the door's crack. Placing her hand on the door, she pushes.

Then, a hand twists into her hair and drags her backward. She struggles for balance, tries to turn.

She's thrown onto the hard tile floor.

She rolls with the force, tries to protect her belly and unborn child, raises the pistol before realizing she doesn't have it.

She struggles to stand and face her attacker.

The guard somehow slipped his bonds and stands before her holding a gun. Either she dropped it, or he had a backup.

She raises her hands.

The guard fires.

The bullet tears into her abdomen. The impact steals her wind. The pain sears, scalds, molten, breath-stealing. She tries to stand, hears another shot.

She collapses on her side, blood pools on the floor. Didn't feel the second round, she thinks, losing too much blood, too fast.

She presses her wound, looks toward her attacker.

He lies motionless, spread-eagled, gun beside him.

She crawls to the weapon, knows Drake is near.

Then he's over her. A sardonic smile on a beautiful face.

Her head throbs.

Her throat feels swollen.

Her mind fills with a sound like locusts.

She musters her strength, crawls forward, collapses, struggles forward again.

Her vision fades. Her mind grows numb. She tries to move but hasn't the strength.

She's going to die here. Her and her baby.

Something presses against the back of her head. It's a gun.

She closes her eyes, breathes a prayer.

This is it.

The gun doesn't fire.

She turns.

Beyond the dark gleam of the pistol is Thaddeus Drake.

His expression is one a tiger wears before devouring its prey.

A perfect smile gleams darkness. "One shouldn't open old wounds."

CHAPTER 15

NEW YORK, NEW YORK

"She's lost a lot of blood."

"Did you get that IV?"

"Yes, full blast."

"Okay, let's get her up here."

Rhyme cries out as the EMT's lift her onto the gurney. She struggles for consciousness, now as fleeting as coherent thought.

"My baby," she says.

She hears the voice, someone speaking with police. "Rhyme Carter," he says, "I think she was here to clean the office, although I don't know why because no one's been here for some time. Probably just needed the money."

Rhyme looks for Drake. If he's here, it will be a scandal. When she doesn't see him, she knows he's gone.

"And the deceased?" It's a policeman with a beer gut that make his buttons look like they'll pop from the strain. "Does he work here?"

"Yes sir. He's security, too. I don't know him very well, though, he's only been here a couple of weeks."

"What do you think happened?"

"My guess? One of those nutty Octavio guys came back to get

something, found the cleaning lady and the guard, tried to kill them both."

"What'd he take?" the fat policeman asks.

"No idea. I never come up here."

The gurney rises and locks in place. This is not gentle, and Rhyme cries out.

Large white pads are piled on her abdomen; blood seeping through.

"Ma'am," the EMT says, "do you have any allergies?"

"No," Rhyme cries. "Please save my baby."

"I'm just going to give you some morphine."

She feels the drug seep into her body and dull her mind. "No!" she says. She doesn't want to lose consciousness.

"You'll be fine." The EMT flashes a boyish smile.

"My baby," she mumbles, then everything fades.

She wakes in a room, stark white and sterile. Someone speaks.

"Just closing up, shouldn't be a minute. Shame, though."

Panic fuses with grief. Dread, then shock tear through her. She tries to rise, tries to lash out.

"Goddammit, Mike! Give her more juice! She's waking up."

"Sorry. Sorry." The IV line vibrates. "Okay, that should do it."

This room is dark, and pale. She lies in a bed, an ungodly number of tubes strung to her body. A gray, worn curtain bunches against the wall to her right as various machines beep and ping. Occasionally she feels pressure on her left arm, a blood pressure cuff, inflating automatically. An empty bedside table sits nearby, and beyond that, an open door leads to a hallway that's well lit in beige and taupe.

She moves her hand to her belly. It feels swollen, but not full. Not pregnant.

Her heart shreds like the bullet through her abdomen.

Her cry is pure anguish. A wail of despair, loss, of remorse and hate. It flies from her soul, fills the room, streaks down the corridor. It empties her, kills her, her resolve, her love, her hopes. It is agony fully developed, grief in purest form. Ears hum with the volume, her back arches as salty tears stream down her face and onto the bed.

A nurse is there, speaking in quiet tones.

"I know. It's okay. It's going to be okay."

Rhyme tries to sit, and the nurse reaches for her, tries to calm her and keep her in bed.

Rhyme grabs her, squeezes tight. The nurse seems alarmed at first, then realizes what's happening.

She accepts the hug, holding Rhyme close as she weeps.

CHAPTER 16

NEW YORK, NEW YORK

She walks the hospital's halls. It's been a few days, but the tears never stop. She leans on a cane, shuffles step by step holding a beige rail for support.

The day's bustle has evaporated, and the halls are empty and quiet. She enjoys this time of night, if there can still be joy. It's quiet and peaceful.

She winces, her wound stings but it's no match for the smoking hole in her heart.

The guard killed her baby, robbed her of the life she'd built, destroyed any chance at normalcy. She thinks of Emery. Is he still alive, or has Drake ended him?

She draws close to her room, is amazed at how exhausted she's become after walking such a short distance. She has to sleep, has to recover as quickly as possible.

She remembers Emery coming to see her, remembers breaking his heart.

"Leave and never come back," she said. His shock was unimaginable, burnt into her mind, carved on her soul. She shakes her head, tries to lose the memory.

It's the only way, she thinks, the only way to keep him safe. Drake isn't the kind to forgive. Ruthless, merciless, cold; these serve to better describe the gloved man, despite what the world thinks.

A huge bouquet sits on the bedside table. Red roses, white lilies, carnations in blue and yellow and green, long lilacs rise to fill the room with the sweetest fragrance.

Rhyme's struck by this, struck by the innocence of her pleasure. The pure, sweet scent, the kaleidoscope of blossoms, something alive, natural, a metaphor for what her life now lacks.

Emery, she thinks, my sweetest love. Please be safe and happy.

She smells the flowers, feels the sutures stretch and the sharp pain that follows.

"You're a tad rusty."

She continues to inhale the flower's sweetness, the ripe elegance of their beauty.

Then she turns.

Thaddeus Drake sits in the room's lone chair, one leg crossed over the other.

She subdues her anger. She's in no state to fight him when she hasn't even the strength to walk the length of the hallway.

She pastes a smile on her face. "It seems so," she says, "or you'd be dead."

Drake chuckles. "I retain a few tricks of which you're unaware," he says. "In fact, you're lucky you didn't kill me. That would've gone very badly for you."

She feels her face harden, her portion of malice break through. "You killed my baby," she says.

He doesn't react in any way she can see. "Hardly," he says. "The only fault I can accept is that I was a few seconds too late. I knew you were coming. Expected to have a chat with you. I also expected that you'd dispatch the security guard with your usual efficiency. I was as surprised as you by his presence." He holds her eyes; his concern seems genuine. "I'd never hurt you or your baby." He pauses here, glances down. "I'm very sorry that happened."

"I came to kill you," she says, "came to protect my family from you."

"As expected," Drake says, "but the line for that particular wish is long. People have tried for centuries, yet none have succeeded."

"Centuries?" she scoffs. "A little dramatic, don't you think?"

Drake glances at the floor, then toward the ceiling like his thoughts are far away. "How I wish I was," he says. "You see, I cannot die. I am immortal. Cursed by God to wander for eternity."

Rhyme laughs, holds her wound. "What a bunch of bullshit."

Drake glances at the Omega on his wrist. "I apologize for my haste, and incidentally, I applaud your aplomb, but we had a deal, and you broke that deal. You tried to kill me, and although I can probably guess what drove you to such measures, I'm struck by the realization that you have only yourself to blame."

The words smash her heart like a sledge. She holds it in, can't afford to betray emotion where Drake's concerned. The man is beautiful no doubt, and cunning. A dark angel with a murderer's soul. He wants another deal, she thinks. Should I mention Emery? Perhaps through some dumb luck, Drake hasn't given him any notice. Perhaps he's still alive, even safe. She watches Drake and weighs her options. Do I say something and put Emery in this madman's sights, or remain silent and hear him out? Drake would know she'd gotten pregnant by someone. Would've kept tabs on her despite their deal. Would know of Emery, his job, his efforts in ruining Octavio. It'd be naïve to think anything else, and naïve she is not, no longer the librarian from Carter's Glen.

She makes her decision.

"Is Emery alive?"

The corners of his mouth turn up, a brief flicker but enough.

With that, she knows, and some weight lifts from her heart. He's alive. There's still hope.

"Indeed, my dear Rhyme, he is." Drake frowns here, looks at his Omega again. "But I'm afraid he'll not survive the night. As we speak, an associate is on his way to introduce your lover to the afterlife."

Her face flushes. She glances around for something to lash out with, realizes she has a cane in her hand, starts to lift it.

"I'd stay calm," Drake says. "He can still be saved. That is, if you cooperate."

Rhyme lowers the cane, leans on it, looks to the floor, feels outmatched but willing to fight on. "What do you want?"

"Are we bargaining for his life or for my other desire?" Drake asks.

"Emery's life. You can kill us all before you get the other." She feels a snarl, erases it with a force of will.

"Very well then." Drake stands. "Here's my offer. If you want to save Emery's life, which, by the way, won't be very long due to his, let's say, habits." He raises a gloved hand here. "Full disclosure," he says, "I'd hate for you to make a decision without all the facts."

"I know my husband's weaknesses."

"Of course, of course," Drake says. "Pardon me, just trying to be civil."

"Spare me," she says. "I think you're bluffing."

Drake nods, removes the glove from his left hand and presses a button on his phone. It rings a single time. Drake looks at the screen, then speaks. "Are you in position?"

"Aye."

"Might I ask you to show me the target?"

Drake moves to Rhyme, angles the phone so she can see.

The screen shows her apartment building. The phone jiggles and Rhyme realizes it's being held close to the scope of a sniper rifle. The picture zooms in on a window and she can see the scope's reticle centered on Emery's head. He sits by the window in her favorite chair, raises a bottle to his mouth and takes a long pull.

Her blood runs cold, she thinks again of attacking but realizes she's cornered.

"Continue as planned," Drake says and hangs up. He replaces the glove, then looks at her in silence.

Breathing comes fast as she searches for a way out of this trap. Drake isn't bluffing.

She sighs, looks down. "What is it you want?"

Drake glances at his watch again. "To spare Emery?"

She nods.

"Marry me?"

She swoons, uses the cane to stop from falling.

Drake comes, holds her arm, helps her to sit on the bed.

She jerks away, weakly slaps at his face.

Drake chuckles. "Such fire, my dear. Such passion."

"I'm already married, you ass."

Drake grins. "There are many ways to fix that."

Her face heats. "I'll never do it," she hisses. "Kill him." A weak attempt to call his bluff, she knows he'll see through it.

"Very well then," he says, "do have a nice recovery." He turns, heads for the door.

"Wait," she says. "Isn't there another way?"

Drake pauses, turns toward her, displays a frown. "I'm afraid not. You see, in my very long life, only God himself has ever bested me. That is, until you. I'd term our arrangement a draw. A stalemate, if you will." He crosses the room and resumes his seat. "I see you're surprised," he says, "but it's true. And there's so much more to say on the subject." Here, he glances at his Omega. "But time is running out for our *dear* Emery."

"How much time?" she blurts.

"Not much," Drake says, "I'm afraid I must press you for an answer. Perhaps this will help." He reaches into his suit and produces a small box. Then he kneels on one knee and opens it to reveal the largest diamond she's ever seen.

"Rhyme," he says, "will you marry me?"

She sees the Omega, its second hand sweeping around its face. Emery's fate lies in her next words. She looks at Drake. He appears pleasant, even sincere.

She knows better.

"You'll assure no harm comes to Emery? In any way?"

Drake smiles. "I'll see to it personally."

A tear rolls down her cheek.

"Okay, then," she says. "I will."

CHAPTER 17

MARYLAND, UNITED STATES

Present day

"I thought a stop necessary before we proceed," Cain says.

"I thought we were meeting the president."

Cain doesn't miss a beat. "In due time, dear Emery. If my biography is to be complete, a little stop is in order."

"Okay. Where?"

Cain points ahead.

"Looks like a house," I say. "A mansion, really."

We turn onto a long drive and wind through pasture lands. A cow looks at us, mulls its cud, eyes dull.

"Yes," Cain says, "quite typical. You see I needed privacy to accomplish my goals here."

The grounds are huge, manicured, surrounded by a lovely white fence. Cattle and sheep graze, seem unaffected by the relentless heat. I see the telltale signs of security, the long black SUV's, the occasional guard dressed as gardener or handyman.

"Why the heavy guns?"

Cain shakes his head. "Times aren't like they used to be. I need security to keep prying eyes away. They've done a marvelous job, though, and we've had no incidents since we started."

"Which was?"

Cain rubs his chin. "I'd say around the same time this nation was born. About seventeen seventy-six."

I nod, again flabbergasted, then check the recording app on my phone and jot some details in my notebook.

We pass a large building huddled near a copse of trees, surrounded by chain link with razor wire.

"What's that?"

Cain waves a hand. "That's already served its purpose."

"Which was?"

"In due time, dear, curious Emery."

The limo follows a sweeping, wide arc, and we stop in front of the enormous house.

The place is grand, beautiful, a country estate. "Looks a bit like the White House," I say. "With all the security, you'd think the president is here waiting for us."

Cain chuckles, then gives me that look. "I assure you our security is better than what the U.S. president commands." He starts forward, up a wide flight of brick steps to a wood-planked porch with wrap around railing. He rings the doorbell.

The man who answers is surprising. He wears a tie-dye shirt with a picture of a hand making the peace sign. He looks a bit dazed, a bit confused. Surely this man can't be why we're here.

"Emery, this is Bill," Cain says. "Bill, say hello to Emery."

The man nods, scratches at a short beard. "Hello, Emery. I'm Bill."

I glance at Cain, give a WTF expression.

"Dear Bill is a treasured guest of mine. He's been with us now for the better part of thirty years."

As Cain speaks, Bill turns and disappears into the depths of the house.

"A prisoner?" I ask.

"Dear Emery, no!" Cain exclaims. "Again, you think me a monster.

Bill is here of his own free will. He can leave at any time but never has."

"Why not?"

Cain looks perplexed. "Well, um, I can't exactly say. Let's go ask."

We walk into a large foyer. Before us, a grand staircase ascends in rich carpet to the second floor which spans the first and provides a view such that anyone looking down can see the happenings below.

From the foyer, we turn left and enter an oversized room jammed with thousands upon thousands of books. I look up and gasp. Two stories above, a large oval skylight sheds sunrays through heavy, antique windows trimmed in white.

Two beautiful mahogany desks command the place. They sit on carpet of a floral pattern—Turkish or Persian, silk, finely weaved—and are littered with papers, piles of books half-a-dozen tall, McDonald's bags, assorted writing instruments, legal pads and even a microscope. Tall shelves surround us, simply stuffed with books. And no cheap paperbacks; each volume is hardback, leather bound. *Adventures of Huckleberry Finn, Brave New World, Last of the Mohicans*. I move to the desk, examine more titles. Books by Nietzsche, Freud, Kant. Then religious texts, the *Tao Te Ching*, the *Holy Bible*; the *Koran, Tora, Bhagavad Ghita*; the *Vedas*. Every one of them dog-eared and worn.

"Thirty years," I say.

Cain motions. "You should see the upstairs. Bill seems quite content here, wants for nothing, similar to the Children of the Rocks."

The name reminds me of Sebastian, the blonde boy I'd met and subsequently watched perform the cleansing ritual that allowed Cain entrance to the Temple.

"And how are the Children?" I ask.

Cain gives me the stupid-questions look. "I'm quite sure I don't know."

"You haven't visited there since…" I trail off, not wanting to remind him of the beat down he took at the hands of the Archangel Michael.

"I dismissed them after their purpose had been served," he says.

I stutter a bit, think of Cain's history. I pull the Percs from my pocket and take two. I won't ask, have convinced myself I don't want to know. Although I know all too well without asking. He's scattered them to the wind. *Dismissed*, to Cain, means "abandoned". Cain's magic thesaurus, a personal vocabulary of the unthinkable.

There's an awkward pause as I look at him then avert my eyes to the rest of the room.

To my right a spiral staircase leads to a second-floor balcony that encloses the entire second story. It too is filled with books.

I catch the unmistakable odor of marijuana, then look up to see a pair of dirty feet hanging over the edge. I can't see the rest of the man, but certainly this is Bill.

Cain grins and motions. We move up the staircase and halfway around the balcony to where Bill sits.

A joint smokes in his left hand. In his right he holds the *Book of the Dead*. It looks cheap, printed on pulp, new as if ordered online. On the floor are various comic books, Archie and Jughead, Captain America, Venom.

He looks up as we approach. "Why does gravity push us down *just* enough?" He elongates the word *just* but has no discernable accent. His eyes are dark and gold, a calmness that makes me think the weed is working its magic.

"Bill, can you tell Emery why you're here?"

"Mostly for the weed," Bill says, then chuckles.

"Would you like to go have lunch with us today?" Cain asks.

Bill shakes his head, drags on the joint. "I'd rather not," he says through held breath.

"We're meeting with the president. Would you like to join us for that?"

Smoke flows from Bill's mouth, he shakes his head, waves a hand. "That is well beneath me."

Cain laughs. "Dear Bill, you're such a delight!"

Cain turns to me, shows the movie-star smile. "Not bad for a clone, wouldn't you say?"

I snicker and take in the dope-smoking hippie. Cain's expression is serious.

"You're kidding, right?"

"Not a bit, dear Emery. Bill here is a clone. A magnificent accomplishment that will serve my goals quite well."

I take another look at the man, his hair is brown, shoulder length. He wears cut off shorts without shoes.

"Um," I say, "goals? You cloned a hippie to accomplish your goals."

"I did, can't you see?"

And suddenly I do see. Cain's cloning people, building an army. To what end? To control Earth? My mind fills with science fiction images. A clone army, scattering across the globe, doing Cain's bidding; mindless minions dealing death and destruction with their... their... joints? Their roach clips? Their dirty feet and peace sign t-shirts?

"Why?" I say.

Cain gives my favorite look. "All will be revealed in due time. I'd like you to take some time and try to guess, though." His look is mischievous. "A little brain teaser for you. A hint: no man can comprehend the mind of God." He turns to Bill. "Have a blessed day, dear Bill. We have to go now."

Bill flashes his eyes, barely glances from his book. "Peace and love, dudes."

Chapter 18

Camp David, Maryland

I've never been to Camp David, despite that as a young reporter I'd requested an interview with the president on numerous occasions. I sit in an armchair made of lodgepole pine, rough and thick. It's spacious and comfortable. In front of me is a long, low coffee table and past that, an armchair identical to mine in which Cain sits. To my left is a long couch featuring soft, flannel cushions and matching throw pillows.

Books are stacked on the coffee table, and I peek at the top one: *Birds of North America* it says, with a picture of a parakeet, a raptor and an eagle on its cover. Around me the walls are covered in wooden panels, floor to ceiling, broken in the corners and near the floor by flat, gray stones. To my right, past a single pillar, is a beautiful stone fireplace.

Cain seems deep in thought but looks as put together as ever. Navy suit with pinstripe tie in gold. His hands are clasped in his lap and he looks straight ahead, seems unaware of even where he is.

I can't get used to the white hair, and when he glances at me, the icy stare of those blue eyes makes my blood run cold as if they've reduced my temperature to somewhere near zero.

The man can do marvelous things, though. Always has a plan,

always ahead of everyone else. This includes marrying my wife, which I've considered at length. Somehow, he convinced her to divorce me and marry him. Somehow, she was convinced to abandon all we'd made together. I watch the white-haired man. Although I'm well aware of his gifts, his ability to calm people, get them to agree to things they wouldn't normally agree to, I can't imagine Rhyme being so duped.

There's a lot to her, that woman, my ex-wife, and if I'm honest with myself, I have to take most of the blame for her departure.

Although the right cross had been a surprise, completely out of character for her, the rest makes sense. I'd given up my family for the booze and the story, the drugs and the chase. What sane woman would want to stay married to a man like that?

Tina Turner's voice leaps into my head. *What's love got to do with it?* Indeed, my dear Tina, as Cain would say, what, in fact, does love got to do with it? When you're married to an absent man, when his arrival only underscores how he loves the chemicals more than you. I mean, that'll erode any love, even one I thought as deep and special as ours.

In the end, though, and let's do be honest for those watching at home, I took her for granted. Even though I married a complete goddess, an angel straight from Heaven, I still couldn't resist jacking it up. I'm reminded of my dream in the hospital, the war in Heaven. Those beautiful creatures, pure elegance, living on a different plane of grandeur and beauty. In my thoughts, Rhyme was born from that. Had to be. No doubt. Even now I know I still love her and even her marriage to the monster with the white hair won't change that. And that's it, the sum of all the noise in my head. Despite anything else, my love for her remains.

"Seems our Emery has taken another kick to the clackers, Lenny."

"It's amazing he can even walk," says Vince.

The home audience is loving this, I'm sure.

I suppress a scowl and push away thoughts of her.

Then I wonder if Slabav knows what Cain's up to.

I lean back, cross my legs and wait. Through the window I see the patrols, Secret Service wearing dark coats. They must be hot, I think.

The heat has been relentless lately. Five other Secret Service agents are in the room with us. They're dressed in hunting attire, thick vests above stout trousers. They seem bored, but as I watch, I notice their eyes miss nothing. They remain ever vigilant.

Sun pours through the window, the air feels stifled. I pull at my tie, hope my discomfort isn't too obvious, hope I'm not sweating too much and staining my suit.

Tom Carpenter enters the room. The President of the United States, he is a stern man by all appearances, not too tall but not too short. I'd describe him as thick, which I know sounds dumb, but the man's neck is thick, his hands are thick, his shoulders, his hips. Even his eyebrows, which are neatly trimmed, appear thick. He wears a tweed hunting jacket over a button-up flannel shirt in red and yellow. Gray corduroys complete the picture and are rolled a single time at the ankle above tan hunting boots.

His thickness leads the way and I think he must work out, which makes sense for a thirty-plus year military man and former army general. I'm sure his intelligence is off the charts.

Cain rises from the chair across from me. I stand as well, and the president shakes my hand with a firm grip. "Mr. Merrick," he says, "a pleasure to meet you. I've always enjoyed your reporting."

I must be blushing and have to admit I'm a little starstruck. "Mr. President," I say, feeling very diplomatic.

He turns to Cain. "Mr. Drake," he says, shaking Cain's hand.

"I am Cain now."

The president grins. "I heard. I was there when you materialized at the treaty signing in Jerusalem." He winks. "Pretty good trick. Cain." He exaggerates Cain's name as he speaks it, as if to punctuate he understands the rebranding. "Do you mind telling me how you did it? I can figure out how you faked your own death, but how did you disarm security? Change their weapons to burning lumps? How did you produce the light from the sky? I'd be interested in using some of those tricks myself."

Cain chuckles. "I'm happy to share," he says, smiles. Then he speaks with complete solemnity, a televangelist on full display. "I am a divine instrument of almighty God."

I can't decide who to look at. My eyes dart from one man to the other. President Carpenter searches Cain's features, then he releases a hardy laugh.

"Of course," he says, "I probably wouldn't tell me either!" He clasps Cain's shoulder as he speaks, then adds with a wink. "I wouldn't try those tricks here." He glances at the Secret Service members. "These guys are good."

I look at them in turn, three men and two women, all very serious, very poised and capable. But they're no match for the immortal. If they knew the truth of Cain, they'd never allow him in the same country as the president.

"It's nice to see you again," the president says.

A look of confusion crosses Cain's face. "Have we met?"

I'm surprised at his audacity and look to the floor. The question doesn't seem like one you'd ask a sitting president. If the guy implies you've met before, then you should just agree. Right?

The president seems unphased. "You don't remember? You were giving a speech in Berlin while I was visiting as secretary of state."

Cain's raises his chin in the air, half a nod. "Of course," he says, "how could I forget? It's very nice to see you again, President Carpenter."

"Call me Tom," he says. "Mind if I sit?"

This again surprises me; this guy operates on a different level. Why would the president ask to sit? I mean, he's the boss, this is his compound.

Tom moves to the couch as Cain and I resume our seats.

"I apologize, but I only have a few minutes," the president says. "Turkey season just opened, and me and the Secret Service boys are going to see what we can bag. That is, if the heat hasn't killed them all off." He smiles here, thick lips over thick teeth.

Cain nods, leans forward. "Of course. This shouldn't take long. I've been appointed as special counsel for the State of Israel. As part of my duties I thought it prudent to enlist your support, in person, for our mutual benefit."

Tom laughs. "You mean the money we send isn't enough?" He glances at me, then back to Cain. He wears his power well and it's interesting to see how Cain reacts.

Cain retains his smile, his calm demeanor. "That's always appreciated, of course."

I find myself immediately wondering how much of those funds are siphoned by X'chasei.

"But I'm afraid we may need military support," Cain continues. "Our intelligence tells us an attack is pending that may involve the Russians as well as various regional players."

The president nods, mulls the statement. "The Russians? Our intelligence knows nothing of this. Are you sure?"

"We have it on good authority. It seems they're planning a blitzkrieg of sorts. An unbridled attempt to attack and occupy Israel. They're currently massing, organizing. If this occurs, it will bring great instability to the region, effect the energy supply, global politics. Your enemies will have new friends, and if they can take Israel, who can tell what's next?"

"That isn't an attack, it's a joint exercise. We're well aware of what they're doing. You're mistaken."

Cain's smile is disarming. "Let's say I'm correct. I have reason to believe an attack is imminent."

Carpenter nods. "Okay. For argument's sake, let's assume the intel is wrong. What you're asking for is American involvement in a Middle Eastern war. Do you have any idea how unpopular that will be? It's political suicide. And during an election year."

Cain holds the man's eyes. "So, we can count on your support?"

The president's smile vanishes. "I'll look into it, even start an investigation if that helps, but I won't support a war in Israel."

"But you have much to gain," Cain says.

"Such as?"

"Influence over the great nation of Israel. Not to mention

Mideastern oil. We've realized our great mistake and are taking measures to correct those mistakes."

This raises the president's thick eyebrows. "Measures?" he says. "What measures?"

"We are no longer content to be a regional player counting on others for our security. We've come a long way but remain beset by enemies on all sides. Really, nothing has changed since our inception, even with President Carter's Camp David Accords in 1978. Our history teaches us vigilance. It teaches our enemies will always attack; doesn't matter if it's this year or this decade. It's a foregone conclusion and thus makes it impossible to keep our people safe. We've transitioned from war to peace. Muslim, Jew, and Christian are now allied in Israel and have accepted that co-existence is better than perpetual war. Our influence continues to grow, and we are taking steps not for our defense, but for our offense. We will no longer suffer incursions and harassment. To that end, I've already enlisted the aid of the King of Jordan, the Saudis, most of the region's leaders. Even the leader of Hamas and the Muslim Brotherhood supports us. We control Iran. Iraq will follow shortly, as will Turkey. We aim to create a single state, one that discourages violence and extremism, one that *encourages* tolerance and peace. Times are changing, Tom, and it would be wise to support us instead of risking the loss of our support during your time of need."

The president's expression mirrors mine, one of complete awe. It seems Cain's been up to things, and I wonder if his gifts have come to bear on these nations. Tom's expression shows he never expected the meeting to develop like this.

"Has the prime minister signed off on this?" Tom asks. "Does Slabav know what you're saying? Because Israel sounds like the aggressor."

Cain leans back in his chair, crosses his left leg over his knee. "I can assure you I speak for him. He asked me to tell you this under conditions of complete secrecy."

The president's eyes focus on the bird book. He's definitely not thinking about birds.

I adjust my position and look to Cain, who watches the president and waits.

Finally, Tom smiles, moves his gaze from the book to Cain. "*If* all you say is true," he says, "and I have every reason to believe it isn't, you will have our very limited support." He shakes his head. "I can't support a war in the Mideast, I think you know that. But I also see an opportunity if war occurs. I'll ask for a promise of resources from you, oil specifically. It seems our thirst for that stuff is never-ending. *If* all you say should come to pass, I won't commit troops but will use diplomatic means, threats if you will, to support you. If it goes bad, it's all on you. The United States will deal with the aftermath, which very well may be the demise of the Israeli state." He glances at me and his features become stern. He switches his focus to Cain. "I feel the need to warn against such action and will be calling Laslo later to tell him this personally."

Cain smiles. "Of course."

"I'll also expect a token of our friendship *if* this actually happens. By that, I mean the lion's share of resources and a complete cessation of terrorism against my country."

Cain nods. "Of course."

"But, with the very remote chance that *I'm* wrong, I wish to be crystal clear. You'll get no troops of any kind, even advisors. If Israel takes this path, it will be alone. I'm not sure it can be done, Israel against the world, and I need to have deniability if it all goes to shit."

Cain stands, extends his hand. "Happy hunting."

The president stands, as do I. He shakes our hands and walks us to the door of the cabin. We exchange the customary departure comments and are ushered by the Secret Service out of the cabin and into our vehicles.

CHAPTER 19

WASHINGTON, D.C.

The next day, Cain asks me to meet him in front of the mansion. I stand on the walk near the huge arc that serves as a driveway. Some sort of stone, probably expensive and hand cut, if I've learned anything about the very wealthy. The day is humid and cloudy with occasional bursts of sunshine. I expect the usual stretch limo, but as I stand there baking, I hear the noise of a far-off engine.

It sounds like a tiger, a deep rumble with an occasional roar. Then at the end of the long drive I see it. A sports car the color of red hedging toward brown. It purrs as it nears, and when it's close, I realize it's an Aston Martin DB11.

"Hey Vince, what's the difference between an Aston Martin and a junkie?"

"I don't know, Lenny."

"The Aston only injects fuel." The home audience roars as the car pulls to a stop in front of me.

I have no idea what to do. Is this Cain? Not likely, considering his love for limos. I stand like a dumb ass staring at the car's lines. This is the Macallan of motorcars. The Omega of automobiles. It looks like a tiger about to pounce and I know one thing as I stare at it: junkies aren't allowed in Astons, breaks some sort of rule, I'm certain.

"Probably a federal law against it," Lenny says.

The passenger's window lowers, and I bend to peer inside.

"Don't just stand there, get in."

It's Rhyme. Her luscious smile and flowing auburn locks call to me from the driver's seat. I can't describe how good she looks behind the wheel of this car. I mean, I'd only ever seen her in a Subaru and she'd never wanted to drive my BMW when we were together.

Her green eyes beckon even as her expression is one of hope mixed with subtle anguish.

Now I know why Cain sent me down here. Shopping. With Rhyme. And her scent.

The home audience is intrigued at this point I'm sure, as I hesitate, glance at the mansion, look down at my feet, then back at Rhyme.

"I think he's gonna go for it, Vince."

And go for it, I shall. I imagine jumping in the car and her stomping the gas. We race away to corners of the Earth where X'chasei has no influence and no one's ever heard of Cain.

I slide into the passenger's seat, close the door. Then her scent rolls over me, and I find myself frozen, basking in the fragrance, lilac and vanilla. A weird thing about smell is it can stir up memories long forgotten. Rhyme straight from the shower. Rhyme's clothes, her hair. The vanilla like homemade ice cream, the lilac like fresh cut branches, intoxicating, clean. Ever-present when she hugged me, brought me coffee, walked around the city.

I'm reaching for my seat belt when she tromps on the gas. I'm pinned to my seat as we fly down the long drive. Tall, manicured trees become blurs as we rocket ahead.

I glance over, see her smile, pure jubilance. Elegant hands grip the steering wheel as her head presses into the seat back. We're nearing the end of the drive. Need to go right or left, there's no option for straight. I fumble for my seat belt, glance out the windshield, back at her, back to the windshield.

Then she turns the wheel hard and we glide through a left that plants my face against the window of the passenger door. She presses the accelerator, and I'm again pressed to the back of my seat.

I hear her giggle, see her smile grow.

"You're gonna get a ticket," I say.

"You'd better buckle up," she says, then gives the wheel a quick right-left turn. The motion rocks me both ways, and I double my efforts with the safety belt.

We approach a huge gate, the entrance to this estate. It's closed and I glance frantic to Rhyme, who isn't slowing at all. I snap the safety belt, feel reassured with the click of its clasp. I push both hands on the dash, eyes locked on the gate.

"Rhyme, Rhyme, Rhyme," is all I can say.

Then the gate starts to open. Slowly. Rhyme hammers the gas pedal and I feel the turbo engage. Just when I thought we were at max acceleration, I'm thrown into the back of my seat, the tiger in the engine box roaring as we rocket.

"Looks like he's gonna pee his pants, Vince."

I may very well pee my pants, I think.

The gate opens in increments. I have the thought that rich people can afford a faster gate.

Rhyme's expression hasn't changed. It's one of pure joy and I feel my heart soak it in, realize I can't remember the last time I'd seen her wear this jubilance.

I look ahead, we're not going to make it. The gate's only open about four feet and I'm certain the car won't get through.

"Rhyme, Rhyme, Rhyme!"

We shoot through like a charging tiger, avoid the gate on either side by less than an inch. I look to my left, to the guard house adjacent to the slow gate. A security man stands in the window. Instead of looking surprised, he gives us a thumbs up.

"Yeeeeeee!" Rhyme screams, and I find myself laughing, thinking about nothing but my beating heart and the thrill of being with her again.

She takes another left at speed, then allows the vehicle to slow to a pace just slower than that of a comet.

A few more breathtaking turns and we're cruising on I-495 at ninety-plus miles per hour. I relax a bit, assure myself I haven't lost control of my bladder. Then she glances at me, holds my eyes for a second before returning her gaze to the road.

"Nice to see you, Mr. Merrick," she says. "And thank you for being my companion for the day." She glances at me and I smile. I can't take my eyes off her, can't pull my stare away from this woman with whom I've shared so much.

I swallow hard, soak her in. "The pleasure is mine."

My youth was spent in a trailer park. Never-ending rows of rectangular homes made of cheap metal and sitting on wheels. I remember when money was tight, which it always was, my mother sold the wheels for extra cash. I think she got about three-hundred bucks, which to us was a fortune.

This was back when McDonald's was newer, a time when small towns had businesses that weren't chains. We celebrated our windfall that day at McDonald's. Drive-thru only because my mother had some hang-up about eating inside, some issue about what people would think of our poverty, which we wore on our faces, in our hair, on our bodies. Poverty's one of those things that builds character but ruins self-worth.

So, we'd sit and eat and joke about things around us. We'd marvel at the sign, the golden arches, which at the time read OVER ONE MILLION SERVED.

"A million people," my mom would say, "isn't that something?"

Those were good days—or at least as good as those days could get. Impoverished as we were, things were simple, and we'd hide from those places we couldn't afford.

Today I feel the same way.

Tysons Corner Center, a place for rich people to buy things they don't need. But then, as I watch them pass, I realize they haven't had to think of *needs* for a while, if ever.

We arrive at valet with an elephant in the back seat. During the drive we'd exchanged pleasantries, talked of old times, never once giving the elephant any attention. Never once speaking of Cain and all that transpired since the day she'd clocked me and left.

I want to bring it up.

But I don't want to bring it up.

I'm interested in her reasons.

I'm also terrified by what she might say.

We stroll through the mall, duck into shops that look like they've spent a fortune on lighting alone. Rhyme buys the occasional thing, and I hold her bags as she collects them. Money seems no object, and I watch as she spends over thirty-thousand dollars on a bracelet that's caught her fancy.

We exit the jeweler. "Oh, I forgot something," she says. "Wait here." Then she disappears back into the store.

I stand, and watch the people pass. All seem well-heeled and those who aren't stick out like a paisley giraffe, or an elephant, as the case may be. I bet *those* people have warm memories of McDonald's.

I smell her before she arrives, the familiar vanilla and lilac. I think of Cain enjoying that scent, this beauty and all she is. The smile, the can-do attitude, the naughty body and luscious lips. I look over the crowd and see an exit. I think to escape, to run from this, get as far away as possible. Hell, I may even stop at McDonald's.

Then she's next to me. She hooks her arm around mine, smiles up at me. "Hungry?" she says.

We go to a steak place close to Saks Fifth Avenue.

I order scotch, single malt, Macallan, straight up. As soon as it arrives, I gulp it down and order another.

"You should just get two at a time," she says.

I look at her, expect the look that says she thinks I'm a junkie. But her face tells me she's not being sarcastic at all, just giving helpful advice. I also remember she *knows* I'm a junkie.

"You think she knows what a loser he is?" Lenny says.

"Indeed. How could she not?" says Vince.

As it happens, the elephant has managed to extricate himself from the Aston's back seat and has accompanied us all through the galleria. I decide to face him, made bold by the scotch.

"So, what's with you and Cain?"

She glances at me, seems ready for the question. "You're angry."

I swirl the scotch in my glass, look back at her. "How could I not be?"

She smiles, teeth glistening, mouth stretched and beautiful. Around her neck, a pendant hangs from a silver chain. I look closer, see it's a beautiful labarum, vibrant maroon on a pearl background. It's brilliant, looks expensive, jiggles when she talks. She's resplendent, more beautiful than I remembered, more beautiful even than the night we'd first met. The night I stared at her until dawn.

"He's the worst person on the planet," I say.

"You've noticed." She fingers the necklace, glances down. "You always were a good reporter."

She's trying to make light of it. Trying to get me laughing so I'll return to ignoring the pachyderm at our table.

I swirl my scotch some more, think about swallowing my words.

But I can't. I'm a caveman fighting a mammoth.

"Why?" I say, which seems to sum up all the questions rattling through my head.

She takes me in, her gaze disconcerting. I'm reminded of her power. If you push her too far, you'll get more than you asked for.

She sips her wine, a white, sets her glass on the table and gives me a look that says something's coming I don't want to hear. Her face becomes hard. "Listen," she says, "I haven't had a good day since the day I left you. I'd like this to be a good day. I'd like you to cooperate. Can we just be together today?"

My thoughts are silenced by these few sentences. Sentences packed with such meaning, such exposure. They tell me she misses me. They tell me she hadn't wanted to leave. They tell me she's with Cain for some other reason. That she's sacrificed something important. In those words, she tells me she needs a day to forget about everything. To pretend things aren't as they are.

I feel a sense of honor as I consider her words. She's chosen me today. If I'm smart, I'll see that too, just enjoy the moments in front of us now.

"He'll fuck it up," Lenny says.

I can't help but smile, feel some relief at her words and all the meanings I've ascribed to them. "Yes," I say. "We can."

She smiles, slides a small box toward me.

"A gift," she says.

I remove the thin blue ribbon and open it. Inside is a silver ring, much larger than a wedding band. It has a black onyx centerpiece, upon which is an etching of an angel. Its wings are spread wide, and it holds a spear. I'm reminded of my dream, of Michael the Archangel.

"Try it on," she says.

I put it on my right ring finger. "A perfect fit," I say, "but you shouldn't have."

She holds my eyes. "I know, but," she glances away here, "it looked like you needed a present."

I examine the ring, it feels smooth, well crafted, expensive.

"I love it," I say.

"I've always felt I have a guardian angel, and I wanted you to have one too."

I laugh. "This is going to protect me?"

She giggles, shrugs. "Can't hurt."

We spend the rest of the meal talking about the past. Laughing about our good times, ignoring the elephant. I must have five or six glasses of Macallan, and she's gone through the better part of a bottle of white.

The check arrives and she reaches for it, but I stop her and retrieve my wallet, stuffed with cash. I place the bills in the bifold the waiter hands me, then add a huge extra tip.

"Why Mr. Merrick," she says, "such a big spender."

I blush a little. We both know it's Cain's money.

We exit the restaurant, and she turns into Saks, motions me to follow.

"There's something I want to show you."

Up an escalator, and we're surrounded by evening gowns. Sequins shine under the store's lights, every color and pattern represented. She selects one and disappears into a dressing room.

Why these places never have a place where waiting men can sit, I'll never know. So, I stand near the dressing room, my heart beating fast.

The door to the dressing room creaks a bit, and I see her eyes. "Um, can you help zip me?"

I enter and zip up the dress. We both look in the mirror.

I stand, eyes on her, mouth open. I look good in the duds that were in my room, even manage to pass for someone who belongs here.

She, however, is radiant.

The dress is dark maroon, sequined with a plunging neckline that enhances her curves. It flows to the floor, pauses only to embrace whatever part of her it touches. Its sleeves flow down to her wrists and end in a ring of transparent lace. She is lithe and the dress multiplies and reflects her refinement. Auburn hair cascades over her shoulders as the labarum shines, a brilliant star just below her neck.

"What do you think?" she says.

Now, if I verbalize the thoughts I'm having at this moment, I'll never stop talking. I think of the wonder she is. How the dress amplifies her magnificence, lets the world know someone truly amazing has arrived. I think so much more, but mostly I think of regret. The loss of her. My stupidity. Our journey together, gone terribly wrong.

I know better than to say these things, and I'm sure the home audience is disappointed when I say only one word. "Overwhelming."

Our eyes meet in the mirror's reflection.

She turns, moves close.

Her lips meet mine and my mind implodes. I'm lost, adrift on this feeling. I hear the little sound she used to make, the petite moan as our tongues intermingle. We are in the moment. Together again. Entwined. One.

She pushes herself away, stares at me. Her lips are moist and inviting. Her cheeks are flushed. She breathes hard, her eyes searching mine. Her expression is raw passion, pure indulgence.

As I stare, I feel the kiss linger as if tattooed. My mind is blank as she fills my vision with radiance and jubilation. I'm tingling. I'm awed. I'm panting.

I look to the floor, try to collect myself.

She steps forward, holds my face in both hands, gently raises my head. "I've missed you, Emery."

CHAPTER 20

WASHINGTON, D.C.

"They won't last as long as the Romans, although they're really not so different," Cain says.

The next day, we sit in the back of the limousine. Cain has the shades pulled for some reason. Blue eyes peer from under his brow, seem to glow in fact, and I think in the dull light he rather looks like a vampire. Brilliant white hair adds to the picture and contrasts beautifully with the dimly lit interior. The shades hadn't needed to be pulled as the relentless sun has gone on hiatus, making the day cloudy and dark.

"It's rather remarkable," he says, "but they've outdone that lost empire."

My notepad sits in my lap, my iPhone is set to record. These days I need to take every opportunity to tape the man.

I glance up, try to remember if I'd packed my Percs. "How's that?"

Cain looks at me as if I've missed the obvious. "It's easy, dear Emery, you Americans think recorded history didn't start until the day you were born." He smiles, stares at me for a second. "You think prior to that, everything was just a void. Incredibly short-sighted really. The Romans only lasted about a thousand years, but I think the U.S. will be lucky to make it three-hundred."

My expression must show I'm missing the point.

"Don't you see? They've muddled it up. Every bit as corrupt and self-absorbed as the Romans of old. Their inability to get things done is astonishing. No one gets along and the politicians serve only themselves. Like Rome, the people are an afterthought, and why not when there are such riches to gain?"

I consider the fact, his error in logic. I'm living proof those riches are not so easily gained.

"Grand ideas at the start, to be sure," he continues. "But I fear now those ideas are wasted, the experiment hopeless." He pauses here, glances out the window toward the mansion's entrance. "I had high hopes for that little band of criminals and their experiment to forge a democracy." He looks at me, his expression solemn. He places his right hand over his heart. "Of the people, by the people and for the people." He stares at me for another second, then reveals that smile. I half expect to see fangs.

"Do you think we could raise a blind or two?" I say.

He continues as if I haven't said a word. "I hoped for their success with such fervor that I even leveraged X'chasei's resources a time or two on their behalf. Do you really think the folks at Valley Forge survived the winter without aid? Do you think this band of ruffians could've defeated the mighty British without help?" He looks at me here, holds my gaze in his icy blue eyes. "If you do, you're as big a fool as that president of theirs."

"What was there to gain?"

He chuckles at this, shakes his head. He's amused I can't see all he sees. That I haven't the centuries behind me, lack the understanding to grasp such subtle complexities.

He sips his drink, pulls a Treasurer from the tin and lights it. "Vast resources, dear Emery. They were on the verge of discovering they inhabited a continent ripe with treasure." He raises a finger here. "And one protected on two sides by oceans. So unlike Europe, so easily defensible and separate from the main. It's not hard to connect the dots. To see the potential for wealth. At first my interest was purely financial, but then I became intrigued by their experiment, curious to see if it could work. To see if they could outdo the Romans. I wondered if humans could put aside being human, for once, and pull together beneath a banner of brotherhood and national pride." He glances at the mansion again, adjusts the Labarum cufflink on his right shirtsleeve. "I know now I wasted my time. They've failed, interested in only wealth." He glances at me, then at my notepad. "Well," he says, "wealth for those who have it."

"And for those who don't?"

His laugh sounds like a silver bell. "Those spend their time complaining about how poor they are." I wave my hand in front of me, the cigarette smoke is a thick haze within the limo's limited confines. "Their ideas of equality are noble, but I'm afraid their execution is lacking."

"So, you're disappointed?"

"Indeed," he says. "They've humanized what was good. To a person, they spend their time sounding noble, as if they actually care about such lofty goals as equality and democracy." He leans forward here, rests his elbows on his knees, drink held with both hands. The cigarette forms lazy coils above the fingers of his right hand. "It's all theater, my boy. A charade of argument and counterargument. Everyone's opinion serves only themselves and when differing opinions clash, it becomes a race to see who can take the higher road." He draws on the butt again, blows more smoke. He motions at the wafting vapor. "It's all fog. All white noise. In the end, I'm afraid, their avarice knows no bounds. Capitalism isn't a bad concept and could probably be quite successful if humans were created differently. But it seems God had other things in mind. Gone is the generation of World War Two. That generation knew sacrifice, understood America's strength was purchased through the efforts of *all* its people. Now these Americans think only of themselves. And that invades them like a cancer. I could name, one after another, the civilizations who fell to that sort of selfishness. You Americans like to patrol the world, to bonk people on the head with your nightsticks. Then to make high-road excuses for your actions while blaming everyone else for what fails to enrich you further. You say you're the home of the free, but as I've watched this failed experiment, I've seen this freedom become more and more slim, seen it slowly stripped from the citizenry in the name of good causes. I'm actually surprised there's not been another revolution over there."

"Why don't you start one?"

He probes my expression to see if I'm serious. Then he says, "Because I do not invest in lost causes, dear Emery. If Americans actually believed all men were created equal, then there'd be no more discussion on the matter. You see? It would just be, just exist." He leans back, sips his drink. "But it doesn't. Everything has become political so those in power can retain that power and keep the populous enslaved. Utter poppycock." He takes another drag from his smoke.

"Does X'chasei still exist there?"

Cain leans back, flashes that stare, looks toward the mansion. "Oh, it exists everywhere. You can't imagine the breadth of that empire. But there I use it less and less as I watch the country die. X'chasei is well-integrated, I assure you. Like a gun in a box, not needed presently but useful when the time comes."

"And you're not exploiting that?"

He chuckles, snuffs the cigarette. "Once I saw the truth of their avarice, I knew it was done. My guess is they'll probably implode. From race, or religion, or some other nonsense that shouldn't be an issue in a place where all beings are free and equal." He swirls the glass in his hand, shakes his head, speaks as if speaking only to himself. "I'm afraid their time has come but they just don't know it." He looks at me. "I can tell you with some certainty that when they fall, it will be someone else's fault. Americans sacrifice nothing, just live in a constant chase of fulfillment and consumerism. The infinite I. A cosmic self-absorption. They forget the lessons of history." He nods a single time, then shakes his head again. "That's if they ever knew them. They think nothing existed before they revolted from the British. But they've forgotten history repeats itself. They've forgotten the barbarity of the past, the lesson no empire lasts. This will be their undoing, and still, as they burn, they'll fail to see the truth."

"And how do you feel about that?"

Cain's eyes flash, giving me an expression I've not seen before. One of surprise, one that tells me he doesn't often get asked about his feelings.

"I don't consider it a loss," he says. "It doesn't change my plans. In fact, with them gone, my tasks become easier."

I chuckle, write in my notepad. "You act like they'll be gone tomorrow."

"Yes, dear Emery, you consummate American. I've witnessed history and can assure you she's an impatient teacher."

"And you spoke of your plans, care to refresh my memory?"

"I believe you've written this down before. Please check your notes."

"I will, but I was just wondering if they've changed. I mean, things have certainly changed since your return. Your hair, your eyes. Seems as if you have supernatural powers that go beyond your gifts. I watched the video of what happened in Jerusalem. The white horse, the blinding light from the heavens, the way you handled security, took the place over, what's that about?"

His glass is halfway to his mouth. "And he seemed like such a bright boy," he says in a quiet voice. "Dear Emery, you simply *must* reconsider your addictions."

He's toying with me, like I'm a child. I think it over, think of his plans, or at least what I know of them.

"You plan to take God's place," I say. "If I remember correctly."

He raises his glass, drains it. Looks at me, shakes his head as if disappointed. "My dear Emery," he says, "I don't *plan* to take God's place, I've already *taken* it."

The words hit me like a punch in the chest. I look at my notepad as I consider his statement. I have no evidence with which to dispute his claim. I mean, other than it just sounds crazy. As I ponder his words, I realize the evidence, in fact, only confirms what he's saying.

"You've become a god?" I say. "Did that happen after you were killed?"

"Indeed, it did."

"Like Gandalf the Grey becoming Gandalf the White?"

"Who's Gandalf the White?"

"J.R.R. Tolkien, *The Lord of the Rings*. A fictional character."

He shakes his head, actually tsk's me. "Dear Emery, I am *not* fictional. I died and was reborn. I returned on Easter Sunday to announce my presence to my subjects. There is no earthly power that can threaten me, no means for humanity to resist my will. I *have* become God. Not *a* god, but *the* God. It's all as was prophesied, and you humans, so self-absorbed, fail to see it. Like the U.S. president, you think it some sort of parlor trick."

I think to challenge him here, to have him perform some miracle or something. Then I remember when I'd challenged him before. Back in Dubai, when I'd asked to see his mark. What I'd garnered from that particular line of inquiry. I snap my mouth closed, consider another question. Not very journalistic, but certainly safe.

"So," I say, "gods marry mortals? How very Greek. Can I expect Zeus or Poseidon next?"

He laughs. "Your sarcasm is always appreciated, dear Emery. They say it to be a true sign of intelligence. Your classic defense mechanism." He places his glass in the cupholder on the limo's right side, looks straight into my eyes. "I know how much you hate me for marrying her. But I also promised you would be in my favor when I returned as God, and I do not wish ill will between us. So, I'll speak as honestly as possible. I love Rhyme. Of that, there is no doubt."

I interrupt him with a snort. "As if you could love anything."

He continues, acts like my comment requires no consideration. "She's an amazing woman, dear Emery, and I'm afraid you know only a fraction of those things of which she's capable. You're a fool for letting her go, for chasing your addictions, for treating her with such indelicacy. If you'd have been smarter, we probably wouldn't know each other. Wouldn't even be having this conversation. But alas, you were not, and despite your obvious flaws and selfishness, she still loves you." The comment surprises me, I feel it invade my expression as Cain continues. "I'm working to change that and believe in time she'll fully embrace me." He seems genuine, even friendly. "I'm sorry for your loss, but only partly. I never expected to marry a human, never expected a lot of things my journey has held. But now, as *God*," he emphasizes this word, "I cannot suffer such distractions as pity for you. You've always been in a hurry to die, and I alone saved you from that fate. I sincerely hope we can find a mutual understanding, that you'll stay in my favor. But the choice is entirely yours. My hope is that you'll be able to set aside the portion of malice you hold for me. But," he pauses here, "if you cannot, it changes nothing. You'll still serve at my pleasure. Like all mortals, that is your lot."

I'm not sure if his gifts are working on me, but what he says makes sense. I even feel a glimmer of fondness for the man. Feel like a chosen disciple of this new god. I think of Rhyme, can still feel her lips on mine. I think to tell Cain of this little indiscretion as a way to rub his pompous nose in it. She still prefers me, of that I'm certain and he's admitted it. I'm amazed at how he can underestimate certain innate human qualities. How he can be so self-assured in his power as a *god*.

I redirect my questions. "I see your gloves are gone."

He looks at his right hand. The mark looks puckered and dead, wilted like a dried-out daisy. "I've no need to hide anymore. No need to consider what mortals think."

"Is that why you refused all the interviews from, like, everyone on the planet?"

"Precisely," he says, flashing his hypnotic smile. "I've no need to talk myself up, as the commoners say. Very soon the world will see my power, and all will be as it was prophesied. One need only look to history to see everything will happen as it was ordained."

"Are you talking about the Bible? The one you created when you were Constantine?"

"I prefer to say I commissioned it, but yes, if nothing else the Bible serves as a history book. The trick is understanding it."

I remember my ride to Damascus with Igneus. When he'd tried to explain the concept of omniscience. I raise my eyes from my notepad.

Cain bends a shade, looks out the window at the mansion. The light hits him in such a way he appears enlightened, irradiated, haloed like a god. He is Zeus surveying his kingdom from Olympus, strong, proud, beautiful, invincible.

"No man can comprehend the mind of God," I say.

He turns his gaze to me, nods. "Precisely."

CHAPTER 21

WASHINGTON, D.C.

Cain looks again towards the mansion, then hits the intercom button. "Do proceed, Jules," he says. "I was hoping Rhyme would come see us off. Alas, she must be busy with her duties."

The limo starts down the long drive at a much slower pace than Rhyme in her Aston.

I suppress the urge to look out the rear window like a lost orphan. "Is she not coming with us?"

Cain refills his glass, then retrieves another one and fills it halfway. He hands me the scotch. I nod and accept. "I'm afraid not," he says. "She has business here."

"What business?"

He looks as if he can barely suffer my boldness. Which prompts me to say, "You do want your wife included in your biography?"

He stares for a second, nods. "Of course," he says, "she's a critical part of my life." He seems a bit deflated as we drive away. "She's Israel's Ambassador to the United States."

Now it's my turn to deflate. She's staying behind, which means she'll not be near me. The thought fills me with dread, drains all energy from my body, fills me with the desire to return to my sanctum and sleep for days on end. Quite a pair, Cain and I, both of us pining for the same woman. Like two lost puppies wandering the streets, waiting for her to give us a treat, a pat on the head. Maybe he does love her. Maybe she's managed to crack his icy heart. I consider his words, "I hope you can accept this new arrangement." He thinks the decision is mine, that Rhyme has no say in the matter. I think to the dressing room, her words, "I've missed you, Emery." I know she's already chosen, know her love for me survives. That she hasn't abandoned me and that I cannot abandon her.

I long to speak with her, to hold her, to mourn our baby, to despair in all that's happened and find healing entwined in each other's arms and hearts.

Cain notices the change in my posture. "Now, now, dear Emery, we'll only be apart for a short time." His face is caring, even empathetic. "I'm glad you're still capable of being her friend and displaying such fondness, though. Makes me feel like she'll be in good hands when I'm not around."

Oh, she'll be in good hands, I think.

"Have you ever been married?" I ask. "During all those centuries there must've been a special lady or two?" I speak halfheartedly, poking fun, but I'm also curious as to the answer.

Cain considers the question, sips his whisky. "I was married once. Thought I'd give it a try. It was rather expected for emperors to marry." He sighs as smoke wafts. "It didn't work out the greatest. After, I was so broken, I thought God made me impotent as part of my exile. Just never another desire. Not a single craving. I did manage to obtain my objectives, though, so an even trade I suppose. I know it sounds sensational but all very true. And don't think Longinus didn't try to tempt me with various women, harlots, even queens."

I nod, knowing full well the appetites of the Roman. I also feel joy rise in my chest. Cain's impotent!

"Alas, though," he continues, "once I became God, everything changed. Rhyme and I are very passionate. I even think that perhaps we can have children of our own someday."

My joy swirls away like water in a toilet. That's what I get for poking fun, a red-hot knife through the heart. Vince and Lenny crack up as jealousy bubbles over and fills my soul. I feel jilted, as if I stand at the foot of their bed, watching their intimacy.

I stare at Cain, my full contempt obvious. He returns a small smile, a look of pity. Then I realize how inadequate I feel. My appearance, my actions, my addictions, my poverty, the sum of what I have to offer. Paltry in comparison to Cain. His youth, his physique, his smile, his power. The way he dresses, his infinite wealth, the smoothness and sophistication.

I'm an alley cat, mangy and foraging.

He's a lion without natural predators.

"Dear Emery," he says, "don't look so downtrodden. Life has a way of yielding good things. You are in my favor and deserve a boon. Say the word and I'll present you with a host of beauties from which to choose. Choose one or choose a harem. I assure you they will all be delightful, sumptuous and open-minded. Speak your desire, and it shall be yours."

"I want my wife back."

He chuckles but seems otherwise unaffected. "Of course, you do. Very natural in fact, to want to make amends. But I'm afraid that's a wish I cannot grant. Rhyme's made her choice, and my advice to you is to move on."

I start to speak, to let him know exactly which choice Rhyme made, but I'm beaten by the ring of his phone.

He looks at the screen and then at me. "What a delight," he says, glancing up at me. "It's Laslo. I'll put it on speaker."

Slabav's voice comes through the line.

"What in the name of God are you doing!" The PM's voice is harsh, and it surprises me. I've never heard anyone use this kind of tone with Cain and live to see the next day.

"Dear Laslo, you seem upset."

"Upset is an understatement. I just received a call from President Carpenter, who told me you enlisted his aid in some unknown war. Promised him resources, told him we were taking over the region? Have you lost your mind?"

"Laslo," Cain says, "do calm…"

"Shut your mouth!" Laslo screams. "You'll do as you're told and nothing more. Am I clear?"

Cain's mouth opens to a wide O, he holds his right hand to his cheek. The action is theatrical, even comical. Despite my feelings toward the monster, I snicker at the pose.

"You are," Cain says. "But unfortunately, I have one more stop to make before I return to Jerusalem. Trust me, Laslo, all of this is for Israel's benefit."

"I decide that, you ass!" Slabav is enraged, screaming. "I decide what's in this country's best interest!"

Cain again chuckles. "Dear Laslo, I wasn't referring to our nation, I was referring to your son."

There's dead silence.

Cain raises his eyebrows, looks at me, looks at the phone as if the connection has dropped.

When Laslo finally speaks his tone is much more sedate. "My son?"

"I'll explain when I return," Cain says and hangs up.

Then he looks at me, his expression gleeful. Blue eyes light the car's interior even as a glimmer of sun creeps through the blinds.

"Dear Emery," he says, "I do hope my biography mentions the morons with which I'm forced to deal."

Chapter 22

Jerusalem, Israel

The phone seems to ring a thousand times before it's answered.

"Laslo, how nice to hear from you. It's been a long time." It's the headmaster at Israel's high school, Leyada. A Jewish education at the finest institution.

"I must be quick, Moshe," Laslo says. "Is Israel well?" The phone slips in Laslo's hands, his palms are sweating.

The headmaster sounds confused. "Well, I'm sure he is. I just saw him this morning."

"Please check on him this instant."

"But I…"

Laslo feels the tension in his voice. "Now, please!" He inhales, forces calm. "Please, Moshe."

"Okay. Hold."

A bead of sweat trickles down his forehead and into his eye. He presses the intercom button on his desk, wipes his eyes with the same hand.

"Yes sir." His secretary sounds like she's in a tin can.

"Send more agents to Leyada. My son is in danger."

There's a pause. "Right away."

Laslo sits in the chair behind his desk. The music is pleasant as he holds but does nothing to calm his panic. If something happened to Israel, Cain will pay. I'll not be controlled by this man.

He thinks to call Khalifa, maybe he can help. Perhaps together they can handle Cain.

His knee bounces up and down as his hand taps the papers on his desk.

He stands again. The wait is unbearable.

Then the headmaster picks up. "Laslo, I'm afraid Israel has fainted."

"What?" Laslo yells. "What happened?"

"His teacher reports he was giving a presentation and then collapsed. He's uninjured though, and says he feels well enough to finish the day."

"No! I've sent some people to get him."

"I saw him myself and he looks fit," the headmaster says.

"He's in danger, Moshe, someone will be there directly. Tell his security people to prepare him for departure. We need to get him out of there. Lock down the school."

"Are you serious, Laslo? We've had no—"

"Do it!" Laslo hangs up the phone, looks at the gathering thunderheads outside his office. In minutes he'll get the call saying Israel is safe. Just have to sweat it out until I get the news, he thinks.

Then he hears a creak behind him. It's a sound he's heard before, a sound that one of the chairs facing his desk makes when someone sits in it.

He turns to see the intruder, and sweat openly flows.

It's Longinus, Cain's associate.

"How did you get in here?" Laslo says.

The giant chuckles, rubs the stubble on his face with a huge hand. "If I've a mind, I can be gettin' anywhere," he says. "Anon and agin, 'tis better me here than at Leyada. Eh?"

Laslo's phone rings.

Longinus nods at it. "Ye should answer."

"Hello?" Laslo says.

"We've got him, sir. Israel is safe."

Laslo hangs up. Looks at the giant across from him.

"'Tis well?" Longinus says.

Laslo nods. "It is."

"Tomorrow twilight ye'll be meetin' with Cain. Aye?"

"Aye, er, yes," Laslo says.

"Do non be meddlin'. Aye?"

"Yes." Laslo says.

"All is well?" Longinus says.

"All is well," Laslo replies.

The chair groans as the giant stands and plods from the room.

Laslo wipes the sweat from his face with trembling hands.

CHAPTER 23

WASHINGTON, D.C.

The knock at the door is expected, room service. Rhyme checks her phone, ten AM. She pulls the soft terry robe close to her body and ties the silk sash in a knot.

The suite at the D.C. St. Regis is comfortable and well accommodated. Done with expensive furniture in pastel blue over a thick carpet the color of the ocean after a storm. A gold chandelier hangs in the room's center but appears useless as a large, arced window sends plenty of sunlight through gold-checked curtains.

She exits the main bedroom, a room all its own, then passes pastel chairs, a beautiful Victorian desk, and a small, round dining table. She squeezes the robe closed at the neck and answers the door.

"Your order, ma'am," the man says. He wears black pants over matching shoes shined to a high gloss. Luxury shoes, expensive. His shirt is white, covered by a smart, tailored vest in deep maroon. A bow tie completes the appearance. Rhyme notices it isn't a clip-on, but one that requires the wearer to have a knowledge of the complexities of tying a bow tie.

She steps aside and the man enters pushing a small cart. "I hope you're enjoying your stay," he says, nearing the dining table. He arranges the dishes, a small white plate, fork and knife on either side, spotless cloth napkin. "Looks like it's going to be a lovely day."

Rhyme feels a tingle in the nape of her neck. An old feeling she'd thought disused and forgotten. A kind of sixth sense, intuition, a warning. Something isn't right.

Sunlight splays wide rays through the window and makes a bright square on the room's lush carpet. The man busies himself, arranges the modest breakfast: an oat muffin, some orange juice, coffee. He seems to be taking his time, not acting like normal waiters who enter with a sense of purpose, then speed through their task anxious to collect their tip.

This waiter is unassuming, even casual.

But the shoes don't fit. What waiter, even at a five-star place like this, can afford shoes this expensive? And the bow tie, the expert knot, what service staffer would be skilled at such a thing?

Painful experience has taught her to trust her instincts and she adjusts her position, noting the waiter's dominant hand.

Through the years Rhyme has learned most people prefer their dominant side. She's learned that when expecting the unexpected, preparation has no equal. She's been caught by surprise too many times, has suffered severe consequences as a result.

The waiter is right-handed, which tells her he'll prefer an assault that comes from his left. She moves behind him, in a direct line with his right shoulder. If he's up to something, he'll spin to his left in order to give his dominant hand the most room.

He seems unaware of her motion as he pours steaming black coffee into a small white cup. He snaps a napkin, folds it to a tight V, and places it atop a round, white plate.

Rhyme watches him work, examines every detail, looks for even a small advantage, anything out of place, any clue to reinforce her already enhanced sense of danger.

Then she sees it, a thin black strap jutting from the rear shoulder of his vest. It sticks out about an eighth of an inch, but Rhyme knows what it is and what it holds. She imagines the line of the strap, circling the man's left shoulder to join another strap in the center of his back, making an X.

A shoulder holster, which means he has a weapon just under his left armpit, possibly one under the right as well.

She knows she has only a few seconds and examines her options.

The man turns to his left just as she anticipates. She steps close, brings her right leg between his feet and reaches into his vest. She feels rusty, slow, hasn't needed these skills in some time.

The man's eyes widen, then narrow an instant later. A normal response here is to attack, she thinks. He'll try and push me back, to create distance with which to work.

He does just that, but with unexpected speed. His hands go for her throat, stabbing for her neck. She steps close, sliding between outstretched arms, an inch from his face, and slams her knee into his groin.

He gasps and doubles over.

He'll try to grab me now, she thinks. A giant bear hug. If he's a pro, he'll fight, ignoring the enormous pain in his testicles. Professionals never give up, ever, are willing to die to complete their mission.

His arms close around her even as his face changes to bulging purple. Rhyme moves, fluid and elegant, ducking the hug, taking two steps back.

She holds his black revolver. Its color mutes the window's natural light. It appears cold and deadly. She levels it, prepared to empty it into the man's chest if he continues.

He shuffles a step, then crumbles to a knee overcome by the pain in his groin.

Rhyme smiles, happy she doesn't have testicles, such an obvious target, such an immense weakness.

"Poor fella," she says. "I bet that hurt."

Dark eyes glimmer rage. The man steams from a purple face.

He lowers his head, seems to give up.

Rhyme knows better.

The man's weight is on his left knee. His head lags and gives the appearance of being subdued. She knows what's next. None of these guys are one-trick ponies, not the good ones anyway.

He doubles over, bends with his abdomen, tries to conceal what Rhyme knows is coming. He's trying to block her view, his hand tracing down his right leg to retrieve god knows what from his right ankle. Could be another gun, a poison dart, a dagger, pepper spray, a taser.

She sees through it all, thinks to shoot the man and end the conjecture. Such a beautiful carpet, seafoam blue, plush, lovely on the toes. It'd be a shame to stain it with blood. Besides, the man needs to answer some questions.

But first, he needs to accept defeat.

She racks the pistol. A cartridge ejects, spinning from the chamber to land on the thick carpet. The action serves two purposes. First, when acquiring the pistol, Rhyme hadn't known if there was a round in the chamber. That is, if the pistol is ready to fire. A distinct disadvantage as the man who carried it would've known its status and could use that knowledge to his advantage. If she assumes a round is ready to go and attempts to fire, she'll be surprised when it doesn't and lose precious seconds attempting to chamber a round. Seconds the man can use to his own advantage. She'd been taught better, taught by the best, won't repay such wisdom with simple mistakes.

Second, the pistol is a Glock, lightweight, made in Austria. A Glock 43, if she has to guess, Vickers tactical version, judging by the feel of the extended magazine and custom slide lock. The good thing about racking a round is the sound it makes. Anyone close knows immediately what the sound means, and she doubts this man expects to hear it. Not from a pretty woman in a hotel bathrobe ordering juice and muffins from room service.

The man freezes, raises his head. He looks like he's going to vomit although his color has improved a bit.

She nods. "I wouldn't," she says. "Take it out and drop it."

A second goes by. Rhyme knows he's considering a full rush, considering the distance between them, her stance, watching the gun to see if it trembles in her clutches. He's looking for weakness, seeking advantage.

He produces another revolver, smaller, tactical, the Mossad version of a .22 caliber handgun. He's Israeli and she startles. The thought is unimaginable.

She's recently been appointed as the Israeli ambassador. Would they send a Mossad agent? She can't begin to guess why the man's here or what he could want. The questions tumble along, cascade through her mind like a waterfall. She forces them away, thinks about what she knows for certain. The man's highly trained. Deadly. Unpredictable. She can't lower her guard for a single instant.

"Toss it over," she nods, slightly squeezing the Glock's trigger safety.

He raises it, holds the grip loose between thumb and index finger. "Careful," she says, "don't try it."

She sees his anger, knows the calculations whirling through his mind. He's been overcome by a woman and isn't happy about it.

This, sometimes, is hard for men, especially tough guy commandos who kill for the government. Some can't take it, can't wrap their mind around the possibility of being bested by a female. When it happens, it throws them into a crazed, irrational state.

Certainly, Rhyme has seen this before, always caused by something as inane as outsmarting a male. Always made worse when she bested them physically. Most just can't see past their own inflamed ego. Their misguided perception that the part that makes them male has anything at all to do with ability.

Whatever the reason, Rhyme has learned not to underestimate the reaction and to always, always expect it. For them, women are weak, meant to be mothers and lovers, not capable on levels that include combat or intelligence.

His eyes dart back and forth as if he's reading something. She knows they don't miss anything. She also knows that she hasn't missed anything. He's subdued, a cornered lion to be gently defanged and treated in such a way as to not further damage his already bruised and childish ego.

A few seconds pass. Rhyme is steady, ready to end the man's life at the first sign of threat.

He tosses the gun, and it bounces across the carpet to land by her feet.

Her tension reduces a half measure. He still has tricks though, is no less dangerous. She knows he'll always be looking for an advantage, will be ready to seize it the moment it presents.

She'd be a fool to think there's nothing more concealed beneath his uniform. A knife perhaps, something deadly to be sure.

"Stay where you are," she says. She doesn't want him to rise, doesn't want him anywhere but on his knees where it will be harder for him to stand and either bolt for the door or at her.

She steps backwards, feels the Victorian desk at her hip. She reaches behind and slides the phone forward, keeping it in her line of vision as she watches the man. She can't afford to divert her eyes for even a second. Can't afford to give him even that much time.

"Look at the floor," she says.

The man lowers his head and Rhyme glances at the numerous buttons on the clunky hotel phone. She keeps her gun trained as she pokes the 0 button with her left hand.

The man sighs, seems to deflate. She's been waiting for this, visible confirmation that he knows he's beat.

The phone buzzes twice before a voice comes on. "Yes, Miss Carter, how may we help you?"

"I'll need the pol…"

The door explodes in a shower of splintered wood and flying fragments, then hangs by a single hinge. Two men rush in, pistols drawn. The agent turns, startled, not expecting this. He leaps like a jungle cat, faster than Rhyme can believe, toward the intruders.

The shots are sharp, painful in the enclosed space, shrill pops from flaming pistols. The agent is almost on them, dashing through the small distance between. She hears more shots. Sees the agent stagger and fall.

He collapses on the carpet as two men stand just inside the door, pistols drawn, faces covered in tight, black neoprene masks.

They turn their weapons toward her.

She has to act. These are neither police nor government agents. No, these are a different variety altogether.

The pistol jumps in her hand as she fires four shots. The first is aimed high center mass, the other three designed to send the men running for cover. She dives left, toward the suite's bedroom.

She hears a gurgling sound, then a thud. She's hit one, has only one more with which to deal.

Unless there are others.

The remaining man enters the room and fires just as Rhyme dives over the bed, into the two-foot space between it and the wall beyond. Muffled shots enter the bed's mattress; wood and plaster shower down from the wall above.

This is bad.

She's trapped, pinned down, knows the man will continue to fire, will keep her pinned and cowering until he can close the distance and shoot her point-blank. She doesn't have much of a chance cramped where she is, has only seconds to come up with something before she dies.

A thought forms, a long shot at best but better than no shot.

She lies flat, rolls on her left shoulder and slides her right arm from the robe. More shots strike the wall above, more debris falls. He's closing, peppering bullets to keep her pinned.

She rolls right, slides her left arm from the robe. She's nude now, completely disrobed.

Her attacker will expect something dramatic and clever. He'll expect her to either pop up and fire wild, or stay flat until the last possible second, then poke around the bed's end for a surprise attack.

Rhyme plans neither.

She rolls the robe into a loose ball and places it atop her lower legs. The Glock is ready in her right hand. She knows a round is chambered; the pistol ready to fire. She'll only get one chance and better not mess it up.

She lies motionless. Feels chilled, exposed as she is. She inhales, controls her breathing, focuses her eyes loosely above her.

Another shot hits the wall as splinters fly from a smoking hole. The attacker spaces his shots at random. She counts, sees seven holes. A couple went into the mattress, she thinks. A couple more to kill the agent. She hadn't heard him reload. He probably has only one or two shots left unless he's using an extended clip, or something special-made. Or has another gun.

She can't rely on the calculations, can't risk her life based on the number of shots fired. Too many variables, too little time. This guy is too well-trained to give a clue to his position, too well-trained to use all his bullets and force a reload.

She hears the smallest shuffle, a single foot pressing into the carpet. It could be anything really, that sound. Could just be her imagination or wishful thinking, but Rhyme has learned to trust her instincts above all. Has learned to act on the slightest hunch and her sense of intuition.

She guesses the man's centered at the foot of the bed.

She kicks with both legs, hard and fast.

The robe flies into the air.

As her legs drop, she uses the momentum to propel her body to a sitting position, minimizing exposure while maximizing sight lines. If the man isn't where she's guessed, she'll be dead.

Her head pops above the bed and she hears two shots. Sees the man closer to her hiding spot than she'd thought.

He's facing left, gun leveled, firing at the robe as it floats back to the floor.

Rhyme aims, fires twice.

The bullets strike the man's temple, one behind the other. The impact, dull, as he hits the floor.

She pauses, gun ready, scanning for other attackers, seeing no one. Naked, she eases around the bed, poised, ready for anything; more agents at the door, more who've entered as she was pinned down.

Blood trickles from the man's temple. So much for the carpet. She steps over him and stalks across the room, alert to every sound, ready for other assailants.

The other men lie where they dropped, no longer a threat, dead.

She passes them, pokes her head into the hall and looks both ways. It's deserted.

The long, shrill sound of sirens demand her attention. Police have been summoned.

She moves to the first agent, searches his waiter uniform. She finds a hotel staff ID with someone else's picture on it, stolen. She checks his pockets, finds a small leather wallet with his identification. Daniel Peretz, from Washington, D.C. She searches further, finds a small set of lockpicks, a few American dollars. She palms the lockpicks, a slim silver rake and tensioner.

Sirens grow closer by the second. She does the calculation, guesses about three minutes until the room fills with police.

She moves to the other man, searches the body, finds his billfold. Mohammed Ashani of Arlington, Virginia. She stares at the ID, tries to connect the pieces, strains to make them fit as they spread farther apart.

She steps across the room, kneels by the man at the end of the bed. A search reveals him to be Bahri Boutros, also of Arlington.

The pieces spread farther. An unknown operative and two Muslims from Arlington. Obviously fake IDs for them, but why had they come? And why had the other agent? And why had the other two killed him? Had they expected him or been surprised? Had they expected her? Obviously yes, they'd kicked the door down. She'd been their target. But why? What had she done to incite such attention? And why attack so brazenly, in broad daylight?

She moves to the window, looks down at the hotel driveway's wide arc. Three police cars arrive in single file. Five officers leap from the vehicles.

She has only a minute now, isn't prepared to answer questions for which she has no answers.

A shiver traces her spine as she realizes she's nude. She goes to the closet, puts on the extra robe. Then she ducks in the bathroom, pulls a band from her makeup case, and ties her hair in a tall bun atop her head.

She goes to the Victorian desk, grabs her purse. A sequined bag just large enough to hold a thin, rectangular pocketbook. The bag contains very little of importance and she dumps its contents onto the desk. Lipstick, a pack of Kleenex, a few coins. She replaces them with her pocketbook, the Glock and the lockpicks. Obviously, the first agent considered picking the lock to her room, probably while she slept. She wonders why he changed his plan. Shudders at the thought of him finding her asleep.

Down the hall, the elevator chimes. The police have arrived and will be rushing the room in just a second.

She races into the hall, screaming at the top of her lungs, sprinting toward the officers.

She sobs, flies toward them, panicked. They lower their weapons, motion her past, tell her to wait in the lobby. Then, guns drawn, they move toward the room with careful patience.

Rhyme sobs for effect as she enters the elevator and thumbs the button for the second floor.

CHAPTER 24

WASHINGTON, D.C.

Chaos is what she needs.

It won't take long for the police to check the hotel's records and know they're looking for one Rhyme Carter, person of interest. Once it's discovered she's the new Israeli ambassador, she'll find herself at the center of an international incident.

With any luck, they'll find her purse missing and think the motive was robbery, maybe even a kidnapping to exploit her position. Missing persons don't get as much attention as triple homicide suspects. This buys her time.

She tries to puzzle it out. Did the old ambassador send the agent? Must harbor some resentment, so summarily replaced. Perhaps he'd ordered the attack?

Weak, she thinks and rules it out. It's a long way to go to secure one's position. There has to be another answer.

The hotel's fire alarm blares, has the effect of setting everyone in a frenzy. This is the exact outcome she'd wanted when she'd stopped on the second floor and triggered it. Chaos means opportunity, and cover, provides movement without suspicion, explains a woman in a bathrobe rushing through the lobby mid-morning. But she needs to rise to levels much higher than the alarm's shrill cry.

She exits the elevator and enters the lobby, a grand and spacious area, elegant, decorated in the old French style. Multi-tiered chandeliers cast brilliance from gems that hang in circled rows. Dark rafters, gilded in gold, run the span of the ceiling with embossed reliefs of French design. The windows are massive here, three of them, adorned with sumptuous curtains in dark maroon. Couches on polished wooden bases hold pillows patterned in diamonds of red and gold. Armchairs with busy patterns and high backs sit around low tables made of glass, trimmed with gold. Below it all a dark, patterned carpet of gold and aquamarine, just starting to show signs of wear.

Rhyme focuses on the amount of people flowing through the space. She's not the only one in a bathrobe. Others wear workout clothes or pajamas. Some in mismatched outfits, a sport coat over swim trunks, dress shoes with sweatpants.

She glances around, choosing her landmarks, looking for other attackers, gauging the distance and risks of the places she needs to hit before leaving the hotel.

She must disappear. She tucks the purse beneath her robe, tucks it deep under her right arm, feels the blunt metal of the hidden Glock, mentally gauges the time it will take to retrieve the weapon and use it.

Six police officers enter the lobby. The one in front barks orders. "Mitchell, get up there and see what's going on." Then he speaks into his radio. "Barnes, status report."

"We're going to need a coroner," Barnes replies.

The lead cop rolls his eyes. "Great," he says. "How many?"

"Three," Barnes replies.

Rhyme walks past, head down. The lobby is full now as more people reach the first floor and head toward the exit.

"Is fire coming?" the boss asks.

"Roger that," the radio squawks. "Should be here any minute."

Rhyme passes the concierge desk and pauses as more police enter, pushing past guests who attempt to exit.

Rhyme slides back, presses herself against the wall. This is a good vantage point but not one where she can linger. One can always count on chaos for concealment, to buy a few needed moments. She looks right, sees her target, three valets gawking at the cacophony before them. They exchange comments, occasionally giggle, smile calmly at any who notice them. Their attention is focused on the lobby before them, on the hundreds of people. They're completely distracted.

Rhyme eyes her target, a podium in dark mahogany behind the valets. Its single door sits ajar, presumably so the valets don't have to keep unlocking it every time they need a vehicle.

Shoddy, she thinks. Have to be quick, stay alert.

She steps from the wall, slides behind the podium then reaches blindly and grabs a set of keys. She slides them in her bathrobe pocket and simultaneously lowers her head.

"Excuse me," she says, passing between the three.

The valets act surprised, step aside so she can pass.

They haven't seen; she's clear.

She joins the crowd, exits the lobby. Heads left out the door, behind the gathering crowd, toward valet parking. A couple of bystanders glance at her, realize she's wearing a hotel robe, then turn their attention to the growing legion of police.

At the end of the arced drive, she turns left, follows the sidewalk a short way, then turns left again and sees a series of traffic cones. A sign reads: RESERVED FOR VALET.

She slides the key from her pocket, glances at the fob. A BMW. She places her thumb on the panic button and moves into the lot.

Fifteen vehicles, all parked close in a lot reserved for about thirty cars.

She thumbs the panic button, moves between the cars, waits for one to come alive.

She hadn't seen anything but police cars when she'd left the building and hopes she didn't miss any. Sometimes valets are tipped handsomely for keeping certain vehicles close. It was dumb to take only one set of keys. She's rusty, should've grabbed a few.

She moves through the lot, clicks the panic button every few seconds. All luxury models are represented, Bentley, BMW, Porsche, Mercedes.

She nears a silver Land Rover, then hears the shrill warble of an alarm. She glances around, sees no one. Chaos doing its job, demanding everyone's attention, providing cover and time.

She walks between the Land Rover and a gray Mercedes to a dark blue BMW 7-series. Lights flash as it cries its warning to the day.

Rhyme presses the panic button again and the alarm stops. At any other time, she wouldn't have taken such a risk, but with all the noise of the police and fire vehicles, she doubts anyone even heard the alarm.

She hits unlock, then enters the posh interior.

Not out of the woods yet, she thinks. Even now police will be blocking the road, gathering together bystanders, cordoning off the area.

The engine jumps to life and Rhyme fastens her safety belt, puts the car in reverse, and backs out of the parking space.

She takes a glance at the hotel. It looks like they're prepping for a parade. Police direct traffic and shout directions at driver's who slow for an eyeful.

She turns left, moving away from the hotel, takes a right on I street, follows it to Pennsylvania Avenue, where she takes another right.

She follows this around Washington Circle, continuing until she sees the street she's looking for, Twenty-Fifth Street.

Here she turns right, follows the road until it bends to the right. Her target comes into view, a PLANET AID donation bin. A large yellow box with two stout drawers designed to allow driver's the courtesy of dropping donations without ever having to leave their vehicle. She's been here numerous times and it's never failed. Funny how nothing changes while everything changes.

The bin looks the same, surrounded by garbage bags in white and black and gray, all stuffed with discarded clothing and hand-me downs. She pulls close, just another car dropping off a donation. No one will question a luxury car here. She eyes the bags around the bin, looks to see if any contain items for women or, barring that, items for adults.

A purple stiletto pokes from the top of one bag. It looks adult size. She unbuckles, leans out and pulls it in the car. Another bag looks to hold an apron and worn flannel robe. She grabs it too, tossing it with the other one in the back seat.

Hopefully some of this will fit.

She drives off, turns left on Twenty-Second Street, then follows it to O Street where she pulls the car to the curb, then checks her surroundings.

There's no sign she's been followed. No one seems to notice or care what she's up to. She slides over the center console and into the back seat.

Rummaging through the first bag, she finds old socks, gym shorts, faded with the occasional hole, and a few pairs of worn Converse sneakers. The second bag contains a nice house robe, a few tops made for a child, three faded T-shirts and various hand and bath towels.

She slips on a white T-shirt with a picture of the Washington Monument. The bags don't hold much resembling slacks. She eyes the gym shorts, selects a pair that look like they came straight from a 1980's sitcom, blue with a wide white stripe down the side and a quarter-size hole near the waistband.

She slips these on, then tries the gym shoes, all of which are too big. No matter, she thinks, not willing to walk D.C. without footwear. She slips on a pair that used to be white and ties them tight. They feel cavernous and her feet don't come close to filling them.

She stuffs the hotel robe in a bag, ties the top of each in a knot, then drives back to the donation bin where she tosses them out as she passes.

She still has to get to her destination, which as it happens, will be a great place to ditch the car.

After that, she'll be a ghost.

Crispy's Scrap Yard has always been a place where few dare tread. A square mile of old vehicles, semis, vans, RVs, cars of every imaginable type, crushed and stacked on both sides of a narrow dirt road.

This used to be a You-wrench-it type place where backyard mechanics could find an elusive part for their cars. Using their own tools, they'd remove the part from a scrapyard vehicle and pay for it on their way out.

Rhyme hasn't been here for years and imagines demand for such products has dropped considerably. New vehicles, more reliant on computers, have gradually replaced the old vehicles that end up here.

The sign reads WORLD-FAMOUS CRISPY'S, written in a sweeping hand with red cursive, the apostrophe, Y, and S are faded to a point where they're barely readable.

Below the sign are two gates secured by a rusty chain and large padlock. Odd for the place to be closed this time of day, she thinks. Unless it's closed permanently. She accelerates, heads up the deserted street, eyes the piles of crushed vehicles behind the chain link. A quarter mile up, she turns onto another dirt road and examines the fence. A half mile later, she sees what she's looking for.

She pulls next to the rusted fence, collects her purse and exits. Unmowed grass surrounds it, but the gap she's seen will allow entrance. She moves toward a section curled with age, receding from the ground about six inches. She tromps the grass as close to the ground as possible, then pushes her purse under. Then, she lies on her back, pushes up on the fence's bottom and squeezes underneath.

The fence is old but still requires considerable effort to fit through. She could've never done this while wearing the hotel bathrobe. Now, avoiding injury is her number one concern. After that, well, she'll deal with things as they come. The trip might well be for naught, a side stop without relief or aid.

Inside, she brushes dirt and grass from her clothes, then retrieves her purse and checks its contents. She moves into the scrapyard and calculates her position.

She used to know the place well and hopes it hasn't changed too much. She places herself on the scrapyard's left perimeter, at about the center point. From here she needs to head further into its bowels, toward section A3.

Years ago, her past life as a librarian had come in handy, and she'd helped update the place for the You-wrench-it crowd. Helped assure it was easier for them to find the vehicles for which they were looking by creating a grid system. She'd taken the square-mile facility and broke it into squares, each approximately an eighth of a mile.

But it's been years and much has changed. Nothing looks familiar. A blind search, looking for A3. Should be along the fence to her left, perhaps a quarter mile or so up.

She sets off, tripping occasionally over too big sneakers but making steady progress through the cathedral of piled junkers.

The roads are run down, uncared for, large ruts with deep puddles, some spanning the entirety of the dirt road. Her choices become narrow: go through them and soak her feet or attempt to climb a massive, rusted pile for a better view.

Ill-fitting shoes are never a good idea, let alone wet ones. Climbing atop of a pile of shaky steel gives the advantage of elevation and view. If she does this, she'll find herself elevated by about fifty feet. A true bird's-eye view.

But the danger will be vast. Piled cars are notoriously unstable. Climbing the pile, then standing on top will be risky and foolish. Not an option that reeks intelligence.

She considers going back the way she'd come, looking for a more passable route. Not a good option either. It's easy to get lost in this labyrinth.

She wades into the puddle, feels water and mud fill her shoes. The water is cold, the grit sharp beneath her feet.

Walking on stones, she thinks. Perfect.

She slogs along, staying left. In the old days, the grids were labeled, now she sees no signs or landmarks. She feels desperate, like the entire idea is a bust.

A cloud of dust rolls into the air accompanied by the sound of grating metal, then the resounding crash of steel on steel. Somewhere to her right, a stack of cars has toppled. A reminder of the inherent risks of this place. She has to be alert, attentive. If she's crushed, she may never be found. Emery will never know what's become of her.

She follows the dirt path, wades the puddles, tired and dirty, the day's heat stealing her energy. She's kept herself in good shape but has no food or water, hasn't expected to take this long here.

The dirt road curves slightly left, back toward the fence. A distant memory triggers. This is section A3. She stops, surveys the piles of twisted metal on both sides. Five cars high on the left, six cars high on the right. A flash of yellow catches her eye, the curved hood of a punch bug. Yes, this *is* the place. Her goal is a little farther.

Surrounded by the forgotten skeletons of once-loved vehicles, devoid of the sound of bird or cricket, the puddled road stretches before her, takes her deeper into the rusted labyrinth.

She rounds the bend, slows her pace. Examines each stack until she finally sees it, the crushed shell of a Datsun hatchback. It sits at the base of a stack of six cars. A Bondo-dappled hood juts from beneath the pile of vehicles. Poking through the hood, a single piece of rebar. She remembers driving the rod through the vehicle and into the ground. A way to secure the pile's base and support the cars stacked above it.

She moves to it, glances at the vehicles above her, mentally plans an escape route if the stack happens to collapse.

The Datsun's hood is split in the middle. Jutting from the right side, rebar rises three feet. The cars above it have shifted and now rest atop the rebar. The pole bends slightly with the weight, the full crush of the cars resting on the slim, rusted rod. This makes things trickier.

It's a miracle it's held this long, she thinks, examining the stack above the Datsun.

The other side of the Datsun's hood shows its years. Rusted through in some places, dented, faded, covered with dust and dead bugs. It should open easily, she thinks. She remembers using a metal grinder to part the hood in two. She also remembers fastening stainless steel hinges to the outer side of it. She'd planned it carefully, although never expected to be back here after so long. Hinges shine from the depths of shadow. They look good, simply *must* be serviceable.

No time to waste, she grasps the hood and applies gentle upward pressure, watching for any shift from the tons of rusted steel above her. The hood creaks like an old rocking chair, opens about an inch. Above her the stack sways a bit but holds. Years ago, this hatch would've moved easily, but weather and time have taken their toll. Her problem isn't the hinges but years of decay on the beat-down hood.

It requires more force. She eyes the rebar, glances up at the pile, then repositions her feet for a more rapid get away. She applies more pressure.

The compartment squeals and gives another inch.

Almost there. Another six inches should do it. She peers through the gap and sees nothing. Encouraged, she applies a bit more pressure, takes a tad more risk.

She feels something hard on the back of her head, knows immediately it's a shotgun.

"Turn around, pretty lady." A man's voice, rough, scraggly.

She raises her hands, turns to look down the dark gullet of dual shotgun barrels. The man wears a ball cap that bears the image of a Scuba flag: an orange square with a diagonal white line, running corner to corner, top left to bottom right. Beneath the image, the words MUFF DIVER in large blue letters.

He's probably the ugliest man she's ever seen.

Gray eyes peer through a cascade of scars, like melted wax turned to skin. It's thick, rippled, and smooth, covering his forehead, nose, and the left side of his face. He holds the shotgun steady and comfortable with hands heavily scarred to the elbows.

The scars tell a story, say something about the man. He's endured unimaginable pain and isn't a quitter. He's not a stranger to hard times, possibly thrives on them.

The barrels don't waver, an inch from her forehead. One twitch and that's it for her. She considers her options. Attack, run, surrender? She calculates her odds, realizes she's out of tricks. There are no options. No way to disarm him without getting blown away.

She looks to her purse which sits on the ground fifty feet away. She'd placed it there so if the cars collapsed, she wouldn't lose it and, more importantly, the Glock it conceals.

Rookie mistake. Better to be killed with a gun in your hand than without. She'd devoted her full attention to her task and none to situational awareness. Thus, she'd been completely ambushed and never heard it coming.

How stupid, she thinks; I'm as rusty as the cars above me.

"George's monument has never looked better," he says.

She glances down, realizes her sweat has turned the white shirt transparent. She's become a scrapyard sex symbol, a pulp fiction damsel.

She grins, drops her hands. "Screw you, Crispy."

CHAPTER 25

OUTSKIRTS OF WASHINGTON, D.C.

"You gonna help me with this?" Rhyme says, nodding at the stack of cars.

Crispy lowers the shotgun, wears the grin Rhyme can never quite figure out, half smile, half contemplating philosopher. "And have them down on my head? Not a chance."

He turns, crosses to her purse, picks it up. "Why you ridin' dirty?" This is a term he'd always used for carrying a gun. "Thought you'd moved on to a quieter life?"

Rhyme moves toward him, glances at the precarious stack of cars. "So did I."

He holds her eyes, seems to read her thoughts. He's always had the ability to smell her bullshit miles off, a talent developed in the military. He tosses her the shotgun, peels off his shirt, tosses that as well, then turns his back. "You know, after what I did for you, I deserve a peek."

Rhyme leans the shotgun against her hip, strips her shirt and replaces it with his, a dusty bowling shirt with the word REGGIE on an oval above the left pocket. "Not a chance, old man, you'd probably die from pure awe."

Crispy laughs, turns toward her. "I missed you, kid," he says. "I'm

177

guessing you ain't here to reminisce about the old days. Apparently, not every lesson I taught stuck. You shouldn't have come back."

She gives him a grand hug. "Probably not," she says. "I just came to get my bag, then I'll be on my way. Don't want to cause you any trouble."

He glances toward the sky, pulls a cheroot from his back pocket and a silver Zippo from his front. He takes his time lighting it. "Here?" he says. "You stashed your bag under *this* rust pile?"

She grins. "Yep, right under your nose."

He draws deep, tries to blow a smoke ring, then gives the same philosopher's grin. "I moved it," he says, draws on the smoke. "Oh, don't look so shocked. You didn't really think you got one by me?"

Rhyme stares at the ugly little man, examines the scars, the pervert hat, the unreadable grin and squinted eyes. "Actually, I did."

Crispy cackles, spins on his heels, and walks off. "Let's go get it," he says, "but you'll have to show me your boobs."

"Not a chance."

"Damn! Dinner, then?"

"That I can do," she says.

"I've been craving that stroganoff you used to make. Craving it for years."

"Consider it done."

"Hot damn!" He does a little jig. "Don't forget the damn shotgun either, FNG."

She laughs, FNG, Fucking New Guy, his favorite term for her. She props the shotgun on her shoulder and follows after, watching as he rummages through her purse and produces the Glock.

He whirls and empties the clip into the bent rebar jutting from the Datsun's hood. Every shot hits home, some make the sound of a ricochet, twanging like a bent gong.

Above the rebar, the stack wobbles, then collapses.

Crispy laughs like hell. The pile topples with a sound akin to cheese graters through a woodchipper.

He eyes the gun, whistles. "Hell of a firearm," he says, moving up the puddled road. "Strange it isn't a Sig, though. Do you like it?"

She follows, glances at the rising dust plume above the toppled cars. "It does the job."

CHAPTER 26

OUTSKIRTS OF WASHINGTON, D.C.

The screen door creaks as he pulls it open. "Welcome to Casa Crispy," he says. "We do hope you enjoy your time and can manage to stay out of trouble. The kitchen is that way, needs a woman's touch no doubt. You sure you're up for this?"

"I'd love to cook for you," she says, "but I'd feel more comfortable if I had my stash."

Crispy looks surprised, acts like he forgot. "Of course, kid. That's why you came, ain't it?"

The last sentence isn't lost on Rhyme and although Crispy isn't one to display emotion, his words are tinged with a certain amount of hurt.

She steps toward him. "Listen," she says, "you know why I never came back, don't you?" He seems uncomfortable, averts his eyes, a man who doesn't like to speak about such things. "I knew you'd make it, despite what the doctors said, but couldn't live with the thought of putting you in more danger. Especially after you saved my life. After you were injured so horribly. I left to deal with it all, to deal with Octavio and save us both."

Crispy seems trapped, stands before her looking vulnerable. This man and emotion have never been a good fit. "Did you bury the fuckers?"

"No," she says. "I made a deal with them. Made an offer they had no choice but to accept."

"Dancing with the devil," he says, holding her gaze. "Hope it was worth it."

"In some ways," she replies. She wants to tell him about Emery and Cain. Wants to spend the next few days explaining all that's happened since they'd parted ways. Crispy would understand; he'd also offer any help she needs. Always had, always will. The man almost died for her. Had survived only due to a limitless wealth of gall and a nature as tough as boot leather. Crispy is old school, the old school's headmaster, in fact. Its dean and entire alumni.

Crispy nods and moves across the room. They'd come to a shack in the middle of the property, surrounded on all sides by a half mile of rusted metal. The place he lives fits him. To the left, is an old cot. A khaki-green wool blanket stretches across its frame. The bed's made with military precision, and Rhyme knows if she tries to bounce a quarter on the surface, it will fly high and proud.

An old footlocker sits in front of the bed. Upon it are two candles and an empty pack of cheroots. Rhyme doesn't see an ashtray and wonders where he flicks his ashes. The floor is tidy, swept and without signs of dirt.

In front of the footlocker is a green Adirondack chair, faded but serviceable. That's how Crispy likes things, clean, dry and serviceable.

She steps to her right, to a three-drawered dresser made of brown wood, cheap. An American flag hangs on the wall secured with drywall screws. Atop the dresser is a framed picture of the two of them, standing in the woods, smiling into a sunny day. She remembers the afternoon, the happiness she'd felt, the safety and sense the man had brought to her life after it all went to shit. Crispy has served her well, like a father, brother, mentor, friend. He'd replaced her father after he'd died and, although he'd never known the man, Rhyme believes her dad must've somehow sent him to her.

Crispy made her strong, resilient, and capable. Had hardened her soft spots and shown that her limitations were self-imposed. He'd then taught her how to push past them. How to endure in the face of adversity, how to overcome obstacles and mostly, how to be self-reliant. He'd disposed of that librarian from Carter's Glen and replaced her with who Rhyme had become.

She moves to the chair, sits. A memory enters. Branch, her first love. A kind, gentle, and capable man. A man she thought would always be nearby. She was young then, thought she'd experienced loss, thought she knew how. Branch was ever-present, fully alive, sweet, and hard as nails. She hasn't thought of him for a long time, and now it makes her heart hurt. Makes her remember the good and the bad. Makes her think of the day Crispy saved her. The day Branch died. One of the most horrible days of her life. Love lost while still fresh. A future obliterated, happiness vaporized in its concussion.

A single second can change everything. What was that? Seven years ago? More?

Crispy reads her mind, puts a hand on her shoulder. Pale gray eyes look down on her. "You're not still living with all that?"

She looks up, manages a smile. "Lest we forget," she says.

He holds her eyes a second more. The scars make his expression tense, the left side of his mouth pulled up at the corner. "Can't argue with Kipling."

She knows he's uncomfortable but trying to be compassionate. It isn't his strong suit, but she loves him for it and mourns his suffering. Mourns the way their lives have changed since she'd run afoul of Octavio and Cain.

He crosses the room, opens a door not readily apparent, one he's taken pains to conceal from casual eyes. He drags out a Pelican case.

"There you go," he says, "just as you left it. I updated the wrapper to make it a little more waterproof."

"My spot was better," she says.

"Yep," he says, "until the cars fall on it. Then ain't worth a shit."

She slides the chair in front of the box, pulls the hard clasps until they click open. Inside is everything she needs. Two Sig Sauer M-11 pistols, shoulder holster, ammo, tactical clothing, boots, fake ID, Jet-boil, wigs in blonde and black, mascara, lipstick in two shades, bras, undies, survival knife, a bottle of Levaquin, 550 cord, binoculars and five-thousand dollars in twenty-dollar bills.

Outside a dog barks. "I'm gonna step out while you change," he says. "Feed that hound."

"You have a guard dog?"

"Yep," he says. "Mangy mutt ain't good for nothing. Look how well it warned me you were here. Truth be told, I think the thing hates me. Always looks like it's on the verge of a nervous breakdown." The scars on his face stretch to a smile. "I'll be back in a few."

"Hold it," she says, tossing keys at him. "Would you mind bringing up the car and disposing of it?"

The grin returns. He'll play along, she knows. He affects an upscale accent. "Of course, madame. And when I return, might we have a bite of dinner?"

Rhyme becomes socialite heiress. "Splendid idea, Mr. Crispy, the concierge said the stroganoff was to die for."

Crispy winks and heads outside into the scrapyard.

The next morning, Rhyme takes a shower. Crispy's shower, three Buicks standing straight up on their front bumpers. A garden hose fastened to the wall about five feet up. The water is cold, and by the time she finishes, she's shivering despite the sun. She dresses, sliding into the black pants and shirt from the Pelican case. She dries her feet, slips on socks and an old pair of her favorite jump boots, steel-toed; good for kicking ass, as Crispy would say.

She heads inside, knows the smell immediately. Crispy's diner is open. Always the same menu, Spam and eggs sunny side up.

"I didn't know you could still buy that stuff," she says. "Can't be good for you."

"You're done with your shower?" He looks over his shoulder, cocks his nose in the air. "Damn! I missed seeing you naked."

Smiling, she takes the spatula from his hand. "I better do this," she says. "Wouldn't want you to reignite."

His cackle fills the small space. "High-larious!"

Like everything in this place, the kitchen is well kept and tidy. He moves to a cupboard and produces two coffee cups. One has a quote. I DRANK WHAT? -SOCRATES. The other is plastic, formerly purple, stained by years of coffee running through it.

"What's your plan, kid? I got the feeling you didn't want to discuss it at dinner."

"Nope," she says. "If you want to keep a secret, tell no one."

He laughs at the comment. "Now who could've taught you that bullshit?"

She loads two plates with Spam and eggs, sets them on the footlocker. "Yeah, I wonder who that sage was."

Crispy takes a plate, pulls a knife from his pocket and slices the Spam, then slides a bite into his mouth. "Jesus H. Christ," he says. "The perfect food. Just never gets old."

Rhyme tries a nibble, mentally asks the age-old question, What is Spam?

"You comin' back?" Crispy asks.

"Who said I was leaving?"

He gives her the philosopher smile. An expression that holds amusement, confusion, intelligence and wariness all within its borders. He says nothing, returns her stare. Another lesson he'd taught her, never bullshit a bullshitter.

"Okay, yes," she says after a few seconds. "I'm leaving. I have to deal with some stuff."

"Uh oh," he says.

"It's not like that. Won't be anything too dangerous."

He nods.

"Seriously, just have to make a call, figure some things out."

He nods, glances at the shoulder holster, the two Sig's strapped to either side of her chest.

"Just being careful," she says.

He nods. "Uh huh."

"I'll be back, though. We need to catch up."

He nods again. Says nothing.

"Would you quit nodding. If you want to say something, then just say it."

"You know what I'm going to say."

She stares at him, searches her memory. She can't hide the look of realization as she remembers his favorite verse. "I'm not saying it."

He nods, "Okay."

She stares at him, knows what he wants, remembers the times she used to read him Cummings as he sat framed in moonlight, feet propped on a log, sucking his cheroot, listening with glossed eyes and apt ears.

"You suck," she says.

"Uh huh," he nods again.

"Ugh!" she says. "Okay. Hope I can remember it." She knows she'll never forget.

She starts.

> *Women and men, both little and small,*
> *Cared for anyone not at all,*
> *They sowed their isn't, they reaped their same,*
> *Sun moon stars rain.*

She finishes, looks at him, hopes it was enough, hopes he hadn't wanted her to recite the whole thing. His look is far away, star-eyed, someone who's just returned from UFO abduction.

He puts his plate down, then moves to her and gives a gentle embrace. "Be careful, kid. I'll be seeing you." He pushes her to arm's length, holds her eyes. She gets the feeling he's memorizing her, acting like they'll never see each other again, tracing her features, taking a mental photograph. The look is unbearable, devoid of emotion. If she didn't know Crispy, she'd think nothing of it. But Crispy is a man who shows his feelings on his face, the gray eyes, the philosopher smile, the way he nods, the things he *doesn't* say. She'd lived with him for a long time, feels completely safe in his company and completely off-put by his stare. To tell him she'll probably never return would be an insult to him and all he'd done for her. To offer excuses or, really, words of any kind, would cheapen the love they share.

He moves off without a word, through the squeaky door, and into the guts of the scrapyard.

CHAPTER 27

BERLIN, GERMANY

April 1945

"Stinks!" Longinus stoops to fit down the narrow stairs.

"Smells of almonds," Cain says, "perhaps our work will be easier than anticipated."

"Yeah, everything's easy with this lunatic," Igneus says.

At the bottom of the stairs, they enter a rectangular room that runs off to their left. It's a lounge of sorts, complete with wood-paneled walls. Across from them, in the room's center, is an entryway flanked by German guards. These snap to attention as Cain approaches.

"Heil Hitler," they say in unison. Cain moves past without a word.

They step into a short alcove constructed of concrete; six-feet thick. A stout steel door blocks their path, a wheeled handle at its center and above that, a large keyhole.

Igneus produces a black skeleton key, which he inserts into the lock and turns. A heavy click follows, and he grasps the wheeled handle. His face goes red as he expels his effort without effect.

Longinus chuckles.

"Anon and agin, do ye be needin' help?"

Igneus steps aside, looks disgusted, somewhat crestfallen.

Longinus's muscles bulge as he turns the wheel, then pulls the heavy door. Then, the whoosh of displaced air and a giant siphon; the door opens fully.

This is the Führerbunker. A place for Hitler to hide from the bombs and assassination attempts that have plagued him throughout his years as Germany's Chancellor.

Longinus steps to the side as Cain squeezes past. Deeper into the bunker is another lounge area with eight folding chairs and two bright, yellow side tables. Two Nazi officers sit here but stand when they see Cain.

He motions them to sit, then moves to a door on the room's opposite end, the door to the bunker's conference room.

They've met here before, he and Hitler, have hatched plans in this very cell to conquer the world and hasten Cain's efforts to fulfill prophecy. A peaceable kingdom, Abel suggested. The perfect sacrificial lamb, a way to present God a choice: free the immortals of their prison or abandon his chosen people.

A shame really, Cain thinks, that it ended up this way. If only God had given some sign He even noticed the atrocities committed against His chosen ones.

The words waft through the centuries, their truth ripe in Cain's mind, ever-present, profound, true from the day he'd slain Abel to this one.

God prefers blood.

Apparently prefers it by the gallon, quart, and jug. God remained passive as the blood of His people rolled down His throat. Oceans of it have been spilled. All for God's notice, to complete Cain's plan. God's people, sacrificed by the millions as God remained silent. As if He'd turned a blind eye, as if He has no compassion for His own creation.

He prefers the endless crimson flow, is addicted to it like Doyle's Sherlock Holmes is addicted to opiates.

Cain steps into the conference room, sees Hitler at a table, head in hands. Four others sit with him, two officers and two women.

Adolf sees him, stands. The others stand as well. Then Adolf reaches under the table and produces a long spear. He tosses it on the conference table with a clatter.

It's Longinus's spear. The spear that killed Christ. A relic said to have such power that no army can stand against it.

"Scheisse," Hitler hisses. "This does nothing!" He speaks German; his words, crisp and throaty.

"You expected?" Cain says.

Hitler looks astonished, beady eyes shifting. "I expected it to work! I expected it to win the war! To wield an invincible weapon and rule as is my destiny. I expected to use it to perfect humanity and rid the world of its toxins. You promised this relic, said it would make me invincible." The others back away from the table toward the walls. "It does nothing!" Hitler screams. "Holds no power at all! Germany is in shambles and I am ruined."

"And how's Eva?" Cain asks.

Hitler blinks, looks around. "She's dead! I found her on the couch in my study. She used cyanide. Never said a word, just killed herself." A wisp of hair covers his left eye, bobs with each syllable. "Himmler has gone to the Allies. I am deserted."

Cain flashes his smile. "It appears that way," he says. "Even now the Russians are merely a stone's throw from your door."

Hitler levels a finger. "I blame you! You and your promises!" If nothing else, the little man is courageous when he thinks he's in charge.

But the facade is cracking, his obvious mental deficiencies taking hold.

Cain waves his hand at the others. They look relieved and hurry from the room. "My dear Adolf, if you must lay blame at someone's feet, let them be your own."

Hitler reacts as if he's been slapped. His eyes narrow, lips curl into a pitiful snarl.

"If you examine the facts," Cain continues, "you'll see I've delivered all that was asked. The only failure is you. You were to conquer the world. I gave you the tools and support to do that. Now you stand before me, spitting insults, whining that all have deserted the cause." Cain shakes his head. "I'm afraid you just weren't up to the task."

He moves close to the little man.

Rage flashes in Adolf's eyes, his thin mustache twitches with anger.

"I'm afraid your time has come," Cain says. "It seems those around you have more courage than their own dear Führer. Even as we speak, they clamber out of this place, anxious to surrender and denounce you." He looks at his gloves, brushes one of them lightly. "You're the last rat on a water-filled ship, and I too have grown tired of you, tired of your grandiose attitude, your feeble spirit."

Hitler's eyes go to Longinus, then twitch back to Cain. He draws a Walther PPK from the holster on his hip, levels it at the gloved man.

"I'll not die alone," he says. "When I'm captured, I'll be sure the world knows of you and your organization." He backs away as he speaks, toward a door at the room's far end. *"You'll* be held accountable. *You* will hang in the streets when the world hears of your role in all this."

Cain smiles, nods at the pistol. "Dear Adolf, do listen to reason. I'd like you to have a quick death."

Adolf reaches the door and bolts through. Longinus glances at Cain, then chases after.

Cain picks up the spear and follows. Up a short flight of stairs, he enters a garden of sorts. Explosions rattle the ground, mortar fire drawing close. The Russians on their way.

The garden is lush and green and German. A thin hedge surrounds a confine about twenty by twenty. Two benches rest on either side; between them a small, cobbled walkway leads to a lattice gate.

Hitler backs toward the gate, pistol pointed at Longinus. His eyes are wild, darting back and forth as he seeks escape.

Longinus steps toward him and Hitler fires twice. The huge Roman crumples.

Hitler smiles as he watches, wears success in his posture, seems to grow bold, inflate. Killing Longinus has empowered him, and he steps forward, gun leveled, a confident expression on his face.

"You're a fool, Cain! You shouldn't have followed," he says. "I'll blame all of this on you, claim I was merely a puppet in your hands. I've prepared documents to back me up. Forged your signature, recorded all the ties between our organizations. All I require now is your body. When the Russians take me, I'll tell them I killed you because you wouldn't end the war. And they'll believe me, they'll have to, I'm too valuable. In the end, the world just needs someone to blame. And I'll deliver that in the grandest of style. I'll befriend my enemies. Yes! Be for them an endless source of intelligence." He chuckles here, nods his head. "All the blame will fall on X'chasei, and I'll be of such use that, in the end, they'll lock me up on some estate where I'll live quite happily to the end of my days." He looks to the sky, purses his lips. "Yes. I may even return to my art."

He appears elated. The plan in his head perfectly formed and ready to implement.

"I'll tell them *you* poisoned Eva, just like *you* gassed all the Jews. I'll tell them no one could subdue your giant friend here, either. My men will back me, they'll be too worried about their own skin. It's going to be perfect. I regret you won't be here to see it."

He empties the pistol into Cain's chest.

Cain feels the impact, falls to one knee, accepts the pain even as he feels his body revolt at the invasion. Hitler continues to pull the trigger. Click, click, click.

Igneus appears, sees the two men on the ground.

"Stop, Jew!" Hitler hisses. His eyes are panicked, sweat streams over his face. "Don't come any closer!"

Cain raises his head, stares at the insane little man.

Longinus stands, brushes his pants, retrieves the spear from the ground.

"Stay back!" Hitler yells. His eyes are crazed, his face contorted and panicked.

"Seems ye be out've bullets," Longinus says.

Hitler steps back, pulls a dagger from his belt.

Igneus laughs. "You won't be needing that." A huge smile splits a frail face.

Hitler looks confused, then, in an instant, terrified.

The dagger drops as he claws his abdomen.

He falls to his knees as flames burst through his uniform and spread with astonishing speed. He shrieks like a feral cat, legs kicking, hands slapping, a desperate effort to squelch the fire.

In seconds he's an ashen pile lying in the garden's center.

A Nazi officer appears from the bunker and approaches Cain. He clicks his heels together, gives a single, precise nod.

This is Heinz Linge, an officer of the SS and Hitler's personal valet.

Cain rises, brushes the dirt from his trousers. "Is everything in order?"

"Ja." The SS man briefly glances at the blood on Cain's shirtfront.

"And your story?" Cain asks.

"Perfektioniert." Perfected.

Cain smiles. "Excellent. In a short while, you'll be captured and turned over to the NKVD. The Soviets will interrogate you, but not harshly. Stick to your story and your time with them will be both healthy and comfortable."

The SS man nods. "I understand."

"Auf wiedersehen, dear Heinz."

"Auf wiedersehen," Heinz says. He turns, crosses the garden and disappears into the bunker.

———

Jerusalem, Israel

Present day

I stare at the relic, amazed it looks so plain. An iron spearhead, about sixteen inches long, bound with bronze wire to an ordinary wooden pole. I'm underwhelmed.

I glance at the Roman, judge to see if his expression is one where he's going to kill me or one more forgiving. His beard has grown since we parted three days ago. He leans back, clasps his hands behind his head. This has the effect of fully brandishing his huge chest, which reminds me of the hood of an Oldsmobile we had when I was a kid. His expression is non-threatening. I relax a bit.

"What did ye expect?" Longinus asks.

"I don't know," I say. "The spear that killed Christ. I just expected some glowing, gargantuan comic book relic." I motion toward it. "This looks so basic, like a—"

"A centurion's spear?"

"Exactly," I say. "This looks like something made en masse and issued to thousands of soldiers with no spear any more special than any other."

"Aye. 'Tis but a common antique. Anon and agin, I do non see why Cain w'be wastin' his time."

Longinus rises. I tense. Then he walks to the bar.

We sit in the same room where I'd first become re-acquainted with Rhyme, where she'd streaked down the stairs to save my life. The spear lies on the oval table and appears unassuming. The Roman returns with whisky and two glasses.

"Should we?" I say. "Cain should be here anytime."

The Roman fills the glasses with scotch, then raises his. "Drink! And live among the good."

This is unexpected, but I need to claim good fortune while it floats before me. I raise my glass. "Amen!" I say, and we both drink.

The Roman appears in better sorts today, and I consider that perhaps he's rethought our relationship. Perhaps he's forgiven me for my past affront concerning all that happened outside the Temple.

I have three Percs on board and the scotch helps to keep thoughts of Rhyme to a minimum. Perhaps I can use this chance to ingratiate myself with the hulk. Friends like him are handy and hard to find, exceedingly hard as I think about it.

Then Cain enters. He paces to the table's head, glances at the spear, nods to both of us.

"I see you've started without me," he says, nods at our drinks.

I head for the bar. "I'll get another glass."

I grab a crystal tumbler, then return to the table. Longinus fills it with scotch, and I hand it to Cain.

"My dearest friends," Cain says, "today we start down a road different from the one last traveled. This road leads to paradise. To goals fulfilled and the joys of tenacity." He pauses, looks at us in turn. "For some of us, it's been centuries; for others a very short while. But we *have* succeeded. We *have* endured. We *have* overcome." He pauses, grins. "After today things will change in a way neither of you will believe." He holds Longinus's eyes here, searches them as if determining the man's loyalty. "I encourage you to remain hearty through all that's to come and, above all, I encourage you to maintain your trust in me. When you doubt, as mortals do." He looks at me here with an odd expression, as if he's forgotten something. "Remember, I have things under control. Remember everything happens as I have ordained and through the prophecies of old. Our journey hasn't been easy, but it has been provident, decreed even, destined. I've taken God's place, as I said I would." He motions to us. "I've chosen you as my disciples. When we find Igneus, he'll join us, and together we shall rule a kingdom where peace and harmony abound. There are hard times ahead, but realize, they're just the natural birthing process of that which is ordained."

He stops here, raises his glass, drinks. I feel like I should applaud, then see Longinus drink. I drink as well and find, as I lower my glass, I'm smiling. I don't know if it's that old feeling of specialness sneaking up on me or just the Percs mixing with the scotch. I think of Rhyme, her smile, her scent. My smile grows.

Longinus grins, and I follow suit. We are knights preparing for battle. Or at least that's the sense I get. Then I'm struck by the fact, I'm the only mortal here. Struck by the fact that all Cain has said has come to pass. If he is indeed God, then there could be worse things. Perhaps his gifts are clouding my judgment, but I don't think they are. Vince and Lenny have remained silent on the subject and seem to only interject when I'm under duress.

I realize the limits of my mortality. The fact that I'm living proof of the human condition: that we're all born knowing we'll die. It seems so much more than a statement as I stand among the immortals. I think to the future. Are these men my salvation? Have I endured their mad antics to be rewarded now? Is Cain really God? Can such a thing even happen?

What happens next erases my doubt.

Cain drains his glass in a single pull. Odd for him, I think. He hefts Longinus's spear, holds it erect before him, its shaft on the floor. The iron tip appears dull despite the room's brightness.

His eyes fix on that tip.

I down my drink, set the glass on the table.

"Longinus," Cain says.

The Roman walks around the table and stands next to Cain. Cain hands him the spear and his huge hand wraps around the shaft.

Cain lifts his right hand and slides his index finger over the spear's razor edge. A trickle of blood appears and rolls down the blade. Cain slides his bleeding finger up until he reaches the spear's sharp tip.

Then his mark blooms, as if rising above his skin in three dimensions. It hovers over the spear, fills the room with a blinding redness. I squint against it, lower my head. My eyes burn, impossible to keep open.

I smell flesh, taste metal. My ears fill with the sounds of a million souls rising in agony.

There's a sizzling pop. My hair stands on end, gooseflesh erupts on my body.

Then I'm simply standing again by the oval table with Jerusalem's sunlight streaming through the windows. My glass stands empty before me.

I look to Cain, see that hypnotic smile. Blue eyes dance, his hair stands on end, brighter than I've ever seen it.

Then I look at Longinus.

Where, seconds ago, stood a hulking centurion of ancient Rome, there now stands a GQ model with dark features. He is slim, about the same size as Cain. Gone are the bulging muscles, the enormous chest, the massive legs, the broad head. The man before me exudes all the elegance and beauty of the angels from my dream. He looks at me, smiles, and I feel suddenly agreeable to anything he might ask.

Cain beams. "I've empowered you, my dear Longinus. Your service has been rewarded. You have been loyal and deserve these riches."

Then I notice the spear.

What, moments before, had been an ordinary pike, now gleams in gold from tip to base. The spearhead glimmers, almost too bright to look at directly. The wooden shaft has turned to some sort of metal, shining in gold, splaying its rainbow to all corners of the room. Thin lines run the length of the shaft, mimic the Zentangle of Cain's mark. Endless rays coalesce, intersect with millions of triangles, a dizzying multitude tumbling end over end, one into another. Streams of crimson and laser blue course through, radiate, intersect, spin and dazzle.

I look to Cain, then to Longinus.

"Longinus?" I say. "Is it you?"

His expression is quizzical, the same expression Cain gives when I've asked a dumb question.

"Aye, dear Emery. 'Tis me. Who were you expectin'?"

Chapter 28

C rispy disappears into piles of rust.

Rhyme hopes it isn't the last time she'll see him. It's been a long time, and she hasn't told enough of her story to appease his curiosity.

She moves her belongings from the Pelican case to a small leather duffle, brown and well-aged. If the bag could talk, it'd have some stories.

She strips off ten, twenty-dollar bills, slides them in her pocket. Then feels inside the bag searching for the hidden zipper. She places the remaining bills inside, along with her diplomatic identification. She zips it closed, piles clothes over it.

Marge Shanahan, the fake ID says, from Sioux Falls, South Dakota. She goes over the particulars, memorizing date of birth, address, height, weight, organ donor status, etc. As always, the devil's in the details.

The last item in the Pelican case is a thin neoprene jacket in dark blue. She pulls it on and zips it, takes a moment to regain the feel of the dual Sigs under the jacket. They feel odd, out of place, and this makes her feel odd. The M-11s had been her companions for so long and through so much, she never imagined they'd feel foreign. She wonders what Crispy would say about how rusty she's become.

The leather bag is heavy as she hefts it and leaves the shack.

Crispy brought up her truck last night, from God knows where. Despite the haphazard look of the scrapyard, Crispy knows it like a mother knows her baby's hands. God knows what's become of the BMW.

She sees her truck and smiles. A favorite for some years, given to her by Crispy. A 1978 Ford Bronco, two tone, brown and white, with a hard top. Rhyme tosses in the duffle.

The vehicle's interior is immaculate as if just detailed. She rubs her hand along the paint, smooth as silk, recently waxed. Crispy's been up to stuff. She glances over her shoulder, expects him to be there with his crooked smile.

But there's no sign of him, he's still in the scrapyard doing whatever he does.

She shuts the door as she enters. Beneath the driver's seat she feels the metal box, a drawer that opens by pushing a simple button. She pulls the Glock from her waistband, sets it inside, then slides it closed. Never hurts to have a backup, especially if you're being hunted.

Eight cylinders spark to life. She pushes the accelerator, hears the engine roar. She has to admit, she's revving the engine as an attempt to call Crispy back. It'd be nice to hug him again, say goodbye properly.

A scan of the mirrors shows no sign of him. In that way, as in all ways, Crispy is peculiar. Perhaps he's had too many painful goodbyes in his life. Perhaps he doesn't believe in making a big thing out of it. He's never been one to stand and wave as someone drives off.

Checking the mirrors again, she puts the Bronco in drive and heads out through the open gate, turns left down the dirt road, then onto the highway. She checks the fuel level, completely full. She's certain she'll find all the fluids and mechanicals of the vehicle in perfect order too. That's how Crispy shows he cares. Not with words. She smiles. Then frowns, thinking about his scars, his life in the old scrapyard, his diet of Spam and eggs, his concern for an old hound or a naïve librarian.

She presses the accelerator, heads to the nearest electronics store for a disposable cell phone. After that she heads north, away from D.C. and deep into the countryside.

Backroads wind through rolling hills and lush trees. This is farmland, rural, beautiful. When she's gone far enough, feels she's been unpredictable enough to keep her location secret, she pulls down a side road, then left onto the next road. This is a thoroughfare for farm equipment, dusty and bumpy, well concealed. She hopes she hasn't gone too far, can still get a cell signal.

Emery answers on the second ring.

"You're not going to believe this." They speak at the same time.

Rhyme laughs. It feels good to hear him, to know they share the same thoughts.

"You go first," she says.

"Okay," he says, talking fast, excited. "Cain changed Longinus, created some relic out of his spear, the spear that killed Christ. Cain says it's unstoppable. And Longinus, well, he's not Longinus anymore. He's been changed. Looks like Cain's brother, elegant, handsome, *small.*"

"Small? Longinus?"

"That's what I'm saying, he's no longer this big brute. He's now normal sized. The darndest thing I ever saw. Remember Cain told him to get his spear? Well, we get back from D.C. and Cain rubs some of his own blood on its tip. Have you ever seen it?"

"The spear? No."

"It looks like something you'd see in a museum, something from Roman times. Dirty, old, rusted, fragile. Ancient really. Longinus tells me it ain't worth a shit, that it holds no power, then Cain does this David Copperfield thing, rubs his blood on the spear's edge, and suddenly it transforms to this golden, shining relic. Then I look at Longinus, and he's magically transformed into this handsome, slim man. So similar to Cain, it's uncanny. Even his speech is a mix of his and Cain's."

Rhyme listens with rapt attention, hasn't the prepaid minutes to ask a lot of questions. "That sounds unbelievable. Are you sure it's not some trick?"

"Rhyme, how could it be? It happened right before my eyes. I'm still trying to process it."

"For what purpose?" she says. "Why would Cain do that?"

"Hmm, let me think. Cain creates golden relics and transforms the human body. It's probably something charitable and altruistic."

She chuckles, his sarcasm is kicking in. "Be serious."

"Who knows?" he says. "The game's afoot, as Holmes would say, but none of it can be good. I mean, why would Cain go to all the trouble if he didn't have a plan? And when Cain has a plan, people die. A lot of people die."

"But you don't know?"

"Nope, no idea. Longinus doesn't speak much now, seems to live in his own head space and won't answer my questions."

"And Cain?"

"He told me I'd be going somewhere with Longinus. Won't say anymore other than that. We're leaving in a few minutes. I'm so glad you called."

He's nervous. She knows his mannerisms, knows his tics. "You sound scared."

"I am! Igneus warned me, said, 'With these guys, it's always worse than you think,' and I can think of some pretty bad things, I mean, it's not like he changed the spear *and* Longinus to host a birthday party or something. Has to be sinister. My mind runs with the possibilities. Oh, and I handled Longinus's sword, found a key in the pommel. Have no idea what that means but managed to put it back before Longinus caught me. I mean, holy shit, right? A key to what? Anyway, the worst part is knowing whatever my mind conjures won't be nearly as bad as the reality. I mean, Jesus, Rhyme, let's think…"

"Emery."

"…about the implications…"

"Emery."

He stops.

"I've only got a few minutes on this phone. Had to get a prepaid so I wouldn't be tracked."

"Tracked? By who? Cain? I'm confused."

"I was attacked, Emery. At the St. Regis. Three men attacked me. I barely escaped."

Emery stutters. "What? Attacked? Like physically?"

"Yes physically, guns and everything. Attacked like trying to kill me."

"Where are you? Are you safe? Are you hurt? I'll get a plane and come get you tonight."

The concern warms her. "I'll be fine, just have to find a space to hole up and sort this out."

"Does Cain know?" He laughs here, mocks, answers his own question. "Of course, he does! He sent them. Had to be him."

"Doesn't make sense. Why would he do that?"

"Because he's a *psychopath*. Why does he do anything?"

"Maybe," she says, frowns, not buying it, wondering if she should. "I mean, I can't say Cain *didn't* send them. Just doesn't click right in my head."

"Where are you now?"

"I can't say. I'm safe, but I need some time to plan my next move. None of this adds up. Longinus, this spear, being attacked. I'll contact you soon. After I get a new phone."

"Rhyme, listen. There are people *hunting* you. You have to assume more are coming, how can you possibly stay safe? I can be there tonight. I can keep you safe."

Rhyme tries not to laugh. The man she loves is earnest, and his intent comes from a pure place. He's also ignorant as to her past. If he came for her, he'd inevitably wind up injured or dead. He'd absolutely slow her down and blow any cover she could hope for. No, she needs to stay alone. The less Emery knows of her whereabouts, the better.

"I'll be fine, dear," she says. "I've got all I need."

The pause lasts a few seconds. She knows Emery doesn't like her answer.

She also knows he'll accept it; knows he has no choice.

"Okay," he says, "but call as soon as you can."

She's struck with the urge to say, "I love you," wonders if he thinks the same. Old habits? Muscle memory?

She suppresses the words but knows the full truth in her heart. "I will. Be safe, Emery."

He sighs, frustrated. "You too."

She ends the call, then dials the number for her husband, Cain.

He talks before she can speak.

"Dearest Rhyme, what a pleasure. I was just telling Mr. Slabav here how hard it is to kill you. It seems one of his agents has turned up dead, and consequently, he's become very cross. A fellow named Daniel, as it seems. Did you two happen to meet?"

Chapter 29

Jerusalem, Israel

Jonas and Ishmael are angels, no doubt about it. Over the last few days, they'd visited multiple times and Sebastian has grown vigorous. The lad has more energy, has become normal to the point Igneus has a hard time getting him to rest.

Igneus sits in a faded red lawn chair, a chair provided by Jonas. Ishmael sits in a similar chair of faded green, watches Sebastian and Jonas play a pick-up game of soccer.

Sebastian boots the ball, and it skids across the garage's concrete. Jonas retrieves it, bumps it to his left foot and boots it back.

Igneus is overjoyed to the point where he finds himself contemplating the very word *overjoyed* to see if it's strong enough. His emotions are closer to elation.

The boy is healthy. Eating well, drinking well, exuberant. Igneus marvels this is the same boy that was so sick just a few days ago.

A small, rusty barbecue puffs smoke in the air. Igneus smells the meat, sausages sizzling, almost done.

To celebrate the boy's recovery, Jonas and Ishmael prepared a little party. At first, Igneus considered the gesture odd, but as he spoke with them, he discovered they were all each other had. Orphaned as boys, Jonas found odd jobs to provide for his younger sibling. Turns out he'd done some time in the military and was a proficient leader. Through hard work, he'd become the manager of this parking garage and had hopes of someday owning it.

The job had allowed him to offer his brother something more, an education, an esteemed profession. Jonas sacrificed so his brother could succeed, and the more Igneus grows to know these men, the more admiration he holds for them.

Jonas kicks, and the shot rockets toward Sebastian with such speed, the boy has no choice but to catch it.

"Whoa," Jonas says, "you should be the keeper for the national team."

Sebastian wears jubilation. "Do you think so!"

"I really do," Jonas says. "Did you guys see that catch?"

Igneus claps. "Quite marvelous."

Ishmael nods. "An amazing catch. You have quite a gift." He stands, attends to the grill. "Hope you boys are hungry? I know I am."

Sebastian sprints to the doctor's side. Ishmael lifts the lid, and the smell of sausage surrounds them.

"Oh boy," Sebastian says. "I can't wait to eat!" He grabs a plastic fork from a table of concrete block and wood scraps, then reaches to poke a sausage. Ishmael swats him with a pair of tongs.

"Back, savage! There'll be none until they're cooked!" They both laugh and soon are in a sword fight, Sebastian wielding the fork like a dagger and Ishmael parrying with the tongs.

Igneus can't help but laugh. Hasn't had this much fun in, well, centuries. Sebastian is his life, and he just can't imagine a day when that won't be the case. The boy fills his soul, lifts him to heights he'd never thought possible, reminds him love exists and remains the greatest of all things.

Sebastian ducks under Ishmael's tongs, holds the plastic fork to the doctor's chest. "Now the death blow!"

Ishmael raises his hands, affects a British accent. "Alas, I've been thrown asunder. Smote by the terrible savage and his fork of doom. Please show mercy, good sir, and enjoy a bounty of undercooked sausages dripping with bacterial toxins."

Sebastian howls and embraces the man in a bear hug. "How's this for mercy?"

Ishmael returns the embrace, a grand smile on his face.

Igneus sips from a plastic cup, watches them play. This place has been good for them. As if God had seen they needed companionship and sent Jonas and Ishmael.

Sebastian returns to the soccer ball. Tries to dribble past Jonas. He whirls to his left, feints right, then taps the ball left. Jonas steals it and dribbles away.

"Dad! Come join us!" Sebastian yells. He's taken to calling Igneus Dad, and Igneus has accepted it as the new norm and hasn't tried to dissuade the boy. They both know the truth of their blood.

They also both know another truth. That they have only each other. In Igneus's estimation, that makes them a family.

Igneus glances at his ankle, then holds up his walking stick. "Sorry, son. Seems my ankle's still mending." This is a constant thought. His shoulder has mended completely, mended within hours, didn't even leave a scar. Once Ishmael reduced it, he'd not had another problem.

But the ankle is something entirely different. It's remained painful, causing Igneus to rely on the stout walking stick Jonas gave him.

Why hasn't it healed like the shoulder, like every other injury over the centuries? And why has the shoulder healed normally, or at least normally by Igneus's standards, but the ankle remains a disability? Is he becoming mortal? Growing old? Will future injuries refuse to heal and eventually make him an invalid?

Ishmael announces the food is properly cooked, and they take their places at the makeshift table. Igneus nods his head and prays aloud and all are silent until he finishes. Then Sebastian tears into the food, reaching across the table for some bread, skewering two sausages with his fork, then grabbing a handful of potato chips.

This becomes a sort of game, each of them battling one another to collect various food items. Igneus wins a sausage. Ishmael fakes for the bread, then grabs the bag of chips. Jonas and Igneus have a tug of war with a plastic jug of lemonade.

There is laughter. There is love. This is their new family, and although they haven't much beside dreams, they are together and joyful, sharing a meal on the second floor of a mostly empty parking garage, sitting in faded, creaky chairs, safe from the rain and evil running Jerusalem's streets.

Jonas is the first to hear the gunfire.

He holds a sausage halfway to his mouth, head cocked, listening. He sprints to the garage's side. Looks down from the second floor at the street below.

A stream of people flee in one direction. In the distance, the rapid chatter of automatic weapons, like two-by-fours smacked together repeatedly.

"What's going on?" Sebastian says, moving close to Jonas.

"I'm not sure but I intend to find out." Jonas moves across the garage, then stops at the top of the stairs. "Stay put. I'll be back."

"I'm coming with you," Ishmael says, ignoring Jonas's protest.

From the second floor, Sebastian and Igneus watch people stream past. Those who can run, do. Those who can't, try. Something is forcing them on, and as they watch, the gunfire grows loud, gets closer.

People are panicked, carrying suitcases, boxes, plastic bags bulging with personal possessions.

Igneus sees the fear on Sebastian's face.

Do they return to the closet or join the crowd and flee?

Can't make that decision until Jonas and Ishmael return.

"You should eat," Igneus says. "Finish your meal quickly."

"No way," Sebastian responds. "I want to see what's going on." The boy is bold, brave even, bristling with the recklessness of youth. Whatever's going on, Igneus will have to make certain Sebastian doesn't get involved.

The crowd thins to a trickle, as if their exodus has been somehow thwarted. These few wear bloodied clothes, some limp slowly. Too slowly. *Run*, he thinks. *Hide!* Igneus suppresses his confusion, focuses on faces, searches the thinning throng for Jonas and Ishmael, wonders what's taking them so long.

Gunfire continues, closer than before. Below, a few people fall and lie motionless, gunned down by unknown assailants closing fast.

"Get away from the edge," Igneus says, pushes Sebastian back.

Sebastian's features cloud, confused.

"We should go to our closet," Igneus says.

Sebastian's expression says he has no intention of returning to the closet.

"Jonas and Ishmael will know where to find us," Igneus says.

Sebastian's face twists. "I'm going to find out what's happening," he says and tromps toward the stairs.

More gunfire erupts, closer, echoing against the concrete, bouncing through Igneus's mind. "Sebastian, don't!"

The boy stops, and Igneus limps to him. They stand fifty feet from the protection of the closet. He has to calm the lad, coax him back to safety. He glances around, reviews his options.

Like most parking garages this one has multiple stairwells. Perhaps he and the boy can escape through one of the other exits, the one farthest from the upheaval and violence.

He makes some assumptions. They stand with a stairwell to their right about two hundred feet away. Behind them is the concrete overlook they've just deserted. Their closet is left, about fifty feet. Farther up and on the right is another stairwell and then two more flights of stairs directly ahead about one-hundred yards and separated by, perhaps, fifty yards. The garage is a rectangle with four flights of stairs, all accessible from the street. If Igneus concentrates on the sound of gunfire, they should be able to take the stairwell the farthest away to make the safest escape.

He knows the area well; knows he stands a better than average chance if they get moving. But it means deserting their friends. He also doesn't know how fast he can go, still hobbled by his injury. The walking stick is no replacement for a healthy limb.

I'm supposed to heal. Have always healed! What's going on?

He decides. They'll retreat to the safety of the closet and wait for Jonas and Ishmael. It's the only possible solution, the only possible option.

The walking stick makes neat clicks as they head for the closet. He has to keep Sebastian focused on getting there, on helping him.

"Sebastian, let me hold your arm."

Sebastian moves close, offers his arm.

Then, there's a sound behind them, a rough cry, hoarse. "Halt!"

A man with an assault rifle stares them down. He wears a military hat with a strange round emblem, has just reached the top of the stairs. Gunfire erupts from below. Igneus hopes the sound means the attackers have encountered some resistance but knows it probably means they're murdering more people.

Igneus steps in front of Sebastian. "Leave us!"

The soldier reveals a toothless grin, ascends the stairwell's last step. Igneus glances around. There's just this single man. No others have come up. He's probably been sent to sweep the garage, to look for others. He and Sebastian have been too slow, have taken too much time considering their options.

The soldier raises the rifle, takes aim. Igneus braces, pulls the boy behind him.

The sound deafens, bounds off the concrete to menace their ears.

The soldier collapses and Jonas appears. He carries an assault rifle, a wisp of smoke flowing from the barrel. Ishmael, close behind, looks appalled, steps around the body as if it might bite.

Sebastian races to them, is picked up by Jonas and carried to the closet. Jonas shoves the boy in, shouts, "Stay put!" Then slams the door.

Ishmael comes to Igneus, helps him limp for the safety of the closet.

The place erupts with a flurry of flying bullets and concrete shards. Igneus hunkers down, as Jonas returns fire. He's exposed, has no barrier from which to protect from the barrage. He moves to the makeshift table and upends it, sausages and chips flying, using the plywood as a shield.

Jonas moves like a cat, fires with effortless precision. Flames burst from the barrel to drop any who move forward. Jonas is frighteningly comfortable with the rifle, exudes a calm grace, a certain demeanor that Igneus has seen at various times through the centuries. He's comfortable with death, comfortable in combat, moves like a man who kills with ruthless intent. It's the attackers who need protection.

With each bark of his weapon, they drop. Jonas's face is pure focus; each movement, precise and measured. Igneus realizes he's seen this grace of movement before, employed by another precision killer. The man moves like Longinus, is as comfortable killing as the giant Roman.

Jonas concentrates his fire on the invading force as Igneus and Ishmael hunker behind the plywood. They're too far from the closet and there's too much shrapnel to attempt to move there. Jonas steps forward, streams bullets through the lot, moving frequently, each step measured, effortless.

More soldiers appear. Three of four stairwells hold them now, and they pour in. Jonas fires, focused, determined, as if he hasn't considered these soldiers want to kill him.

He abruptly changes directions, then draws close to Igneus and Ishmael.

He fires more slowly now, seems to pick his shots more carefully.

With the number of soldiers streaming up the stairs, this defense won't last very long.

Jonas reaches the plywood, ducks beside them, smoke rolling from the rifle's barrel.

"I'm almost out of bullets," he says. "I'll have to rush them, try to scare them off so I can grab another weapon and reload. When I do, you guys get Sebastian and make a break for it."

Just then Sebastian bursts from the closet, eyes wild, face crazed, sprinting across the garage toward the stairs.

Jonas leaps toward him, misses by a fraction. Bullets fly, careen off concrete as the place fills with flying lead.

Jonas sprints after the boy.

Igneus freezes, panic invades.

The stairs are now filled with soldiers, firing at will, indiscriminately. Guns chattering as they advance.

Sebastian runs wild, darts panicked and without direction.

Igneus limps forward, screams, "Sebastian!"

Jonas is on one knee, firing as fast as he can.

Then he stops and looks at the weapon, tries to fire again.

He's out of bullets.

Sebastian turns, runs straight toward Igneus. Behind him, the soldiers pour in, rifles leveled. All aimed at the crazed boy.

Igneus puts the rest together. Soldiers filling the boy with bullets, turning their weapons on the rest of them. Sebastian falling, eyes drained of life, youth ravaged, razed like the Children's compound.

Thoughts of safety fade. His hand tightens on the walking stick.

Then everything slows.

Jonas's mouth moves but takes many seconds to form a word. Igneus hears only elongated vowels and consonants. Bullets trace past at speeds so slow, he could reach out and simply swat them down.

He sees Ishmael, eyes wide, soaked with fear, mouth open, yelling.

He watches Jonas's eyes dart, searching for another weapon, more ammo.

The enemy fires.

Shell casings drift from their weapons to sparkle and spin in the air. Slow arcs of hot brass that drift into space. Rifles recoil as long flames leap then take a few seconds to quench. Igneus traces every movement, is attune to every single thing in this space.

Sebastian is wide-eyed now, sprinting, terrified. Behind him a slow stream of bullets chase. He'll never make it.

Then, Igneus's mind fills with a phrase, soothing, measured, serene. A message from far off.

My God will provide all my needs.

Jonas rises, sprints toward the enemy, gun held like a club.

Igneus steps forward.

Soldiers pour in, undaunted now, unopposed. Bits of stones fly by, hang before him, weightless and lazy.

Igneus feels the power rip through him, flood his mind, overwhelm his soul.

The thought is clear, a point well made.

No force can oppose him.

He fills to bursting. Skin ripples with gooseflesh, conscious thought ceases.

His body becomes whole.

He raises the walking stick.

He is a tool of God.

CHAPTER 30

JERUSALEM, ISRAEL

Laslo Slabav stares out the window of the conference room in the Prime Minister's office building. He waits for Cain. Outside, storm clouds roll like troops on an endless march. Gray ghosts cascading through an endless limit of sky. Lightning creases their heads, rolls along their bodies, pass from one to another and streak to the ground. The procession is without end, and he can't shake the feeling the foul weather portends something dark.

Oshi Khalifa enters. He wears khakis today, which surprises Laslo. He hasn't seen the man in these clothes for some time. Laslo rises, greets him with a broad smile. They share a friendly embrace.

"Blessings to you, my friend," Khalifa says, "may God grant you peace and health."

Laslo smiles. "And to you, my dear friend. I'm glad you came."

"You said it was urgent."

"It is. I'm expecting Drake presently." He pauses, remembers the man goes by Cain now. "I mean Cain, presently. He's asked for a meeting, and I thought it beneficial if we're both here."

Khalifa moves to the table, sits. "Of course, Laslo, it's my pleasure to meet with you both. What items shall we discuss?"

Laslo takes a seat, slides the ever-present legal pad a bit to the left and a bit closer. "I'm not sure what he's doing, Oshi. I believe he's up to no good and he'll destroy the peace that we've worked so hard to achieve. I believe he wants to undo all we've done."

Khalifa's eyebrows raise. "You can't be serious? He's the one who made it possible to begin with. Without him none of this would've happened. I can't imagine he'd cast that aside."

Laslo leans back, considers his friend's words. "I think it's possible. I also think he has his own agenda. I'd go so far as to say he thinks *he's* in charge of *us*, in charge of everything. I've had my men look into it. We can't explain how he did what he did at the Temple the day we signed the treaty." He looks at his friend, makes a minor adjustment to the legal pad's angle, glances back. "Don't you find that odd? Shouldn't he share his plans with us, be forthcoming?"

Khalifa's eyes are far off as he ponders the question. "Perhaps," he says, "but then I'm struck by all he's accomplished. The man seems to operate with a deeper understanding of this region. In the end, his results are astounding. He has a gift for motivating people."

"Or killing them without a second thought."

Khalifa nods, adjusts the blouse of his khaki uniform. "Yes. But then, I'm not sure I can blame him. He has little patience for those who don't cooperate. Rather iron-fisted, but I think he realizes sometimes people need that. Need to be led. Talks, summits, treaties, none of those were needed, nor have they born fruit." Khalifa makes a fist with his right hand and holds it in front of him. "An iron hand wins the day. At least you and I were smart enough to see his power, and we've been rewarded generously, and with more than riches." His smile seems strained, his words well-considered. "We've become renowned for our efforts, Laslo. We enjoy the same notoriety Drake did. The whole planet knows our names. Our people enjoy peace. Our religions cooperate and flourish." He shakes his head. "I have a hard time seeing the problem Cain poses."

Laslo studies his friend.

Khalifa isn't wrong.

Perhaps I've become so accustomed to worry, I'm unable to enjoy the benefits of peace.

"Do you know he's been meeting with other leaders?" Laslo says. "That he met with the U.S. president? He's met with all the leaders in the Mideast. I can't help but feel he's executing some plan, especially since he's been doing all of this without our knowledge." He glances at Khalifa, studies the man's expression. "I find my trust in him suffering, Oshi. It's like he still wears those gloves, but I can't tell what they conceal. I can't shake the feeling something wicked races toward us."

Khalifa's eyes narrow, his lips stretch over a thin face. Laslo recognizes the look, has seen it a hundred times before. But those were times of stress, times when their feud was on full-scale. That strained grimace has all but disappeared as their friendship blooms, as their people find peace. Perhaps he's planning something, perhaps he and Cain have joined forces.

Laslo keeps his expression clear, then chastises himself for his mistrust. Oshi has proven to be a wise leader and solid ally. There's no reason to consider him a threat.

"I've been remiss in my thanks for your help, Oshi. Jews from all over the world are relocating without incident, happy to finally practice their culture in peace. And a large part of that is due to you. I'd hate to miss the opportunity to give you my thanks."

The tension slides from Khalifa's face. He nods, smiles. "Think nothing of it, Laslo," he says. "Soon all will be as it should be."

"Gentleman, I see you're early." Cain sweeps through the door. A force of his own, the brightness of his energy fills the room. He shakes Khalifa's hand, offers some words. Then turns to Slabav and reveals a smile that both gleams and disarms.

"No greeting, Laslo?" Cain says. "Rather impolite, I'd say."

Laslo stands and puts both hands on the table. "You threatened my son," he says. "I've had to move him somewhere safe."

Cain places his hand over his heart, looks shocked. "Dear Laslo, whatever do you suggest? I've made no such threat."

Laslo ignores the comment. "I have some questions I want answered, Cain." Fully take charge, he thinks; what Cain needs is a solid hand, an iron fist. "I don't know what you're up to, but I can't believe it's a coincidence my son fainted at the exact moment you advised me to consider his best interests."

Cain starts to speak but is silenced by Laslo's raised hand. "Let me finish."

Laslo waits, stares at him, has to make sure Cain knows who's in charge.

"You've yet to adequately explain your antics at the Temple on Easter. Then you convince me to employ you as a spokesperson, where you travel the world making bargains with other leaders. Bargains of which I have no knowledge. I don't know what you're up to, but you will explain these things to my satisfaction, or you'll be sitting in a prison cell until I decide what to do with you."

Cain nods a single time, points to a chair. "May I sit?"

Laslo suppresses a winning smile, then takes a chair himself. The fact Cain asked permission to sit means he knows who's in charge. That he's accepted his place and is deferent enough to realize his answers better be good.

Cain assumes the chair as four men enter the room dressed in casual business attire. All dark colors, navy, brown, black. A security detail to be sure. Laslo nods at the team's leader, turns back to Cain.

"Now that I have your attention," Laslo says, "I'd like some answers. But be warned, if I find those answers lacking," he motions to the security detail, "these men will take you to prison." He watches Cain's face, waits for a reaction. This man is no match for the career politician or the security men in the room.

Cain sits, hands clasped on the table before him. He appears unphased, as if he's waiting for a nice cup of tea. "Laslo—" Cain starts, but is silenced again by a raised hand and stern shake of the PM's head.

"Here are the rules," Laslo says. "You'll answer what I ask quickly and honestly. If you have any comments, any other, let's say, musings, I'd advise you to shut your mouth." He pauses for effect, has to make sure the man has no doubts about the seriousness of the situation.

"Is that clear enough?"

Cain's eyes lose some of their humor. A glimmer of fire flashes over icy orbs.

He's getting angry, Laslo thinks. He's trapped and he knows it.

"Perfectly clear," Cain says.

"Shall we begin?" Laslo asks. A rhetorical question, he knows, but one that serves to enforce control.

Cain nods.

"First, what are you up to?" Laslo says. "What plans are you making and not divulging?"

Cain's smile is astonishing, disarming. His lips part to reveal perfect white teeth. He is the epitome of calm. "Dear Laslo," Cain says, "I'm up to nothing save elevating your nation to its true status. Haven't you realized the time has come for Israel to lead the world? We've become a shining example of what can be achieved when people put aside their petty differences."

Laslo adjusts his tie and squares the legal pad. "And you've decided this? All on your own? Israel will lead the world because Cain's ordained it?" He leans forward, elbows on the table. "I don't believe you. In fact, I believe your actions serve only *your own* purposes, only the interests of Cain or Drake or whoever the hell you are now. You told President Carpenter that war is at hand. Why would you say such a thing when peace reigns in totality?"

Cain glances at his fingernails, then to Khalifa, then at the PM. "Was I incorrect in my assumption that you'll need the support of the U.S. when war comes?"

"You're evading the question." Laslo glances at the security men, has a notion to order Cain's arrest that instant. He leans back in his seat, adjusts the legal pad again, clears his throat. "I'm asking about war and what you know about it," he says. "Who threatens us? What is it you know? I'll have my answers Cain, or I'll see you rot in a jail cell."

"Dear Laslo, I know many things, things you could never imagine. Things you could never hope to grasp." Cain looks at the security men. One of them has moved aside his suit jacket to reveal a pistol.

"Alas," Cain continues, "I wouldn't want to rot in prison, after all."

He grins at Khalifa, looks back to the PM. "It's my job to answer questions," Cain says, "of that you were very clear, and I apologize if I seem aloof." He shakes his head here, chuckles. "Let me be as frank as possible, dear Laslo. Today your country will be invaded by a coalition of nations that have formed an alliance to stamp out Israel's growing influence." His voice is calm. "Their plan is to invade the country. To take control of its resources. To obliterate its heritage and to slaughter its people." He pauses, his words hang in silence. "It'll be a surprise attack. One executed with such speed and force, you can't possibly withstand it." He holds Laslo's eyes. "Israel will fall within three days. The factions that oppose you have operatives hidden within the masses of Jews relocating here. A Trojan horse of sorts and excellent cover to be sure. When the order is given, these will create an instant ground force. Israel will be besieged by planes, missiles, rockets, tanks, and anything else you can think of. They're counting on the element of surprise. Their force of numbers. By the time the world notices, it will be too late, Israel will be nothing but discarded detritus atop history's bone pile."

The corners of Laslo's mouth twitch as eyes dart back and forth "That can't be true. What? How—" So many questions race through his mind. When's the attack? From what direction? How can Israel prepare? What can be done? He adjusts his position, pulls the legal pad close, looks at the security men, at Khalifa.

Then, a calming thought enters. A thought that brings him to his senses and eases his rattled nerves. He's taken Cain at face value. There's been no intelligence to suggest such an attack. This is nothing more than Cain's attempt to wrest control. A gambit to avoid prison. Cain's a liar, bluffing, desperate. These are antics, a ploy to turn Slabav's attention elsewhere.

Laslo allows a grin to form, his eyes soften. He can't wait to see the look on Cain's face, to see the gleaming smile disappear when he orders his arrest.

His next words are said in a mocking tone. "I see," he says, "very interesting. And to whom do we have to thank for such a grand invasion?"

Blue eyes sparkle as they meet Slabav's. Brilliant white hair seems to illuminate further. The smile disappears. "You have only your dear friend Oshi to thank."

Slabav is stunned, instantly dismisses the idea. "Nonsense," he says. "Complete balderdash." He turns to his friend. Sees the full truth in Khalifa's expression.

He's been betrayed.

Khalifa frowns, the strained expression returns full force.

Slabav has to ask, has to hear his friend speak the words. "Is that true, Oshi?"

Oshi doesn't move, just stares ahead.

Finally, he nods. "I'm afraid so."

Beware the bearer of gifts, for a dagger they may conceal.

Slabav stands, realizes he's trembling. He leans toward Khalifa, lowers his stance to look in his deceitful eyes. "Why on earth would you betray us?" he says. "For what purpose?"

Oshi stands.

Security men tense, step forward, all guns show from beneath open suit coats.

Laslo raises a hand; they stop.

"Did you think I was going to let you rape my culture, Laslo?" Khalifa says. "Did you think I aligned with you out of some level of friendship or goodness?" The hatred is plain on his face. "Part of my bargain was to assist in getting the Jews all in one place." He glances at Cain. "A bargain made with this devil. A bargain he backed out of, bade me to be patient, told me the time would come but at some date to be determined." He shifts his gaze between them. His pose is stoic, rooted. "I've waited long enough. Far too long, in fact. Things are in motion that cannot be stopped." He looks at Laslo, points a finger. "While you were giving speeches about tolerance, granting interviews, prancing around like a prized peacock, I was gathering the support I needed to *truly* solve this mess." He laughs, holds his gaze on the PM. "You're a fool, Laslo! You were never a warrior and know nothing of a warrior's ways. When Cain backed out, I realized I had all the support I needed. That he'd handed me Israel on a silver platter. All his meetings with these leaders, their pledges of support, of protection." He turns to Cain. "All a ruse, Cain. And right under your nose. Did you not question the ease with which you convinced them to support you? How easy it was to secure good intentions and promises of protection?" He pauses, lets the questions sink in. "It was me the whole time. I was behind all of it." His words hang in the air as he trades glances between Laslo and Cain. "It disturbs me to tell you this," he says, "but no one supports you. They're all with *me*! Have promised their allegiance to *me*! They've denounced you and your empty words," he motions to Cain, "your ridiculous appearance, your shows of fake power. Even now they race toward us, swift and devastating. Israel is beset on all sides and from every direction. Very soon your nation will be but a memory." He fully confronts the PM. "You're no leader, Laslo. A leader has will, vision, passion. You have none of those." He scoffs, shakes his head, holds Laslo's eyes. "You're just a politician," he says. "All you'll ever be is a politician. Don't you see? A leader was needed, so I took charge. I provided the will you lack. The courage to see it done. The vision to move forward and change the Earth. I alone have the fortitude to finally claim the throne for my people, the true heirs of this land." His smile is broad now. The man beams. "Laslo, I'm afraid you'll go down in history as a failure." He whips his head toward Cain. "And you will be denounced as an evildoer and taken into custody." He raises his index finger as if he's forgotten an important detail. "But there's good news. News from which you can take heart." His eyes shift between them. "After the invasion, you'll both be tried, convicted of course, then beheaded in public and on television for the whole world to see. Your sacrifice will mark the beginning of this new order. They'll probably even make a holiday of it."

Laslo trembles, holds the conference table for support. "Arrest them both."

Two security men move for Khalifa, as two move for Cain.

Cain raises a hand. "There'll be none of that."

The men cease their motion. Stern looks frozen on their faces, hands suspended midway to their guns.

Laslo stares for a second, wonders why they aren't following his order. Then he looks close, realizes they can't follow his order. They can't even move. That they've been somehow suspended, all four of them frozen in time like statues.

He hears explosions, low, resonant, far away. He hopes it's thunder, glances at the marching clouds outside. It sounds like a fireworks finale, overlapping, loud, fast.

He glances at Cain, then at Khalifa.

Khalifa's face is stretched with shock as he stares at the frozen security detail. It changes to one of realization. He looks to Cain, relaxes, smiles. "You know you're beat," he says. "I knew, once everything was revealed, you'd try to join us." He sighs, looks to the ceiling, then back at Cain. He pulls a silver pistol from his suit. "But I'm afraid it's too late. I don't know what tricks you've employed to survive this long, but I promise you, these bullets are real, and you will die the coward that you are."

Fire leaps as Khalifa empties the weapon.

The bullets strike Cain center mass, full in the chest, eight shots.

Slabav realizes what's happened. Khalifa's organization has infiltrated them, this is an inside job. He looks to Cain without shock or remorse. Khalifa's done them both a favor. One less thorn to deal with.

But Cain doesn't fall, doesn't appear to have felt the bullets' impact. Slabav stares, expecting blood to bloom through Cain's expensive shirt.

Cain flashes his smile, shakes his head. "Hardly," he says.

Smoke rolls from Khalifa's pistol. His smile disappears, his eyes betray confusion.

Cain's brilliance becomes more intense. His hair more radiant, glistening, swirling. He raises a hand, then makes a downward motion.

Slabav steps back, watches Khalifa disintegrate, his form billions of shiny particles floating in the air like so much dust, each speck brilliant, spinning. They coalesce for a second, then spread and twist like a live model of DNA.

Laslo stares, filled with questions, hands trembling, head throbbing.

The cloud spins like party glitter frozen in time and space. Laslo thinks to reach for it, to cup his hands and pull some for himself. Before he can, it coalesces once more, races in unison toward a single millimeter at the mass's center. There's a small spark, a tiny puff of smoke, the smell of cordite and, somehow, malice. Then all the particles merge to a single focus and disappear entirely.

Laslo's mouth hangs open. Khalifa is gone. His clothes haven't even survived.

He looks to the security men still frozen in place, then slowly turns to Cain.

Cain tugs his lapels a single time, adjusts his seat at the conference table.

He glances at his watch, looks up at Slabav. "Have you any other questions?"

CHAPTER 31

JERUSALEM, ISRAEL

"Dad!" Sebastian screams.

The gunfire deafens and his ears ring. Tears pour as he sprints toward Igneus inches in front of the mass of streaming bullets.

Igneus raises the stick, its energy palpable, thick, dazzling.

The building shakes. Cracks appear on concrete walls.

The floor fragments, then buckles.

Around them pipes burst, reveal a myriad of rainbow wires, spew water like fountains.

Igneus is rooted, staff raised high.

Spears of light leap from the wood.

Then the sound of falling stone, as if a mass of boulders rolls down a mountain side. Dust fills the air as light leaps at the enemy in spiked shards.

Pipe and concrete splinter like balsa wood.

Jonas dives for Sebastian, puts himself between the child and soldiers.

Igneus barely notices.

The building surges, shakes like a wicked carnival ride.

Bullets drop, soldiers fall.

Cracks spread, then split like torn tissue. Soldiers drop through, screams trailing as tons of rubble crash down.

Water pours as more pipes explode.

The garage fills with light, tangible, palpable.

The roof peels away to expose an angry sky.

Then all becomes black. All becomes chaos. The walls collapse as the garage itself buckles, then falls in.

Igneus stands above it all, a lighthouse in a tempest, rays flowing in all directions, muscles tense, chaos denied.

Jonas pulls Sebastian close, calls blindly for Ishmael.

Then a flash so bright, a single second of dazzling, abrupt light.

All is silent.

<hr>

Sebastian feels rain on his face. He holds Igneus's hand and stands on a small ridge of concrete that is now the entirety of the garage's second floor.

Ishmael and Jonas join them, eyes wide as they survey the destruction.

Igneus stands on the edge, looking down.

Below, dead soldiers stare at a leaden sky. Limbs jut from cracks in the rubble as blood flows through to congeal in large pools.

Sebastian looks at Igneus, senses a change. A boundless confidence, a power fully bloomed. His walking stick is black now, charred and rough. Smoke rises from it to flow into the storm.

Ishmael stares at the carnage, glances at Igneus. "What. Was. That?"

Jonas says nothing, just stares at the frail Jew.

Igneus looks serene, unharmed. "Let's go."

CHAPTER 32

JERUSALEM, ISRAEL

"Have you any other questions?"

Cain sits relaxed at the conference table, his face calm.

Slabav shakes his head, stares at the spot where Khalifa stood. The silver pistol is all that remains. He tries to wrap his mind around it. One second there, the next, a spinning tower of sparkles and the man's gone.

From the street below comes gunfire. He moves to the window, looks down at the scene. Hundreds of soldiers stream toward the building. Their assault rifles spit fire and kill any who stand in their way, threat or not.

This is the force Khalifa spoke of.

"We're under attack," he says.

Cain nods. "It's well in hand, dear Laslo. I've sealed the building."

The four security men haven't moved. They share stern expressions, expressions of action. Suddenly, they animate, look around as if they've just been deposited from another planet. The leader recovers, steps forward, stumbles, then reaches for a Khalifa that's no longer there. The others move toward Cain.

"Stop!" Slabav says. "Change of plans. We're under attack. Get downstairs and help the others, give me a status report as soon as you can." The four blink as if he speaks a foreign language.

"Go!" Laslo yells.

They blink again, look at one another, then hustle from the room and down the hall.

Laslo turns to Cain. One more card to play, he thinks. An ace in the hole.

He effects a calm demeanor, one of control, of power. "I forgot to say congratulations."

"For?"

"Your marriage, of course. I hear she's a fine woman and I hope you two will be very happy."

"We are," Cain says, "and thank you for your wishes."

Laslo wants to smile but frowns instead. It's time to drop the bomb on the smug idiot. "It's a shame she's dead."

Cain raises his eyes. "Is she now?"

Laslo collects himself, wills the politician within to the forefront. He's not beat yet. "I've sent a man to collect her in Washington. A man who doesn't fail. One of my best. Soon," Laslo says, "I'll get the call she's been captured or killed. After that, you and I will re-examine our relationship."

Outside gunfire barks with more frequency.

Cain glances at the window. The bright aura of his hair has diminished a bit, and Laslo wonders if it's an indication of the man's thoughts or emotions.

"I know of your man," Cain says. "Khalifa sent two as well." He pulls his iPhone from his pocket, places it on the table. "I'm afraid you've both underestimated your measure of Rhyme." He shakes his head. "I'm sure your man is already dead. As are his."

Slabav tries to keep the shock from his face. Cain, a skilled diplomat, a worthy adversary, is probably lying. Whatever they say in this room, Laslo thinks, doesn't matter at all. All that matters is what's happening thousands of miles away. His agent against Cain's wife. Laslo's never been a gambler, but if he has to wager, he'll bet the farm on his agent.

"You knew?" Slabav says. "Then you must've warned her, added security, moved her to a safe place." He stares at Cain, tries to read his expression, tries to see what those pale blue eyes conceal. Then he laughs. "I'm afraid I have to call your bluff. I know your wife hasn't changed hotels. That there's been no extra security at the Saint Regis." He shakes his head, chuckles. "I can't imagine you'd know all this and just leave her to be captured. I'm certain her suffering doesn't figure into your plan." He pauses, takes the chair at the table's head. The gunshots outside distract, but he forces them away, has to deal with the most proximal threat first. "I can only surmise that you're lying and know nothing of this. Soon, your wife will be in custody, if she isn't already. I'll get the confirmation any minute."

Cain tips back his head and laughs. "You've never met my wife," he says. "She requires no warning. She'd probably be upset if I gave her one. She does so love a challenge."

Cain seems unaffected by the clatter of fighting outside.

Laslo thinks about it, his mind clambering with all there is to consider. Cain said he'd secured the building. How? Had he done that on his way in? Does he have other operatives with him? Certainly, the man possesses supernatural powers, perhaps he'd secured the place with something otherworldly.

Slabav stares at him, an enigma. He'd just been shot in the chest eight times but has no marks save some holes in his shirt. He must wear a bulletproof vest. But then what of Khalifa, how had he pulled that off? Slabav's mind swims, overwhelmed with so much, so many details, trying to strategize in the midst of too much.

Slabav's phone rings and he can't suppress his smile. Now Cain will be brought to heel. He pushes the speaker button, wants Cain to hear the conversation. Wants to watch his face and stupid white hair deflate as he hears the news.

"Slabav here," he says.

"Our asset in Washington is dead."

Slabav feels his face flush, avoids looking at Cain. "Daniel? Can't be," he says, "just not possible."

"Daniel. Yes sir. Mission failed. Two others found dead as well. The female has disappeared."

Slabav feels the vibration through the table's wood. Looks up to see Cain lift his phone and thumb the button.

"Dearest Rhyme, what a pleasure. I was just telling Mr. Slabav here how hard it is to kill you. It seems one of his agents turned up dead, and consequently, he's become very cross. A fellow named Daniel, as it seems. Did you two happen to meet?"

Cain stands, crosses to the window. "Oh, I see. How very smart of you."

Slabav can't hear the other side of the conversation and it doesn't matter. All is lost. His ace is a dud. He glances at the silver pistol on the floor a few feet away. Gunfire draws ever closer as Cain looks out the window.

Perhaps if I shoot him in the head, Slabav thinks. He remembers the video; the day Cain was assassinated. He remembers Cain's arrival at the treaty signing. The white horse, the heavenly light. He looks to where Khalifa stood, thinks of the security detail frozen in place. He thinks of Israel, his son, and what Cain can do to him.

Realization fills him. He's powerless.

Cain turns from the window, motions Slabav over.

Below the streets are filled with fighters who wear different uniforms but are obviously of the same force. They fire indiscriminately, moving forward, their numbers growing by the second. Slabav's countrymen lie bleeding in the street. Men, women, children, some move, try to crawl, are quickly assassinated by the gathering mass.

Cain watches the carnage, speaks into the phone with a pleasant, even loving, voice. "Of course, my dear. I'd like you to return to Washington. Go to our home there, change into something nice, then meet with President Carpenter on Slabav's behalf. By now he should have word about the attack here and will probably have some demands before he offers aid. When he mentions those demands, I want you to refuse them entirely. Tell him by day's end the entire Middle East will be Israel. Make it clear the United States will receive nothing from our administration."

Laslo watches, mind swimming, questions unanswered, power slipping away. Cain has him and he knows the only way to save his country and his son is to bow to the man, to acknowledge his authority. He steels his resolve. Sometimes wars take time and sometimes the strategic man must grasp patience until opportunities are more plentiful.

In the street, the fighting continues. A one-sided fight, a complete sneak attack. All Khalifa said is true. He watches a thousand soldiers surround the building, unopposed, rifles raised, howling their victory to the night.

At least Cain's victory won't last long. Soon the invading army will raid the place and take them both in custody. Even with Cain's power, Laslo doesn't see a way to avoid that. He knows the region's leaders, knows their mindset. Even with Khalifa dead, he and Cain will be arrested, tried and beheaded in public. Another madman will rise and take Khalifa's place, then continue the sacking of Israel and the extermination of its citizens.

The army fires at the office's bulletproof glass. Some of the combatants have seen him and scream their observations to the others. They fire as one, seeing Slabav peering down from the window, knowing he's trapped.

Then, a flash of light splits the darkness. Lightning perhaps, but rather close. A flashbang maybe? Why, when the army has everything under control down there?

He examines the street, sees a man stride into view. He's thin, emaciated really, moving forward without fear, fully confident.

The army turns on him. Their faces wear glee, their eyes, contempt.

A thousand weapons bark as a wall of bullets speed toward him.

Laslo feels sorry for him, sorry for his death. He's certainly brave. Or stupid.

White light crackles the darkness to illuminate the scene below. The man faces the army, bent branch raised. He's bald, thin, not who one would expect to confront such a force.

The stick resonates, glows, reflects on the man's scalp, his crinkled brow, his angry face.

A white beam flies from the staff, rockets straight into the army.

Screams follow, bodies fly, consumed by fire.

The light grows, concentrates, swirls like a spinning mist, then spreads to the remaining combatants and up the side streets in all directions.

More screams, more fire, more dead.

The force, thousands strong, decimated.

Laslo's breath comes in rapid bursts, his knees feel shaky. What force is this? More of Cain's antics? More of his power? His breath fogs the window. Below, the bald man appears as a stick figure leaning on a tree branch.

Laslo squints at the light, watches it disappear behind the city's buildings and roll through its streets. Below, the street is silent. Thousands lie dead, rifles melted into linear clumps beside them.

He looks to the horizon, sees the light spread, gain speed, and move through the city.

The thin man leans on the stick, speaks with a child. Two men join him. One has a rifle and seems on full alert. The other runs toward bodies, ignores any in uniform. He kneels next to a woman who was caught in the army's path. He places a hand on her neck, then opens a scraggly backpack and starts to treat her wounds.

Laslo's legs quiver, his body revolts. He's unable to process what he's seen. Unable to deal with such sudden changes, so many changes, so many unknowns.

He flops to the floor.

Cain stands at the window speaking with his wife.

He watches the carnage without expression. "Good news, my dear," he says. "I've found Igneus."

CHAPTER 33

CARTER'S GLEN, NEW YORK

I t all started here.

Poplars line the street as the Bronco creeps along. The night is humid, and Rhyme rolls down the window to inhale the freshness of the maples. Streetlights on tall wooden poles add a conical glow to cluttered yards and dingy picket fences.

Various trucks are parked here, magnetic signs stuck to their doors. KEN'S CARPENTRY, J&L LANDSCAPING. The trucks of people who work for a living. Honest people, dependable, rising early and working until the sun disallows further effort.

She knows most of them by name, wonders if they'd remember her.

Ahead on the right is Sycamore Lane. A long, winding road that goes for miles and takes a person deep into New York's hilly landscape, ultimately to Canada.

She turns onto it, notes the asphalt needs repaired as she bumps along. On her left, she passes the Galbreath house, further up she passes farmland, pays regard to the barbed wire border used to keep cattle in or intruders out. Perhaps both.

About three miles up, it comes in to view, the burnt husk of her childhood home. She presses the brakes, stops in front. Much has changed, yet much is the same. In her memories she hears the laughter, feels the warmth.

A tilted mailbox sits next to a drive that's short and wide. Imprinted on its side, in cursive, THE CARTER'S. Flowers, bright yellow and dark purple, surround the name. Hand painted, the drawing of a child. Her parents made a big deal when she painted that. What was she then? Nine perhaps. She reads the letters, feels the sting of tears well in her eyes.

This has to be cathartic, right? Gazing upon the place where her formative years were spent. The place where she lay in her twin bed staring at the closet, waiting for monsters to tumble out and eat her whole. A little girl then, growing to a woman.

She follows the driveway with her eyes. It leads to three wide steps that used to be white. They're covered by soot now, and the handrail has partially collapsed. The portico above the porch is equally destroyed and partially obscures the screen door. It's a frame only, the screen burnt out by the fire.

A four-pane window looks over the porch and is surrounded by light blue siding. She remembers when she and her dad had painted the place. Three weeks over one summer. They'd taken their time, had fun, completed the job to her mother's exacting specifications. Light blue, professional, no drips. Painted in her mother's favorite color.

She'd enjoyed the work, the time with her father. That summer was a blessed time. Of course, like most things, when you're living in such a time, you can't possibly process or really internalize the qualities they hold, the memories they form. Can't possibly have the capacity to cherish the time while you're living it. Her father's laughter, spilled paint dripping from his fingers, him chasing her around the yard until he got close enough to tap her nose and turn its tip powder blue. Sun-warmed days, talking about books read, songs listened to, gossip heard.

She'd lived those days in joy, at least had that to remember, viewed through the lens of a child, thinking they'd never end.

No one told her times change, *things* change. That parents age, children grow up, that seasons race on delicate wings, flipping pages that wither and rot.

Or are consumed by fire.

No one mentioned you have but one chance in these moments. A single shot to cherish times together. No one bothered to say, once the moments pass, all that remains are fleeting specters. Memories longed for, seductive but never quite right.

Crickets announce their presence to the night, and the creaking chorus drifts into the SUV. She stares at the place, lost in thought. Can almost see her father lugging the next bucket of paint around the side of the house; his body tilted from the weight, overalls covered in splotches, a twinkle in his eye and smile on his face. It was hard work, but he loved it. And Rhyme loved him, so the math was simple. Time spent with him made her feel content, protected, warm. A feeling she thought would always be.

That's until they came for him.

She traces the frame of the porch, the white-washed handrail, the cracked pillar rising to the second floor. Above the porch, the roof is slanted, leads to a single window that was Rhyme's bedroom. She remembers crawling through to sit on rough shingles and stare at the stars. Sometimes her father would join her, groaning as he slid out and crawled next to her. He'd point out constellations, or at least the ones he knew, which consisted of only the Big Dipper and Orion's belt. They'd make up names for the rest. Fat Barney, Tussled Peak, Morbius the Snaggletoothed. They'd spin ancient tales about the origins of the fake constellations, assign to them a meaning used by fictitious mariners as they sailed off to win the day or rescue the damsel.

She'd discovered her love for stories on that roof. Lying under an impossible number of stars and reading books by the light of an Eveready. She'd experienced Mark Twain's Mississippi, Aldous Huxley's dystopia, E.E. Cummings's double speak, and S.E. Hinton's Pony Boy. On weekends she'd read, legs covered with a blanket, head resting on a heart-shaped pillow they'd found at a Target in Westhaven, until sleep found her and took her to the land of dreams.

Now all that remains are charred trestles and broken glass. The window appears as a pocked eye in a mushroom socket, tilted like the entrance to some dark lord's labyrinth. The roof has collapsed, and she can't imagine what creatures now inhabit the home. She thinks of them, a raccoon family for some reason, sharing happiness and scrounged treasures, planting seeds among walls that suffered so much death.

She's not sure why she came here. Her time would probably be better spent at the cemetery, in front of her parent's graves, paying respects. Don Henley lyrics float through her mind. *"Those days are gone forever; I should just let them go."*

And she should.

But she can't. Has known from the day they'd come for her father, that the actions of those involved matters. They'd destroyed her peace, her slice of happiness. Not much in terms of wealth, but all to her. They'd stolen her parents, her joy, her life.

She presses the accelerator, leaves her memories floating over the home, hovering beneath those beloved stars. A quarter mile up she turns left, drives another two miles, passes the cemetery's iron gate. She doesn't look, has relived enough for one night. Perhaps before she leaves, she'll stop by.

Maybe I like torturing myself, she thinks. Maybe part of me longs for sorrow like a starving prisoner longs for moldy bread. She speeds past, pushes away thoughts of her last interaction with her father, of the secret he'd left buried in the woods behind the cemetery.

Another mile and she turns left, goes miles farther before the big green sign comes into view. WELCOME TO CARTER'S GLEN, it says. Beneath that, A HAPPY PLACE.

The words make her grin for some reason, and she wonders if the families remaining are indeed happy. All the industry has dried up. At least it's not full of chain restaurants and big box stores, she thinks. She's been through enough of the country to know that small towns have become a rarity today, that every place looks the same, that only the names change.

People spend what little they have to acquire things they think they need without a single thought as to what makes *them* truly happy. Her father thought them great fools for their love of possessions. Rhyme agrees. Happiness isn't material, can't be bought. It's rather a state of being, defined by the person who seeks it. The most obvious things in life get obliterated when one doesn't know oneself. When one doesn't know what makes *them* happy.

Adverts are tricks. Commercials, manipulation. All based on a false premise that if you make money, you'll be happy. If you buy this thing, you'll find joy. Such a shame, the masses duped. Purchase the right thing and when strangers see it, they'll envy. The default being envy equals happiness.

Truth is, none of those things are worth the cost of the match to burn them.

She stops as the town's only traffic light turns from amber to red. To her right, the pizza place, Ciccarelli's; to her left, a laundromat. Customers sit in cheap, metal chairs, watch machines toss clothes through a tight loop. They bury their faces in their phones and wait for the buzzer to announce their garments are ready.

More evidence of the downfall of Carter's Glen, she thinks. If the people here could afford washing machines, the laundromat would be empty and the pizza place flourishing. If the people here could afford something as basic as a washer and dryer, then they'd have money to spend on pizza. But the pizza joint is deserted, a large pane overlooking the street as red neon flashes the words FRESH-BAKED. A kid leans on the counter, her face also buried in her phone.

The light turns green. She looks right, sees the sign for the Giggleshmertz Institute, or Giggleshit's as the town folk call it. Memories dump in her lap. Dr. Giggleshmertz and his psychiatric institute, Carter's Glen's claim to fame. She remembers the man, his devices, his ruddy cheeks and fat body stuffed in an expensive suit.

She remembers smoke coiling from the barrel of the first pistol she'd ever shot. The first pistol she'd ever pointed at another human. The first pistol she'd killed with. The first man she'd killed.

"The path of your life is unwritten," her father would tell her, "and you're the author." Ten years ago, Rhyme landed the job as Carter's Glen's new librarian. Recently graduated, she lived with her parents to save a few bucks. Back then she'd drove a Honda Civic because it was economical and reliable. Things should've played from there, should've happened as they do for everyone else. She'd meet someone, get married, have a family, raise her children in Carter's Glen around parents she so dearly loved.

But things went terribly wrong.

She'd found herself on a runaway rocket ship, propelled down a runway paved with deceit and murder. She was forced to leave Carter's Glen, forced to learn of arms and tactics, martial arts and lockpicking. She'd learned how to live off the land, how to blend in any environment. How to survive. How to kill. Her eyes, shocked open by her parent's murderers. Held open, dried, bloodshot, by her father's secret and his charge to her. "Protect this at all costs."

Those people wanted that secret, envied its promise of power and wealth. They came for it, murdered her parents, destroyed her home. But they'd made a mistake. They hadn't calculated Rhyme's promise to her father, the weight of such a thing, the totality of her commitment. They came time and again, forcing her down unexpected paths that eventually led to the shadowed worlds of Octavio and X'chasei, to Cain and to Emery.

More deserted store fronts, signs taped to windows announcing, LEASE SPECIALS and PRIME LOCATION. She drifts through the few blocks of the downtown district. Past Cutler's place, a local beer joint whose patrons sit on the curb, sipping Genesee Cream Ale and talking about how their town/life/marriage/home is going to shit.

On her right, the library comes into view. The one place she knows better than any other, the one place she can be safe and think a bit. A former courthouse, and thought to be haunted, it looms in stone and shadow. The bushes are lit from hidden bulbs that shine over the rough stonework three stories high and lead one's eyes across the rows of windows on each floor. A dim light shines through these, added security such that an intruder can be more easily seen by a bystander.

How she loved this place. The best years of her life had been spent here, organizing books and periodicals, greeting customers, attending to the many tasks an old building bids. She'd improved the place in her time. Added banks of computers to a little used space on the third floor. She'd instituted DVD's for loan, children's courses on reading, even a place for the town's special interest groups to gather. She'd become a staple of Carter's Glen, spending more time in the library than what her meager salary bought and without minding a single second. This was her happy place, all tucked into a quaint little town in the hill country of New York State. Carter's Glen had been her life, had held everything dear to her. How did it go so wrong?

She uses a forgotten path to drive the Bronco behind the library and into a preserve. From there, she exploits a little-known secret on the gothic fence surrounding the grounds. Now, she listens, smells, waits. Studies the grounds behind the library and mentally marks anything that's changed over the years. The grounds are wide, well kept. Landscape lighting shines on the sidewalk, down stairs leading from the library's rear door to a path of stone block.

From the stairs, the path leads about twenty feet, then becomes a wide, long circle that spans the rear grounds and goes around to meet with itself back at the steps. The circle is bisected in the middle, leading in a straight line from the steps to a large gazebo. Five white pillars under a shingled roof. Two rustic wood benches facing each other. Angled beams of moonlight beckon one to respite with a good novel.

The scene is from a love story. The surrounding woods, the chirping sounds of the night, silvery light flowing over, causing benches to appear melancholy, even lonely.

A cartoon princess springs from the library and falls into her lover's arms. They'll sing of love, pledge eternal oaths. Overwhelmed by passion, they'll probably make love.

Cheeks flush as she thinks of Emery. His doggedness, his tenacity. His cute butt and inviting lips. His strong hands, his acuity, his long-suffering manner. She thinks of the kiss they shared, thinks how romantic it would be if they could spend an evening sitting in this enchanted gazebo, catching up, holding hands, making love.

She allows herself the thought, crouched by the fence, peering at the gazebo. Emery in a tuxedo, offering a bowl of ice cream. His eyes glow in the night. His smile welcomes, loves. She goes to him, feels his arms around her. He whispers how he's missed her, how nothing else matters.

Their kiss is passionate, his hands on the small of her back, pulling her close. Their breathing rapid, running away from them on thin beams to dance among the stars and speed them in their journey together. Their hearts are full, together again, just as it should be.

She stares at the spot, imagines him in her mind. Soon, they'll be together. Forever and always.

A full moon tonight. That's going to be a problem. She kicks herself for not checking the weather. She's rusty, and a little rattled if she has to be honest with herself. After her talk with Cain, she planned on fulfilling his wishes, performing her duties. But after surveilling their house in D.C., she decided it too risky. Too many questions, not enough answers. Certainly not enough answers for her to risk returning to the mansion.

She'd arrived above their D.C. home on a long narrow ridge with enough trees to provide ample cover and allow her to view the place from a safe distance. Through her binoculars, she saw Cain's men, X'chasei troops, patrolling the grounds in untimed intervals.

Perhaps Cain *is* trying to protect her? Perhaps he's as good as his word. She chuckles at the thought. Even when Cain speaks truth there's always, always, some ulterior motive. The man's a master manipulator. A maestro of the complex machinery of an organization like X'chasei. Even with world politics, the man is a master conductor, applying subtle pressure here, giving rewards there, planting his agents, and generally controlling every detail of everything. No, there's no way she's returning to that house, returning to a place directly beneath Cain's thumb.

In a way, the attack at the St. Regis had been a blessing. Cain has no way to find her now, no way to know her whereabouts. He'd never think she'd return to Carter's Glen; it's just been too long since she's been here.

She crouches by the big oak, the moon's light changing green grass to something gray and dull. She checks her pistols. Safe, tucked in their holster on each side. Probably not needed tonight but always a nice measure of security. She needs some time alone with a computer. Some time to try and sort these things out.

She steps from the oak's shadow and moves swiftly to the library's rear wall. She crouches behind a bush, peers around the building's corner toward the main road. No cars this time of night. She closes her eyes, hears only crickets, smells only mowed grass.

The building's stone grinds against her back as she looks up at her target. The third floor, the computer lab she'd installed. Five vast windows overlook the courtyard. A dim light shines from within. This will be impossible to climb. The stone is thick and will provide a semblance of a handhold, but what will she do when she gets to a window? Break it? Risk the sound being heard and reported? No, she thinks, there's another way, a way she'd used years ago.

She moves through the damp mulch of the library's landscaping. The chips deaden the sound of her steps and make her silent. There are six bushes, spotlights every twelve feet serve to illuminate and beautify.

She moves toward the first light, keeping to the shadows. She crouches next to it, then claws through the mulch until she finds the light's electrical cord. A quick cut with her knife and the light goes dead. She crawls past on all fours, moves to the light at the fourth bush and cuts that cord as well. Anyone driving past the library won't even notice the lights are out. Anyone coming around the back will already know she's here. She crawls forward, close to the wall, between the third and fourth bush.

Here she digs, pulls away as much mulch as possible until she gets to the soft earth beneath. Then she pulls at clumps of dirt chastising herself for not remembering a digging tool. This is certainly quieter than the sound of a shovel and sometimes hard work is what it takes to attain one's objectives. Sweat breaks over her face as she pulls the dirt away, scoops with both hands as quick and silent as possible.

Then she feels the hatch, about two-by-two feet. In the old days, this is the place where they'd shovel coal to the basement to heat the entire building. She clears the remainder of dirt and mulch, then grasps the handle and pulls it open.

She looks into darkness, hopes not much has changed in the room below.

She pulls a small Petzl headlamp from her jacket and places it on her head. She looks down before hitting the switch. Below is dusky concrete covered with dirt and mouse droppings. She looks both ways, then swings her feet over the edge and drops into the room.

She glances up, thinks to close the hatch but isn't sure if it can be opened from this side. She shakes her head, doesn't like the risk but has no choice. Turning her head, she guides the light around the room.

It's as she remembered. A square room about eight by eight with another hatch affixed to the left wall leading to where the furnace used to be. To her right, four shelves bolted to the wall. These hold old paint cans and a few dusty bins. A broom sits propped against them.

She looks to the room's door, iron of some sort, rusty even back then. She presses an ear to the cold metal. This is the risky part; she has no idea if the library has a security system. If it does, there's almost no chance the hatch is wired to it. There may, however, be cameras waiting in the hall beyond, motion sensors, security lights. She might trip an alarm when she opens the door or when she steps into the hall.

She considers her options, weighs the risk of each. She can attempt to crawl through the hatch into the furnace room, but then where? She could exit back to the library's grounds and attempt a different route, but that will only increase exposure and waste time.

This is a gamble, playing the odds. She's willing to bet as part of Carter's Glen's downfall, funding has been cut to the library. She doubts the town council has diverted resources into a security system, especially for a place with nothing much in it. She'd never known a time when the place was a target of thieves. She also knows it was never robbed during her tenure as librarian. Since that time, she'd known plenty of thieves. Knows they'd never consider a library a fat score. What's there to steal? Books? Old DVDs? Perhaps an outdated computer or two? She considers the wager, places her bet on the tight fists of the town's council.

The old door is heavy but opens easier than she expects. Despite the room's dust, someone has kept the door oiled and operable. She switches off her headlamp and slides the door open. The hall here is short, spans only about a quarter of the library's footprint. The basement of the place has two separate sections, the one she's in, for servants and custodians, for those who once stoked the furnace and did the chores. And the other that holds what used to be the prison, inmates awaiting sentencing or punishment.

This is a tremendous advantage; the old servants' area allows access to the entire library through a series of stairwells. From the door, she turns left, relieved no alarm has been tripped. Yet. A grin crosses her face as she adjusts her pistols and switches on the headlamp. She should be home free with easy access to the stairs leading to the third floor.

She stays low, moves quick to the single door at the hallways end. It opens easily and she ascends the stairs with caution, looks for cameras, motion sensors, anything that might trip an alarm and give her away.

There's nothing as she passes the landing to the ground floor, then past the second floor without incident or alarm. On the third floor, she approaches the door and cracks it ajar.

The room appears little used and in need of a paint job, fresh carpet, and some new chairs. Vast, it takes up the entirety of the third floor. Long tables sit in the room's center, a good place for the meetings held here, which Rhyme assumes are ongoing. A poor town's library is generally free of charge for locals organizing tedious events.

Rhyme looks to the rear wall. Three computer stations sit beneath broad windows that overlook the library's rear grounds. They're divided by wood partitions. She steps in, looks for cameras. She sees none and breathes a sigh. The floor needs a good sweeping; the town council has probably cut funding for a custodian. The current librarian, Stella Stevens, if Rhyme remembers right, the woman who'd replaced her, if she's still here, is now expected to rely on volunteers or do the work herself.

The moon casts broad beams onto bookshelves lining the room's walls. It provides enough light to see her way. Across the room are broad double doors, each made of wood, adorned with stout brass handles. This used to be the private chamber of the presiding judge, back in the old days, and Rhyme knows the stairs lead to the second and first floors, granting easy access to the massive double doors of those levels.

She presses the button, and the headlamp goes dark. She moves to the first computer, sits in an old metal folding chair, and flips the switch. A few seconds later, the screen comes alive, casting more light into the room than she prefers. The light will act as a beacon to curious busybodies. The front windows are a concern too, and she looks to see if they have shades that can be drawn. There are none.

This is too big a risk, she has to find another way. She slips off her jacket, covers her head and the computer monitor, creates a tent to obscure the beacon from wandering eyes.

She pulls up a web browser and is confronted with a password icon beneath a block for USERNAME. It's prefilled with the word COMMONUSER. She knows how libraries in small towns operate. Security for computers like this, designed for public use, is generally lax. The password should be easy. She thinks it over, wonders if the computer has a lock-out function, if entering the wrong word too many times will lock the system down.

No choice, she thinks, have to try. She types CARTER'S GLEN, gets a message she's entered the wrong password. She leans back, switches on her headlamp as if its brightness will help spark an idea. Then she remembers the old password she'd created for public users. Something so easy it's impossible to mess up. Something so easy it couldn't possibly remain in use after all these years. She types PASSWORD1.

The computer hums and presents her with the home screen. She's in, perhaps the headlamp aided in some magical way, she thinks. The place has always felt magical. Voodoo actually, letters becoming words, words arranged in sentences to form paragraphs. Those collecting to build chapters and express thought. Thoughts shared across generations. If magic doesn't lie there, then the world is truly without hope.

She clicks to a search engine. In the block, she types LONGINUS.

Emery said Cain created a weapon of immense power. That he did so using Longinus's spear. He spoke of handling Longinus's sword, of finding an ancient key in the pommel. Something about that, Rhyme thinks. Something that nags at her intuition and strokes the hairs on the nape of her neck. There's something there. The key means something, as does the spear. When she'd heard those words, she knew she'd have to dig up more on the Roman. Of course, Emery might've been speaking in hyperbole. Could've confused Cain's thoughts or motives about the purpose of the key or plans for the spear. But she doubts that's the case. Emery's a reporter. Has been a reporter his entire life. Has not one, but two Pulitzers. When he describes something, one can rest assure it's free of hyperbole or fantasy. He deals in facts and reports without bias. She has to assume he hasn't lost that instinct, the ability to communicate what he's seen in such a manner that it can be taken as fact. Provided he wasn't too high.

If Longinus's spear has become a super weapon, if Cain has plans for the thing, then it can only be the Spear of Destiny.

She remembers reading about such a relic, a weapon so powerful no army can stand against it. Thought to be the spear that killed Christ, imbued with the power of God and used to defend His flock.

She remembers Longinus saying it "Wasn't worth a shit." She surmises Cain and Longinus have tried to use it before but without effect.

She mulls the point, the fluorescence of the computer screen filling the space beneath the jacket. Emery said Cain mixed his own blood on the tip of the spear, said when he did, Longinus's entire appearance changed as did the appearance of the spear.

What does Cain's blood have to do with this? And why would it make a difference after all these centuries? It's a fact that Longinus is the centurion who killed Christ. It makes sense the Roman would know where the spear is kept and how to retrieve it. It also follows he probably didn't think it held any special powers and just hid it away somewhere as a relic. Longinus likes his weapons close, has always appeared uncomfortable without his sword at hand. Did that apply to his spear? X'chasei is a vast organization and Longinus can store the spear anywhere in the world. But where? She was there when Cain told the Roman to go and retrieve it. The centurion was gone for three days. And what of the key? What secret does that hold? Does it have anything to do with the spear? Anything to do with anything at all?

Thin threads, she thinks. Knowing Longinus and his proclivities, he could've partied for two days, then gone to some X'chasei repository and retrieved the relic.

But that doesn't make sense, either. Cain is always watching, would've been quite cross had Longinus dallied in his orders. Longinus is a lot of things, but one thing he isn't is a guy who doesn't follow orders, especially when they come from Cain.

She sighs, sits up straight, listens for any odd noise. It's easy to become distracted when deep in thought. Besides, she's rusty and knows the weakness has to be accounted for and minimized as much as possible.

She types SPEAR OF DESTINY into the search engine. Have to start somewhere, may as well start with that.

The computer hums as the page loads. The connection is slow but ample. She clicks on the articles, gleans as much as she can from each. She's looking for breadcrumbs, a hidden path to the answers.

The space is quiet, empty, dark. Rhyme feels the library's embrace, an old comfortable armchair. She feels content in the looming solitude. This is her happy place. This is going to be fun.

CHAPTER 34

CARTER'S GLEN, NEW YORK

Stella Stevens presses the joint to her lips, feels the marijuana calm her aching legs. The bath feels nice, luxurious. The only thing about this apartment that can possibly feel luxurious.

She lowers herself in the water, feels her flesh erupt in goosebumps as her body embraces the heat.

She starts to fade, thinks about Jacobs, the Sprocket Man. It's a bit embarrassing, hung up on a man with such a nickname. But at her age she can't be so choosy about who she dates and her chances to find a companion. She sighs, takes another drag, filling her lungs and choking back a cough. Is he the guy for me? The owner of Carter's Glen's shitty little bicycle repair shop? She could do worse, especially around here. She exhales, feels the smoke flow over her lips. Probably can't do better, though, not in this town. She considers moving, realizes she's too old and too lazy for such an endeavor.

She glances out the bathroom door, realizes she's left her phone on the end table she'd purchased from Target last week. She hopes he'll call. Perhaps he has a mind to share her tub and her weed. She imagines him joining her, his hands soapy, sliding over her skin, gently grasping her neck as he moves in for a kiss.

Her hand dips beneath the bubbles. Even if he doesn't call, she can still have a good time. She lowers herself in the tub, opens her legs.

At first, the beep is distant, and she thinks it's the weed. When it persists, her hand rises above the water and she leans forward, looks into the living room.

She almost kills herself getting out of the tub, slipping on the tile floor, using the toilet as a brace. She exits the bathroom, heads into the living area where she stands, listening. It's coming from the bedroom.

Cold air washes over her as she enters her room. The sound comes from beneath her bed. She kneels, peers under, sees the device.

The weed is doing its thing as she stares and tries to focus her thoughts. Then she remembers, years ago, when she'd been made an offer she couldn't refuse. A thousand a month to monitor a single alarm. If tripped, call someone. When was that? It's hard to concentrate. Back when the other librarian went psycho and killed some people, then fled town never to be heard from again.

What was the man's name? Morlock, Moredred, Limerick. Something that starts with an L or an M. She remembers the man, strong, handsome, confident. A man of military caliber, a catch if she could've reeled him in.

She retrieves the device, a small receiver with a blinking red light. She rubs away the dust and examines it. No buttons, no dials, just the beep and the blinking red light. She leans back on her haunches, bare breasts covered in goosebumps. She's amazed the thing still works. Who knows how long it's been under the bed?

She returns to the bathroom, grabs the robe from the back of the door, slips it on, then shivers some more. The robe is black and lacy, mostly see through, a representation of a trade she'd made with Victoria's Secret. A trade many women make, now that she thinks about it. Comfort for sensuality, warmth for seduction. A bad trade by all measures, for even if she could attract a man like Jacobs to her bed, she'd be clad in the garment for only about four seconds before it became a heap on the floor.

She shakes her head; weed causes her mind to wander. "You have one job," she says aloud. "Easy money at stake." She tries to remember the man's name. The task seems impossible after so long. Nonsense fills her mind, Limbstick, Merrier, Montezuma.

Wait, he gave me a card. What kind of librarian would misplace such a thing? Probably put it where I'll know exactly where it is. But where?

She moves across the living room, back to her bedroom. It smells of sandalwood in here, Sprocket Man's favorite. Just in case. The bed is small, well made, pillows of purple and white lie against a cheap brass head frame. She moves to the closet, peers inside.

On the top shelf is the Nike box where she keeps important items. If it isn't in there, it's gone forever. She takes it to the bed.

The box contains her birth certificate, last will and testament, a letter from Jacobs (probably written while drunk), her diary (mostly blank), a picture of her parents, a clipping from the Carter's Glen Daily announcing her hire as the new librarian, and a black business card.

Relief washes over her. The weed enhances the feeling, makes it torrential. The card has a weird symbol, an oblong O with three dots in the center. Beneath that, it reads, OCTAVIO CORPORATION. The man's name isn't on it, but her mind still tries, Monty, Morgan. She flips it over, sees the number.

She moves to the living room, dials the phone.

It's answered on the first ring. "Report."

"Um," she says, "this is Stella Stevens. I was told to call if the alarm at the library went off."

"Location?"

"Carter's Glen," she says, "Um, New York."

There's a pause, some typing, then, "Roger that."

The line goes dead as Stella sits with the phone to her ear. She shivers again, wonders if weed lowers one's internal temperature.

She stands, adjusts the silky robe, then thinks, fuck it, and lets it fall to the floor.

She takes a single step before her phone rings. "Baby Come Back" by the Seventies band Player. The name reminds her of Jacobs, a player if there ever was one. That's the reason she chose it as her ring tone, as a reminder. The singer is smooth, calming, enhances the effect of the weed or perhaps the other way around. Player sings their song to the naked librarian, begging her to come back.

She answers.

It's Jacobs.

"Hey gorgeous, what're you up to?"

A smile blooms. "Hey yourself."

CHAPTER 35

CARTER'S GLEN, NEW YORK

Rhyme's back aches from the cheap metal chair. The jacket remains draped over her head, her face bathed in the bright glow of the computer screen. It's been two hours, and her mouth's as dry as the pages of an old book. She wishes she would've brought along some water. Of course, she can head downstairs to the library's vending machines. They must still be here, even after all these years. They provide a modest source of income to the library. She considers the risk, then discards the thought.

She's been fortunate to this point. Or as Crispy would say, she's "exploited the intersection of preparation and opportunity." Her knowledge of the building, combined with the town council's tight fists, had allowed her to come up the back way without encountering security. Likewise, the third floor is void of camera or motion sensor. Worrying over nothing, she thinks. The place doesn't have a security system at all.

The last two hours have been productive, but still, there's something missing. Turns out Longinus and his spear are quite famous. As the legend goes, Longinus was basically blind during the time of Christ, had eyesight worsening as he aged. But when he'd run the Savior through, a miracle occurred. Some of Christ's blood splashed in his eyes and restored his sight. According to the legend, the event was a turning point for the Roman and caused him to realize that Jesus was, in fact, the true Messiah. After that, he'd spent the days until his death spreading the gospel.

What a joke, she thinks. The legend has Cain written all over it. Her husband, a diabolical spider at the center of a tremendous web. His many limbs poised on silky strands, sensing even the slightest vibration and responding accordingly. Rhyme heard Cain's own tale straight from his mouth. Cast out, made immortal, guided by his brother, Abel, who came to him in dreams and visions.

He'd collected the few other immortals to his cause, Longinus, Igneus. Had reigned as the Emperor Constantine and commissioned the first Bible. A false Bible, Rhyme knew, holding only what Cain wanted and none of what he didn't.

Cain had always used Longinus for his own purposes, had created history to match the legend, to match Cain's own ambitions. An accounting of Longinus's life and eventual death: all fiction. Only winners write history.

How Cain uses him now is a mystery, but after the story Emery told, her inclination is that the spear may be the key to the whole thing. The ultimate undoing of Cain. A means to put the man in his final resting place once and for all.

She continues her thought experiment, tracks Longinus through the web pages, attempting to find out where he keeps the relic. The options are many.

In St. Peters Basilica, Rome, Italy, there stands a statue of Saint Longinus. Turns out the Roman is revered as a saint by the Catholics. Rhyme never knew that, despite being Catholic. She stares at a picture of the statue. It shows a man in flowing robes holding a spear with his right hand, his left outstretched as if preaching to a mass of people. It holds an honored place in St. Peter's, one of four statues surrounding the Papal Altar.

The statue was carved in 1643 by an artist named Bernini. The same artist who'd created the apse above the Longinus statue that serves as reliquary, a place that holds relics assigned to the saint with which they are associated.

The pictures of the statue are beautiful, the carving splendid, the details rich and subtle. She marvels at the years it must've taken to accomplish. Her thoughts turn to the reliquary. Does Longinus keep his spear there, returning only when he needs it? She mulls it over as her intuition remains silent. Storing it there doesn't really make sense. Why would Longinus keep it in such a public place? A place that would grant limited access even with the power of X'chasei. There's no doubt X'chasei has infiltrated the Vatican. Hell, they may even control the Pope, but keeping a relic of such power in a place like the Basilica reeks of Cain and his machinations. She knows Longinus well enough to know he wouldn't be caught dead in church, and certainly wouldn't be comfortable storing his spear in such a place. Let the Catholics believe what they wish; it's easy to display fragments of metal and say they came from the spear that killed Christ.

Not an option, she thinks, Longinus wouldn't store his spear in St. Peter's.

The internet offers other ideas, other churches and museums claiming to own the Spear of Destiny. The Museum Manoogian in Armenia, for one; a church in Vienna, for another. The latter holds more promise than the former. The legend states the lance in Vienna had come directly from Constantine the Great, Rhyme's current husband, and was even used by him during his rise to power. The legend goes on from there, states Hitler used the relic during his rise to power and throughout the subsequent World War.

She considers the option as she stretches her back. There are problems with the theory. First, Cain wouldn't have needed a magical relic to rise to power as Constantine. By then X'chasei was well-established, and, well, Cain just gets his way when he wants something. Certainly, history books would've mentioned a lance of great power, one that laid low entire armies.

As for Hitler, again there's no recorded history of such a weapon being used in battle. Add the fact that Longinus himself said the relic was useless. The math becomes basic. The relic had no power until such time as Cain added his own blood to it. If that's true, that Cain's blood is what imbued the lance with power, then why didn't Cain attempt that in all the prior centuries. Perhaps he did, and it had no effect. Perhaps he didn't, and if so, then why now? She doubts Cain would have access to the power of such a relic and not use it.

As brilliant as the man is, he can't tell the future. His moves run more toward molding the present to his desires, creating the future he wants in the process. If the lance had been used at any point in recorded history, then it would've been a *major* event. A singular earth-shaking moment akin to dropping the H-bomb on Nagasaki. It wouldn't have gone unnoticed, would've been recorded by someone, probably scores of people, then passed down through written and oral histories.

An event like that would serve to make the relic the all-time, number-one, sought-after item in history. Ever. This power wouldn't have been ignored, and Cain would've already conquered the world.

Doesn't add up, something changed. Something the books and histories don't know, have never known.

She considers her facts. Longinus's relic, powerless until modern times, given power by Cain's blood. Cain knows of the relic and orders Longinus to go get it. Longinus has a key in the pommel of his sword. Longinus is gone for three days, during which he uses the key to open some secret vault and retrieve the relic. She's adding here, assuming, making an ASS out of U and ME, as Crispy would say.

She leans back, rubs her temples, then the back of her neck. She turns off the monitor, lowers the jacket from her head, feels the library's coolness. Outside the sable darkness of night has become the blue gray of morning. She has to go, but before she does, she has to make sure she has plenty to mull over.

Nothing makes sense. Probably the way Cain wants it. She remembers the words of Doyle's famous sleuth, Sherlock Holmes. "When you've eliminated all which is impossible, then whatever remains, however improbable, must be the truth." A smart guy, Doyle, probably smarter than me. Although she doubts even he could deal with Cain.

With Cain, everything is possible.

She clicks through the open windows on the screen. Rereads an article that speaks of the relationship between Pope Innocent and a Turkish Sultan by the name of Beyazid II. The article states the Pope wanted to stop the Turk's advance on Rome but was at a loss on how to do so. To that end, he'd made a deal with the Sultan. The Pope imprisoned one of the Sultan's rivals in exchange for a yearly ransom paid to the church. Part of the deal included the Holy Lance.

This story has Cain written all over it.

Rhyme's intuition prickles as she wonders about the Roman's origin. It makes sense he'd keep it somewhere he's comfortable, but where on the great green Earth could that be? She wonders from where Longinus originally hailed. One would think the obvious answer to be Rome or its surroundings. But really, if one looks at history, even as flawed as the record is, one discovers the Roman army was made from many, many peoples from many, many regions.

Following that line of thought, Longinus could be from anywhere conquered by the Romans. The thought does little to narrow her options but does shrink them to a smaller footprint than the entire Earth.

Then she has a thought, remembers the day she'd met the hulking Roman. He'd introduced himself as Longinus from Misthli, which, at the time, sounded no more than just a clever moniker.

Now it feels entirely different.

She flips her jacket over the monitor, then covers her head, recreating the tent to keep the computer's light to a minimum. Time is running out.

She turns on the monitor, types MISTHLI into the search engine. It returns nothing of interest. Then she types, LONGINUS OF MISTHLI. Again, nothing important, no further clues. She rubs her eyes, stifles a yawn. Her brain no longer fires on all cylinders. Time to try the obvious. WHERE WAS SAINT LONGINUS BORN. The computer hums, and the screen shows numerous listings with the word CAPPADOCIA.

Finally, a lead. She scans the articles using the rule of threes. If she can find three articles from reputable sources that say the same thing, then she can accept them as probable fact. This turns out to be easier than expected and she finds it's a widely held belief that Longinus came from Cappadocia.

But where is Cappadocia and why hadn't he introduced himself as Longinus of Cappadocia? She types, MISTHLI, CAPPADOCIA, and her answer appears.

Cappadocia is a region of Turkey that contained the city of Misthli, long since vanished and now part of Goreme National Park. It's located near the town of Goreme in Turkey and known for numerous communities, all of which exist in the hollowed cones of earth for which the region is known. Entire cities underground, homes, churches, markets, all underground.

Her pulse rises, excitement, a payoff for her research.

Now to check the time frame. Misthli was settled sometime around 400 BC and survived until deserted by the Turkish government in 1923. It'd been incorporated into the Roman Empire starting around 100 BC.

The timeline fits! Longinus is from Misthli, Turkey, now Cappadocia. Her intuition becomes a live wire, electrified, buzzing in her head. She's found her truth, knows her answers.

Now to check transit times. Her fingers fly across the keyboard like hounds on a scent. It takes fourteen hours to drive from Jerusalem to Cappadocia, but only a few hours to fly. She doesn't know how Longinus traveled, but due to his size, he generally prefers to use one of X'chasei's private jets.

So, assume three hours to fly there, say another day to get his spear, then three hours back. But why had it taken him three days? Maybe he was visiting family. She chuckles. Any family Longinus had would be long dead. She rules it out as a nonsense thought. There must be another reason.

She rubs her eyes, thinks how a hot cup of coffee would do her good right now. It's a good time for a break; she's tired, and the computer seems to be running more slowly by the second. She glances at the monitor, countless windows remain open. No wonder the machine's getting bogged down.

She starts to click them closed. Time to wrap it up anyway. She's found a way in, can return at her leisure. She makes a mental note to get another prepaid cell phone so she can call Emery and discuss what she's found.

Stifling a yawn, she clicks closed the windows.

There's no mistaking the next thing she feels.

A pistol pressed to the back of her head.

CHAPTER 36

MOUNT TABOR, ISRAEL

I turn up a paved road that begins to wind and ascend. Outside, the landscape of the valley begins to change. More forest now, more mountainous, many meadows with the occasional bovine nibbling short grass. The road has endless switchbacks, and as we ascend, it becomes more and more difficult to enjoy the scenery. We climb higher and higher, switchback after switchback.

Just when I think I'm going to have to stop and stretch my legs, perhaps throw up, Longinus points to the right. I guide our SUV into a wide, square parking lot. To our left are a few old buildings. Beyond them a church rises into the sky.

"Where are we?"

Longinus exits the vehicle and walks to the back. I hit the button and the hatch raises. He ducks in, retrieves his spear and plods away toward the ancient church.

He looks ridiculous, contrasts with the surroundings in a comical way. Like seeing someone on the street carrying Poseidon's trident. Doesn't make sense and sparks a lot of questions. He has a peculiar gait, actually the same gait as his former self, like he's been marching since the day of his birth. This only adds to the effect, makes it even more absurd. Here's a supermodel fresh from a fashion shoot, marching toward an ancient church while carrying a golden spear that spans above him by a few inches. None of it fits. In fact, its oddly comic in this new, slim Longinus. He exudes poise with effortless intent, and I expect him to glide everywhere, for his feet to hover just above the ground as if he's been elevated. A modern angel, glam and sleek.

I exit, hear the bleep-bleep of the car alarm as I press the button on the key fob. I follow him, across the parking lot, and onto a wide, smooth sidewalk. To my left, six large cypress trees present their leaves to a sun hidden by clouds. To my right, I pass three buildings. All appear old, but not as ancient as the church.

On the way in, we'd driven through a giant stone archway that bore the symbol of the Franciscans. I take in the buildings, wonder if they're dorms or offices. I'd love to spend some time exploring, maybe even knock on a few doors and strike up a discussion with whoever answers. The reporter's way; knock and hope.

We continue on, past a two-story, L-shaped building. A steepled roof of red tile appears maroon in the day's darkness. Small windows span its second story, and in them I hope to see a monk. I pass through a pair of short stone columns and continue down the long side of the L-shaped building to my right.

Past a small garden, then a copse of small evergreens that attempt to hide a short, rounded catacomb of weathered stone. I glance to my left, notice some ruins. I wonder what they're from, what history the place holds. I pull my notebook and jot a reminder to research this place more fully.

A strong breeze pushes against me. There's no time to dally. Longinus is well ahead of me now, almost at the church. I pick up my pace. It's going to storm anyway, and I may as well be inside than soaking wet. I mean, I wouldn't want to ruin my suit.

The path changes to a gloss of flat, smooth stones, level and ancient. It widens and presents a clear view of the church. A sign reads, CHURCH OF THE TRANSFIGURATION which makes me wonder what has been transfigured, the church or those who enter. Perhaps it's speaking of Longinus. He's been recently transfigured, has changed entirely. Perhaps that's why we're here, to complete his metamorphosis.

I grow close to the ancient building, then stop and stare.

Contentment sneaks into my psyche. This place is amazing. I take a step, then stumble a bit and almost fall. I glance around to see if anyone noticed. Only a few people are here, tourists probably, far too busy taking pictures to notice me.

Longinus plods on, spear in hand, moving with purpose, focused.

He's going to have to wait, I think, as I direct my gaze to the church and marvel at its beauty and craftsmanship. It's a huge block, rises three stories. Facade towers guard the basilica's entrance, and as I look closer, I see each holds a huge bronze bell on its top floor. I lower my gaze to the narthex, an intricate arch spanning between the bell towers and rising to a thick stone point. This is a facade of sorts, appearing robust from the front, but passing under it, I realize its depth is about the same as the stones with which it's made. Perhaps two feet.

I enter a small courtyard, flanked on both sides by the base of each bell tower. The stones are perfectly set, perfectly symmetrical. Whoever made this place had a real talent for masonry. The church appears stout, impregnable really, as much fortress as religious site.

I stare up at the basilica, stone walls in tan and brown. Above the entrance, the building looms into the sky. I see a large rectangular plaque on the wall above the entrance. It's engraved, in Latin perhaps, but I can't read it. I can, however, make out the reference: MATTH XVII. I scribble the reference in my notepad, likely a Bible verse, then look above the engraving to a set of three wide, decorative panels. They're divided in thirds by two spiraling stone pillars. Above them, I see the steepled roof of the basilica. It bears another etching of the Franciscan symbol.

I direct my attention to the church's doors. They're old and wooden, dark and thick. They appear engraved and I move toward them, anxious now to take a good look.

The doors are really dark, almost black, and this surprises me. You'd think a church would be happy and bright and welcoming, especially its entrance. These doors are tall, perhaps twelve feet, and not quite as wide as one would think a cathedral's doors should be. Each is inset with four panels, and each panel holds a different version of the Franciscan symbol, which looks to me like a Celtic plus sign. Then I realize I've seen the symbol before. Seen it in the Vatican when I was with the Apostle. It's a Templar symbol, but the ones I'd seen were always red. I wonder about the relationship between the Franciscans and the Templars, the history of the order and how they coexisted, if they coexisted. I'm afraid I'm not a very good Catholic. A good Catholic would know such things.

A raindrop hits my ear. Above me, dark clouds pout, sliding silently toward some unknown destination.

Longinus clears his throat. A dainty and polite sound compared to the old Longinus but one that's successful in getting my attention. He stands by the church's entrance, a fashion model posing with a golden relic. His expression reveals impatience, but in a kind way, if that's possible. I give him a smile and shake my head, then move toward him.

A man hurries through the doors, heads toward us. The heavy fabric of his robe rushes behind. He seems frantic and impatient, as if he's been waiting all day.

"Cain called," he says. "We must hurry." He has a well-trimmed beard and intense blue eyes.

"The roof?" Longinus replies. The man holds his gaze on Longinus for a second more than is comfortable in polite society, then motions us to follow.

Inside, the basilica's ceiling is massive and steepled. Dark rafters run its span and outline the structure's pointed roof. Beneath this, a series of arches at floor level on both sides. The interior is built from the same stone as the exterior, and I think the place must have been a fortress originally. Rows of long benches fill dark, wooden floors. A broad aisle runs between them toward two altars, one above the other, the lower one placed beneath and just past a huge stone arch that's engraved and formal. The upper altar stands above, radiates grandeur, a place reserved for special occasions. A mosaic of Christ rises above both. He's pictured with some men I can't place.

I head down the aisle, intent on examining all of this in more detail. The monk grabs my arm, spins me around to face his piercing eyes. His smile quivers at the corners; he looks close to a nervous breakdown.

"Please," he says, then pauses, forces the smile wider, swallows. "Follow me." He spins and moves to the right of the church's entrance, through a great iron door. We find ourselves on the lowest level of one of the bell towers.

The monk rushes across the square space to another door, then produces a key and slides it into the lock. He gives us a quick glance and I can't help but feel he's making sure I haven't escaped.

Soon we're climbing ancient stone steps. Ahead of me Longinus ascends with an uncustomary grace, a step behind the monk. I hurry after them both until we go through another door and enter the bell tower proper. It's large, open to air on three sides with a dusky bronze bell hanging in its center, catching what little light the day will give, then bouncing it back toward us.

I wonder what this bell has to do with our task here. I turn to ask, just in time to see Longinus disappear over the bell tower's back wall and into the gloom of the day.

I rush to the spot, peer over. There's a small platform suspended about thirty feet above the ground. It leads to a flight of very narrow, metal stairs that climb to the church's roof. Longinus plods up, spear held in front. I'm reminded of a prince on his way to confront a dragon. I'm reminded of a painting by Raphael.

The monk pushes at my back. "Go on! Go on!"

I glance over my shoulder, gauge that the monk won't suffer further discussion. I climb over and step onto the small platform.

My feet hit the damp metal and I fall on my ass. It makes a muted gong sound like a Three Stooges' special effect.

When I look up, the monk's blue eyes peer down. He can't mask his frustration. His arm pops out and he waves at me to move along. He's holding his patience, but just barely. His expression tells me he wishes I would've fallen all the way down.

I stand, hold a slim, rusted rail for support. The steps before me are narrow, wet, and I get the impression that if I fall, I'll be falling a long way.

Longinus has reached the top and is making his way up the sloped roof. I take my time, climbing the slick steps slowly and carefully. Safety trumps the monk's impatience. I manage to reach the final step without busting my ass again.

Here I stare at the basilica's long, steep roof. It appears treacherous, and I doubt even a mountain goat could traverse it.

The elegant frame of Longinus reaches the ridge, and moves right, toward the farthest end of the structure. How he keeps his balance is a mystery, and I again place the blame on Cain. He's probably imbued the Roman with super-footing or something.

I, however, have not been granted such powers and feel my next few steps will be my last. I glance down the stairs, think to turn back. Then Longinus calls to me.

"Come on!"

I brace up my courage and take the first step. I somehow manage a second step and even a third. I refuse to look around, concentrating solely on my ascension to the relative safety of the roof's ridge. My feet slide a bit as I pick my way, but I manage to maintain traction until, at last, I'm straddling the structure's ridge.

Longinus is almost at the far side of the roof. Don't let me slow you down, I think. The wind is stronger up here, flowing freely and without obstruction. It buffets me and even at this distance I hear the rattle of the shaking stairs I've just left.

I check my balance against the wild breeze, then start to move to where Longinus stands. I can't see the ground from here, only steep angles on both sides. I imagine myself sliding headlong down the slick stone roof, then I do. I slip and fall backwards, but just before I enter the death slide, I manage to twist my body and land hard on the roof's peak.

Air rushes from me with a harsh whoosh. My ribs sing a song of pain. I'm spread-eagled now, a pathetic windvane atop the devious structure. I push myself up, manage to breathe again, then stand motionless on the ridge. I can't see a way forward, or at least a way where I don't die. I steel my resolve; I'm not going to let this damn roof defeat me. I glance both ways, search for a less treacherous path to the Roman.

I see nothing.

I inhale, then expel all my breath. A meditation of sorts, or perhaps my last rites. I step forward on shaky legs, walk the tight rope that is this narrow ridge. I'm a newborn fawn taking its first steps. I have about a foot of space to work with and it's all wet and slippery.

"Look at this dipshit," Lenny says.

"Right you are, Lenny. The adventures of Danger McStupid," Vince says.

Ahead of me, Longinus waits. He hasn't seemed to notice the steep incline, the long fall. Benefits of immortality, I think. If he fell, he'd probably just stand up and dust himself off.

He wears a look of amusement, his slim frame cuts a sharp silhouette against the brooding sky behind. He is sharp angles, lean lines.

After a few moments, a couple of harrowing slips, I finally catch up. I want to grab the Roman, use him as an anchor. I realize then that this new Longinus hasn't the weight to manage me, lacks the hulking musculature of the man I once knew.

I do my best to balance on my own, think a Chinese acrobat would have a hard time managing what I've just done.

Then the wind gusts and shakes my confidence in my perch. I make sure my feet are centered on the small walkway, then flash a look at Longinus. Before I can speak, the view steals my breath.

The vast landscape of Israel greets me, spreads beneath an angry sky to offer greens and browns to the atmosphere, as if opening itself to the pending storm.

I stand atop the basilica, which stands atop a huge rounded mountain. The view blooms three hundred and sixty degrees. I can see for eons, possibly forever. Behind me, the long roof I've just endured leads back to the parking lot and down the mountain. Before me is everything else.

The valley blooms. To the north, rolling hills dot the landscape and interrupt the smooth flatness of the spreading valley. Beyond these, the shadowy peaks of Israel's northern mountains. They reach for the thunderheads and attempt to blend their verdancy with the clouds' bruised faces.

To my left, the valley glides along, heads south toward Jerusalem and borders the Mediterranean Sea to the west. I can see for hundreds of miles, maybe thousands. I can see the entire nation, maybe even the nations around us.

I check my balance again, pry my eyes from the view, and ask Longinus why we're here. He doesn't respond. Just stands at the edge of the roof, precariously posed above the vast valley.

He leans on his spear, its shaft propped on the roof's thin ridge. The relic catches the odd sun beam, then magnifies and splays the pattern onto the roof and out over the valley. The spear is beautiful, radiant. Red and blue lines race through myriad etchings, spinning, swirling. I divert my gaze, afraid if I watch too closely, I'll lose my balance and be tossed from the precipice.

I venture a step toward the Roman. The church has been built right to the very edge of the mountain, and I look down to see a long drop, more than three-hundred feet if I have to guess. I'm surrounded by danger; the drop before me, the roof's steep angles on both sides, the wind jostling with indiscriminate malice, and the slippery catwalk that leads back to the bell tower. If only Rhyme could see me. I check my footing, then step away from the edge.

Longinus is visibly tense, suddenly appears more alert, more focused. He's found something and stands like a blood hound catching a scent. He looks north, eyes fixed on a single point. I follow his gaze, squint into the wind and through the darkened haze.

Has Cain imbued the Roman with enhanced vision as well? I strain my eyes but see nothing but the beauty of Israel.

Longinus is riveted, though. The sharp angles of his face turned gold by the spear's brilliance. Eyes fixed on some distant point, a model smoldering before the flash of the camera.

I continue scanning north, occasionally glancing at him.

Now, I've never seen an invasion. Never witnessed a military force on the move, but when I do, there's no mistaking it. A single dot appears on the horizon, black and distant, moving toward us, flying. Another joins the first. Then still another and another until the expanse above the horizon fills with little black dots. Thousands of them, perhaps tens of thousands, moving toward the valley, crossing the mountains and speeding toward Jerusalem with great haste.

CHAPTER 37

CARTER'S GLEN, NEW YORK

Rhyme raises her hands, feels the pressure of the gun against her head.

"FBI, ma'am," a voice says. "I apologize but we're forced to detain you on a number of charges starting with the murder of three men in Washington."

Rhyme says nothing, watches the reflection in the computer screen. Two men, one standing behind and to the left of the other. The one in back says nothing, hopes not to be noticed, gains the advantage of surprise should Rhyme attempt anything.

"Please put your hands behind your head."

Rhyme considers the implications of following the order. If she complies, she'll be cuffed and disarmed, then taken to the local jail until such time as she can be transported to Washington. The whole process will take days, even weeks, time she doesn't have.

How'd they find her anyway? She stares at the screen, considers the question. The only way would be an advanced security system, something along the lines of what the Pentagon uses, infrared, noting only body heat. Supremely effective and easy to conceal. She must've missed it.

She doubts they'll shoot a woman in the back of the head, so she takes a risk, stands, slowly turns. The move serves to lessen her disadvantage, allows her to survey the room and the G-men.

"Can I see some ID?" She leans back on the table, jacket held with both hands.

At the sight of the twin Sigs strapped to her body, the man in back steps forward, draws his own weapon. The other agent holds up his hand and stops him. "Of course, ma'am," he says. He produces a leather bifold from his suit pocket, then flips it open.

Rhyme examines the credentials. "Agent Elroy," she says. "Hmm, I always wondered what happened to the kid from the Jetsons."

She's buying time, knows these guys are legitimate, knows they're highly trained and won't tolerate her nonsense much longer.

"Very funny," Elroy says. He replaces the bifold in his suit. "Please put your hands on your head and turn around."

Second time he's asked. In her experience, there won't be a third. She considers the risk of her next move. She needs to take advantage of the fact they expect her to go for her guns. The agent in back holds his weapon on her. If he fires, he won't miss.

Disadvantages: rusty, outnumbered, physically weaker, covered by a gun.

Advantages: the Sigs. She can think of nothing else.

The odds aren't good, nowhere close to being in her favor. She considers tossing her jacket in Elroy's face, then moving to her left. The move would place Elroy between the other agent and her.

Crispy wouldn't approve. First, he'd say, it's expected. Second, you might end up dead. Third, if you end up dead, the mission fails.

She turns, drops the jacket on the floor, raises her hands. She clasps her fingers behind her head and sticks her ass out a little. She doubts feminine wiles will work on these guys, but she might be surprised.

Then another plan forms, only a fraction better than the first, but better enough to decrease her chances of being shot.

Elroy's hand grips her right wrist. She feels his left leg slide between hers. The agent isn't being pervy, but following his training, positioning himself so that if she turns, he has the advantage of a low center of gravity and an easy way of tripping her up.

She feels the handcuff clamp on her wrist, not as tight as usual. A classic mistake by male agents, being gentler with a female perp.

She's expected this, counted on it.

The fraction of room within the handcuff will set her up perfectly.

Just as the handcuff clicks in place, she places both feet on the computer table and pushes backward. This would usually mean she's propelling herself right into the agent's arms. But she knows his training, knows the move he'll employ. He'd had her clamp her hands behind her head so that when they were cuffed, if she resisted, all he had to do was pull down and she'd fall backwards onto the floor.

From there she'd be easy to detain. An effective technique if done on anyone else, anyone not trained in the harsh, unorthodox style of Crispy.

As she pushes off the table, the agent pulls hard on the handcuffs, toward the ground. This is exactly what she needs, extra force to propel her where she wants to be. She flips backwards in a tight arc, twists her body at the same time, feels her wrist pivot inside the cuff. Now she's facing the agent. His face is baffled, surprised, open mouthed, trying to think.

Rookie move, no time to think in a situation like this. The agent holds the handcuff's other end. Rhyme seizes it, twists it from his hand, clamps it hard to his wrist.

Judging by his expression, she's surprised him again. The move has added to her list of advantages. First, she's surprised them, a distinct advantage. Second, Elroy's thinking, which means she's already won. Third, she can now use him as a shield between her and the other agent.

Rhyme uses the handcuff to leverage Elroy's arm out and away from his body, then she steps under it and behind him. She pulls him close, twists his arm up between his shoulders.

Elroy cries out as she presses the move. The other agent steps forward, angles for a shot, but Rhyme stays a half second ahead of him, uses Elroy as a shield.

Elroy strains against the pain, pulls his body forward, has no idea how much his strength is helping her. He pulls away, struggles to move forward against the pain of his twisted arm. Rhyme uses the movement to launch herself at the second agent. The man's face registers his surprise. He fires his pistol.

Her right shoulder bursts with pain. She's been hit.

Her foot shoots around Elroy's side to impact the bridge of the other agent's nose.

He drops to the cold stone floor, unconscious, blood running.

Elroy panics, reverses directions, propels his body backwards. This is his Hail Mary, a desperate attempt to regain control.

Rhyme expects the move, so predictable.

As Elroy lunges backward, she steps to his right, pulls his handcuffed arm in front of him. Without her as a brace he starts to fall back. She twists, ignores the pain in her shoulder, palms Elroy's forehead as he falls, gives it a little extra speed.

The impact is hollow, like a baseball against a brick wall.

Elroy's eyes roll up in their sockets, then flutter shut.

She kneels beside him, blood flowing down her arm. A pulse check gives good news. He's not dead.

Not as rusty as I think.

She pulls up her sleeve and examines the wound. About four inches long, superficial. A graze she can attend to later. Crispy would be cussing her to blue blazes right now.

Searching Elroy's pocket, she finds the handcuff keys. His service weapon lies on the floor. She unlocks the handcuff, then quickly removes the magazine and the chambered round from his gun.

She crosses to the other agent, searches his pocket, empties his gun and takes his handcuffs and keys as well. She drags the man to where Elroy lies. Working silent and fast, she cuffs each agent's wrist to the other's ankle.

The men lie askew on the floor, a weird game of Twister. The way she'd cuffed them will make it almost impossible for them to walk and will buy her extra time to disappear.

The FBI's involved. This isn't good.

She puts on her jacket, applies pressure to her wound to squelch the bleeding. Then she retrieves both agents' service weapons. Returning to the computer, she closes the remaining windows and clears the browser history.

Down the stairs and out the hatch, which she closes, replacing as much dirt and mulch over the lid as she can scoop.

Outside, she rushes to the library's back door and drops the two empty pistols on the steps. Then she moves down the sidewalk, through the gazebo and through the gothic fence.

She enters the Bronco, reverses back up the path to the road.

Dawn is, at most, thirty minutes away, but it's still early enough that the road is empty. At this time of day, the town's workmen should be just stirring from their beds.

She turns left, keeps the Bronco at the posted speed limit.

On the way out she sees the town's sign. THANKS FOR VISITING OUR HAPPY PLACE.

CHAPTER 38

MOUNT TABOR, ISRAEL

I blink at them, try to figure out just why the hell we're here if this is an invasion. Cain certainly knows that the Roman's unique talents lie in ground warfare. Wouldn't he be the very person you'd want to face the onslaught and command your forces? Why would Cain want him perched on the very precipice of this ancient church?

I think to ask him what's going on, to engage him solely for the purpose of easing my own fears. But when I turn my head, my mouth snaps shut. His expression shows a level of concentration I've never seen the man achieve. He's calculating, sizing up, planning some defense. His face is calm. His eyes focused like he's hypnotized. Wind bustles his suit in rough gusts, ruffles his hair; he leans on the marvelous spear and watches the swarm approach.

I stare at the dots, a swarm so thick it's difficult to see the clouds above the sea in the distance. Dark lines streak from the impossible mass and race to the ground. Bursts of flame follow as rolling balls of smoke rise to the sky. A second later, I hear the explosions. The cacophony of war.

A mass of military vehicles rolls out of the mountains. Like army ants, organized, endless, moving. Tanks, it seems, with helicopters above. I hear their cannons, see puffs of gray as they belch their payload into the land ahead.

"We should call Cain," I say.

I feel helpless, detached. Perhaps he'd sent us here to keep us safe. Or perhaps he's ordered the invasion himself. I stand behind the Roman, worry about my balance, watch the swarm teem over Israel's countryside. They fill my vision and multiply by the second. I look south, toward Jerusalem. I wonder if they're being attacked as well.

The mass pours into the valley below, growing in size and scope, their sounds clear, their intent transparent.

I try to estimate the size and realize the word army doesn't capture the magnitude of this force. Planes of every type, too numerous to count, fill the sky; thousands of vehicles invade the valley. As if a hundred nations have joined forces with the sole intent of invading Israel.

I'm standing in the midst of another war, but not a war of angels, a war of men.

A sleek, gray fighter streaks past, close. I wobble, almost fall. The engine screams, high-pitched, deafening. It spits flames into the land around us and is gone in a flash.

Steel locusts buzz across the valley, shrieking, ravenous. The air clots with sound and smoke, the ground trembles with their wrath. They streak toward us, shriek past like Hell's doors have been thrown open.

"Longinus!" I yell above howling engines, exploding rockets. "We need to get out of here!"

The Roman doesn't look, doesn't even twitch.

I look to the swarming locusts, see a pair of fighters break from the mass and turn through a long arc, then make straight for the church.

Straight for us.

I gauge the distance, guess their intent. There's no way they don't see us. Just no way this church isn't their target.

I grab Longinus's arm, pull, try to get him to follow me to some safer place.

My efforts fail to move him a single centimeter. I'm surprised. He's small now, not the hulking Roman I've grown to know. I should be able to move him easily, but it feels like pulling a concrete post. Despite his stature, I can't budge the man. It's as if his former density has been packed down to fit this smaller frame.

"Surprise, surprise," Lenny says.

"What a maroon," says Vince.

"Shut up!" I yell.

The fighters close at astonishing speed, arrows sprinting toward their targets. I can almost hear the pilots speak. *Target acquired. Fire at will.*

In a few seconds I'll be killed, blown off this roof never to see Rhyme again, never to share another kiss or enjoy her scent. I mourn this, feel great rage fill my soul. I won't be able to say goodbye or to tell her all I should've said long ago.

I face the jets, stand tall, stare into the face of my doom, gray raptors with pointed beaks. I won't be intimidated, refuse to fill my final breaths with fear. Rage fills me like lightning, changes me to a brash, confident and foolish street fighter.

I'll die, chin out and eyes open.

Fire spits from their wings. Shrapnel hits the roof. Chunks of stone strike my body.

I force myself steady, eyes forward and focused.

Missiles drop from each fighter's wings.

Cain's sent me here to die, an elegant way to separate me from Rhyme.

The fighters streak toward us, beyond them the rest of the swarm. The sky is filled with them, their smoke, flying missiles and chattering bullets.

They've come to raze Israel. To enslave its people and decimate its sites.

The missiles hang in the air. Their tails ignite, their lazy drift corrects. They are alive, correcting their line, flowing through a wide coil to streak toward us.

They won't miss. The church will be destroyed and so will we.

Or, at least, me.

Wind races over as if chased from the valley. I close my eyes, feel its push, feel it flee for calmer skies.

The fighters blaze past close enough to touch. The backwash hits, a gust of air that tries to throw me to the ground, blows my suit like a sheet on a line.

I lean in, watch the missiles, wait for death.

A war cry raises, loud as the fighter's cannons, clear and rapturous as a symphony's crescendo. All the instruments rising to a fever pitch of melody and resonance, a booming tumult of passion and focus.

My hands shoot to my ears.

Longinus throws me down on the narrow ridge of the hard roof.

I clamber, manage to catch the ridge and stop myself from falling.

I look up.

He stands in his true form. Longinus, wrath of the Roman empire, larger than I've ever seen him, a barbarian, a gladiator. He fills my vision, his eyes focused, blazing, a deadly scowl creasing his lips. His muscles strain, bulge, quiver. His suit becomes strips of fabric that billow behind as fragments fly away on the wind.

The spear is alive now, brighter than before, brighter than anything on Earth. Neon red, laser blue, speeding along the shaft's etched lines, too fast to follow.

He raises the pike, spins it a single time, then holds it above him. Veins bulge on his forehead as he fights the relic. More pop from engorged arms and neck. His teeth are clenched. His eyes squeezed shut as he wrestles the spear. His face is equal parts agony and concentration. Sweat streams, soaks the long, black hair flowing in the wind. He's facing the swarm, meeting them head on.

He groans two words. "Hold. On."

I look for something to grab, gauge the distance to the ladder we'd come up. There's nothing that can hold me, no point to which I can cling. I look to the Roman and his monstrous legs. The roof's stone cracks beneath him and his footing looks precarious. I see his agony, his focus, the superhuman effort he exerts.

"Hold." The single word is almost too much for him.

I wrap my arms around his leg, a toddler hitching a ride on my father's limb.

It feels like a live wire. Otherworldly energy sizzles through my core, fills my head with visions, centuries of anguish, eons of blood, ages of malice.

I see Christ on the cross, bloody face raised to the sky.

Skin sizzles as my hair dances.

I see Cain, maniacal, laughing, fangs bared, skin red.

I smell burning flesh. Is it mine or the Roman's?

Longinus moves his leg a centimeter closer.

I ignore the pain and squeeze for all I'm worth.

It starts to rain.

The drops sting my face, sizzle against the relic's energy. Lightning strikes a foot in front of us. Shards of stone fly through the air. My jacket bristles, then smolders.

The wind's a gale now, a hurricane making landfall, a blitz of vertical rain and horizontal shrapnel. The sky is black and pours its displeasure over the Earth, over Israel.

I look up at the Roman.

He is Zeus returned, an ascended Olympian with flowing hair and bulging muscle. A Greek god no longer suffering the antics of petty mortals.

The missiles arc, rise above the church's roof, streak toward us, seconds from impact.

His muscles become taut within my grasp, hard as steel, hard as the man who bears them.

A groan escapes as fire sizzles from the relic to streak through the rain.

It flashes, streams, blinds. The rockets explode in a flash of yellow and crimson. Debris tumbles past, clatters over the roof to the ground below.

The Roman's gaze is fury, pure effort of will.

He wields the golden spear as it spits fire. I follow the blazing trail, watch it split, then smash into the fighters. They explode in a shower of burnt ember and black smoke, pieces floating to the Earth like so much ash.

I breathe a prayer, think of Rhyme, can't believe I'm alive.

Fear makes me weak, but I gain my feet. I'm surrounded by a death cloud, the swarm filling the sky before me.

"No way he survives, Vince."

"Right you are, Lenny."

Fighters streak by, ignore us entirely.

The swarm's everywhere, land, air and sea. The valley below has filled with tanks and trucks and military transports of every kind. Above them, thousands of aircraft, maybe more.

I see long gray ships in the distance. They fire inland, a barrage that turns the verdant valley to something flaming and dead.

We can't win, I know. We've downed two fighters. Two.

"We've gotta go!"

Either the Roman doesn't hear me or can't.

I glance to the valley as sweat drips from my nose, mixes with the rain.

Longinus has saved us, and the rest of the force hasn't noticed.

They flow over the valley like ants on an apple, an endless onslaught. Mud flies from their tracks as fire leaps from their turrets to explode ahead. The sky teems with helicopters, above them jets, and bombers above that.

I blink at the sight, lick my lips with a dry tongue, rub various scrapes and lacerations. I struggle to absorb the enormity, ludicrous in its proportions. Enough firepower to consume the entire Earth.

Longinus pours his efforts into the relic, muscles bulge like they'll tear through his very skin. He leans into the spear. Smoke rolls from his hands, streams away on the wind. His hair smolders as a giant hand squeezes the weapon's shaft. Colors blur, pick up speed, overwhelm the golden brilliance.

Helicopters break from the throng and head toward us. Ten of them.

"So much for them not noticing," Lenny says.

"You're toast," says Vince.

The choppers remind me of wasps, hulking machines with thick pods on their sides. They buffet in the wind. Lightning shreds the sky behind and around them. They blaze forward, toward us.

The air around me fills with an eerie haze.

A fog in deep magenta absorbs the day's darkness, the howling wind, the relentless downpour. It engulfs like a monarch's robe as it spreads to cover the roof. It becomes thick, a veiled mist surrounding the church from ground to precipice.

Longinus continues his fight, grips the spear with mighty hands, seems to control it a fraction better than before. His hair streams behind in a black mop, his tattered suit reveals thick scars that streak his torso. Sweat flies, glistening droplets made purple by the mist.

His face is pure concentration, jaws locked, eyes narrow as muscles strive to control the relic. Giant legs seem rooted to the church, riveted in place, anchored by the Roman's sheer will. They strain, tremble, barely hold him upright even as the relic tries to lay him low. The entirety of his body contracts, flexes, bulging veins over knotted muscle.

The helicopters hover before us, giant wasps ready to sting.

They fire in unison, every cannon, every bullet, unloading fully.

Spots appear in the haze, small dimples that ripple where missile and bullet make impact.

They strike the magenta dome and fall to the valley floor.

Longinus has created a force field, an impenetrable umbrella of regal mist.

I grin at him, a faithful sidekick. I fear the relic might overwhelm his considerable strength. He's still human, still has a limit of endurance. I'm astonished he's come this far.

Massive arms shake, his legs quiver, sweat pours down his reddened face.

The relic is winning. Longinus squats, seems pushed by a giant hand that is the spear's energy. His breath comes in gasps as massive legs tremble against the relic's power.

I step close, place both hands on his low back. Then I push, my feet slipping on the roof's stone.

I will not fall. I've determined that; whatever comes, I'll stand fast and do what I can.

I push with everything I have, try to give the giant some small support. His weight crushes into me. My feet slide, my arms start to tingle, then sizzle with energy.

He doesn't notice my efforts. His head tilts to the sky as droplets fall from him like a summer rain.

I feel him push back, feel him lower a little.

My legs shake as I double my effort, my hands start to slip.

I press on as a roar escapes my throat.

I level my shoulder, press against his haunches, force my legs to find purchase.

Longinus groans, something deep, guttural, a lion in a cave.

Bolts of lightning hit the roof with a thundering crack. Shrapnel slices my forehead and I feel the blood start.

Longinus straightens, heaves. I hear his cry, louder than the first, louder than the choppers and thunder and wind. A cry of anguish fused with rage, a cry of desperation and finality.

I go deaf as his wail flows over the church and into the swarm.

I can't hold much longer. My vision is magenta, and I can't tell if it's from the mist or my own blood. The spear's energy grows, flows around us, engulfs and assaults as if offended by our efforts against it.

Dark clouds congeal and descend over the valley, over the swarm. Like being underwater and looking to the surface. Rain falls in thick gray lines as clouds boil and buffet.

The wind howls, ravages, tries to dislodge us from our perch.

I hear a sound like cold bacon dropped in hot grease.

Smoke pours from my shoes and the slick, wet stone bubbles at my feet.

The area dries in a single second.

The rain doubles its efforts, each drop turning to vapor as it lands.

The Roman's back is as hot as a branding iron, sears my shoulder as I push.

I lower my head, expel my last bit of strength.

The Roman's cry fills Israel.

I'm engulfed in redness, pure energy in bloody crimson, white hot, writhing through my psyche like a python, alive and vicious.

My face blisters from the heat. My eyes weep from the onslaught of wind and steam and mist.

The spear crackles, red hot, glowing.

Across the valley, a million lightning bolts rain. A sudden burst lasting only a single second.

The helicopters vaporize.

The valley glows fire red.

Northern mountains turn a crisp fuchsia as smoke pours from their peaks and floats into a boiling sky.

For as far as I can see, lightning falls, a million bolts jagged and brilliant. All becomes crimson, the world is ablaze.

Then, the spear goes quiet. Its energy vanishes.

I feel Longinus droop, then fall to one knee.

I collapse beside him, completely exhausted, pushed beyond my limit, certainly beyond the limit of any junkie anywhere. Ever.

Aircraft fall like so many raindrops. Jet fighters, transports, bombers, helicopters, all struck down by the Spear of Destiny. They drift, fall slowly in fluttering coils until they explode into the Earth.

Lightning runs across the valley, flows over the mountains, devours all in its path whether on air, land or sea. Everything is fire, everywhere crimson death, a tsunami of destruction.

My legs tremble as I sit on the perch. They search for the strength to hold me in place.

Then, they refuse to bear me further.

I start to slide.

I've no strength left, not even to save myself.

A giant hand grabs me and plants me on the ridge. It holds me a second, then releases.

I look to Longinus, but he's no longer there.

The supermodel stares back at me, wears smoking slacks burnt off to mid-thigh.

He grasps my shoulder, gives it a playful shake, then gives a glamour-model smile.

I reach inside what's left of my suit jacket and retrieve my Percs. The bottle is partially melted but the pills seem fine.

I down four and offer the bottle to the Roman.

"Non," he says, and waves it away.

CHAPTER 39

JERUSALEM, ISRAEL

Igneus leans on his staff. Around him, bodies litter the street like newspapers blown on the wind. Thousands lie inert and smoldering. A thick stench rises as if their spirits have become confused and huddle terrified near their former shells.

He looks down the street, watches as Jonas and Ishmael attend to injured civilians. Sirens scream in the distance, echo off the city's concrete and glass, bound over rooftops and up forgotten alleys.

The power was both indescribable and unstoppable. God's tool indeed. Now, how to tell Sebastian.

The child stands to his right, looks to the sky above the mass of the dead. He doesn't speak, just stares in a manner that says he's seen too much.

The boy has suffered in his short life, more than any child should. Forced from the sterile steel bastion that served as home for the Children of the Rocks. Then into a parking garage where they'd discovered a semblance of something close to normal, where they'd been happy.

At least up until its annihilation.

Now he stands amid burning corpses, the battle's aftermath. All he's witnessed, Igneus thinks; a lifetime's quota of misery, of death, of deceit.

Igneus grasps his chin and gently turns until their eyes meet. The boy is pure, his eyes clear, lucid, displaying no trauma, or sadness, or duress.

"Are you okay?" Igneus asks.

"I feel it, too."

Sebastian looks like a cherub, a beacon from God that says some things on this planet remain yet unspoiled. He is kind, lively, energetic, hopeful, youthful.

And earnest. He looks at Igneus as blue eyes betray sadness and an underlying fear. Igneus feels the emotion like it's his own, feels a visceral connection with the lad. Feels his hope, his contentment, a fine ribbon of tension. He sees the child's visions flowing, vivid in detail.

Peace abounds. There is purity here. The whiteness of a cleared ledger. Clouds of silver roll toward a pink horizon. Beyond that, flocks of birds, a verdant beyond with forests of deep green. Shoulders of white foam ride waterfalls that splash to timeless rivers, which bulge their banks and race toward enormous oceans of white-tipped blue.

"We're chosen, Father," Sebastian says. "Anointed."

Igneus stares at the boy, tussles his hair. "I know."

And he does know. Knows beyond any question their time is at hand. Some call it destiny. An understanding of what lies ahead and what must be done. Impossible to ignore.

It is certainty, it is fate.

Igneus traces the lad's features, tries to memorize his face. He envies the boy and his images, wishes his own were the same. He caresses his cheek, embraces the child, tries to print his emotions on the lad's heart.

When the worst comes, they'll face it, together. "God's given us each other. Let us be worthy of His trust."

The boy squeezes tight, lingers for a few seconds, basks in the affection. From this point forward they shall not want for food or protection. He closes his eyes, squeezes. This feeling, so foreign after centuries of vapor, centuries of beastly nightmares, of plans, manipulation, murder, genocide.

This moment is everything, and Igneus awes at its wonders.

He's become a father, has been given a charge to teach and nourish.

And it is the best of things. The absolute finest moment of his life.

"Dear Igneus!"

Igneus opens his eyes. He knows the voice. He steps in front of Sebastian.

"How nice to see you! I was so worried."

Igneus marvels at the changes. Cain's hair shines like a silver sun, bright white, perfectly groomed. He glides up the street in an expertly tailored suit, steps around bodies, barely notices the thousands dead around him. He's immune to the rancor, this street as killing field. His shoes twinkle deep black, shined to a high gloss. A perfectly knotted tie completes the portrait, complements a carriage of ease and power, a disarming comfort among the horrific.

"Seems we have some cleaning up to do," Cain says. His smile is warm as he stands before them.

Igneus knows the deception. A buried trap on a narrow path, designed to maim, then consume.

Sebastian steps forward, whispers something to himself, then speaks clearly. His voice is not that of a twelve-year-old boy, but an echo, larger than the boy by leagues.

"Away, foul beast."

Igneus glances at the lad, blinks. The boy just spoke the words that formed in his own mind.

Cain's smile slices the darkness, a mega-star backstage waiting for the curtain to part. "Sebastian, my boy!" He bends at the waist, places his hands on his knees, lowers himself to speak to the lad.

Igneus squeezes his staff, feels its power; he has nothing to fear.

"Look how you've grown," Cain says. "I was just in the process of sending a team to collect you and all the other children." He frowns a bit here; his hair loses some of its shimmer. "Then all this occurred. I hope you'll forgive my tardiness. You were always my favorite."

Igneus places a hand on Sebastian's shoulder. "Enough, devil, you have no power here. Be gone and plague us no more."

Cain's expression shifts, a fraction of movement at the corner of his mouth. Anger glows within eyes of blue steel, then changes to a look of concern. "Dear Igneus, my dear friend, do not offer such bitterness after all the lives we've shared. I seek only our reunion and, as always, hold your best interests at heart."

Igneus knows the expression, knows Cain's powers. Words, tempting, mesmerizing, toxic. He glances past Cain; sees Ishmael and Jonas move through smoldering corpses to those who need care.

"I know who you are," Igneus says, "I see through your deception. You, who are condemned to wander, to plague the Earth, to claim dominion. I will see you thrown down. I will expose your true nature to the world. You are a deceiver of nations, a minion of the dark, and I will suffer you no more. Away, foul creature, back to the depths that spawned you."

Igneus feels his belly burn, feels a passion in his soul that pushes the words through his throat. He's no longer impressed by his own boldness, as if the quality was inherent from his first breath.

Cain offers that winning smile, seems unperturbed. The glow of his hair fades, yet icy blue eyes retain a portion of malice. "I see," he says, then draws inches from Igneus's face.

His voice becomes a rough file over solid iron. Lips curl, reveal fangs. His face glows a dark sanguine. Heat radiates, a force malicious and awesome. Crystal eyes become feline, eyebrows crease to a sharp point. His words are hissed, flow from some other place.

"By all the forces at my command, by all that suffer and toil, by all that lament the night and beg God's mercy, I will see you at the appointed time and will steal the last breath of your miserable life. I will sup on your misery and drink of your terror. Before your very eyes shall I smite the boy, then I shall throw you asunder, in the light of day, for all the world to see. You will be my power and I your ruin. Your terror shall nourish my legions, and through your agony, your despair, your complete helplessness, will my power become unstoppable."

Igneus stares into the face of evil. Feels the man's fire, the swirling malice.

A liar with empty words and hollow threats.

Igneus stands unafraid, solid as his convictions.

He feels something peculiar, as if suddenly surrounded by a field of pure electricity. His hair prickles, then stands atop tingling skin. The impulse grows, throbs, pulses.

The power is neither his nor Cain's.

It's the boy.

The child's hair bristles like quills on a porcupine, each strand electrified, sparks leaping between.

Sebastian's eyes turn up, then inward. His face is angelic, calm.

His voice is an echo through deep caverns, a rushing wind, hollow, powerful, unquenchable. He's a prophet in a tempest, shouting his message from the mountain tops.

Energy surges.

Cain flies, cartwheels over bloodied asphalt and tumbles through burning corpses.

Jonas and Ishmael watch, mouths agape, as Cain streaks past, then smashes into the side of a battered and smoking blue car.

Seconds tick. Cain rises, brushes his tattered suit, shakes his head. Smoke rolls as he stumbles a step, then stops and adjusts the remnants of his tie.

His mark turns the night blood orange, its beams flow into the mist from atop his hand. Ishmael and Jonas drop to their knees, cower behind the corpses of the decimated. Other survivors muster what courage they can, screaming, rising, limping toward safety.

Igneus hears them weep, hears the pleas of terrified survivors.

This light, pure evil, pure despair. Intent on destruction, intent on conquest. The absence of hope, the abandonment of goodness. He remembers the feeling, the complete disorientation, the unbridled terror.

He raises his staff.

White-hot beams surge, rise, coil.

His words are whispered, but everyone hears.

"I rebuke thee."

Epilogue

The heavens blaze blistering orange as beings like vapor leap from their perches. Mountains rise through jagged layers to stretch flickering fingers toward the inferno. Clouds are fire here, the air, a molten mix of toxin and despair, a fetid soup of the age's agony and humanity's fall from grace.

Cain listens to the suffering billions, inhales deep the aromas, acrid brimstone, charred flesh. Grotesque imps flee at his approach and fill the space with the fluttering sounds of leathered wings. Beyond, mountains blaze maroon as lava cascades down their slopes to form bubbling rivers. The occasional soul pops above percolating ooze to gasp fetid fumes then howl that foulness back into the cacophony.

Mountains loom, spew fire in long arcs that trail like the tails of a kite. Jagged lines run to the distance, mountains, layer upon layer, black tipped and razor-sharp for as far as the eye can see. Deep maroon and blackest sable form shadows that rise and consume the fleeing imps as they race away.

Above him, demons sizzle on their roosts, like gargoyles they sit, motionless, unaffected. Tendrils of soot become a thick fog that rises around them. Saliva drips from their fangs, ropes of foam dangle from stretched mouths. Heartless eyes burn as they scan the plains. Some lick their paws or talons, bask like cats on an afternoon nap. At Cain's approach, scarred wings rise, then pump the fetid air, carry the creatures into the filthy clouds. They circle, stay well away, moving with learned caution. They know their power doesn't affect him, know beyond any doubt their master has returned.

Cain's rage knows no limit. The place is an inferno, the masses seething beneath. Shrieks rise in a wondrous chorus of pure despair. He leaps in the air, his form changing to furious dragon, bigger by leagues than the largest demon. Massive wings glide on vapored soot and ride the heat up and up. He circles, temper growing, fire streaming from his mouth to vaporize the place's inhabitants as they scream their pleas for mercy.

There is comfort here. A fine feeling of flame and fear, of punishment delivered and wrath conveyed. He circles high, vaporizes a group of imps then watches as their husks blaze toward the lava rivers below. They squeal and pop, toxic kernels that burst to nothingness.

He glides over the landscape, circles, touches down only to snag a soul then rend it with monstrous talons. Igneus is to blame. The frail man has banished him, and Cain's mind rages with the impossibility of that piss ant laying him low.

What power has he stumbled upon? With what entity has he joined? His staff appeared as nothing but an old stick, a thick branch from a local tree. Certainly not imbued with anything extraordinary.

But the power had come from Igneus. And Sebastian, the shit-caked little whelp who'd sent him tumbling through a pile of corpses. A boy who'd slapped him like an irritating gnat.

He hears the call, soothing, commanding, a call he can't ignore. Gigantic wings turn through a wide arc. He glides ahead, enters an enormous cave atop the tallest mountain.

The ground shakes as he lands.

"How very theatrical," his master says. "I remember when I used to do that. Simply marvelous."

Cain shifts his form, returns to that which is comfortable. He runs his hands over his suit, dark maroon in power stripes above oxfords in oxblood. He adjusts his tie, glances for a mirror to check his appearance.

"You're an endless joy," Lucifer says.

Cain turns, lowers to one knee. "I've failed, my lord. I've been banished."

Broad wings spread behind the being as he moves. A sharp tail cracks ash-soaked air like a bullwhip. He is glorious and Cain marvels, full of envy. This being has the answers, has bested God repeatedly, has guided Cain, shown him the errors of his many wasted centuries.

He is master of the hopeless, lord of hell, fallen angel, Lucifer.

He changes form to that of Cain's father, Adam. The square jaw, the sharp, dark eyes, the broad shoulders, hands, strong but gentle. "Nonsense, my son," he says. "You've not failed, you've learned. God makes his moves, creates allies where he needs them. But never forget, the Earth is *my* realm and *I alone* decide what horrors to exact upon His sheep. That's my purpose, to test."

He motions Cain to rise. "Walk with me."

They exit to stand on a broad precipice overlooking the expanse. Demons do their work with terrible efficiency. "You know this all exists because of man?" Lucifer chuckles. "So easily duped. If I hadn't seeded all this in their puny little gourds, none of it would be possible." He pauses here, scans the horizon as a flaming breeze caresses and embraces them both.

"It's about fear really," he continues, "one tends to create that which they most fear. It's the power of the mind, of suggestion. Good needs evil, as evil needs good. There has to be a foil. A patsy if you will. For instance, when I was given dominion over the Earth, I could've burned it all in a single day if that was my wish."

"But what fun is that?" Cain says.

Lucifer's laugh is a stark contrast to the oceans of horror before them. "Exactly!" He gives Cain a slap on the back. "Quite precisely correct, my son. No fun indeed. Isn't it more fun to keep them in constant pain? To ply them against one another and always, always keep them battling? Too many sheep in the corral makes for a crowded stable. I prefer a concept grander; the liar, the cheat, the man so full of greed, or lust, or power, that he'll do anything for more. Technology has made this so simple it barely interests me. It was I who instilled the concept of happiness." He glances at Cain. "All vapor, you know, blown away on the slightest breeze, but quite effective. They don't know the Earth *is* Hell. That I've made it that way with God's permission." He laughs again, behind him a backdrop of smoke and misery.

"You should hear them, *How can God let this happen?* Always sending hopeful messages to the cosmos, prayers of wanton avarice and perceived needs. It was easy to separate the holy from the masses. Easy to throw them down or get them to change course. In the end they mattered very little. If they didn't go along, I'd just hasten their death. Send them to their God. A way to dilute the waters. I told them the car they drive matters, the house they live in matters, the clothes they wear matters. I showed them envy in such a way that they still don't see it. I taught them greed without saying a word." His chuckle is hypnotic. "Deadly sins and all that. I'm sure you catch my point. I'm inspired by you. You learned early the nature of God and His tricks. A no-win proposition if you ask me, but the brilliance is that *you* did exactly what *I* did. Overt action is too obvious and usually fails miserably. But sleight of hand, well, that's something, my boy. Sun Tzu taught you well. Win the war without fighting, without risking a single ally. I watched you do it, turning their joys into sorrows, their cravings to traps. Using their truth against them. Simply brilliant, really, and not the musings of an average man. Reminds me of myself, if I must say, a quick learner where the sheep are involved. Which reminds me, I simply must take you to a couple of bedsides. Have you witnessed one of the sheep in their final bleating moments? No? So delicious when they realize they've wasted their life chasing smoke. It's generally right at the end, but so tasty when they realize it's too late. Do you know what the number one wish of the soon-to-be-deceased is?"

Cain shakes his head.

"More time, my boy. That's it. Never more money, or work, or sex, or drugs, or fame. Never a newer car or bigger house. Always, they beg for more time. Will give anything for a single day more."

He looks over the flame and vapor. "Created in God's image, but never seeing their perfection. Turns out God's an idiot, and likewise, the sheep follow the shepherd."

Cain hangs mesmerized by the man bearing his father's features.

"Ah well," he says. "I've talked enough." He steps away. "If it's not too much bother, I'd like to impart some advice. The Apostle's Revelation is a road map; follow that, and you'll not go astray."

"I don't understand," Cain says, "I changed the book, adapted it for my own purposes."

Lucifer smiles, Adam's smile, comforting, loving. "Of course," he says, then looks away and shakes his head a single time as if disappointed. "You'll get there soon enough," he says. "For now, realize your friend Igneus is a prophet of God, as is the child, Sebastian. They can't be subdued. By you or anyone. Although, I think it'd be rather sporting to toss a force at them and see what happens. Perhaps Longinus and his new relic can make it interesting. Either way, don't waste your time with them. They have their own role to play." He raises a finger. "I almost forgot. There's footage of Igneus destroying the army in Jerusalem. I've taken the liberty of disseminating it throughout the world. All lines of communication must remain open. Be sure to take credit for this victory. Your new Longinus should excel at that. You don't see it yet, but we have all we need to win this war. Bide your time, enhance your power, and do what you must. But, above all, take heart, your conquest is almost complete, your destiny almost fulfilled. Soon, we'll rule all firmaments forevermore."

As his words trail off, he becomes a flickering image, fades as Cain stares into the horror.

A smile blooms.

"Why do birds suddenly appear, every time you are near?" Bill sings loud. He likes the Carpenters' classic.

He rises, puffs the joint. Sends a plume of smoke into a shelf of old books. He's moved onto the Bible, King James Version. Whoever that was. It's his favorite. The one with the red letters.

He moves to the staircase and descends to the main floor. "Why do stars fall down from the sky…" He starts to hum as he searches for the wine glass buried under all the papers and tomes on the mahogany desk.

"Shoot, empty. My kingdom for more wine." He yells into the library's emptiness, then assumes a broad mahogany armchair with a green leather cushion. He opens the Bible, looks for the red words.

"Blessed are the peacemakers."

He sits back, puffs the joint, glances at the empty wine glass.

Peacemakers. Like Drake, like Jesus. God bless them. He reads on, skips everything but the red. He likes the red, likes that Jesus said these words.

Of course, there are other great men, other martyrs and peacemakers.

The Sicilian Martyrs, executed in 180 AD.

Jan Hus, who said, "I would not for a chapel of gold retreat from the truth."

Dirk Willems, who, in 1569, successfully escaped across a frozen moat, but turned back to save a guard who'd fallen through the ice. He was recaptured and martyred for his "persisting obstinance".

He thinks about these men, wishes he would've known them, feels like he does because he's read about them.

He likes the red letters. He likes the peacemakers.

Smoke glides through pursed lips as he reaches for the wine glass and takes a long drink. It's wonderful, tasty, sharp, fruity. He doesn't know who refilled it.

He returns to the red, joint hanging from his lips.

Near Washington, D.C.

INCOMING…

The word blinks in electric turquoise, floods his wrinkled face in a dusky jade glow. Above, a fluorescent light flickers, makes his head ache.

This job should provide enough money to disappear forever.

On the screen, pixelated letters: HIGH PRIORITY. FEMALE, 34, MURDER, TREASON, ESPIONAGE. LAST SEEN HEADING NORTHWEST FROM D.C. APPROACH WITH CAUTION. ARMED AND DANGEROUS. APPREHEND ALIVE.

An icon appears, gets clicked. Then, an image starts to form.

He props his feet on the cheap desk, feels it shift under the weight. Panel walls surround, an arsenal on dust-covered ivory. Three Glocks, two shotguns, assault rifles, flashbangs, hand grenades, knives, tactical flashlights, body armor.

Think I'll take the big boy.

The rifle feels heavy, solid, deadly. He pulls the bolt; clean, dry and serviceable. Smooth. Ready. The sniper's choice, Barrett M82, made to reach out and ruin your day.

This should be fun, if the demons stay away.

Let's see: ammo, cold weather gear, poncho, double Glocks, MRE's, what the hell, a shotgun never hurts. His chuckle sounds joyless. His mouth feels dry. The computer's fan thrums at high speed. The room's hot. *Need to install that vent.* He shakes his head, sighs, glances at the computer.

Her image fills the outdated screen.

Auburn hair cascades as lips form a sly smile, a twinkle that says she's up to something.

And those eyes. Like a cat's, glowing, feminine emeralds hold a tint of malice, a touch of mystery.

High priority.

Alive if possible.

This *will* be fun.

END

Turn the Page for an Excerpt

EMBERS OF SHADOW

———————————

AGES OF MALICE, BOOK III

LLOYD JEFFRIES

Embers of Shadow
Ages of Malice, Book III

Outskirts of Washington, D.C.

Words fly, breathless, trying to say everything at once. "Mr. President, I have information about my husband. I know his secrets. You must know the truth."

Carpenter regards her with a smirk. "Do tell, Mrs. Cain."

Relief washes over her. Once she explains everything, they can overcome her lunatic husband.

"He can't be killed." She speaks quickly, rushed, has to get out as much as possible as fast as possible. "He's immortal, punished by God. He's been alive since the beginning of humanity. That's why he's Cain. He's the real Cain. From the Bible. He can't be killed and never, ever fails. How do you think all this happened? All these world events? He's been planning this for centuries. Using trial and error to improve his methods. He heads an organization that controls every aspect of the world. You have to capture and put him away before it's too late."

Carpenter's expression is dubious. He looks around the hangar, then back at her. "You're telling me I can't kill your husband because he's immortal?" he says. "Nice try, but you'll have to do better than that." He chuckles, shakes his head. "You know, I expected you to say something crazy to save his skin, and incidentally, I like the extra touch of making him a Bible character, but still, don't you think you're trying a bit too hard to save the man you love?"

"I don't love him," Rhyme blurts. "I married him to protect the man I *do* love. It's a long story."

"I'm sure it is, and probably as full of lies as this one."

"I'm not lying. He's been alive forever, was Constantine the Great, created the Bible, changed it for his own purposes. He's bent on ruling the world and will succeed if you don't listen."

The president looks on. "Uh huh."

"You have to believe me!" she blurts, looks down, inhales, collects herself. "I know it sounds fantastic, but it's true. If you don't act, if you refuse to do *exactly* what I tell you, all will be lost. You can't beat him. No one can beat him. But you *can* capture him. He *can* be neutralized."

The president shakes his head, waves a hand. "I've had enough," he says. "If you want to play games, we can play all night."

"But…"

Tiny lights twinkle through her vision as he slaps her face. "Shut your mouth!" he says. "You're here by your own devices, your own decisions." His voice lowers, sounds thick and scratchy. "You think this is our first rodeo? *We* always win, Miss Carter. That's what we do; get our man and get our way." He motions around the hangar. "Normally, I don't like to be associated with such things, but I *will* know the truth, one way or the other. Your husband's making waves. Has taken control of all the oil in the Middle East and Russia. I must admit, it's impressive the speed at which he's done it." He starts to pace, speaks as if giving a speech. "He's upset the world order and if we can't get it under control, things are going to get very bad, very fast."

He moves close, leans down, glides a hand through her hair in a gentle caress, holds her eyes, caresses her throbbing cheek. "Your husband won't listen to reason and seems hell-bent on his present course. Normally, it'd be enough to just let him know we have you in custody, but, unfortunately, times are such that there really isn't any other option than drastic measures. NATO has been forced to act and make no mistake, we *will* regain control of the region, then we'll convince the Chinese to abandon Russia."

"But you can't! You'll never win. You don't understand…"

His head snaps toward her and she flinches, braces for another slap.

Then, he snickers. "I'm afraid this is set in stone and there's really no way to stop it. We don't need Cain captured; we *need* him dead. He's too big a threat for us to sit on our hands while he demands fealty from the world. I'm sure you know he's proclaimed himself God. He's even asked me to surrender the US. Can you believe that? Your husband has quite a pair on him, but I'm sure, of all things, that, you know."

Agent Elroy approaches, whispers in the president's ear.

"Thank you," Carpenter says, then turns back to Rhyme. "I'm told we're all set here." He adjusts his tie. "Mr. Jenkins?"

Another shadow breaks the light and moves to stand by the president. The man is small-framed, short. A pencil mustache sits above thin lips. His hair is combed in such a way as to cover the swathe of baldness atop his head. Beads of sweat appear on his forehead. He peers at her through eyes like a game hen, gives the appearance of one whose life has been only laughter and ridicule.

President Carpenter continues. "We learned something from our Muslim friends," he says. "You know, the terrorists who'd film their captives while doing inhumane things. They taught us terror and, although not official policy, it's a useful tool when time is of the essence. Fortunately, Mr. Jenkins here is very, very good at this sort of thing. He'll start slowly and film everything. Then he'll send snippets to your husband with a polite request to renounce his authority and turn himself in. If Cain refuses, Mr. Jenkins will send more footage. Things will get worse and worse for you tonight, Mrs. Cain. Jenkins here is known for being methodical, exacting. For his, let's say, patience. I believe you'll find him unpleasant and, I want to be very honest here, you'll not survive the night, no matter what Cain does.

"You see, it doesn't really work if we just remove a finger and stop. Or just waterboard you and stop. The pause gives you time to collect yourself, to rest and mentally prepare for the next round. We've found this to be ineffective.

"What *is* effective is doing it all in one go, sending the highlights to the person with whom we're negotiating. In this case, your husband. By the time he does as we wish, you'll be long dead." He grins again. "That's an added bonus, no pesky witnesses running to the press and causing trouble. Not that the press would help, we've controlled them for a long time now. But, as you know, sometimes someone gets through, and we can't allow that to happen."

He stoops, whispers in her ear, smells of expensive cologne. "We're very, very good at this."

He stands, steps away, raises his voice. "Keep up the good work everyone," he says, "and please support Mr. Jenkins in any way you can."

He turns to Rhyme. "It's a pleasure to make your acquaintance, Mrs. Cain. I'll give your regards to your husband, just before *he* dies."

Words flow fast, desperate. "Mr. President please, just listen. If you go against him, he'll destroy you. Don't you see? Think of the country, the people. There's another way. Mr. President!"

A fist slams her nose. The chair slides back an inch as her vision blurs with stars and tears. Blood runs from her nostrils, drips on her shirt.

President Carpenter enters an SUV, and two agents climb in with him. They pull off, two other SUVs following, one behind, one in front.

Rhyme strains through blurred vision, updates her calculations. Eleven agents now, plus Jenkins. Three SUVs remain.

Jenkins stands before her, shakes his hand. "I don't like to hit women," he says, "but for you I made an exception."

Two agents drag a large Pelican case across the hangar's floor. Mr. Jenkins moves to it and draws a small, steel briefcase. He strolls toward her, swings the case wide, whistles a song from the Broadway show: *A Chorus Line.* He takes his time, consciously places each foot on the concrete so it yields the maximum echo from the hangar's walls.

Then, he kneels, opens the case, and turns it toward her.

Implements shine and shimmer in the beam of the spotlights. The tools inside are sharp, polished to a high sheen, encased in black foam, lovingly cared for. She sees something round, like a gear with sharp teeth. Then something that looks like a saw, about twelve inches long with an etched steel handle. Next to that lies an angled prod of some sort, a large version of a dental scraper. Then, at the top of the case, resting in its own cut out of black foam, is a large, steel phallus. Its end tapers to the shape of an arrow, appears as sharp as a straight razor, about five inches wide.

She gasps, stares at the tools, searches for courage, fights the grip of pure panic.

Jenkins follows her eyes, retrieves the phallus, holds it close to her, turns it slowly so it gleams in his hand. Light rolls over its length to reflect on her face.

"I see you've picked a favorite," he says. He leans close, his whisper sweaty, terrifying. "It's my favorite too. Men *and* women both *love* this one." He eyes it, savors the look and feel. "I'll save it for last. It'll be a highlight for both of us."

An agent places a plastic bucket next to her chair.

She glances toward it, wonders what horrors lie in its depths.

"Thank you, my good sir," Jenkins says, then turns to Rhyme. "I see you're wondering what the bucket's for." He purses his lips, rolls his eyes up. A look of relish, of pure joy, of expectation and craving fusing to a savory flush of fulfilled desire. "Let's say it's for souvenirs. I'll let your imagination fill in the blanks."

He crosses to the camera, pulls a hanky from his pocket, polishes the lens. "The record is three days," he says. "Let's see if you can beat it…"

Dear Reader

Thank you for reading *A Measure of Rhyme,*
Book II of the epic series, *Ages of Malice.*

Please take a moment to leave a quick star review and spread the word
to your fellow readers. By sharing your opinion, you not only share
your experience, but you lend credibility to me as an indie author and
generate trust in others that they're getting a story worthy of their time.

The saga continues with *Embers of Shadow,*
Ages of Malice, Book III, available Spring 2024.

Follow Lloyd for free short stories, get news, and more at:
https://lloydjeffries.com

About the Author

Lloyd Jeffries enjoys dark comedies, philosophy, clever turns of phrase, religious studies and thought experiments involving the esoteric and legendary. A decorated veteran of numerous conflicts, he served in the U.S. military and has practiced Emergency, Trauma and Wilderness medicine for more than twenty years. He hides out in Florida with his family and Buck the Wonder Dog.

A Measure of Rhyme is book II in his epic series,
AGES OF MALICE.

Join Lloyd to get news and more:

www.lloydjeffries.com

X x.com/LloydJeffries2

9 798985 526950